Praise for *You, Me & the Sea*

'This is escapism in the best possible way.
You, Me & the Sea is such an immersive, affecting
novel – I absolutely loved it! Escaping to the island
setting was utter bliss. I can't tell you how much
happiness the descriptions of the sea, the sky and
the landscape brought me. The love story is beautiful;
I cared so much about both of them. This book gave
me a huge amount of comfort at a very tricky time.'

Marian Keyes

'I absolutely loved *You, Me & the Sea*. Its beautifully
evoked wild setting, tense, detailed writing, suspenseful
storytelling and finely drawn characters work together
to make it a very special read. Rachel and Fraser,
each such a wounded soul, gradually build an inspiring
relationship between them. This immensely
deserving novel should be a huge success.'

Rachel Hore

'I couldn't put down this amazing book.
It's a comfort and a breathtaking romance – aka
sizzling hot! – with beautifully atmospheric scenery.
What a perfect escape!'

Alex Brown

YOU, ME & THE SEA

Also by Elizabeth Haynes

Into the Darkest Corner
Revenge of the Tide
Human Remains
Under a Silent Moon
Behind Closed Doors
Never Alone
The Murder of Harriet Monckton

YOU, ME & THE SEA

ELIZABETH HAYNES

First published in 2021 by
Myriad Editions
www.myriadeditions.com

Myriad Editions
An imprint of New Internationalist Publications
The Old Music Hall, 106–108 Cowley Rd,
Oxford OX4 1JE

First printing
1 3 5 7 9 10 8 6 4 2

A CIP catalogue record for this book
is available from the British Library

ISBN (paperback): 978-1-912408-75-7
ISBN (ebook): 978-1-912408-76-4

Map of the Isle of Must by Jo Hinton Malivoire

Designed and typeset in Stempel Garamond
by WatchWord Editorial Services

Printed and bound in Great Britain
by Clays Ltd, Elcograf S.p.A

there is
what you think
you are

and then there is

more

L. E. Bowman
The Evolution of a Girl

Part One

April

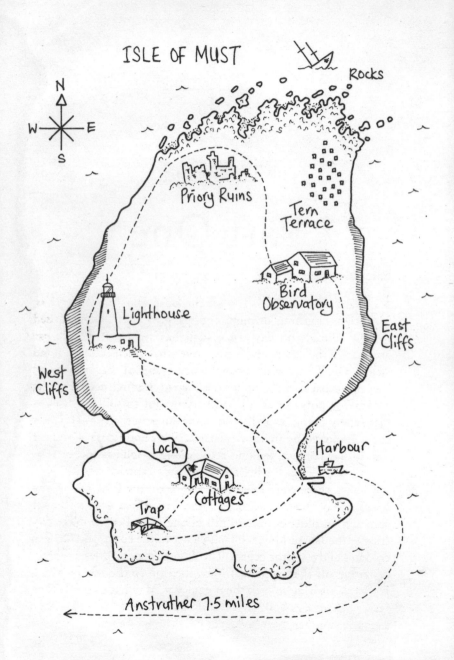

1

The Island

Rachel

It's nearly eleven. Rachel is on the boat, the *Island Princess*, it's called, churning through choppy grey seas. It's supposed to take tourists on day trips, so it has seats and a little bar area inside the cabin, and a tiny toilet that smells of diesel and sick. Craig Dunwoody brought her a cup of tea earlier and then went back to the upper deck again, leaving her clutching a steaming polystyrene cup and trying not to spill it. Craig is technically going to be her boss, she supposes, although really she's employed by the Forth Islands Trust and Craig is just her day-to-day contact, the one who's going to tell her what to do.

Besides Craig, Rachel and the boat's captain, whose name is Robert, there were five other people on the boat when they set off, all of them tourists: a mother and father with a teenage son, and an older couple in full hiking gear. People make day trips to the Isle of May, which is closer to the coast, and has seal colonies and a visitor centre. The *Island Princess* does a circuit, dropping off the trippers at May, then on to the Isle of Must, and back via May to pick them up again. May has two full-time reserve managers and several volunteers doing various things over the summer months. Craig has told her all this.

Robert doesn't talk much. He said hello and helped her aboard and that was about it.

The boat had stopped at May after about an hour. It was grey and rocky, with a steep, winding path leading up from the concrete jetty against which they moored. The tourists disembarked. On the jetty a young man in a green knitted pullover, with something monogrammed on his right chest, had greeted them. Rachel had been expecting him to lead the tourists up the path, but he'd waited for them all to get off and then Craig had handed across three of the plastic storage boxes, the sort you use for moving offices, which were then stacked neatly on the jetty. Once the boat began to chug out of the harbour again, the young man had stood on a wooden box and begun to give a talk.

Rachel had watched all of this without comment, dazed with tiredness and the effort of fighting the constant low-level anxiety. She had slept a little better last night, shattered from a day spent on trains and buses, but still she had been awake this morning from about four, worried about oversleeping and waking to find her new employer knocking at the door. As it turned out, he'd had to join her for breakfast, because the bed-and-breakfast (and Dawn, the owner) only started serving at eight. Rachel hadn't been particularly hungry but she could smell bacon cooking when she sat down in the dining room, and, being the only guest, didn't want Dawn to have wasted her efforts. So, a full Scottish breakfast, complete with square sausage – a new one on her – and black pudding and bacon 'from the farm'. She'd left the black pudding, ate as much as she could of everything else. Craig had arrived before the food, and Dawn had made him a coffee. They seemed to know each other well. Maybe he put business her way. The birdwatchers, perhaps.

Craig was okay. Hair that would be called strawberry blond on a woman, wispy-fine and receding; pale blue eyes, freckles, quietly spoken. Very grateful to her for taking on the job, flushed and a little sweaty – he had been up for hours, he said, getting everything she needed – and jumping from one topic to the next so that it was hard to take everything in.

'Don't worry,' he'd said. 'I've written all down. You don't have to remember a thing. And you can phone me if you get confused.'

He'd pulled out a crumpled sheaf of A4, folded in the middle, which had dense typescript on most of it, and notes scrawled over the top in red pen. When he'd spewed forth everything he thought she needed to know, only about a tenth of which she could possibly have repeated had anyone wanted to test her on it, he had taken a deep breath and sat back on the raffia chair in the bright little dining room.

'So,' he said, 'you're from Norwich?'

'Yes.'

'I've never been.'

And that was that. A moment later she was sent to grab her backpack from the room while he settled up with Dawn, then he was outside in a battered old Land Rover, the engine ticking over.

At the harbour, which was not very far away, Rachel had helped him stack plastic storage boxes on to the boat, and, once the tourists had piled on, they were away.

Must is another forty minutes beyond May, beyond the Firth of Forth and out into the North Sea. All Rachel can think of is the square sausage and the tea, swilling around inside her. By far the biggest meal she's eaten in months – what was she thinking? To counter the movement of the boat she keeps a fixed eye on the island as it gets larger, making out details. There are not many pictures of Must online, she'd found when she first searched. There were plenty of pictures of the Isle of May, and so she's been imagining it as May's younger sister: more compact, prettier, greener. Instead the island before her is a squat, ugly little thing, a black and green troll crouched in a slate-coloured sea, waves striking it firmly up the arse.

The closer they get to it, however, the more it grows. The back end rises into black granite cliffs, white with foam at the

5

lower levels and pale with the guano of a hundred thousand seabirds higher up. She has seen bigger islands. She has seen bigger cliffs. But this one is going to be her home for the next six months or so, and she needs to like it. She needs it to want her as much as she wants it.

Craig leans over the railing above her. 'Ten minutes,' he says. 'How you doing down there?'

'Fine,' she calls, knowing she's probably green, wishing her make-up bag weren't buried in her rucksack.

She can see more of the island now. The lighthouse is on the nearest side. Further along and about half a mile back is the small bird observatory that houses birdwatchers, and occasionally other people: ecology students and scientists. Her job will be to take care of the observatory, to clean it, and change the beds once a week ready for the next lot. She has to cater for them, too, which is why the *Island Princess* is loaded with food for the birdwatchers who will be arriving on this same boat tomorrow, not to mention bedding and duvets and other fancy shit that apparently they're not used to. It's been sleeping bags and tins of beans they brought themselves, up to now.

Today is Friday. She has just over twenty-four hours to get ready for them.

Rachel looks at the island and tries to imagine living somewhere so very different from the place she has left, her sister's Victorian house just outside Norwich city centre. She has lived in various student digs, house-shares and flats. She has been in towns but mostly cities since she was a child; while the countryside has never been far away, she has never lived in it. And this is properly rural, seven and a half miles off the coast of Scotland, and even the other side of those seven and a half miles of grey choppy sea there's barely a town with nothing but fields behind it. She tries to think how far away she is from her nearest Starbucks. Three and a half hours? It's nearly two hours' boat crossing. What if something happens? What if she panics?

She gets unsteadily to her feet. Craig moves to the front of the boat, picking up a rope and looping it between his hands.

There is a funny smell that gets more pungent as they get closer. It smells alarmingly like shit. Like blocked drains.

The boat rounds the south end of the island and chugs through a narrow channel between the rocks. The swell calms and it feels almost peaceful here, the wash of the boat causing huge pads of seaweed to rise and fall without breaking a wave. Out of the breeze the smell of sewage is even more pronounced and she wrinkles her nose.

Through the thickly salt-encrusted window at the front of the cabin she can see a concrete jetty, and a man and a dog standing on it. Even from this distance she can see he's huge, a real beast of a man, broad-shouldered, beard, short dark curls moving in the breeze. If you were going to picture a lighthouse-keeper – even though that isn't what he is – then you'd probably picture him. He's even taller than she first estimated, she realises as Craig jumps across the gap to the jetty and shakes his hand. Craig is over six foot, and this guy is taller still, by quite a whack. He reminds her of someone she can't quite place.

She smiles at him and waves, but, if he's seen her, he is pretending he hasn't. The dog, however, is staring right at her. It's a big dog, black and shaggy, with the long snout and upright ears of a German shepherd. Maybe it's mixed with collie. She likes dogs. This is good news. There will be at least one other sentient being on the island, even if it can't talk and is already affiliated to someone else. For some reason its presence here is comforting.

Fraser. The man is called Fraser. She doesn't know what the dog is called.

Fraser

You only really start to feel anger once it's gone cold. Before that, it's like something outside you, something unexpected: you watch yourself getting angry and you're almost surprised by it, because that's not you. That's not how you behave. And then, afterwards, you get the numbness and you think, *where did that come from?* and it's almost funny. Or you'd cry if it wasn't quite so hideous.

And then later, much later, days and months afterwards, the anger hasn't resolved and it's fermenting inside you because actually nothing has changed, and then you get sick with it. And you don't know why. You get what they call a stress-related illness, only you're not stressed at all, not when you don't have to go to work and actually at the moment everything's paid for, so you can't claim to be stressed. And then they change it to depression, and you think, *oh, is this what that feels like?* Because you wouldn't have called it that. You wouldn't have called it depression.

Even now he hates that word. It implies a lack of control.

Anger, gone cold and hard like a body that's saponified – turned waxy and soaplike by the passage of water over fat, the passage of time. That's what anger's like, when you can't get rid of it.

They had words, yesterday.

'You've to keep out of her way,' Fraser had said.

'Oh, aye? An' how'm I supposed to do that?'

'You see her, you talk to her. Just don't seek her out. Don't make friends. She doesn't need friends, and neither do you. Get me?'

He'd understood. Fraser could see it in his eyes, the flash of alarm. He didn't see it often these days, but sometimes it was needed, that sharp burst of authority.

Rachel

Despite the relative calm of the harbour the boat is pitching, the jetty rising and falling alarmingly as Rachel tries to judge the right moment to jump. The two men are still talking. The boat's engine shifts into some sort of neutral gear and suddenly it's much less noisy.

'Aye, but it'll have to do for now ...' she hears Craig saying.

Robert comes out of the wheelhouse and shouts something across to the two of them and they both laugh. Even though she can hear the words Rachel's brain cannot form them into any sort of sense and she thinks they must be speaking Gaelic. Or it's Robert's incomprehensible mumbling.

The man – Fraser – looks down at her for the first time in response, frowning. She guesses that Robert said she was a southern softy – or even something more offensive than that, judging by the way he's looking at her.

Fraser leans over and holds out a hand. Rachel mistakes his intention and shakes it, awkwardly, the boat still lurching.

'No,' he says, 'give me your luggage.'

Rachel slips the backpack off her shoulder and tries to hand it to him. It's too heavy really, for her to lift one-handed, but he takes it with ease, slinging it over his shoulder and offering his hand to her again. This time she takes it and he hauls her up on to the jetty. She loses her footing and for a horrible moment she is dangling from Fraser Sutherland's arm, her foot between the boat and the jetty as the boat rises again.

He drops the backpack, grabs the waistband of her jeans with his other hand, and hauls her up just in time.

She is left on the jetty, legs still wobbly from the voyage, heart racing with how close she just came to crushing her foot. He's already turned back to Craig, as if nothing had happened. The dog pushes against her and she looks down into a pair of serious brown doggy eyes. She lets it sniff her hand until it nudges her with its nose and wags its tail and she rubs her cold hand over its head, between its ears. In response it turns and leans the weight of its body against her leg. She feels the warmth through her damp jeans and it is weirdly comforting.

Robert has started moving the stacked boxes into the deck space Rachel has just vacated, and Fraser reaches down and hauls them on to the jetty as quickly as he stacks them.

They have obviously done this before. She feels she should be helping, but Craig is also just standing there watching them, and it takes them less than two minutes.

Robert raises a hand and says something and disappears into the wheelhouse. It might have been a goodbye, although he's scarcely spoken at all today.

Rachel has recovered a little. Remembered her manners.

'You must be Fraser,' she says, offering a hand again. 'I'm Rachel.'

He looks at it, takes a firm grip and a gives it a single, rough shake. Turns away before she has a chance to say anything else, hefting up two of the plastic crates as he does so. *Pleased to meet you too*, she thinks.

The smell is overwhelming, almost stinging her nostrils. She puts a hand over her nose. 'Does it always smell like this?' she asks.

Craig waves a hand at four large stainless steel drums that are on the low cliff above them. 'No,' he says. 'It's the septic tanks.'

'The what?'

'They get emptied once every few years. Helicopter comes to pick them up. Due in the next few days.'

Rachel looks at the tanks. Her stomach lurches.

They carry the crates to the end of the jetty and load them on to the trailer of a quad bike that is sitting there. Fraser brings her rucksack, hooked casually over his massive hand. Without another word he climbs on the quad bike and revs it, then bounces off up the rough track. The dog scampers ahead, knowing to keep out of the way, and Craig and Rachel follow, more slowly. It's steep, and it's not paved either, but potholed and spotted with grassy tufts and patches of loose stones, which makes it challenging to climb. Craig is trying to talk, something about puffins and gulls, but eventually he gives up. Rachel makes it to the top before he does.

The island is about a mile long and half a mile wide, a rough oval in shape, should you be looking at it from Google

Earth, which Rachel has done quite a lot in the last week. The harbour and the lighthouse are in the southern half, the lighthouse on the western side, across the width of the island from the harbour. The bird observatory is on the eastern cliff. They follow the path towards it, which undulates along the top of the cliffs. Everything as far as the eye can see is green, and grey, the colours changing as the sun comes out and disappears again. A few scrubby bushes line the path, bent double by years of growing in the wind, and, overhead, seabirds wheel and call. Nearer the cliff, the noise rises until it's almost deafening. There are almost no level sections to the path. They're either walking uphill or downhill, and their steps thud on the springy turf. As if the island is hollow.

Rachel has been told already not to stray from the path, for fear of collapsing a puffin burrow. The birds mate for life, and return to the same nest site every year. She read that on Wikipedia. Anxious not to disappoint a puffin couple returning from half a year battling Atlantic storms only to find their home destroyed, she is determined to be careful.

She can see the bird observatory on the summit of the next hill, a solid, squat building with whitewashed breeze-block walls. The quad bike is parked outside it and the trailer is empty by the time they get to it. Fraser emerges from the open door with the dog at his heels, and stares at them as if they've been hours.

'I'll give you a call, shall I?' Craig asks him.

'Aye, or I could leave it here.' He's talking about the quad. 'You know how to use it?'

Rachel thinks for a moment he's asking her, but he's talking to Craig.

'Aye, right enough. I'll see you, then,' Craig says, and shakes Fraser's hand.

And Fraser walks off in the direction of the lighthouse without so much as a glance in her direction. The dog stays a moment longer, looking from Rachel to Fraser's retreating back as if it's thinking of staying, then it takes off after him.

'What's the dog called?' she asks.

'Don't know,' he says. 'Come inside, hen.'

How many times must he have been here, and he's never once asked about Fraser's dog?

The boxes have been stacked in a large, open-plan room. An unattractive kitchen is at one end: badly fitted cupboards, a laminate worktop warped and lifting at the edges, revealing the chipboard beneath. The rest of it is a sitting room with various mismatched chairs and sofas, and an ugly stained-pine dining table, marked with several overlapping rings where people have put mugs down without coasters. Bare wooden benches sit either side of it. The breeze-block walls are decorated with posters of birds and pictures of Highland scenery, and one framed picture of Anstruther harbour with the *Island Princess* moored in the foreground, the whole thing faded where it's been in the sun. There is a large, squat woodburner at the far end, and a vast stack of random bits of wood inside a frame which seems to be made out of pallets, nailed together.

The place smells damp, and over the top of that Rachel can still detect the undeniable whiff of shit from the septic tanks.

'I'll give you the tour,' Craig says nervously, perhaps worried by the expression on her face. Although there's not a lot more to see.

There are three bedrooms: a double, a twin, and the smallest room, which has two bunk beds in it. There is a chilly, cheaply tiled bathroom without a bath – just a shower, a toilet and a sink. There is also a separate toilet next door to it. It feels very much like the sort of hostel you'd stay in when your budget amounted to the next step up from free, and her heart sinks. None of the beds are made. There's her first task.

'Right,' she says. 'Am I in the double?'

'I'm sorry?' Craig answers, confused.

They stare at each other, then he seems to follow her train of thought.

'Oh! No, hen, you've a room in the lighthouse.' He chortles with laughter – how hilarious that she thought she was staying in the bird observatory! Nobody had actually said anything

12

about where she was going to sleep. She had just made that assumption.

'With ... Fraser?'

'Aye, with Fraser. Much nicer up there, there's a telly an' everything. Did you think you were down here, on your own?'

Rachel feels something like the beginnings of panic. 'You want me to share with a man I've only just met?'

She has a particular voice that emerges when things go wrong. It comes from nowhere and it's a bit high-pitched, not her usual voice at all. It says things, before she has time to think that saying them out loud is probably not a good idea.

Craig looks slightly horrified. 'Ah,' he says, lamely, 'Fraser's all right once you know him.'

'But I *don't* know him,' she squeaks. 'That's the point.'

For a moment they stare at each other, until she realises that she has no choice. What's she going to do? What *can* she do? Run? Get back on the boat?

'There are other buildings ...' he says. 'There's the old lightkeeper's cottages, the ones we're thinking of making into holiday lets. Maybe you could look, see if you'd rather stay there. But it's a lot of work, so for now you'll have to stay in the lighthouse. And you don't really want to be all on your own. This is a lonely enough place without making it more so.'

They unpack the plastic crates. Craig unloads everything directly on to the counter, as if he's in a hurry to get away as quickly as he can. Rachel starts to put things away, but the cupboards are already occupied: ratty cardboard, cobwebs, a packet of porridge oats with a hole in it, its contents scattered. Everything needs cleaning.

As the plastic crates are emptied they are nested neatly inside each other. Rachel had taken her backpack out of the quad's trailer but now she puts it back in for Craig to cart on to the lighthouse, along with the empty crates, which are going back with the boat.

The birdwatchers have very basic needs when it comes to catering. They'll do their own breakfasts, and there will be bread and ham and cheese and tinned soups and beans for them to make lunch with. Rachel's catering role comes in the evenings, when she will dish up something simple and hearty. Lasagne. Shepherd's pie. Tuna pasta bake. Stew. In between groups of visitors, she will change the beds, clean, and do the laundry. Other than that, there is an extensive list of small but important jobs including checking the level of water in the well which provides the bird observatory with water (a dry spell might mean showers are rationed), making sure the generators are stocked with fuel, collecting driftwood for the woodburner when walking on the beach, litter-picking on the beach (apparently plastic items are washed up constantly; there are two huge metal bins by the jetty which are collected every once in a while and taken to the recycling centre on the mainland), and keeping birds out of the bird observatory. It seems they have a tendency to wander in, if the door's left open. 'Helping the warden as required' is also on there.

She had asked Craig about that over breakfast, scanning through the list and barely taking it in. 'What sort of things will he need help with?'

'Counting birds, most likely. Ringing and netting. Taking pictures. General maintenance.'

All of these things are whirling around Rachel's mind, twisting themselves around the notion that she's sharing a house with a man she's only just met. A man who, she now realises, reminds her of Captain Haddock from *Tintin*, if Captain Haddock had been six foot five and built like a wall.

There is a pile of plastic-wrapped duvets and pillows that were in several of the largest crates.

'You'll need one set for your bed, hen,' Craig tells her. She counts them out. There are two double duvets, so she takes one of those and a pack of pillows and separates it from the rest.

They have finished unloading all the boxes and Craig has shown her the outhouse with the generator, and the washing machine, and the heavy iron grating that covers the well. They are back at the quad.

14

'Backsies?' he asks warily.

Really she would prefer not to have to hold on to him, but it's a fair walk back to the lighthouse and she's tired now, still tired from yesterday's long journey. She throws the duvet and pillows into the trailer along with her backpack, clambers on to the back of the quad and he fires it up, lurching off down the hill and up the other side, nearly tipping her off the back of it. She squeals and grabs at his waist, thinking about helmets and people who've suffered brain injuries following quad accidents, never mind miles out in the North Sea; but, by the time she has opened her eyes and looked at the grey-green landscape bumping past, the lighthouse is looming large ahead of them.

He stops the quad outside the lighthouse and kills the engine. Rachel collects her backpack from the trailer, eases it on to both shoulders. Duvet in one hand, pillow in the other.

'Call me if you have any problems,' he says in a tone that suggests he might even answer.

He manages an awkward jog down the hill to the harbour. The *Island Princess* is waiting for him, rising and falling next to the jetty, ready to head back to May to pick up the tourists.

Already thirty-six hours have passed since she left Lucy in the station car park. It feels like a lifetime ago.

Fraser

Fraser is no more keen to share the lighthouse than Rachel is. He has lived here for the past four years, and the way of life has suited him just fine. He isn't supposed to be on his own, there is supposed to be an assistant, but whoever they were they never appeared and he never bothered to ask, because the answer would have been 'funding issues', as it always was. And he's glad, under the circumstances, to be left to his own devices here. Fraser is not a man who plays by the rules. And, so far, he has been able to do things his way.

Now, thanks to the arrival of a new manager – Marion Scargill – they have this grand scheme in place to earn money from the island. There have always been birdwatchers, scientists, coming and going and staying in the bird observatory for the odd week at a time. They brought sleeping bags and tins of food and they managed well enough with the list of instructions for how to work the generator and how to check the water levels. They paid a nominal sum towards the island's Trust and that was fine, everything was fine. And the island wasn't paying its way; it isn't exciting or pretty like the Isle of May, or dramatic and close enough to see from the shore, like the Bass Rock – it's just another island with puffins and shags and razorbills the same as you get everywhere else, only without the scenery or a visitor centre with a working toilet.

'We were thinking holiday cottages,' Marion says.

It's January. Raining and blowing up a storm outside, and he's at the head office of the Trust, which sounds as though it should be grander than two scruffy offices in a shared building, a bank of mailboxes in the hallway, frayed carpet on the stairs, loose carpet tiles in here. A radiator on full blast, ticking and gurgling.

He stares at her. 'Oh, aye?' he says, thinking, here we go. He has heard this before. Marion, the new broom, all teeth and big hair and a suit that doesn't really fit her. He has nothing against her, right up to the point at which she interferes in the way he manages things.

'We were hoping to get them up and running in time for the season ...'

'The season?'

'April to November ... or maybe all through the winter, too, if there's the demand.'

November, he thinks, good luck with that. And why the fuck would anyone want to come and stay on an island that has, quite literally, nothing but birds to look at? There's no shop, no beach to speak of, not that anyone would want to paddle in the fucking North Sea. Birders, they're one thing – you can trust them to keep to the paths and not trample on ground-nesting birds. They're generally good at clearing up after themselves, and can be called upon to help with the ringing and the counts. But holidaymakers? With poorly trained dogs and kids and … toddlers? With unfenced cliffs round most of the island?

Not to mention the idea that he is fucking busy enough with his job the way it is. Not to mention that he likes his privacy.

He doesn't say any of this. Sits and listens and works the muscles in his jaw, hands balled into fists, tucked into his armpits where she can't see them.

'You don't need to worry,' she says, clearly misreading his silence. 'We're going to employ someone to manage it. Starting with the bird observatory.'

He doesn't want to just keep repeating her words back to her, and he cannot quite trust himself to speak at all in any case, so he stares until she carries on.

'We're going to smarten things up at the observatory – sheets and duvets. And we'll cater for them – hearty meals in the evening so they don't have to cook when they're all tired and cold.'

'Yum,' he says, a lemon-slice of sarcasm in his voice.

'It'll be a long process, of course. We'll have to get the lighthouse cottages refurbished gradually, but hopefully the new person will manage that as well as catering for our first guests. We'll aim to have the first cottage bookings by, say, the beginning of July. The bird observatory bookings will pay for it, and then after that it'll be a healthy profit.'

He almost laughs out loud, but his gritted teeth prevent it. Firstly, she has grossly overestimated the condition of the lightkeeper's cottages. He can almost smell them now – decades of damp, the mess left by marauding birds, the smashed windows with mouldy chipboard covering them, the old flagstone floors mossy and uneven. No plumbing, no electricity. She will have to get planning permission, and, however much she might want it to happen, that could take a long time. Other people have tried to do things with the cottages before – although not, as far as he could recall, anything as profoundly stupid as converting them to holiday cottages – and so far each scheme has been abandoned. Not cost-effective, especially when you have to get all the materials and the construction workers over to the island on a boat. And where are they going to stay, while they're refurbishing?

Secondly, and perhaps more importantly, there is the issue of Someone being employed to manage the bird observatory, as well as this proposed refurbishment. While he is not against this in principle – lord knows he certainly isn't about to start catering for fucking ornithologists, he has more than enough to do – it's more a question of who this person is going to be, and where they are going to be living.

He asks Marion, as politely as he possibly can.

'Oh, in the lighthouse, of course,' she says brightly, and he wants to smash his fist into the wall behind her.

'*I* live in the lighthouse,' he seethes.

'Aye, you do, you live there rent-free as an employee of the Trust, and your colleague will be similarly employed and accommodated. The lighthouse has – what is it? Three bedrooms? Or four?'

There is nothing he can say. Yes, there are fucking four bedrooms, if you count the one with the sloping floorboards and the huge damp patch on the ceiling from the broken tiles on the roof. That one's not what you would call habitable – and the other two are sparsely furnished and chilly, with mattresses that have definitely seen better days. Better decades. Centuries, even.

What Marion has failed to understand is that he has a certain way of life on the island, that he is used to managing on his own. Most of the time there are no birders. They certainly don't come every week.

There are things he has thus far been able to take for granted. Privacy. Peace. Being in control of things. Miles of rough sea between you and the land, like the widest moat you can imagine, and no drawbridge.

The other islands have webcams that people online can view and control. So far the Isle of Must has resisted this intrusion, or has been overlooked, to be more accurate. Everything he does on the island, he does without anyone watching. Without interference. Without comment.

He is used to things the way they are. How is he going to manage, having some guy leaving shavings in the sink, drinking his coffee? What about his vegetable garden? What about the chickens?

He talks himself down from near-raging internal hysteria. None of this, of course, is going to actually happen. The birders he's met and grudgingly interacted with are not the sort who particularly want to be catered for. By the look of them, they probably spend the entire year sleeping in those grubby-looking sleeping bags, moving from one bird hide to another, following migrations and breeding seasons around the coast. They're not going to want duvets and carpets and a lasagne with garlic bread. They're used to eating own-brand baked beans cold out of the tin. And they spend their money on fucking binoculars and camera lenses, from what he can tell – and travelling, probably – not on cosy weeks in 'luxury guest accommodation'.

Marion is talking out of her arse. As usual.

'Of course,' she adds, smiling acidly, 'you could consider managing the bird observatory yourself, as we've discussed previously?'

She sees his face. Allows herself a smirk.

'I thought not.'

By the time she stops talking about recruitment and timescales 'moving forward', he's almost smiling. It'll be fucking hilarious to watch all of this go tits-up, he thinks. As it inevitably will.

And now it's April, and Marion's plans have been set in motion. And this replacement woman has turned up, in a brand new waterproof jacket that swamps her, and boots that have barely had the labels taken off, looking as if a strong gust of wind might blow her off the cliff. He thinks she looks pissed off already. He thinks the big cheery hello and the handshake is all a big fucking act.

Rachel.

Rachel

Yesterday morning Rachel had said goodbye to Lucy and Emily. Ian had had to stay overnight in London for a meeting, so he wasn't there – and she hadn't been surprised, or disappointed. She had liked Ian when Lucy first got together with him, but then gradually over the six – no, almost seven – years they've been together she has decided he is a bit of an arse, and over the past eighteen months this has festered into genuine dislike. It's probably mutual.

She's got worse at hiding it, though. It was something that had been on her mind in the past few weeks, one of the list of things she had been musing over, during the long hours of darkness spent trying to sleep.

How it feels to be childless.

The fact that islands aren't really islands, it's only the sea that defines them. They're land, connected to land seamlessly, it's just that water is over the top.

Things that can only be defined in the presence of another thing.

Mothers are only mothers because they've given birth, only then sometimes they're not.

Lucy cried in the station car park. By rights she should have been at home in a fleecy dressing gown still, because it was early and she had a baby and who could expect anyone to look glamorous at six in the morning when they'd been up most of the night? But Lucy was up and dressed, in snug Boden jeans. She was even wearing a jacket, wheat-coloured linen, artfully creased. She had offered to drive Rachel to the station and Rachel had had no intention of turning that offer down, having spent most of her money on the train tickets. Tears were streaking her make-up and Rachel had looked at her with one raised eyebrow, thinking, who the fuck puts make-up on to say goodbye to their sister at six in the morning?

'Hormones,' Lucy said, flapping her hand, and Rachel, who in the past few months had not thought it possible that she could find any more reason to be annoyed by her only sibling, had suddenly found she could.

Emily was fast asleep in her car seat in the back. Rachel did not turn to look, although she could smell the delicate scent of her. Milk-breath and soft skin.

'You'll be fine,' Lucy said, as if it were Rachel crying and not her. 'Email me,' she said. 'Every day? And I'll send you pictures of Emily.'

Rachel wanted to say, *Don't*. Sometimes it was easier just to keep quiet. 'I'd better go,' she said. 'I don't want to miss the train.'

They had hugged awkwardly across the central console. 'I'll miss you,' Lucy said, into her ear.

'You too.'

And she'd got out of the car, retrieved her backpack from the boot and walked towards the station, trying not to run. It didn't feel like an escape.

It's not an escape if you have nowhere else to go.

Fraser

His mobile rings while he is in the kitchen making coffee. It's Craig, out of breath from tramping back down the hill to the boat. He has left the quad outside instead of putting it in the shed, which is fucking typical. But that's not what he's phoning for – he wants to talk about the girl. Woman. Whatever she is – his new lodger. Housemate.

'Aye, she's nervous about sharing with you. Go easy on her.'

'Why's she nervous?'

'Apparently Marion never told her she'd be sharing. She was thinking she was staying in the bird observatory.'

'And you're just leaving her here?'

'What am I supposed to do? Marion will have my guts if I take her straight back.'

'Fucking Marion.'

'She looked panicky so I told her about the lightkeeper's cottages.'

'They're not fit for a pig to live in.'

'Aye, well, I did mention that as well.'

Fraser makes a sound, a giant pissed-off huff.

'Well,' Craig says, 'I'm sure she'll come round. Just don't, you know, attack her or anything.'

'Fucking as if.'

'I was joking.'

'Yeah, I don't find it funny. Why didn't they just employ a man, for fuck's sake?'

'Because it's not the 1970s, Fraser, you can't actually discriminate like that any more. And besides, I don't think they had any other applicants. Funnily enough.'

Fraser disconnects the call and stomps about in the kitchen, wondering whether he is going to have to watch his language around her and be careful not to startle her all the time. It's been a long time since he has been near a woman for more than a few hours at a time, and he has never actually shared a house with one. There were women on the rigs, years ago, but they had their own quarters and most of them behaved like blokes, which he supposed was their way of dealing with being so vastly outnumbered.

And then there is the other matter. He's going to have to talk to her about it. He will have to get her on side. He will have to get her agreement, and in order to do that he will have to be Nice.

Other than that rather crucial detail, he doesn't have a clue how he is expected to behave.

On his own island. In his own house.

Rachel

Why didn't they just employ a man, for fuck's sake?

Rachel stands in the hallway, silent, awkward. Not wanting to be caught eavesdropping on Fraser's phone conversation. Not wanting their first encounter to be an argument.

Once upon a time she had been good at standing up for herself, and for other people, but she isn't that person any more. Now she is the sort of person who stands frozen to the spot in a chilly hallway listening to the man she is now living with expressing a sentiment so outdated he might have landed straight out of the last century, and she already knows she is going to have to pretend to not have heard because she isn't brave enough to say something about it, and if it's even possible she hates herself just a little bit more.

She waits for further sexist ranting, but there is only an alarming clatter of crockery, as though he's doing the washing-up in a temper.

Awkwardly she opens the door again and closes it firmly, sniffs loudly and eases her backpack to the floor, dropping the duvet and pillow on to the tiles. She pulls off her boots and slots them next to a series of enormous trainers, hiking shoes and wellies. Her boots, which had felt so huge and cumbersome after the shoes she normally wears, look tiny beside them.

Be brave, she thinks.

'Hello? Fraser?'

'Aye,' he says, and steps out from the kitchen, holding a tea towel and a mug.

Rachel takes a deep breath. 'Craig tells me I'm staying here.'

'Aye,' he says again.

'It feels a bit like we've just been landed with each other. Accidental housemates.'

He shrugs, and stares. 'Makes no difference to me. I'm out most of the time.'

'Well, I guess I will be too.'

He smirks, the first time his expression has changed. 'You'll find there's not gonnae be much for you to do.'

'No?'

'You'll be busy on Fridays and Saturdays and the rest of the week sitting on your arse. Room's upstairs,' he says, and turns and heads into the kitchen again.

'Which one?' she asks.

'Any one you like, other than mine.' And then, as an afterthought, 'There's linen and towels in the airing cupboard. Let me know if you need anything.'

She drags her backpack up the stairs. It feels bigger up here, and there are six doors, all closed, along a narrow hallway. The mustard-yellow carpet is thin and badly laid, wrinkled and threadbare in places, the floorboards creaking beneath her feet.

She opens the door at the top of the stairs and finds a bathroom, big enough for a separate shower, a huge rolltop bath that should be trendy but actually is original, rust and limescale staining the ancient enamel in a long trickle from the hot water tap.

It smells of men, of men's things. Shower gel and Lynx. Damp, cracked tiles, a mirror that's so filthy she can barely see her reflection. Black mould has been wiped off the tiles around the sink, settling into the grout. She looks at the toilet, seat up. Can't quite bring herself to look down into the pan because she already knows it won't have seen bleach in a long while. Lowers the seat and wipes it with a wad of toilet paper before using it.

Next to the bathroom is the airing cupboard. She moves on to the next door.

It's clearly his room. She shuts the door again quickly.

That leaves three rooms to explore, and after a few minutes she sees that she has the choice of a large double the other side of the bathroom, with blue flowery wallpaper, a wardrobe that looks like the gateway to Narnia and a basin in the corner which hangs at an angle off the wall; a smaller room at the back with bare floorboards, a bed with a stained mattress and a large damp patch on the ceiling; or the room next to his: yellow wallpaper, a flat-pack wardrobe and a chest of drawers, a view over the harbour from the large sash window, and a cast-iron double bed with a mattress that at least looks newer. There is a blanket folded on the armchair.

She sits on the bed in the yellow room for a while, wondering if she should go and sleep in the bird observatory tonight at least, when there's nobody in it. There is a moment where she thinks, not for the first time: *what have I done?*

She pulls her phone out of her back pocket and looks at it, thinking that she might have a message from Mel or even Lucy, something to take her mind off the fact that she's on a rock miles from anywhere and so far out of her depth she's in danger of drowning, a little bit.

No signal at all. Not even one bar.

Ten minutes pass with her staring at the wallpaper, then she forces herself to get up. In the airing cupboard she finds several sets of sheets and pillowcases, chooses one. It smells clean but a little musty. Once the birdwatchers are settled in she'll wash it, she thinks. Freshen it up a bit.

When the bed is made up with her new duvet everything feels a little bit less awful, and the sun comes out and floods the room with light. She goes to the window and looks out through the salt-washed glass over to the jetty, the sunlight twinkling on the surface of the water. The *Island Princess* has gone.

She has a sudden pang of something: a gasping panic, a fear of falling, a fear of drowning, a fear of being trapped somewhere small and dark and tight. Strange, when actually she's somewhere so open. The room is big and airy. And yet she feels cornered, trapped. Alone. Not alone enough.

Islands are only islands because of the sea over the top of them, she tells herself again. *I am still connected to the land, the same land that stretches all the way home. To Lucy, to Emily, to Mel, to Mum and Dad.*

She gets a few things out of the backpack to try and make it feel a bit more like home, but quickly gets bored with unpacking. Besides, she might not be here for long. It's only until Julia takes over. That might be anything from a few weeks to a few months. She doesn't want to start to feel at home only to get her marching orders. She takes the present out of her bag, the one Dad gave her from the drinks cabinet before she left. Does Fraser deserve it? He's clearly a misogynist twat, after all. But what's she going to do, drink it herself?

'It's a good one,' he had said to her.

'Dad! You got that for Christmas.'

'Never mind, I'll get another. Can't hurt, you know,' he said opaquely, 'to oil the cogs.'

When she leaves the bedroom she can smell freshly brewed coffee. Fraser is in the kitchen and there is a large filter coffee machine, and a grinder, and a bag of beans. He is leaning back against the worktop with a mug in his hand. The dog is lying in a dog bed near the range cooker, head between its paws, looking at her.

She gives him the whisky and thinks he likes it. She is careful to say that she brought it for him, rather than bought it. After what she overheard, she wouldn't spend money on a gift for him, and now begrudges her dad losing his Christmas present.

'What's your dog called?' she asks, and adds, to make a point, 'Craig didn't know.'

'Bess,' he says.

At the sound of her name Bess lifts her head and looks at her master with those brown, intelligent eyes. Rachel drops to one knee and Bess wags her tail and dips her head so she can fuss her.

'Hello, Bess,' she says. 'You're a good girl, aren't you?'

26

'Made you a coffee,' Fraser says. What he means, of course, is that he made himself a coffee and there is some left over. She is not fooled.

'Thanks.' There is a mug tree so she helps herself, finds the fridge and adds to the cup from a bottle of semi-skimmed. Then takes a deep breath and decides to get it over with.

'So, this is weird.'

'Aye,' he says, drinking.

'I've never moved in with someone I've just met. It's like I'm in your house.'

He shrugs. 'It's not my house. I just work here, same as you.'

'Do you get your own shopping? I mean, do I owe you for the coffee and the milk?'

'I buy the coffee beans because if I asked Craig to get them he'd get the cheapest ones.'

'So I do owe you for the coffee.' It was good, though. Best she'd had in ages, better than the cafés back home, and some of them were supposed to be all that.

'Don't worry about it. Unless you're planning on drinking ten cups a day.'

'I'll have tea,' she says, getting back to her feet.

Bess looks up at her, and across to Fraser, confused by this new dynamic.

They stand there in silence for a while. Rachel has the distinct impression he's a man of very few words, and for her part she can't think of anything to say. She is not usually like this. She wants to say, *This isn't me – normally I'm chatty and sociable.* But is she? She's been changed so much by everything that's happened. Maybe the island will suit her after all. Maybe she will learn stillness. How to live with herself.

But you can't say any of that to a man you've just met, can you?

Instead she says, 'Can I see the lighthouse?'

Fraser leads her back out into the hallway. She had not paid much attention to the layout on the way in, so distracted was she by the phone conversation she had overheard, but now she sees there are three doors other than the one to the kitchen.

He opens one of the doors, which leads to a smallish living room, a threadbare sofa with sagging cushions, two mismatched armchairs, a woodburner with a stack of logs in a basket next to it, a flatscreen TV on a table next to it.

'Cosy,' she says, for want of something to say.

'That's the radio,' he says, pointing at some electronic equipment on a table behind the sofa.

'Oh,' she says.

'I'll have to show you how to use it. It's for the coastguard, if there's an emergency.'

'Is there no phone signal, then?'

'Sometimes not in a storm.'

'Do you have to use it often?'

'Not really. We test it once a week. But you need to know how to use it, in case.'

He shuts the door again, while she's still wondering what sort of emergency might take down Fraser and leave her the only conscious person able to summon the coastguard, and swallowing down a fresh burst of panic.

Maybe he sees the look in her eyes, because he adds – which doesn't really help – 'It's not just for us to contact them. Sometimes they contact us, too. There's a pager that goes off, in case we're out of the building.'

'Why would they contact us?'

'Emergencies. You know,' he says, vaguely.

The next door, to her surprise, leads down a step into a space with nothing inside it but a huge spiral staircase, and a second door in the far wall. The hallway is cold, the chill of the stone and the height and the openness of it all.

'Where does that go?' she asks, pointing at the other door.

He doesn't answer, but opens it. Beyond is a sort of workshop, not a garage because there isn't a car, but that sort of thing. There is a space in the middle that she guesses is where the quad bike is housed when it's not in use. Beyond that, Rachel can see piles of wood offcuts, toolboxes against the wall, a ladder on hooks, double doors at the back which are propped open. Outside she can see sea, and sky.

'Right,' she says.

He begins to climb the stairs, and she follows him.

It's a long way up, but there's a landing just below the halfway point. He stops there and she thinks he's trying not to show he's out of breath. Indicates the window, and she looks out as best she can through the salty glass at a rather empty view: a bit of land, a bit of grey sea, a bit of grey sky. Wonders if she's supposed to be noticing something.

After a moment or two he continues up the stairs. They're getting narrower, and, just when she's at the point of thinking he's going to have to pause for breath again, the stairs end on a small stone landing. There is a metal stepladder fixed to the wall, and a hatch. He climbs up through the hatch, and she follows.

'Wow,' she says.

Up here there is a view, a proper view. She can see for a long way, even if it is much of the same sort of thing: choppy grey seas, a cloudy sky with a shaft of brilliant sunlight breaking through over the mainland, which looks, from here, closer than you might think.

'May,' he says, indicating a long, flattish island to the west. 'That's the Northumberland coast, over there. And that's Fife. And the rest of it, well, nothing between us and Scandinavia.'

'It's amazing.'

She turns to the light – the lamp – which is a nest of interlocking glass facets, brilliantly clean and beautiful, and the big glass bulb behind it.

'And you don't have to do anything? It's all automated?'

'Aye. An engineer comes every three months.'

She's momentarily distracted by the birds, hanging on the air outside the lamp room, suspended on invisible threads.

'You can see whales, sometimes,' he says, as if he's suddenly wanting her to be impressed.

'Really?'

'Aye, great pods of them. Minke, orca. Sometimes even humpback.'

'Gosh, I'd love to see that.'

'Maybe you will, while you're here.'

'What about the stars?' she says, turning back to the view. 'I bet you get a brilliant view of them on a clear night, don't you?'

'Aye,' he says, flicking a glance at the enormous light bulb right next to her. 'You should come up here and have a look.'

Now he's teasing her. She remembers the comment about employing a man, and stiffens. Stares him out.

'Craig said something about some cottages,' she says.

'Aye, look. See where the loch is? Next to that.' He points, but all she can see is rooftops and a dark strip of water.

'Can I go and see them?'

'Help yourself,' he says. 'They're in a state, though.'

'A state?'

'They're basically derelict.'

She takes a deep breath in. One woman's derelict is another woman's in need of updating, she thinks.

'Perhaps I can have a look later,' she says, turning away. 'I've got the bird observatory to sort out.'

Rachel

There is a surprising amount to do. She is too tired, really, but she can't leave it all until tomorrow morning, and besides, what's she going to do until bedtime? Hang out in the lighthouse with Captain Grumpy?

Rachel makes a cup of tea and sits down with the sheaf of notes Craig left her. At the back is a hand-sketched map of the island, and a printed list of the names of the people who are arriving tomorrow. Five of them. All men. There are no dietary requirements.

Among the notes is a list of suggested evening meals. Jacket potatoes, spag bol, chilli; egg, chips and beans. There are recipes for the spag bol and the chilli. Nothing too complicated, but cooking for six is a bit more than she's used to. Hopefully none of them are going to complain. At the bottom of the meals list someone has written, in a different handwriting, 'BATCH COOKING IS YOUR FRIEND!!'

The following page is about the internet and how to reset the router. Rachel pulls the phone from her back pocket and tries to connect to the bird observatory's wifi, eventually finding the router in the cupboard and resetting it. Green lights come on. Her phone connects, and pings for a few minutes as emails and notifications come through. Mel, Lucy, Ian, various bits of spam. She puts the phone back in her pocket. It would be too easy to sit here and work through all that; she has things to do.

There's a weird smell in the bedrooms, and it takes a while to identify that it's the mattresses, that smell of manmade fabric that has got damp and dried again very slowly. She opens the windows in each of the rooms, and the wind blasts in. Cold, salty, tangy – only marginally better. She goes back to the kitchen and begins a shopping list on the back of Craig's note: Febreze. Some kind of air freshener. It would be hilarious if one of those 'sea air' scented candles turned up, she thinks, smelling nothing like the actual sea air, which in reality has heady notes of drying seaweed and fish.

It is Rachel's job to make the bird observatory *a little more civilised*. Those were the words Marion had used: *make it look a bit more like an upmarket holiday let, and a bit less like a hostel*. She had tried to sound enthusiastic on the phone; interior design is not really her thing. But it is Lucy's, and the week before she came out here they spent a whole evening discussing fabrics and colours and ways to 'zhoozh' things up. Rachel has never really known what that means. Perhaps if she aims to make things look like Lucy's house it will be a good start.

31

In reality, though, she has limited tools to work with. And clearly a tiny budget, if there even is one at all. The bed linen is in one of the plastic crates, still in packets. There are the rest of the duvets and pillows too. It's all cheap stuff, bulk-bought, the duvet covers and pillowcases a dull grey, all of them identical. Plain white fitted sheets, thread count not mentioned but certainly about as low as it gets. Two sets, one for each bed and one to be in the wash. She calculates how long it will take to wash and dry five sets of bedclothes. It'll take at least three washes, probably four – and the washing machine in the generator shed is an ancient one with no 'quick wash' setting that she can fathom. Added to which, there is no dryer, and the weather is damp enough to make drying them in time highly unlikely. Not to mention the environmental cost of using all that water on sheets that are ostensibly clean.

It strikes her for the first time – and probably not the last – that Marion has really not thought all this through.

There's so much to do, Rachel thinks. *I don't know if I can.*

She stands in the kitchen wondering whether it would cost the planet more to take the boat back to the mainland with all this gear and wash and dry everything in a launderette rather than doing it here. There are bales of towels, too, desperately in need of a first wash to make them at least slightly absorbent. In the end she shoves a load full of towels in the washing machine and sets it going. Adds 'detergent etc' to the shopping list because there is only one half-full box of washing powder and no fabric conditioner.

There is an ancient wooden clothes horse in the generator shed, patches of mould on it that she can clean off. Once the towels are washed she will leave them on the clothes horse in the kitchen; hopefully they will dry overnight.

She makes up all the beds with the brand-new bedding, which is frankly exhausting, and then takes a break. It's half-past two, and she's vaguely hungry, so she makes a cheese sandwich and sits to eat it. The sun is bright on the rug in the living room, and from every window she can see sea, sky and birds. It really is a birdwatcher's paradise. In that isolated moment, she can see the appeal.

The kitchen counters are loaded with the shopping. She opens the first cupboard and pulls out the ratty cardboard box. The bottom falls out of it and with it something from inside, something heavy, which explodes on the kitchen floor.

Rachel shrieks and jumps back as clouds of flour envelop her.

Bastard thing.

Not only is it an old bag of flour, but when she eventually finds a dustpan and brush and begins to sweep up the mess she realises with a bolt of shock that it's moving of its own accord. And she looks closer and sees the flour is crawling with insects.

She squeaks again and shrinks back against the cupboards. The bag of flour has been chewed through at the bottom, and mixed in with the mess are what she thinks at first must be wild rice, small grains of black. When she looks closer, she realises it's droppings. Mouse droppings?

She scrambles to her feet. She doesn't mind mice, or insects, particularly; she just doesn't want them here, now, when she's too tired to deal with this on top of everything else. When the first guests are arriving tomorrow and the place is filthy, and damp, and probably a health hazard.

She is not going to cry. Rubs at her eyes, her face feeling gritty under her floury hands. The sudden realisation that the little insects are probably in her hair sends her into a sudden panic and she rushes for the bathroom, for the only mirror in the place, leaving floury footprints all through the main room and the corridor to the bedroom.

Her shocked little face looks back at her, white and grubby and smeared with eye make-up and flour. There is flour in her hair but she can't see anything moving; combs her fingers through it over the sink, shaking her head vigorously and muttering *fuck this shit* under her breath because it somehow helps, a little.

Fuck this place, fuck this shit, fuck it all.

She washes her hands, and her face, and as she stands straight again there is a shadow, suddenly, and then it's gone again. She looks up at the frosted glass window. It was as if someone just walked past.

But Fraser's at the lighthouse, isn't he?

She holds her breath for a moment, her heart thumping, drying her hands on the back of her jeans – which are covered in flour. God, what a complete mess.

It was just a cloud, she thinks. The sun going behind a cloud.

But when she goes back into the main room it's not sunny any more. In fact, through the main window she can see heavy, black clouds over the sea.

She gets out her phone and sends a WhatsApp to Mel.

Jesus this place is shit

A message comes back straight away.

Ur there? Whats happening? Whys it shit?

Bird place is a mess

Just tipped flour everywhere

Bugs and mouse droppings

FML Send gin

Aw babe itll be ok

tired from the journey etc

I don't know if I can do this

yes u bloody can

u r awesome

It's always there, in the background. The panic. The fear. She can hear the voices in the back of her mind already: *Why are you doing this? You're doing it wrong. Nobody likes you.*

She pushes the voices back down, reaches for the dustpan and brush.

All she has to do is get through this. She might not even need to be here very long – just until Julia can take over. You can live with anything for a few weeks, can't you? Just a few weeks. One minute at a time, one hour at a time, one day at a time. Every day will get easier.

Won't it?

2

The Bird Observatory

Rachel

Four positive things about today, Rachel thinks, vigorously wiping down the inside of the cupboard. There seems to be bird shit and various feathers inside, as though something tried to nest in here.

Come on. You can do this.

Number one. I didn't throw up on the boat. That was definitely a win.

Number two. I have clean sheets and a new duvet and my bed is already made, I can get straight in it when I get back to the lighthouse if I want to.

Number three...

She thinks for what seems an age, loses track, finds herself again in that dreamlike state where she's been standing at the kitchen counter with a dishcloth in her hand, staring at the window for an unidentifiable period of time.

Number three. The island's nice. It has cottages.

She disallows that one. She can't express an opinion on the island when she's barely seen half of it, and, actually, is it nice? It's rocky and bare and muddy. It would be nicer if it had a few trees, she thinks. Did it ever have trees? Were they all cut down by some ancient inhabitants? Wasn't Scotland once all forests ... or was that just the mainland? And as for the mythical cottages – she will have to reserve judgment on those until she's seen them.

Number three. I made it here and I can't go back.

She doesn't even bother to think of number four. She has nobody here to answer to, after all. Three will do for now. She thinks of Mel telling her off. She will call Mel later, or perhaps just send another WhatsApp, or email. If she calls, she will end up getting emotional and that will be counterproductive for both of them.

Not that Mel will care, or be surprised. It's how they met, after all.

Melanie Loakes, meet Rachel Long. Rachel, meet Mel. Norwich. Summer, two years ago. Tuesday morning. Twenty to eleven.

Rachel is in the waiting room at the doctor's surgery. Outside it's raining, and Rachel is dressed in pyjama bottoms, a grey T-shirt that she's been wearing for three days and four nights, a pink hoodie that used to belong to Lucy over the top of it. She only got out of bed three minutes before her appointment time, thinking she was going to just leave it, and then talking herself into going. It doesn't matter that she's late. The doctor is about an hour behind schedule. She has flicked through a magazine the way she flicks through TV channels, unable to commit. Now she is staring vacantly at the elderly woman directly opposite her, who is talking to another, younger woman.

'Course I think marriage is a sacred thing, you know? A man and a woman. In a church.'

Rachel hasn't been listening but suddenly she is. Maybe it's the way the younger woman is sitting, upright, staring ahead, her jaw set. She's barely into her twenties, wearing a black denim jacket with a small rainbow pin on the lapel.

Rachel glances around the waiting room and catches the eye of the only other occupant.

There is a strange sort of kinship in that first glance. The unwashed hair, the way her knee is jumping, the bitten nails. But behind the dark eyes is a quiet fury, trained on the older woman who has carried on, oblivious to the silence around her.

'You can't just be marrying people of the same sex, 'tisn't natural. Not what God intended for us, is it? And I know these people aren't believers, but they still shouldn't be ramming it down our throats. I mean, it's everywhere now, isn't it? It's taking over. On the telly. I even saw an ad on the telly the other night – an advert! Of all things! Two women kissing, in a car!'

Abruptly the dark-haired girl gets up and comes to sit next to Rachel. There is a brief, startled moment where they lock eyes. Rachel feels as if she's being challenged. In normal circumstances she shrinks from challenges, but this feels different. She is torn between the desire to say something, to speak out, to tell the old woman that she's homophobic and wrong, and panic at saying anything at all.

But she's not on her own any longer. Her new friend takes her hand, raises it to her lips and kisses it. Then both of them turn towards the old woman and stare. Rachel feels, bizarrely, triumphant.

'Wonderful, I call it,' the dark-haired girl says. 'Love is love.'

The girl opposite them blinks, wide-eyed, mouths something that might be *thank you*.

'Well, really,' the old lady says.

The nurse comes. 'Gemma Hoskins?'

The rainbow pin girl gets up and follows her, and then it's just the three of them. They are still holding hands, with the old lady across from them, looking everywhere except at them, lips furiously pursed.

The dark-haired girl mutters, 'Cat's bum face,' and Rachel loses it, properly loses it: laughs as she hasn't laughed for what feels like years, airless, breathless, shoulders shaking, until she gets a stitch.

The old woman is called in next. They listen to her walking stick tapping up the corridor. 'I'm Mel,' the dark-haired girl says, letting go of Rachel and holding out her hand instead for her to shake.

It's lunchtime when Rachel finally gets out of the surgery, clutching a prescription. She hasn't quite decided if she's going to take it to the pharmacy. Mel is waiting for her outside. They go for a coffee, as if they're properly dressed and normal.

Mel has been depressed all her life, off and on. At the moment she's not too bad. She has been on tablets since she was seventeen.

Rachel is experiencing this for the first time, officially. Her life has been a rollercoaster of highs and lows, but this is the first time she's not been able to handle it, not been able to make herself feel better. She has been spending the days in bed, the nights with the TV on. She is about to be chucked out of the house share she's in, which means she will have to go back and live with her parents, which is about the worst thing she can imagine, which is why she has finally dragged herself to the doctor's.

Three weeks after this first meeting, Rachel moves into Mel's spare room.

Five weeks after this meeting, Rachel gets a job temping at Evans Pharma.

At that point, she is just four months away from the next big fuck-up.

Rachel

It's a quarter-past four. This time tomorrow the boat will be on its way with the first lot of guests. The thought makes Rachel lurch into action again. She is going to have to be methodical about this. She works her way through the building, checking everything works: all the light switches, all the radiators, taps, plug sockets, curtains, cupboards and drawers. The light is out in the bathroom. There are no bulbs in the kitchen, or in the big storage cupboard by the front door which contains cleaning products, a mop and a bucket. She will have to ask Fraser; she adds it to her mental list.

Finally she drags the vacuum cleaner out of the cupboard and cleans the entire place from top to bottom. Not a single cobweb in a corner, not a tiny mote of dust, not a speck of flour anywhere.

After that she looks at her watch again. Five to five. She opens Mel's email. Sent before the WhatsApp.

Date: Friday 5 April 2019
From: Melanie Loakes
To: Rachel Long
Subject: Well???

Hey mate

How are you doing? Did you make it okay? What's the island like? What's the lighthouse bloke like? I'm guessing ancient and bearded?

Seriously babe I'm missing you already. I hope that sea air is better than anything you've breathed in your life. I hope that being on your own is good for you. I hope that you find your happiness again my darling, because you deserve it, you really do.

Julia texted me earlier asking if you'd been in touch. Her mum's gone in for the op today and she's just hanging around waiting, getting herself into a state about everything. I think she'd be made up if you sent her an email if you get a spare minute. She's really worried that you're hating it already.

Write back and tell me how you're doing babes. I'm worried, and I'll stay worried until I hear you're okay.

Peace out,

Mel xx

She's here because of Mel, and Julia – all that had happened just a week ago. A week! It feels like a lifetime.

Norwich city centre. The Birdcage, on Pottergate. Thursday. Late afternoon.

Mel calls her out of the blue, asking if she's free for a drink.

Rachel is always free for a drink, unless she's in bed, and even then she has been known to drag her hair into a plait and go out anyway, especially for Mel.

Rachel has a horrible feeling that Mel's going to tell her that she has decided to move in with Darius, her builder boyfriend. Meanwhile Rachel has been psyching herself up to asking Mel if she can move back into her spare room, the one she lived in last year for a while, before her most recent fuck-up. At the moment Rachel is living in one of Lucy and Ian's rental properties free of charge. Hints have been dropped and those hints are becoming more frequent and less subtle; she's going to need to find somewhere else to live, and staying at Mel's is just about the only thing she'd be able to cope with. Unless she's giving up the house to move in with Darius. They've been together for over a year now.

But it turns out their meeting is not about Mel's relationship status at all. And Mel is about to change her life forever.

'So,' Mel says. 'I had a brainwave.'

'Oh?' And Rachel thinks that she sounds a bit high. She's nervy and breathless, and smiling, and her cheeks are flushed with it.

'It's the "you can do anything" thing. You know? Like we were saying, yesterday.'

'You can,' Rachel says. 'Whatever you want.'

'Not me,' Mel says, leaning forward. 'You. My friend called. Julia. You know, the ecologist?'

Rachel looks blank.

'She's writing her thesis on lichens. She got a job working on this island off the coast of Scotland. Maybe I didn't tell you? Anyway. She got this job, only something's happened.'

There is a pause and Rachel immediately thinks this Julia is probably pregnant. She can't help herself. She has a nose for it. Pregnancy. Babies.

'No, not that,' Mel says, seeing Rachel's face. 'Her mum's been on the waiting list for a kidney transplant forever, and they've found a match, a live donor, and Julia was holding off because there are so many blood tests you have to do, you know, there's always a chance that it won't go ahead…but anyway, it's all systems go, and they're hoping to do the operation on Friday. So Julia can't start the new job because she needs to stay with her mum for the first few weeks or months or whatever after the operation. And the island people are having this massive crisis because they need someone quickly, like, next week, and they can't recruit someone else because they really want to keep the job open for Julia and besides, they didn't like any of the other candidates, or something. They need someone really flexible, temporary. And then I remembered what you said yesterday. About getting away.'

The 'getting away' thing had been in relation to getting away from Lucy and Ian. Preferably getting away from Lucy and Ian's house and back into Mel's spare room. It takes a moment for Rachel to sort through what Mel's said; she's feeling fuzzy, has been awake most of the night, staring at the telly, zoned out. When she pieces it all together the whole idea seems so laughable she thinks she must have missed something.

'You mean…me? Go to Scotland?'

'Yes, you. Of course you.'

She feels the panic rising, and all the things fly at her at once. No. It's too far. She knows nothing about lichens, or Scottish islands. She has never been north of Yorkshire. And, and, and all the things she can't even admit to, about wanting to go and wanting to run away, all at the same time. About how she feels every time she sees a baby. About the sour taste of shame. About the creeping danger of the misery. About how close she has come to ending it.

'Go on, Rach. You'd be perfect for it. And it would get you away from…all this. Give you a chance to get your head straight. And besides, it sounds like the work is piss-easy.'

'What's the job?' Rachel asks.

'The island has a lighthouse, and, like, a hostel thing – not a B&B, it's like a hostel for birdwatchers. Julia was going to be managing the hostel, changing the sheets, doing dinners. I think there's only six beds. And it's not even that busy, even in the summer, but apparently the guy who lives in the lighthouse doesn't want to do it.'

'So – it's living on the island?'

'Yes. All that fresh air! And solitude, too, just you and the gulls and the occasional twitcher. Julia was going to do all this stuff on the ecology of the island, too, and they were really keen on it, but I don't think they'd mind having someone who isn't a naturalist. They've just got all these birdwatchers booked into the hostel and nobody to look after them. They're desperate.'

'And a lighthouse-keeper who sounds a bit difficult.'

Mel looks at her. 'It would take your mind off things. Anyway, he's not the lighthouse-keeper, it's automated; he just lives in it. He's the nature reserve warden, or whatever it's called. Looks after the wildlife.'

'They wouldn't want me,' she says.

'Yes, they absolutely would. Besides, Julia will recommend you; she really wants it to be someone she knows. And it might not be for very long, maybe even six weeks or so, just until Julia's mum can manage without her. And the summer, too; you'll be out of there before the bad weather starts.'

'She doesn't know me,' Rachel says. 'What if I fuck it up? What if I can't manage? What if I have to come back?'

'What if you don't?'

Rachel stares at her. And Mel fishes in her pocket and brings out a square of paper, folded into four. She smooths it out on the table, looks at it, slides it across. *Julia Jones*, it says, and a phone number. And then, underneath, *Must*. As if she had been about to write something else, something to compel

43

Rachel to act. Must call. Must act. Must fucking do something before this gets any worse.

'That's the name of the island,' Mel says. 'Nice, isn't it?'

Before she forgets, Rachel writes a quick email to Julia.

Date: Friday 5 April 2019
From: Rachel Long
To: Julia Jones
Subject: Arrived!

Hi, Julia,

Hope things are okay with your mum. Mel says she has gone for the operation – I hope it goes well.

Just to let you know I got here safely and the island is lovely. I'll keep you updated.

Best wishes

Rachel x

She walks back to the lighthouse the long way round, figuring that later in the week one of the birdwatchers might try and ask her something, and she will look like a prize idiot if she has to admit that she has never been to the north end of the island. She has her fleece on but the wind has picked up and it's colder than she expected, given the sun which is now shining in a cloudless sky. The island is glorious, although the seabirds are something of a hazard: they have no fear of her whatsoever, landing abruptly in front of her and flapping off again without warning, circling overhead in a menacing fashion and dropping shit everywhere. Rachel thinks she should have brought a hat. So far she hasn't been hit, but it must be a matter of time.

Half a mile or so northeast of the bird observatory, Rachel comes across the ruins. She read about them when she did her limited island research; it's a former priory, dating back to the twelfth century. Some crusader built a sanctuary here and founded it. Later on, the island had been a plague refuge, and then later still a shrine, thanks to the miraculous recovery of some of the plague victims, who had been left on the island to die. Over the years the reputation for healing had persisted, but then the weather, and the distance from the mainland, had made the island less appealing and the priory had fallen into disuse. Now little remains but waist-high walls and the large stone altar, almost cave-like, with two vertical stones and a remaining flat stone across the top of them. The grass is dotted with rocks that have probably come from the priory, and now the birds have taken it over.

The north side of the island is different from the south side; the cliffs have fallen away to nothing. In places the rocks give way to sections of beach and it's possible to reach the sea, should something quite so daft become necessary. The waves crash in spumes of glittering white, the noise a dull roar. With no cliffs here, there are fewer seabirds, with the exception of some black birds sitting on the rocks, long, graceful necks and sharp-looking beaks – cormorants? Or gannets – or are they the same thing? She'll have to look them up. She finds a place to sit on the springy turf and watch the roaring waves for a little while as they surge through the spaces between the rocks, white foam racing towards her. Turns her face to the sun, closing her eyes, enjoying the solitude. She finds silence difficult, always has. When things got really bad, she used to sit with her headphones on and an app choosing music for her for hours and hours. Anything to blank it all out.

You might expect it to be peaceful here, and it is, but it's not a silent peace, it's a noisy one. Very noisy. Waves and wind and birds crying, and the ever-present call of the sea.

Something flickers across her closed eyes and she opens them quickly. A bird flying across the sun, probably. But she has an odd feeling now, as though she's being watched. She gets to her feet and brushes her hands across her backside, looks up the long slope towards the bird observatory, and the lighthouse beyond and to the right. Behind it are ominous dark clouds, a smudge of a rainbow.

She needs to get back.

In the distance some movement catches her eye. At first she thinks it must be a bird, but then she sees a figure near the lighthouse, walking up the hill. She can just make out a dark coat, some sort of hat, jeans. It must be Fraser, of course. But he looks different, somehow, from the man she met earlier. Smaller. Skinnier. The figure moves out of sight behind the building.

Of course it's Fraser. Who else could it be?

Rachel

The lighthouse isn't at all what she expected. She had expected a single column, gaily painted with red and white horizontal bands. Over the years she has been dragged on many a post-Sunday lunch bracing walk along the coast, and the lighthouse at Happisburgh was always a marker that indicated a cup of tea and a biscuit was imminent. Happisburgh Lighthouse was what Rachel had been expecting, despite having seen pictures when she had been Googling the island. But this lighthouse looks more like a Victorian parsonage lifted from the North Yorkshire moors and impaled on to a tower, which happens to have a lamp room on the top of it.

It's not unattractive. It just doesn't feel quite right.

Rachel's walk back to the south of the island takes her round the other side of the lighthouse, and there is plenty more to see. A series of outbuildings at the back, set in a rough U shape. And there are chickens! To her absolute delight, she can see four – no, five – big old hens pecking around in the yard. The outer doors to the workshop, which she'd seen when Fraser showed her the back door, are open. Just inside – she hadn't noticed it earlier – is a smaller wooden structure that she guesses must be their coop. She wonders about predators, but then realises that probably there aren't any.

Beyond the sheds is a garden of sorts, raised beds and a wigwam ready for beans. She looks at the beds and tries to guess what's growing, but beyond the canes and something that looks like carrot tops it's hard to tell. It's neat but not obsessively so; weeds grow up around the sleepers that have been used to make the beds.

So: Fraser likes his fresh veg, and his fresh eggs. And his decent coffee.

The veg garden is fenced on one side, presumably for some shelter from the wind, and on the other side of this is a much smaller garden, surrounded by a wall. To her surprise it's a riot of spring colour. Lots of stunted daffodils, hyacinths, still some crocuses. It's a wild, tangled sort of place, everything looking a bit windblown. And at the end of the path, a bed with a single rosebush in it, a leafy climbing rose which is having a good old go at clinging to the wire trellis covering the wall.

And then she finds herself back at the front door.

This time she opens the door without knocking and blasts into the hallway. Her cheeks are pink and stinging from the wind, her ears numb. She takes off her fleece and hangs it on the coat stand by the door, toes off her hiking boots and slots them next to Fraser's giant wellies.

Something smells delicious. She can hear pots and pans banging around in the kitchen. Fraser is stirring something on the stove, a huge black Aga-like thing that looks every bit as intimidating as he is.

'Hello,' she says.

Fraser looks around and then goes back to the pot. 'How did you get on down there?'

'Great. All done, I think.'

'Did you go to the cottages?'

'I didn't get a chance.'

'I can take you down there if you like.'

'That would be great, thanks.'

She has so many questions for him that she doesn't know where to start, but her conversation skills have pretty much

47

dried up over the course of the past year. Apart from necessary conversations with Lucy, and Mel, of course, she sometimes went for days without talking to anyone. But then Fraser clearly doesn't get to talk much, either. They make a fine pair.

He's changed from earlier, into a plain navy T-shirt and jeans. She watches him, eyes dry with tiredness. Is she imagining it, or is there something going on? It's as if she's walked in on something, an argument; it's an uncomfortable prickle on the back of her neck, hanging in the air like static, like a moment of quiet in a classical performance when people aren't sure whether to start clapping. It's as if there is a question she has forgotten to ask. Something she should have done, and hasn't. As if he is angry at her, sulking, and she has no idea why.

'You like curry?' he asks.

'Oh. Yes, I do.'

'Set the table, then. Cutlery in that drawer.'

She finds knives and forks, and neatly ironed cotton napkins in the drawer below. A stack of placemats are on the kitchen table already; she sets two places.

'It smells amazing,' she says, not quite sure how to broach the delicate subject of cooking generally and whether they are going to take turns.

He doesn't answer. He takes two plates out of the bottom of the Aga, which makes her realise that he was always planning to eat with her and it wasn't something he was forced into because she happened to turn up. In fact, she thinks, as he places the two plates on the table, he was probably waiting for her.

As he does so, he looks at the door. As if he's expecting someone else.

'What sort of curry is it?' she asks.

'Vegetable,' he says, and then, through his first forkful of it, 'Butternut squash.'

It's a beautiful meal. Brightly coloured vegetables in a warm saffron-golden sauce, on a bed of steaming white sticky rice. Where's he got a butternut squash from, anyway? Did he grow it? Or is it another one of the 'special' things that Craig has brought him from the mainland? He's given her a huge plateful. She looks at it and remembers the Scottish breakfast she had this morning, which feels now like a year ago. She thinks, *I don't usually eat as much as this in a week.*

She takes a mouthful and the flavours are overwhelming. The heat of it rises a second later – quite the most chilli-laden sauce she's had in a long time.

He keeps glancing at her and looking away again, as if he can't quite settle. As if he can't bring himself to look.

'Too hot for you?'

She wonders if he's deliberately overspiced it, to see her squirm. 'Not at all,' she tells him, with a little half-smile. 'I went to uni in Birmingham.'

They eat in silence for a while.

'What was your degree in?' he asks.

'English.'

She doesn't tell him that she dropped out after the first year, although suddenly she finds a voice and can't stop, rattles on about the nineteenth-century novel, the digs she lived in, the course, the lecturer she got on well with. He doesn't ask anything else – doesn't get a word in. Perhaps that's why she's doing it. Out of nowhere she remembers Julia Jones, whose job she has temporarily taken. Writing a thesis on something relevant, something he would probably be interested in. Fraser isn't interested in feminist critical theory, clearly. She wonders if he's even read a book.

There it is again – the prickly tension on the back of her neck. Fraser hears something that she doesn't, looks up to the doorway.

Fraser

He watches her eat, listens to her talking about Atwood and Woolf and feminist criticism, trying to think of things to say.

He's not used to making small talk. He's never sat at this table with a woman before. All of this is new territory.

He thinks of Julia Jones, and wonders if the conversation would have been any easier over her first meal. Mosses and lichens, he thinks; he'd have thought that on any given day he would take that over English. But Julia isn't here yet, and Rachel is, and he has to make the best of it.

He has no beef with feminists. His mother, who died of cancer five years ago, had been a fearsome wee woman from Paisley who would give him what for if he gave her any cheek, even though he'd towered over her from the age of twelve. She had had Fraser when she was sixteen, and he'd not had a dad or anything resembling one – not counting Uncle Jack, his ma's older brother, who had taken him to Rangers matches a couple of times as a kid – until she had married Douglas, when Fraser was at college. And then Maggie had come along the following year. He'd thought it a bit weird, his ma getting pregnant, but of course when he'd seen the baby it was another matter. She was tiny and vulnerable and held on to his finger with her whole hand.

'She likes you,' Ma had said.

The feeling had been mutual, although for his part it was strained rather by the screeching in the middle of the night; he'd got up a fair few times with her, when Douglas was on nights. For some reason Maggie had settled in Fraser's arms better than she did for anyone else. He liked that – knowing that he had the knack. Or whatever it was. And after his ma and Douglas had got divorced, when Maggie was just ten, he'd been there for the both of them.

Maggie.

His ma never blamed him for what happened, or if she did she never said, which was something that he could hold close to his heart when she was gone. Given that there was nothing else left.

He told her in the hospital, that one day he would kill Jimmy Wright. By then she had been unconscious, the morphine

50

keeping her sedated but, at last, pain-free. If she heard him, she did not, could not respond. Couldn't tell him that he was mad; couldn't order him not to do it. Perhaps that was why he had waited. But he had wanted to tell her, none the less. 'For Maggie,' he'd said, kissing her forehead. 'And for you.'

She had died an hour after he'd left the hospital; one of the nurses, when he came back, told him it happened often that way. 'It's as if they want to slip away without you,' she said. 'So you don't have to see it. She was waiting for you to go, so she could go too.'

While it might have been the sort of thing some people's mothers would do, to avoid fuss of any kind, he couldn't help thinking that his own would have chosen to go out with a bang, with as big an audience as she could gather around her and as much drama as possible, if she'd had any choice in the matter. In reality she had changed the year before, when it all happened. She had aged overnight and shrunk into herself a little bit more with each day that passed. The lump in her breast and the one on her spine and the others they kept finding, until they stopped bothering to look for more – they were just so much scar tissue from her broken heart. It was this that killed her in the end. It wasn't cancer. It was devastation.

She was only fifty-five.

He finds the emotion welling up inside him at the kitchen table. He hasn't thought about his mother in a long time. It has been easier not to. Thinking about Maggie is hard enough.

Rachel has fallen silent, is looking at her empty plate with surprise. 'Plenty more,' he says, waving a fork at the casserole dish. 'Help yourself.'

She takes a further delicate spoonful, and one of rice. 'Thank you.'

He wonders how she managed to eat it all so fast while simultaneously talking, while he's still chewing on Round One.

'Are you a vegetarian, then?' she asks.

'No,' he says. 'Are you?'

'No. I mean, this is great.'

'I thought you might be.' He's not admitting to the fact that he cooked this curry just in case she was, but that's exactly what he did. It's nice enough, though. He'll do it again.

He goes back to eating. 'So what were you doing, before this?'

She looks up, startled. He watches her trying to collect herself, wonders what he's said to provoke that reaction.

'Long story,' she says. Then she adds, 'I did some travelling after uni. Far East, Australia, Thailand. Then I worked for a pharmaceutical company. Then I had a bit of time off. And now I'm here.'

That wasn't a long story at all. In fact it was a notably short one. He waits for her to carry on and tell him about the 'time off', but she doesn't. There is a silence that starts out like a moment of blessed peace after all the talking, but quickly becomes awkward. He fumbles for something to say to change the subject, to make her feel better. To unfreeze her.

'You got family?'

There's a pause while she chews, swallows. 'Yes. Mum and Dad. Older sister.'

'You close?'

'I guess.'

'Boyfriend?' Get that one out of the way, he thinks.

'No. At least – no. You?'

'Ha!' he says. 'No. Nor a girlfriend either.'

'I guess it's not easy, sustaining a relationship when you live out here.'

'I don't do relationships.'

He thinks she might be about to ask him more about that, and to bring that line of conversation to an end he gets to his feet, the chair legs scraping noisily on the tiled floor, making her jump. He puts his plate in the sink and turns on the tap. Then she's beside him, with her plate, and picking up a tea towel to dry.

'That was really good,' she says. 'Shall we take it in turns to cook? I don't mind if we do.'

52

He shrugs. 'I'll cook anyway. You eat it, if you want to.'

He feels her tense beside him and he realises what he said probably sounded ungrateful.

'I mean, you'll be cooking down at the bird observatory. Don't want to do it twice, do you?'

'I suppose not.'

Bess whines at the door, and Rachel goes to let her out. The fresh air fills the kitchen again and he can smell rain on the wind. Tomorrow will be wet, he thinks. He has grown used to reading the island, reading the clouds. He is not always right. But in the morning, whatever the weather, he'll have forgotten his prediction in any case. You deal with it, as it comes. You eat what the boat brings you, you fix things that are broken, you deal with ginger-haired arts graduates that wash up on your island. You wait for the right moment to speak up.

This isn't the right moment. Not yet.

The dog scampers back in, and Rachel closes the door behind her and resumes her drying up.

'What about you?' she asks, as if she's resuming a conversation that broke off minutes before. 'How come you're working here?'

He doesn't answer straight away. He has a sudden desire to tell her, to actually say the words. Nobody has asked him this question, ever. The interactions he has with the birdwatchers, the scientists and the staff from the Forth Islands Trust that turn up every once in a while are all necessarily brief and functional. Even when conversations get a little deeper, it's usually about birds, or seals, or whales, or the tide or the weather or the wildflowers and the dense, springy turf. Nobody has asked him anything personal for, probably, years.

I'm here because I'm going to kill someone. I'm here because I can't be trusted.

He doesn't say it. He thinks of an answer to her question – how come he's here? And that question in particular, of all the questions she could ask him, is the one perhaps he's most desperate to answer, while at the same time not being able to.

He looks at her, briefly, finds those bright blue eyes study-ing him intently, and looks away again.

'That's *my* long story,' he says. And leaves it there.

Rachel

I don't do relationships.

He said that, and Rachel thought to herself that it sounded like a bloody brilliant way of going through life, because relationships generally were shit, weren't they? Although she didn't say this out loud. If she'd followed that policy she might not have gone through the whole Amarjit thing and then she'd be a lot better off now.

He hasn't messaged her for a while now. She'd thought that when he stopped messaging things would get easier, but they haven't. She should have blocked him, but she hasn't. She pretends this is because she is being an adult by being civilised towards him even after everything that happened, because she is a good person, she is kind, and because he sometimes used to cry on the phone to her and she was worried he might hurt himself.

Almost eighteen months have passed since their relationship came to an abrupt end. He has not left his wife. He has not hurt himself.

She'd kept the messages because she had thought about sending them to his wife. Because she deserves to know. And maybe then the woman would leave him, serve him fucking right, and then maybe he'd think twice about doing it to someone else.

But she hasn't done this either, because she also knows that his wife isn't going to leave him, because it turns out she knew about Rachel when it happened and she didn't leave him then. So she would be sending the screenshots of his messages to her for another reason: to hurt her. To make her see that he was still contacting her even after it was supposedly over. And that would surely serve no purpose but to wound. Now, too much time has passed for her to get away with the 'look what your arsehole of a husband is still doing' approach.

Women like to talk about girl code and sisterhood and fixing each other's crowns. Women don't mean to hurt each other, but they still do it. They'd almost rather hurt each other than hurt the bastard who caused the situation in the first place. That's what love does to you.

While Rachel is still wiping things dry, Fraser empties the sink and puts the plates in the cupboard. She watches as everything goes away, trying to memorise where it belongs so she doesn't spend time opening and shutting cupboards and ending up guessing.

'I'm going to bed,' he says, when he's finished, offering Bess a dog biscuit. He makes her sit for it. 'If you're staying up, turn off the light when you're done.'

She looks at her watch. It's just gone nine p.m. but it feels later. She is bone-tired from the stress of the past few days. 'I'm ready for bed too. It's been a long day.'

She leaves him to turn all the lights off and heads for the stairs. In the bedroom, her backpack is still lying on the floor. She pulls things out half-heartedly, hanging a shirt and a hoodie up in the wardrobe that smells very odd. Musty. She finds her washbag and goes to the bathroom, but the door is closed. A strip of light shines from underneath it.

Bess comes up the stairs and looks almost startled to see Rachel there. The dog sits, looks at the closed bathroom door, looks back at Rachel, as though there's a queue and she's not sure if she's joined the back of it.

Rachel waits for a minute on the landing, in case he's about to finish in there and she can nip in to have a wash. His bedroom door is open, the bedside light illuminated. A big bed – kingsize, by the look of it – with a cotton duvet cover on it that might once have been the epitome of '80s masculine black with a red stripe through it, but now is faded to grey. It's crumpled, and the room is certainly lived-in – a pile of books beside the bed – she was wrong about him not being a reader, then – clothes on the chair, although they are folded. Her mind is on other things – on what this room reminds her of. She is looking for something but not really expecting to find it: some explanation of why this man is living here in complete isolation, how he deals with it.

Then her mind swims back to focus on where she is, and then she sees it and can't unsee it.

On the bedside table, next to the pile of books. The oddest thing, and at first glance it doesn't look in any way scary or dodgy, it's just that it looks out of place.

And then she hears steps inside the bathroom and she knows he's about to come on to the landing, and she dives back to her own room and shuts the door.

Just in the nick of time. She can hear him treading the thin carpet between the bathroom and his room next door. Then his door closes, firmly. She sits on the edge of her bed, breathless with terror.

It was a knife.

Not just any knife, one of those huge fuck-off hunting knives with a serrated edge. A weapon.

What's he doing with it? You don't need a knife like that to cut a butternut squash. And in any case, why is it in his bedroom? Next to his bed?

There's only one thing it could mean. He's scared of someone.

And the only person here is her.

Fraser

Fraser lies in bed wondering if he should lock his door.

That the rooms here have locks in the first place is quite strange, given the isolation of the place. You have to trust people if you're going to live with them, miles from anywhere, don't you? If you're going to steal something, where would you even take it? He thinks about locking the door, but she will hear it – the key turning in the lock – and to do so would imply that he is afraid of her; that he thinks that she will come into his room unexpectedly. Or, worse, that he doesn't trust himself not to hurt her without a locked door between them to give him time to come to his senses.

All those rather sweet things she said about it being weird, about her moving in to his house – it was her way of bringing it up. *You're not going to kill me, are you?*

Of course he's not going to kill her. Of course he's not going to hurt her.

Is he?

He has thought a lot about crime, and justice, in the past four years. Violence. Retribution. Guilt. Absolution. Forgiveness. They are abstract concepts, but he has given each of them careful consideration. He has thought about it so much it's borderline obsessive.

And it's not as if he has no experience of violence. If she knew this, if she knew what he is capable of, what he has thought of doing, she would be calling Robert right now and asking for the boat to come back.

On his infrequent trips back to the mainland Fraser spends a long time in the second-hand book shop in Market Street in St Andrews, donating back to them a bag of those he's read and taking another pile away with him – true crime, legal thrillers, a bit of Dickens; sometimes he will just pick books on a whim. The owner has taken to putting books aside for him, ones he thinks he'll enjoy, and invariably he takes the whole pile.

He doesn't know what it is he's looking for, but he's searching each book for it. It's the answer everyone wants, isn't it? Aren't some things we do simply beyond forgiveness? How can anyone ever be forgiven, for taking a life?

Now he's lying there listening to Rachel using the bathroom next door, hearing the rattle of the water through the pipes, hearing her sniff, and cough. He shouldn't be listening but the sounds are so alien to him. In the silent moments he forgets quickly, and then hears something and it makes him jump.

He has been living with this a long time, he thinks.

Living with the ghosts.

Rachel

Rachel wakes up suddenly, disorientated, wondering what has woken her. The room is dark, utterly black, apart from a strange intermittent glow. It takes her a minute to realise that it must be the light from the lighthouse, sweeping the dark skies. In between circuits, she can only just make out the shape of the window. Inky dark, still, outside.

She waits, heart thumping, and then she hears it again. A low moan from somewhere.

It's him, of course; it has to be him. Nobody else here it could be, is there?

Silence, for a while, and then the moan again, which rises and becomes a shout. Is he in pain? What's going on? She picks up her phone and sees that it's half-past two. Then she turns on the bedside light because she can feel herself getting scared, and she wants to see the edges of the room she's in, to get a sense of place.

It comes again, louder, sounding almost afraid. Angry afraid. And a 'No!' to go with it.

Definitely a nightmare, she thinks. She remembers the knife. What if he sleepwalks, too? With a knife?

And then she hears a single word, like a question, rasped out: 'Maggie...?'

She climbs out of bed and opens the door. The hallway is just as it was last night, of course, Fraser's door still firmly closed, the light off. Bess is outside his door on the landing. When the dog sees Rachel she rises to a sit, gives a small whine.

Rachel goes to her and strokes her head reassuringly, then carries on to the bathroom and turns on the light, shutting the door. She uses the loo and pulls the ancient chain, which empties the cistern noisily. Perhaps that will be enough to bring him out of the dream he's having.

When she goes back down the hallway, the light is on under his door.

'Fraser?' Rachel says. 'Are you all right?'

He doesn't reply. She thinks she can hear breathing from the other side of the door, but perhaps it's just the blood roaring in her ears. She heads back to bed and turns off the light, lying there for a long time thinking about it. He has nightmares. Lots of people do. And maybe he's never known about it before because there's been nobody here to wake him up, or be disturbed by the noise.

Now Rachel can't sleep. It's only watching for the strange brightness that comes and goes with a lovely rhythm that's calming her down. It's almost hypnotic.

And of course, now, she can't stop wondering: who is Maggie?

3

Learning

Fraser

Fraser opens his bedroom door to see Bess lying on the landing outside Rachel's room, facing it, her head on her paws. She lifts her head to look at him, and then lowers it again almost immediately. He wonders what she's doing there. The dog usually sleeps downstairs next to the range, where it's warm, or sometimes in his room when the weather is mild. Last night he had closed his door, of course – maybe she objected to being shut out.

Then he remembers something: Rachel outside his door, asking if he was all right. He'd heard her going to the bathroom, and then that. Of course he was all right. Why wouldn't he be?

He must have made some sort of noise. Another nightmare, maybe. He has vague memories of sitting on the edge of the bed, again, head in his hands. Fuck.

The girl is already wary of him, she's made that clear. Although he can't blame her. None of them on the mainland have given a passing thought to how fucking awkward this is, the shoving together of a man and a woman who've never even met, forcing them to share a house and a kitchen and a bathroom in complete isolation. For all she knows, he could be a rapist. For all *he* knows, she might be a psychopath. They hadn't considered that, either, had they?

And he'd been expecting Julia, anyway; he'd been prepared for Julia. She has worked for the Trust before, although he has not met her. He has seen pictures of her on some field trip, holding up a rock which was clearly something significant.

He goes downstairs and puts on some porridge, remembering the moment when he hauled Rachel up on to the jetty by the waistband of her jeans. What an introduction. *Welcome to the island, try not to fall off the boat.*

And here we are, day two, and he still hasn't told her.

He's going to have to tell her today, that's for sure; it can't go on any longer. Although she might not last, might not cope, and there's still a chance she will phone Craig this morning and demand to be taken off the island, especially if he's been shouting obscenities in the night. He will see, when she gets up. If she wants to leave, then she can go and she won't need to be any the wiser.

And Julia will be here before too long, and she will be off looking at her mosses and lichens and he will be left in peace. He understands scientists. He's had plenty of them here on the island over the years. He knows that even while you're talking to them, mostly they are thinking about their subject. And the rest of the time they'd prefer it if you didn't talk to them at all.

Meanwhile, he will try to sleep. Try to stay quiet.

Try not to think about murder.

Rachel

When Rachel wakes up the next day, she can tell from the silence in the lighthouse that Fraser has already gone out.

The kitchen is clean and tidy but there is a pan on the stove with some porridge left in it. He has left her a bowl and a spoon at the place where she sat for dinner last night, so she assumes that the porridge is for her. There is also a mugful of coffee left in the filter jug. Possibly he is saving that for his mid-morning break, but she takes the risk and pours it into a mug, washes up the jug and empties the filter of the steaming coffee grounds.

The porridge is rich and creamy, with a hint of something in it, something alcoholic. It's delicious and warming and fills her up.

She washes the pot and her bowl and dries them, trying to remember which cupboard the clean dishes go in.

Outside it is grey and cold, a strong wind blowing. Rachel is hopeful that the sun might break through later. She pulls on her fleece and boots and sets off for the bird observatory. On the way she sees Fraser, on the clifftop, Bess at his heels. Fraser is looking out to sea with a pair of binoculars and, squinting, she can just make out some birds floating on the waves a few hundred metres off the shoreline. He is too far away to hear her if she were to shout.

The bird observatory is warm, and smells of the chilli she left in the slow cooker overnight. It has developed into a rich-looking sauce and she stirs it, scraping in the dark bits from the edges. Gives it a taste.

Somehow she has added too much salt. Fuck. She grimaces at it, wonders what she can do to fix it; adds another can of chopped tomatoes. Now it looks watery. She gives it another stir, leaves it cooking. Hopefully that will dilute the salt a bit, and by the time they come to eat it this evening it'll be okay. If it's not, she'll have to do jacket potatoes. Or something.

The towels that she left draped over the clothes horse are still slightly damp. She needs a washing line really; a line strung between the bird observatory and the well house would do it – something to catch that breeze on dry days. Otherwise, how is she supposed to dry the linen?

She adds it to the mental list of questions for Craig – she's going to email him later.

If the towels aren't dry by four p.m. then the birdwatchers will have to make do with the remaining towels in the bale, the brand-new, unwashed ones that probably have the absorbency of the plastic bag they came in.

She goes back out of the bird observatory, heading for where she saw Fraser. She turns in a slow circle, buffeted by the wind, looking for him, and eventually sees a figure striding in the direction of the harbour where the boat dropped her off yesterday. She walks in that direction, which thankfully is downhill, but nonetheless she's out of breath when she gets close enough to shout to get his attention.

He turns and sees her, waits for her to catch up. He's heading for a strange-looking structure that she'd wondered about when she'd seen it from the boat – a long, curved thing, a timber framework with netting over it, like the fruit cage that Dad has on his allotment, to stop birds getting at his raspberries. Only much bigger. It's like a tunnel, she realises, getting smaller and narrower at one end. Like a funnel.

'What's this thing?' she asks, giving Bess's head a scratch.

'This? It's a Heligoland trap.'

'A trap?'

'So we can ring birds. Come and look.'

Fraser takes her to the pointed end, where there is a wooden box attached with a flap. He lifts the flap and she leans forward to see: it's empty.

'Passerines fly in and get trapped, then I ring them, record them and release them. But not so many at this time of year. We'll have more later in the summer.'

She wants to ask what a passerine is, she's never heard of one before, but she doesn't want to appear stupid. It seems a big structure to build just to trap one type of bird.

'About half of all birds are passerines,' he says, as if he's reading her thoughts. 'Most garden birds, for example. They have three toes pointing forwards and one back, so they can perch.'

'Like, not a seabird?'

'Shorebirds and waterfowl,' he says. 'Mostly shorebirds, and eider ducks. That's what we get here. But we get plenty of passerines in the summer, some rare ones too.'

She smiles. This is good, she thinks. She has learned something so she won't look quite such an idiot if a birdwatcher asks her a question.

'Will you show me how to do ringing?'

Fraser looks surprised, just for a moment. 'Sure, if you want to. You can help.'

'I'd like to. Besides, it's in my job description that I'm supposed to help you.'

He closes up the trap again and stands awkwardly for a moment, waiting for her to ask something else.

'Oh! Thank you for the porridge. And the coffee.'

He shrugs. 'I can do eggs one day if you prefer.'

'Oh, lovely. From your hens?'

Of course from the hens. Where else is he going to get eggs from? Unless he harvests them from the seabirds' nests.

'Do you have something like a washing line?'

He frowns at her, shakes his head.

'Only, the towels aren't dry. I can't imagine how I'm supposed to dry bedding and towels in a day each week, really. I think if I leave them on the clothes horse they'll just stay damp and get smelly.'

'You can bring them up to the lighthouse,' he says. 'There's a tumble dryer in the workshop. Better check it actually works.'

'Ah, that sounds great. Wouldn't it be better just to hang it all outside, though? It seems a shame to waste this wind.'

He smirks at her. 'Aye, well, you might get it dry right enough, but you'll likely have to wash it all over again. And that's if the wind doesn't take it out to sea first.'

She had forgotten about the seabirds. They would just shit all over everything, wouldn't they? How stupid she feels!

'I can bring the dryer over to the bird observatory,' he says. 'There's no point in you carrying everything there and back, and I don't use it.'

'Really?' she says, suddenly happy again. 'That would be great, thank you. Can I give you a hand?'

He shakes his head but she follows him back up to the lighthouse anyway, and he doesn't seem surprised or perturbed to have her as his shadow. She goes with him round to the workshop at the back. It's much bigger than she'd first thought: she can make out breeze block walls and the door that leads back into the house, a cobweb-threaded UPVC window giving a little light; but it's difficult for her to see much more until he flicks a switch and a fluorescent light overhead reveals the tool chests round the walls, a big workbench, old wardrobes and shelves stuffed with tins of paint, plastic crates, cardboard boxes. The quad bike has been backed in, complete with trailer.

The tumble dryer is near the door and he quickly starts wiping it down, as if he's ashamed to let her see it. He drags it out from the corner it's been living in, and plugs it in – it works. It squeaks painfully, as though it needs some oil somewhere, but, when he pauses it a moment later by opening the door, Rachel can feel a gust of warm, slightly stale air coming from it.

'Great! That's fabulous,' she says.

'Can you get the bottom?' he asks, and between them they lift it over to the quad bike and haul it into the trailer. He tips it over on to its side and ties a ratchet strap around it, presumably to stop it jumping around when they go over the bumps. 'Want me to take it over there now?'

'If you've got time.'

He grunts as if he isn't doing her a massive favour, starts up the quad bike and waits, looking at her expectantly.

'You coming?' he asks at last.

Oh, she thinks, and climbs on the back of it. Is there a way to climb on board without grabbing his shoulder for support? Is there a way to ride the quad without actually holding on to him? If there is, she hasn't found it yet, but actually she is already starting to get used to it, this strange sort of partnership that's come from nowhere. Because what else can they do? He might not like having her in his space, and she might not be comfortable with this new level of solitude, but they have to get through it, don't they?

It's raining now, but Fraser's back is sheltering her from the worst of it. She hunkers down as the quad speeds along the clifftop, seabirds calling at them, affronted at the intrusion. In no time at all the bike is decelerating and he eases up as close to the generator shed as he can. The rain is driving at them sideways and she can hardly see through it, but Fraser doesn't seem in the least bothered.

She takes the bottom of the dryer again. Lifting it out of the trailer is much harder than putting it in; it's heavy, and it's wet, the smooth sides slippery. But she is determined not to look weak, and she lifts it, feeling the pull of her core muscles that are still not as strong as they were, hoping she's not going to have to drop it.

There are three steps up to the building, and a doorway that looks too narrow to get the dryer in. They didn't think about this. She should have measured the doorway first. Will they be able to fit it through the bird observatory porch instead?

But before she can think about this any further he's somehow moved his hands from the side to the back of the dryer and it slides in through the doorway with just a centimetre to spare either side.

'Okay?' he asks. 'You can put it down.'

She tries not to drop it, going for a controlled descent. Her fingertips are screaming with the effort.

'Where d'you want it?'

She looks around. 'I'm just hoping there's a plug socket.'

There is a double one on the far wall – where the washing machine is, of course. He walks the dryer over to it.

'Thanks again,' she says. 'I'll go and get a cloth and give it a wipe down. Do you want a cup of something?' She thinks of the coffee machine in the lighthouse and assumes he's going to decline.

'I'd better get back to work,' he says.

'Right,' she says. 'Thanks again.'

He hesitates for a minute, frowning, hands in his pockets, a silence that's suddenly awkward.

'Is there something wrong?' she asks.

He breathes out, then shakes his head. 'No. We'll – we can talk later.'

'Talk?'

'Doesn't matter. Later.' And he turns to go.

She cleans the dryer as best she can, and dries off the plug and the cable and anything else that looks as if it wouldn't take kindly to being rained on and then connected to the electricity, then she goes to get the towels and lets it run for an experimental half-hour, while she has a cup of tea in the bird observatory. The place is looking better. It could do with something to take that slightly musty smell away, but clean bedding and towels will do that, and now she has a dryer she will be able to get everything washed. She emailed Craig last night, asked him for some fabric freshener and some reed diffusers or something. He hasn't replied.

And now, of course, she keeps thinking about Fraser. He wants to have a word with her. As if she's done something wrong. She only has to be here for a few weeks; surely he can put up with her if it's only temporary? Surely he's not going to tell her to pack her things and go?

Fraser

Murder. He's thought about it a lot, since that night.

He had been asleep in bed when the phone had rung downstairs. He hadn't bothered to get out of bed, and an hour or so later – two-fifteen – there had been a knock at the door. The sort of knock you don't ignore.

His uncle, his face wet with tears, staggering, illuminated in the bright orange of the streetlights. A taxi idling against the kerb. Somewhere a dog barking.

'What the fuck…?'

'It's Maggie. There's been an accident. She's dead.'

The next few hours had passed in a bone-white fog of shock and denial. There had to be a mistake, he'd thought, over and over again, pulling on his jeans and sweater and going to the hospital with Jack. Maggie was, actually, still alive. She was on life support. He didn't see her immediately. The two of them were shown to a small, windowless room where his mother was waiting, red-faced and red-eyed, hands shaking around a fragile scrap of tissue, a cup of tea on the low table in front of her untouched, dark skin congealing on the surface.

They'd sat in a silence punctuated by wet sniffs, none of them able to find words. Two weeks earlier, Jack, who was a heavy drinker, and unpredictable, had had a row with his sister – merely the latest in a long series of incidents between them, but one that had ended in Jack storming out shouting the sort of things that were difficult to come back from. He'd wished death and disease upon her and her friends. He had called her a drunk and a hoor and had told her she'd never see him or her nephews, his sons, again as long as he drew breath.

All of this had been related to Fraser as, supposedly, a neutral party. He had been the go-between for years, the one that kept Jack, and their mum, and Maggie, all linked by a thread even when they'd done their level best to hack through it. Now, the memories of those fierce words still fresh in their minds, brother and sister had apparently lost the ability to communicate, as if they'd have to resolve that particular crisis before they could deal with this one.

A moment later a tired-looking young man in scrubs came in, and sat down. He introduced himself, but Fraser immediately forgot his name. He told them that Maggie had suffered catastrophic internal bleeding. That an artery somewhere had been torn by the impact of the car crash; that it had been impossible to treat her injuries. She was being kept alive, he said, but there was extensive brain damage from which there was no possibility of recovery.

Later, there was talk of organ donation – Fraser brought it up – but that was quickly shut down. She wasn't suitable, they said. But they really appreciated the consideration at such a difficult time, so many families didn't, what a difference it would make, but unfortunately blah blah.

They couldn't use her organs because she was an IV drug user. It was only later that Fraser had realised. She'd been off the gear and back on it several times already and she was still only eighteen. Fraser had thought she was doing better. He'd seen her three days ago and she'd been bright and happy but not high. She'd been talking about a charity that was helping her find a flat. She'd been asking if she could stay at his until the offer came good. He'd even said yes, because she looked as though she was doing great, and even if she'd been rattling how could he ever have said no to her? But he had, in the past. Tough love. Cruel to be kind. Trying to help her 'grow up'.

But how can someone grow up when they're expending all their energy fighting an addiction?

It was only in the days following her death that the full picture began to emerge.

She'd been using. The lad she'd been with – Jimmy Wright, someone who'd supplied her, a local scrote of a dealer – had got her in a car. Jimmy had been similarly off his face, had crashed head-on into a tree. Maggie had been wearing a seatbelt but had still ended up crushed into the dashboard.

Jimmy Wright had a fractured ankle and cuts and bruises, and was back home two days later. Until he was arrested.

He'd got six years for causing death by driving while under the influence of drink or drugs. He got an extra year because he was driving without a licence. Having served a year on remand, and having completed all suggested courses and therapy while in custody, he was out on licence two and a half years after his conviction.

So yes, Fraser knew what it felt like to want to murder someone. He had wanted to track down Jimmy Wright, to tear the smug grin from his face and choke him with it. He'd imagined – awkwardly at first and then with increasing fury, because after all who could interfere with his thoughts? – different ways he could kill him and make him suffer for it. He'd imagined how to get away with it. Where to bury a body, whether you could dismember it and bury it in several different places, or whether you could drop it out to sea. He had thought about sticking the body in a car and torching it. He'd thought about all the possible ways to get away with it, but he'd recognised that such a thing was impossible, unless you were an expert on forensics. There was no way to be certain of not leaving evidence, of not being seen on some CCTV camera somewhere, of there being no witnesses. And besides, it had felt like a dishonourable thing to do, hiding it. Never mind it being a waste of everyone's time. He'd never had much to do with the police but he respected how kind they'd been to his mother. And they had done a good job in getting Wright into custody quickly. It wasn't their fault that the judge had been so lenient in the sentencing.

If you were going to do it – get revenge for something so personal, so desperate – why not just admit to it? Why not just rip the bastard to pieces, then call the police and hand yourself in to them? You'd be in prison for life, or at least for the next thirty years or so – you'd come out an old man – but you'd have done it, got proper justice for her. Got your revenge.

And what else was he supposed to do with his life, now Maggie was gone?

Then he was collared by a journalist at the airport, when he was waiting for a helicopter ride to the rig he was working on at the time. He almost told her to piss off, at first, as he had done all the others. But her approach was different. She offered her condolences, and looked as though she meant them. She asked if he'd considered appealing the sentence, given the information (which was news to him) that Jimmy Wright was suspected of being involved in the supply of a batch of heroin that had contained, among other things, anthrax, and was linked to the deaths of three other addicts in the months before the accident. This had come out a month or so after the sentencing. Fraser had been away, avoiding the news. He was only just going back to work.

'No,' he replied, 'I'm going to kill him.'

'I'm sorry?' The journalist had looked startled. Looked at her phone, which she had held up to his chest, her way of asking permission to record what he was saying. He didn't give a fuck, anyway. He'd not been sleeping since the trial, hadn't slept a full night since Maggie was killed. Maybe she'd caught him off guard. Maybe he had just had enough.

'You heard me. I'm waiting till he gets out. Then I'm going to kill him.'

It made the newspapers – the front page, of the local one.

Two police officers came to talk to him on his next shore leave. They were calm, sympathetic, but very firm. 'You can't go around making threats to kill,' the older one said. 'We can manage a verbal warning this time. We don't want to caution you, or arrest you. Please don't do it again.'

He had tried to stay away from journalists but if someone asked him he was going to give a straight answer. He had dog shit put through his letterbox, although by the time he got back to the flat weeks later it was dried almost to dust, smeared down the back of the door and stuck between a flyer for double glazing and a kebab shop menu. His uncle Jack was assaulted outside a pub by three of Wright's cousins, although he wasn't actually hurt, and was pleased to be able to give one of them a fractured jaw; the other two ran off. The whole thing was captured on CCTV and showed that the initial assault was not his fault. The one with the fractured jaw put in a complaint, but the Procurator Fiscal declined to prosecute Jack for anything.

When Wright was released, back into the arms of his dysfunctional family, Fraser had been living on the island for nearly three years. He'd thought, many times since he came here, about the loch. The dark, still water, and how quickly a body would decompose. Or be consumed.

Out of the blue he got a phone call from a radio chat show – how they got the number, he had no idea – for a comment. He was told that Wright had expressed no remorse, and had been talking to journalists about how he was waiting for the confrontation so that he could show Fraser Sutherland how little he cared for empty threats.

So when Fraser managed to sleep, he dreamed of murder. And he waited for the right time.

Rachel

Rachel heads down towards the harbour at a quarter to four. By then the sun has come out and the wind has dropped, and the island is suddenly looking emerald-bright and sparklingly dramatic against the dark rainclouds heading further out to sea.

There is no sign of the boat. The quad is parked at the bottom of the slope, the way it was yesterday when she arrived, but Fraser is not with it. She goes across to the other side of the concrete jetty, to the tiny white sand beach, striped with black skeins of seaweed. At what must be the tide mark she comes across bits of rubbish and starts to pick them up, remembering vaguely that beach cleans are part of her job description and she might as well, while she's waiting. One of the washed-up items is a blue plastic bucket with a huge crack running through it – she can use this to collect the other bits and pieces. A shred of carrier bag, one of the flimsy green and white striped ones that the corner shop used to provide; a toothbrush, tin cans, the lid from a tub, a broken bottle, a silver crisp packet; a single flip-flop with the thong part of it flapping loose. She looks at it for a long time, wondering who wore it and how far it has travelled to get here, and where its partner is, then it goes in the bucket along with everything else.

Distantly she can hear an engine; she turns back to the jetty and sees Fraser standing there, rock-solid, arms crossed over his massive chest. He is facing out to sea. The boat is coming.

She climbs back up on to the concrete and puts the bucket down beside her. 'Do we have somewhere to dispose of all the beach rubbish?' she asks.

'Aye, those metal bins,' he says, pointing to the end of the jetty. Two tall metal containers that look more like grain silos. 'I try to sort through what's recyclable. Stick your wee bucket over there beside them. I'll have a look after we've sorted this lot out.'

The boat is chugging towards them between the rocks. Rachel feels weirdly elated, seeing it again. A day has passed, her first day, and she's survived it.

The boat's engine is killed abruptly and the *Island Princess* drifts up to bump its fenders against the jetty. A man – Rachel guesses he's one of the birders – throws the rope across to Fraser, who hauls the boat closer before tying it up. Robert is at the stern, throwing a second rope on to the jetty and then jumping off and making fast. On board, the men are gathering backpacks and camera bags and passing them to Fraser, who is creating a pile. Robert holds out a hand and helps them on to dry land. Rachel feels a sudden twist of nerves that she tries to swallow: this is her moment. *Don't fuck it up.*

'Hi! I'm Rachel,' she says, shaking hands. 'Welcome, hi. You got everything?'

She shakes hands with all of them and desperately tries to remember who fits with the names she memorised this morning. Steve, Daniel, Roger, Eugene, Hugh. Roger is tall and thin and looks like a solicitor. Eugene has a grey beard. Daniel looks like a student, the youngest by quite a way. Hugh is good-looking, late forties, looks as though he could be a TV presenter. Steve – she tries to think of something to link to him. Looks like he might be someone's uncle. That doesn't really help; they could all be someone's uncle, apart from Daniel.

Robert stops her briefly and hands over a Morrisons carrier bag. She glances in it: a bottle of Febreze, and a box containing a vanilla reed diffuser. She wrinkles her nose at it – vanilla? –

but then realises she probably looks really ungrateful. 'Thanks, Robert! I appreciate it.'

'Nae bother,' he says. 'See you Friday.'

Fraser has been helping the birdwatchers load the trailer; now he passes her on the jetty and goes to talk to Robert for a moment.

'Have you guys all been here before?' Rachel asks Steve.

'Oh, aye, many times,' he says.

Hugh the TV presenter – maybe something daytime, like an antiques show, or property – chimes in. 'It's going to be quite odd having you around,' he says. English accent. 'Not that we mind, of course, now that we've met you!'

'I'll keep out of your way as much as possible,' she replies, trying for a warm smile.

'Don't worry on my account, hen,' says Eugene, looking at her chest. 'You keep us entertained all day, if you feel like it.'

'Right,' Rachel says, glancing back towards Fraser and suddenly glad that she's not staying in the bird observatory with this lot.

Fraser hasn't heard what Eugene said to her. He and Robert are deep in discussion, heads together. She tries to read Fraser's expression. In that moment he looks up, across at her. She's not being paranoid. They're talking about her.

Fraser

'Got something,' Robert says to him, and Fraser recognises the tone of his voice.

'What is it?'

'Been on the news again,' Robert says. 'And then there's this.'

He hands over a newspaper, folded in half. It's not the front page but a column somewhere inside: he has folded the paper so that it's on top. *One year on: search for missing man 'still a priority', say police.*

'Fuck,' Fraser mutters.

Robert could say something pacifying – *it doesn't matter, don't worry about it* – but they are good friends now. Everything that has passed between them is cemented by this. They have a connection, one of just a few words spoken, twice a week. On his visits back to the mainland, Fraser will go for a drink with Robert and even then they will say very little; they will sit with their pints and watch whatever sport is showing on the TV above the bar. But sometimes connections run so deep there is no need for conversation.

Fraser folds the paper again and tucks it into the inside pocket of his jacket, glancing up towards the quad bike, and Rachel. The birdwatchers have already started up the hill, leaving Rachel behind. She should be with them; what's she waiting for?

'How's she doing? The lassie?'

'Aye, not bad so far.'

'Did you think she'd no' last the day?'

'I did wonder.'

'And she's still here, right enough.'

'She's got more spirit than you'd think.' He looks back at Robert, who's got a strange sort of smile playing about his lips. 'What?' he asks, feeling something rise.

'Maybe she needs to watch out for you,' Robert says, playfully.

'Don't be daft.'

'She's no' worried about that, then?' He nods towards the newspaper, tucked under Fraser's jacket.

Fraser knows instantly what he means. He looks up the hill. Rachel has set off, following the birdwatchers. She has nearly caught up with them already.

'I've not had a chance to tell her,' he says.

'How come?'

'Just hasn't been the right moment. Maybe tonight.'

'You didn't want to tell her in case she took a fit and left?'

'Something like that.'

He shakes Robert by the hand again, and loosens the rope at the bow. Robert unhitches the stern and jumps aboard while Fraser holds the boat steady. The engine rattles into life, a dull roar penetrating the quiet of the harbour. He coils the rope and tosses it on to the deck as the boat eases back into the channel. Robert waves, and then looks behind him to guide the boat out into clear water.

He fires up the quad and overtakes the group on the way to the bird observatory, unloading the baggage while he's waiting for them. There is nothing he can quite put his finger on, but the place looks different already. It's spotlessly clean and tidy, and it smells of something spicy. Clearly she has deployed the slow cooker already. The birdwatchers are lucky bastards, he thinks; he hopes they appreciate the effort she's gone to.

He thinks about waiting for them to catch up, to check that Rachel is all right, but the longer he stands by the quad, the more the newspaper in his pocket is pulling at his attention. He wants to be alone so he can read it properly, take in what it says. He doesn't want Rachel to ask.

This is the problem, living with someone. What if they ask you things, a direct question? You have to reply, don't you? You have to tell them the truth. Even when you haven't admitted the truth to yourself.

Not for the first time, he curses Marion and thinks the same thought all over again: he was better off alone.

Rachel

The kitchen is clean and tidy, everything washed and dried and put away. Her guests are sitting in the main room, thick-socked feet pointing at the woodburner or resting on the coffee table that she wiped this morning, and they are all talking about counting schedules and lists and who is going to do what tomorrow. She hears the names of birds she recognises but couldn't pick out of a bird identity parade, so she's kept quiet. They asked her a few questions, earlier, about whether the puffins have arrived (she hasn't seen one yet, although apparently they have been seen on the water offshore) and something about razorbills that she was not able to answer.

She had some help from Steve in setting the table – in the end she left him to it – but other than that they have ignored her, talking animatedly while she brought out the chilli and the big pot of rice, and some garlic bread. They ate it quickly, all of it, leaving her wondering if the portion size had been too small, even though she had followed the recipe that was supposedly enough for six and had thought it looked like enough for eight people.

Steve had offered her a vote of thanks to which they'd all murmured some sort of assent, but that had been it. She had collected the plates and washed them up, as usual wondering whether the environmental impact of using the clean water to wash up the dishes was less than using the dishwasher. She was pretty certain washing up by hand was better. She would ask Fraser, later.

Once the kitchen is clean she asks Steve what time they're planning to have breakfast. They have a little huddle to consider it and the answer comes back – eight. They'll be going out first, before dawn. It's easier to count birds in silhouette against the sky. She sets the breadmaker to finish at six, asks Steve to get the bread out then so that it will be cool enough to cut when they're ready for breakfast. He shrugs, already engaged in a different conversation about a bird they saw here last year, which some of them are disputing. Rachel wonders if the bread will be left to go soggy in the breadmaker, starts to worry about it, then stops herself. It's their lookout if there's no bread for toast.

Now she heads outside, pulls up her hood because it's raining, turning on the torch and keeping it trained on the rutted path ahead of her. It would not be good if she missed her footing and collapsed a puffin burrow – and in places she is not that far from the sheer cliff face. Two hundred feet down, to the surging white waves, the rocks below the surface.

She can hear the noise of the water crashing far below her, then the roar of the wind as it picks up and the rain gets heavier and drives against her face. She struggles to stay upright. It has got very dark very quickly, thick black clouds, and rain heavy enough to make it difficult to see. She has to hold the hood of her jacket over her head to stop it blowing off, and it takes all her concentration to stick to the path, worrying about being blown over the edge and down to the sea below.

It's terrifying, and cold, and she is just thinking she can't stand it any more when her feet slide out from under her and she slips down the hill on her bottom, while she screams into the wind and throws out her arms and tries to clutch at passing tufts of slippery grass, trying to slow her descent.

At the bottom of the hill she crashes into a soupy puddle, her knee twisted awkwardly underneath her. She lies there for a moment, gasping with shock, her fingers clawing into the grass, trying to assess how close she is to the cliff edge. She is crying now, howling because of fear and tiredness and the humiliation of sliding down the hill, even though nobody was there to see it. She can see her torch a few metres further on where it has rolled to a halt against a tussock of grass, and when she crawls over to retrieve it she realises that it's a good thirty feet or more to the edge. Then her tears turn into a hysterical sort of laughter because she's still alive, and the water and mud has soaked through to her skin.

She's twisted her knee and it hurts, a bit, but otherwise she's all right. Nothing broken. She's in the little valley, the last one before the lighthouse; it's more sheltered than on the top of the cliff, although it's really dark now. To her left the path turns down towards the harbour. It's just a few minutes' walk up the next hill to the lighthouse.

In the hallway she peels off layers of wet jacket and boots. From the kitchen comes the rich scent of some sort of meat cooking.

'What the fuck?' Fraser says, from the kitchen door. 'What happened to you?'

There is no mirror anywhere, and that's probably just as well. Her jeans are covered in mud, her hair plastered across her face, dripping down on to her sweater. She pushes it away and her hand is gritty – she has just smeared mud all over her cheek. 'I slipped.' She sniffs.

'You all right?'

'Twisted my knee, but it's not too bad. I'm fine.' Her voice sounds high and quavery, the noise of the wind still ringing in her ears.

He's looking at her with an odd expression on his face. She hasn't forgotten the ominous threat that he wants to talk to her.

'You want to go and get dry clothes on?' he says. 'Dinner's nearly ready.'

Rachel goes up the stairs, trying not to limp. But by the time she reaches her room the shock of the fall has caught up with her, and her hands are shaking so much that she can't unbutton her sodden jeans. She lets out a sudden, gasping sob, and then another, and eases herself to the floor because she doesn't want to make the bed wet, and rests her face in her hands and cries, and cries.

In the end she manages to get her breathing under control. In for five, out for seven. It takes a while. Shuddering sobs keep catching her out.

She washes her face and has a go at putting on some make-up using the little bathroom mirror, but if anything it makes her look worse. Her eyes are bloodshot and puffy, her cheeks bright pink and scoured from the wind, and the rain, and the peaty mud she rubbed into herself. Finds some clean leggings and a hoodie.

Deep breath. Down the stairs, into the kitchen.

Fraser looks at her.

'What?'

He doesn't answer. Shakes his head, putting down two plates. Some spicy-sweet lamb casserole thing. Couscous. Salad.

'How are your new guests doing?' he asks.

'They thought the bird observatory looked hilarious.'

'Oh, aye?'

She was sure they hadn't meant any harm, but there was something disconcerting about the way they'd hooted at the bed linen and the towels, at the little vase on the windowsill that she'd placed there to break up the lines of the room (planning to put flowers in it if she ever finds any big enough to justify picking). They hadn't said anything about the chilli, good or bad. It was still a little too salty, she had thought, tasting a tiny bit just before she served it up to them, by which point it was far too late to do them jacket potatoes anyway.

'I guess they're used to it being more rough and ready.'

'They've had it that way for years,' he says.

'And they still keep coming. Clearly they didn't mind it how it was. I've no idea why I'm here, really,' she says.

She's chewing, and trying not to think about how much her knee is hurting, when Fraser's massive hand deposits a glass tumbler containing a fingerful of amber liquid on the table in front of her.

She looks up, but he's not looking at her. He sits down at the table with a second glass.

'Thanks,' she says. Her voice sounds horribly hoarse.

'You don't have to keep thanking me,' he says. 'I'll just assume you're grateful. Let me know if I piss you off, or if I say something that upsets you. Right?'

'Okay,' she says. 'Sorry about…it wasn't you. I'm just tired.'

She finishes her plateful and takes a swig of the whisky. It burns her all the way down but it's just right, rich and warm and with notes of toast and burnt caramel.

'Is this the one I brought?' she asks. She'd nearly said *Is this my dad's?* but stopped herself just in time.

'Aye,' he said. 'Nice stuff.'

'It's good,' she says.

'You like your whisky?'

'My dad likes it. He makes us do a tasting thing every Christmas.'

They both take another swig. For the first time, she meets his eyes.

'Makes everything a bit less bleak, I find,' he says.

'I guess it does,' she thinks.

She hasn't had a drink in nearly a year. Or, no, a bit less than that. Because for a few weeks at the beginning she had drunk quite a lot. Lucy didn't know about that, of course. Would have had an absolute fit if she had.

She takes a deep breath in. 'What was it you wanted to talk to me about?'

'What?'

'Earlier. You said "we'll talk later" or something.'

'Oh. Right.'

She thinks he looks nervous. She has a bad feeling suddenly. He's going to say that he can't have her here after all. She's going to have to be sent back.

'So,' he says, 'there's something I should have probably told you.'

And then there's a noise behind her, and she looks around at the doorway and there's a man standing there, and Rachel jumps out of her skin.

4

Lefty

Fraser

Lefty strolls into the kitchen and instantly Fraser wants to kill him. Talk about timing.

'Is this her?' he asks, pointing at Rachel.

'Aye, of course it bloody is,' Fraser says, raising his voice and smacking his palm on the table. 'If you'd just given me another five minutes, you wee shite.'

He sees Rachel flinch at the bang, and regrets it. Her eyes are wide, her face ghost-pale.

'I'll go away again,' Lefty says casually.

'There's no point now, is there?'

Rachel is looking from one of them to the other. Maybe she's realised there's something worse than being stuck in an isolated lighthouse with a man, and that's being stuck with two of them.

Lefty goes to the fridge and gets out a can of Coke, cracks it open and heads back for the door. 'I get when I'm no' wanted,' he says, looking pointedly at their plates.

Fraser watches him leave, gritting his teeth. It's not as if he ever sits down to eat anyway. He glances at Rachel, at her pale face, her huge eyes staring back at the doorway through which Lefty has just disappeared.

'That's Lefty,' he says. When she doesn't speak, he takes a heavy breath in and continues, 'He's not supposed to be here. Nobody knows about him, other than Robert who runs the boat, but best not mention it to him either.'

'What do you mean?' she says. 'What's he doing here, then?'

'He's kind of ... like an assistant.'

'An assistant?'

'Unofficial.'

'How come nobody knows about him?'

Even as he says it, having thought this through for weeks, he realises he's phrasing this all wrong. 'I mean, he's not in trouble or anything like that.'

Maybe that's not even true. But it's too late to take it back.

'Trouble?' she echoes. 'What sort of trouble?'

'He's not – he's just – well ... he had nowhere else to go.'

He sees the confusion chasing across her face. He's painting himself as some kind of philanthropist, a rescuer of homeless youths. She is looking bewildered rather than cross, which he's grateful for, but at the same time it's making him wary. She doesn't know him well enough to be on his side.

'How long's he staying?'

Fraser clears his throat. 'Until someone finds out, and kicks him off the island and back to the shithole he was in before.' He says it and meets her eye, staring her out. Let her be in no doubt: she will either make or break things. If the lad is kicked off the island, she will be the one responsible for his situation worsening beyond measure, not to mention it likely costing Fraser his job, his home and his sanity.

He doesn't like having to trust people, much less women. Much less a woman he has only just met.

'Where does he sleep?' she asked.

'Downstairs. I guess it was a study. It's got a bathroom next to it.'

He sees the relief flicker across her face.

'And he's – he's all right? Is he?'

Fraser has to think about how to answer this. He can understand her concern, in a way, seeing Lefty through a stranger's eyes: he's small but wiry, stronger than he looks, stronger than he used to be; but he's still got that hunted look about him. Scrappy hair that he's cut himself – and he did have wee bald patches for a while, so it looks decidedly uneven – and two missing teeth at the front, the rest of them in bad shape. He's almost certainly never seen a dentist. Fraser, despite being huge, probably looks less of a threat to her than the feral-looking Lefty.

Is he all right? For some reason he doesn't want to lie to her – he hasn't, so far, not really, and he suspects he is so out of practice at having to talk to people that she would see through him instantly – and so, carefully, he says, 'He's had a rough time. If he gives you any trouble, anything at all, you just tell me about it and I'll sort him out. Right?'

'Right,' she says.

He thinks she does not look very reassured. She is still wondering what exactly he might have meant by 'trouble'. But she has no choice, after all. If she calls Marion and tells her that there's a strange extra person on the island, that Fraser's got an assistant, they'll all be back off the island very quickly indeed. And she's only just arrived.

'Any more questions?' he asks.

'Is that what you wanted to talk to me about?'

'Aye. But the wee idiot beat me to it.'

'I thought—' she says, and stops herself.

'You thought what?'

She smiles, the briefest of smiles. 'I thought you were going to tell me I had to leave.'

'Why would I tell you that?'

'Because I fuck things up. It's what I do. It's the only thing I'm good at.'

She smiles again, and he meets her eyes and sees again what's behind them, what he recognised before. Pain. Fear. And some desperate sort of nameless need – a need to do the right thing, a need to belong. And something inside him twists.

Rachel

Rachel has spent her entire life lurching from one fuck-up to the next.

She had been doing okay at school, trying hard, until Lucy's GCSE results came in, and Rachel suddenly realised that her older sister was bright and, by comparison, Rachel wasn't. After that there seemed little point in trying hard; she scraped enough passes to do her A-levels, scraped through those and managed to get on to an English course through clearing. She dropped out at the end of the first year, partly due to an extended period of illness and an unsympathetic tutor, partly because the course was hard and she was struggling with everything, and partly because Lucy had just graduated from Durham with a first and had already been headhunted into Ian's dad's accountancy firm as a junior. Rachel had worked two jobs for a while, trying to earn enough money to stay in her shared house so that she didn't have to go back to Norwich and her parents, but then her housemates had decided they really wanted someone on their course to live with them, so they'd made things difficult for Rachel until she got the hint, and left. Two months back in her old bedroom, staring at the ceiling and going quietly mad.

She got a job at Nando's, which thankfully was nothing short of brilliant. It was hard work but good fun: the staff treated her like family, and she was able to pick up extra shifts here and there until she had saved enough money to go travelling. She made it to Thailand with some friends she'd picked up on the way, got mugged, broke her ankle and had to be brought home to the UK at phenomenal expense, since it turned out her travel insurance didn't cover her for riding mopeds while drunk. Another fuck-up – and her parents had had to pay her medical bills. Probably they still were. She had heard all about it several times.

Back in Norwich, she had tried to get back into Nando's, but they'd had no jobs going. She'd done a bit of temping to keep her out of the house and out of Mum's way, but then the darkness that had been chasing her finally caught up, and she ended up spending days in bed, nights awake, staring at the TV in her room.

And then she'd gone to the doctor to try to get something to help her sleep, and met Mel in the waiting room, and then things had started to get better again.

It was like a rollercoaster, she thought, or maybe it was like the undulating clifftop on the island – the bigger lows led to the bigger highs, and then on the other side of each high there was nothing but another massive low.

On the other side of the high of making a friend, of moving in to Mel's spare room and actually feeling half-sane again, of finding a proper job, a decent job, even if it was just temporary and not especially well paid, was another massive fuck-up.

Amarjit.

Rachel's job was a maternity leave cover as a marketing assistant at Evans Pharma. She had limited office experience, just a few temp jobs which mainly involved those tasks that nobody else wanted to do: mass mailings, filing, copying, shredding. This felt like her first grown-up job. She didn't want to mess it up. She was on time every day, listened, concentrated, remembered people's names, made teas for everyone when she didn't have anything more pressing to do.

She had been in a meeting on her second day, confused but trying not to show it, when in he strolled. The cardio team's head of marketing – Amarjit Singh. She hadn't known who he was, then. Sean, the sales director, made some comment about him turning up late and Amarjit just winked and smiled. And Rachel was trying not to stare, utterly dazzled. He was just beautiful. Light blue fitted shirt, sleeves partly rolled up, one of those heavy, expensive watches a little bit loose on his wrist. Dark hair, neatly trimmed beard, dark eyes, and his smile...bloody hell. He looked as if he'd stepped out from a magazine ad for men's cologne.

Within two weeks she was sleeping with him. Rachel cannot think of it now without cringing.

Amarjit's flat was in a new block in a really smart complex in the city centre. Walking distance from all the bars and clubs, a neat little car park at its base, one space per flat, a few visitors' spaces that were always full. Not that she had a car; but he was always complaining about it: that people with two cars were just using the visitors' spaces, which meant that nobody could ever invite visitors over.

In hindsight, months later, she would wonder which other visitors he was talking about. But then, of course, the complaint had slipped underneath her like a satin sheet, disregarded. Back then she'd felt important, valued; she hadn't heard the things that she should have heard. Did not even register them. Like the wife he'd mentioned very briefly in passing, and she could have sworn that at some point he'd used the word 'separated', or maybe 'ex', but afterwards she could never quite remember the moment he said it, or indeed if he actually had.

There. He had casually invited her to come over to his flat the week after she started. The week after that, she had actually gone. If anyone had asked, Rachel would have said that he was all right, he was a bit of a laugh...that she thought they were mates outside of work. That evening they had been working at an event promoting Caleril to GPs, listening to an American heart surgeon who Rachel had thought was pompous and talking shit. In the bar, afterwards, she told Amarjit this rather loudly and he laughed and told her that the surgeon was a friend of his.

Four drinks in, then several more at a too-crowded bar afterwards, and he said to her, 'Let's get out of here,' and got a taxi with her. They had been talking non-stop. She thought he would drop her at hers; was wondering whether he would want to come in. Whether Mel would be at home or not. Whether the kitchen was a mess. What Mel would have to say about it. Instead the taxi went to his first, and when it stopped he said to her, 'Coming in?'

Despite him taking her to his flat, she had not been expecting sex. Yes, she'd had a massive crush on him, but she had been careful to hide it. He had only ever done what she considered playful flirting; potentially it was nothing more than friendliness. He'd asked her to help out at that event, something not on her job description, not done by her predecessor and beyond her pay grade, and she'd believed that this meant he valued her, that he thought she was worth more than she was being paid. He had told Sean what a great job she was doing.

And then he had opened the door to his flat and she'd gone inside, swaying on her heels down the narrow corridor into the living room at the end. It was small, blandly done in grey and sky-blue, as if he'd bought it furnished from the developer. He'd followed her into the living room and she'd heard a chink, and looked around and he had undone his belt, his trousers, was standing behind her with his hand inside his pants.

She had looked open-mouthed from that to his face.

'You don't have to come,' he said, 'but I'm going to bed.'

He had turned and gone back to one of the doors she had passed.

Now, of course, she thinks that what she should have done was gone back out of the flat, shut the door behind her and called an Uber as she was going down the stairs. It wouldn't have been too awkward. He could still have been her boss. A line had been drawn and she could have chosen not to cross it. He had even said precisely that, *you don't have to come*, and of course she hadn't had to. She hadn't been threatened by him. He hadn't done anything to assault her, or even scare her particularly.

Although, she thinks in hindsight, undressing himself in front of her had more than a whiff of the Weinstein about it. Not to mention their relative power positions at that point.

All of this is academic: because she did not walk out of the flat.

She doesn't want to think about him now.

Instead, her thoughts lurch back to the weird lad who just strolled into the kitchen and strolled back out again. Fraser is talking about something else, about the septic tanks – she had forgotten about them, had almost got used to the smell; they're being emptied on Tuesday, apparently.

For a moment she wonders if that really just happened – the lad walking in – or if she'd had a peculiar hallucination brought on by tiredness. Lefty. His name's Lefty. What sort of a name is that?

'Is your knee okay?' he asks.

She flexes her leg experimentally. 'Throbs a bit,' she says. 'It'll be fine.'

'Want me to take a look?'

'There's nothing to see,' she says, alarmed. As if she's about to pull her leggings down in Fraser's kitchen.

He shrugs. 'Suit yourself.'

To distract her from the awkwardness, she drinks the last of the whisky.

'Want another?'

'No,' she says, getting to her feet. 'Thanks, though. I'm going to get an early night again.'

She takes her plate and the glass to the sink and washes them up, aware of him sitting at the table behind her. It's as though something just happened. Something a little bit predatory. Suddenly that uneasiness is back, sitting uncomfortably on her chest.

If there were another woman here, just one, she would feel a little less vulnerable. But there it is. She's here now. What else can she do but get on with it?

Fraser

In the grubby bathroom mirror, he catches sight of himself while he's cleaning his teeth.

You stupid fucker, he thinks to himself. *Look at you.*

He's handled everything badly from start to finish. He should have told her about Lefty straight away. Because there was no way she was going to leave, was there?

He spits into the sink. Can't bear to look at himself any more. *You idiot.*

Nevertheless, when he speaks to Craig next, he's going to provide him with a shopping list that includes whisky. Maybe several bottles of wine.

Bess is outside on the landing, looking up at him with concern in her brown eyes. He rubs her head, gives her a little ear-scratch, goes into his room and shuts the door. He strips down to shorts and T-shirt and climbs into bed, reads two pages of the Alex North thriller on his bedside table, and then two more. When he's tired enough to be losing focus on the page he replaces the bookmark – a postcard of the house on the rock at Pittenweem, the Isle of May bathed in sunlight behind it – and turns off the light. From next door he hears a sound, that might be a sob. It might be a cough.

The newspaper that Robert left him is on the chest of drawers where he put it earlier. He rereads the article, which doesn't take long. The police have issued an appeal for information, but the tone of the article, a meagre two paragraphs, suggests they aren't especially desperate for a response or even expecting one. There is a grainy image, that familiar CCTV still of a figure in a dark jacket standing next to the driver on a bus. No further trace of him after that. No evidence he has come to any harm. The well-used phrases seem to be even more half-hearted than usual. No mention of a family desperate to know he's safe, because, while there is a family, they clearly don't give a shit.

No mention of where he'd spent the last few years before he disappeared off the face of the earth.

No mention of what he'd done before that.

Rachel

Rachel is in bed, woken once more by a muffled shout from Fraser's room. This time she'd known better than to get up.

Her thoughts wind their way back to the moment Lefty had walked into the kitchen and scared the shit out of her. And the look of him, too. He reminds her of school. Not quite the gang of lads who would regularly shout obscenities at the girls just for fun, the lads who hung around outside the school gates smoking – not them; instead Lefty calls to mind the loners, the ones who had clearly slipped through some sort of net. Every class had them. In particular there was one who joined her class in Year 10, in the middle of term. He'd come from Yarmouth or Thetford or somewhere, didn't talk to anyone, spent lunchtimes strolling around the edge of the field kicking at the turf, avoiding people. Wouldn't make eye contact, even when – proud of herself for being brave and kind – she'd asked him once if he was settling in okay. He'd sworn at her and leered and said something about her legs, and she'd blushed, horrified, and never spoken to him again.

Ryan. That was his name. She couldn't remember his surname.

He'd left in Year 11, before the final set of mocks. Someone said he was fostered. That his mum was in prison. That he was on drugs, or she was – the story varied depending on who was telling it.

Something about Lefty reminds her of Ryan, and this is making her uncomfortable. She'd been a bit scared of him, of Ryan, while at the same time feeling unbearably sad for him. If this was America, she had thought at the time, he might be the sort of loner who would be collecting guns.

Now she thinks how very unkind it was of her to think these things and not do anything about it. Not be the one to make a difference, try harder, speak to him kindly and regularly instead of ignoring him the way all her friends did.

Another thing to be ashamed of. As if she needs another stick to beat herself with.

She wonders what happened to Ryan, and as much as she tries to imagine him off somewhere doing something amazing with a family of his own, a family who love him, she has now made the association of Ryan and Lefty, this weirdo without even a proper name, someone who isn't supposed to be there, someone who doesn't belong. And all she can think is that if Ryan is even still alive he's twitchy and probably on something, and cannot look anyone in the eye.

That thought leads her, suddenly, shockingly, to another: the knife on Fraser's bedside table, how she had wondered last night if he was somehow protecting himself against her.

Maybe it isn't Rachel that Fraser is afraid of. Is it?

Fraser

The next morning Fraser is up and out before dawn. He drags Lefty out of his pit and takes him up past the bird observatory to the plateau that leads down in a gentle slope to the ruins.

Lefty, once he's woken up, is unusually talkative. 'Where are we getting the gravel from?'

'We're getting a load when the helicopter comes.'

'The helicopter for the tanks?'

'It's bringing bags of gravel.'

'They gonnae drop it up here?'

'No. They'll drop it where the tanks are.'

'Can we no' tell them tae drop it up here?'

'Helicopters don't like hovering for too long. So they're dropping the bags down there and picking up the tanks.'

Fraser has had this discussion with various organisations and companies several times. Apparently the newer helicopters need to keep moving around or they overheat; they're at risk of malfunctioning without a constant airflow. He had always thought that hovering was the one thing helicopters were good at, but there you are.

Lefty's attention has moved on. 'What's she like, then?'

Fraser doesn't answer. He still wants to keep Lefty and Rachel separate, if he can. Which, of course, he can't.

'What's she like? The girl?'

'She's got a name.'

'Aye but you hav'nae introduced us, have you?'

'Rachel.'

'What's she like?'

Fraser ignores him, not just because he's already sick of this conversation but because he doesn't really know how to answer. Nothing he thinks of quite covers it.

The sun is just coming up and it's cold and fresh, the air bright and full of birds. The terns will be coming soon. Fraser has, as always, been keeping a close eye on the Isle of May's blog, and the tern terrace they constructed last winter was well used in the spring. Fraser's is going to be better. Not that he's competitive, of course. But Must has more flat terrain at this end of the island than May has. More space for nestboxes. So that's what they're doing, that's the plan. They are going to level the plateau as best they can, cover it with gravel, make boxes to provide the chicks with protection from the weather and predators, and create a nesting habitat for the terns that will be arriving in a month or so.

'You fancy her?'

Abruptly he turns and takes Lefty by the scruff of his jacket, lifting him almost off his feet. Lefty yelps in response, scrabbling at his hands. 'That's enough,' Fraser says, really quite calmly. 'You just stay away. You hear?'

He drops the lad again and they continue in silence, Lefty keeping warily behind him.

They get to the plateau just as the sun streaks across it, highlighting the blades of grass in bright gold. It's really rather beautiful. Almost a shame to cover it in gravel. But the terns need it and, besides, there's nobody but him to appreciate it.

They have already constructed a rough square – he has enough gravel coming to cover ten square metres. He sets

Lefty to work checking for puffin burrows; there are only three, one of which is collapsed and clearly won't be in use this year. They can try to leave the burrows' holes accessible, but chances are the puffins will find a new nest site, grumble about it and give him filthy looks. There have to be sacrifices and, to be fair, the terns have had a far longer migration, and two active burrows are really a small price to pay for the most magnificent tern terrace in the whole of Scotland. Possibly the whole of Europe.

He watches Lefty out of the corner of his eye, thinking that actually he's looking well. Considering how, these days, he refuses Fraser's home-cooked meals and lives off fish finger sandwiches, toasties, oven chips and cans of pop, there is proper colour in his cheeks, a degree of strength in the way he hefts the shovel along the line they've marked, the wind lifting his hair. When he'd first arrived, he'd been barely eight stone, a skinny runt who could barely lift the shovel at all, never mind tread it through the heavy soil.

I did that, he thinks. *Me. I did it. I kept him alive.*

Although not a day goes by without the accompanying rot of self-loathing that goes with it.

The tern terrace is coming along nicely, although Fraser won't say that in front of Lefty. They have finished clearing the space and have laid some of the membrane that will form the base, enabling the gravel surface to drain but preventing weeds from growing through, and staked it firmly in place. For the last hour or so Lefty has been building the wooden boxes that will shelter the young birds from predators and the worst of the winds. All the wood has been cut to size down in the workshop; now it's just a case of hammering the pieces together.

He checks his watch. It's gone nine. From his position here he has a good view of the bird observatory, and he has not seen Rachel yet. Thinks of her request to view the cottages. Thinks that, if she's going to go and look, then he'd better go with her.

Rachel

The lighthouse kitchen is quiet and empty.

On her way through the hall she glanced at the door that must be to Lefty's room, which she had somehow failed to notice hadn't been opened when Fraser gave her the tour. She had assumed it was a cupboard. He hadn't mentioned it, of course. She has been thinking about Lefty a lot since waking up from a confused dream about school and Ryan, lying in the semi-dark with her heart beating, wondering if she's going to end up being knifed by either Lefty or Fraser.

There is porridge in the kitchen, and coffee, and she helps herself to both, sits at the table and checks her phone. An email from Lucy, one from her bank, one from her dad. One line.

How are you doing, chick? Let us know. We miss you.

Dad misses her. Mum doesn't, as far as she can tell.

She can't finish the bowl of porridge, so she swills it out into the sink and washes up.

In the hallway she stands and stares at the closed door. There's no way he's here. She can tell by the cold, frozen silence of the building. Nevertheless, she knocks at the door, echoingly loud in the open hallway.

She tries the door, and it opens on to a messy bedroom. There's an unmade single bed, a chair with random clothes thrown on to it. On the floor by the bed is a plate smeared with drying ketchup, a fork, a pint glass. There is a TV on a chest of drawers and an Xbox console, a controller on the tangled duvet attached to it by a lead that snakes across the floor. A few scattered Xbox cases. The room smells of unwashed clothes, old food, and sweat. There is a window – the curtains are drawn – and on the far side of the room is another door through which she can see a toilet and a shower. The tiles are a lurid floral pattern and the shower curtain, hanging off three hooks, is some dark colour. She closes the door again.

She didn't imagine it, then. Lefty is real. Lefty has been here for quite some time.

And nobody knows he's here.

How has Fraser got away with it?

She's just about to get her boots on and head down to the bird observatory for more cleaning when there's a noise outside and the door opens, and Fraser walks in.

'Ah,' he says, as if he's about to make an announcement. Then he just stops and looks at her.

'Thanks for the porridge,' she says. 'I'm hoping you did leave it for me and you weren't saving it.'

'Aye, I'll leave you breakfast, if you're not gonnae get up.'

'Am I supposed to?'

'No.'

'I probably would have got up earlier if I'd had a full night's sleep,' she says.

'Oh aye? Bed not comfy?'

'The bed's fine,' she says. She thinks about saying something about the shouting, then sees his wary expression and changes her mind. It's rude, she thinks, and maybe unkind, and that's not who she is. 'Just – you know. It's a strange place. I'll get used to it.'

'Aye,' he says.

He helps himself to the remainder of the coffee in the pot, drinks it in three gulps. Bess comes over to the table to say hello, leans damply against her knee while Rachel rubs at her fluffy chest.

'Thought maybe you'd like a walk,' he says from the sink, his back to her.

'A walk?'

'You wanted to see the cottages.'

She thinks about the bird observatory, about the list of things she still has to do before serving dinner to the birders. But there's still the possibility of moving to the cottages, perhaps tomorrow, or even this evening, once she's finished at the observatory. Nothing had happened in the night, other than

Fraser shouting again, but there is still something disturbing her about sharing a house with two men who haven't done much to put her at ease. If she's going to stay on the island – and she is, because she is determined that this is her chance to prove to herself that she can stick at something – then being on her own feels preferable to staying here in the lighthouse.

'Great,' Rachel says. 'It won't take too long, will it?'

'Nah,' he says.

He's already out of the door.

Fraser

The cottages are at the bottom of a ravine that bisects the island at a diagonal, a row of them, with a rough potholed track that leads down to the harbour. The remaining half of the ravine is a deep loch, perhaps thirty metres long and five metres wide, silent black water. At the seaward end of it is a rocky wall, a sort of dam that was built two centuries ago to close the end of the loch, to make it deeper, and stop the water draining to the sea. It had been used as a cooling system when the light was powered by engines. Huge rusting pipes still run from the lochside to the lighthouse, alongside the steep path leading up from the cottages, difficult to negotiate in either direction. The long way round, the track that leads down to the harbour then snakes up from the shore at the other end of the chasm, gives access with the quad. But the path is the most direct route from the lighthouse, and Rachel needs to see the worst of it.

She probably won't even need to go inside the buildings to make that decision. This is what he's hoping for.

Bess has no problem with the slope, but in places the loose stones slide beneath Fraser's feet and he has to steady himself. More than once he has slid down the slope on his arse, gathering momentum all the way. He walks in front of Rachel, thinking that if she slips he might be able to stop her from another fall. In reality the slope is so steep that she would probably take him with her.

He stops when the roof of the cottages is in view, to let her have a proper look.

'Oh,' she says. 'Right. Bloody hell.'

There are three cottages in the terrace, with a fourth, nearest the loch, that has become a storage building for spare cans of fuel for the generator. The two at the harbour end are in the best condition, which isn't saying much. The third one is missing several tiles and part of the floor inside has caved in.

He would have fixed the roof if they had provided him with the wood, and the tools with which to do it. He asked many times, before the floor collapsed, quite willing to patch things up to at least stop the damage getting any worse. They had told him yes, they had even told him to get what he needed the next time he went to the mainland, but he'd never managed to get the agreement in writing that they would reimburse him, and he knew full well that he would pay out the money and they would somehow wriggle out of refunding him, so he'd never done it. As a result, the cottage with the damaged roof has fallen into total disrepair and the remaining two, which were certainly habitable when he first arrived, are now both damp and getting worse every winter.

They have reached the bottom of the ravine. The cottages are right in front of them, in all their dilapidated sadness.

'Oh,' she says, again.

Fraser has no intention of taking the guided tour any further than this, so he stands with his arms folded until she takes herself down to the far end and pushes at the door.

Bess has gone off looking for rabbits, which are plentiful, although she never actually catches any. She likes looking at them, the hunting instinct thankfully overridden by her training. Occasionally he'll trap some, kill them and cook them. It's damage control. The puffins are what the public want him to protect, not the rabbits. There are only so many burrows that the island can accommodate. Besides, he likes a rabbit stew.

He lets Rachel wander in and out, scraping the door across the stone floor, looking up at the rotten floorboards, the bird shit everywhere, the damp, the moss and the pervading smell of mould and decay, and worse besides.

She comes out and goes straight to the next cottage, without meeting his eyes. She's in there for a full five minutes. The longer she's in there, the more he feels it, a twisting anxiety in his gut, because he knows what's in there and if she notices it, if she makes the connection, then there will be trouble. He fidgets from foot to foot and he is about to follow her when she emerges again.

'See what I mean?' he asks, expecting some sort of demand for an explanation, but there isn't one.

'Yes,' she says, 'it's grim.'

She has clearly seen enough. She shuts the door firmly, the way he left it. It takes her considerable effort to close it. It would take a similar effort to open it again, should she want to try.

Rachel starts back up the hill.

There is no sign of Bess and so he whistles for her. She is down at the edge of the loch, not moving.

'Bess!'

He comes up behind the dog slowly, talking to her, not wanting to startle her and provoke her to jump in. What the fuck would he do then? He can't go in there after her.

She whines at the water and he sees something white, moving, just under the surface.

Not for the first time, he thinks about murder. How easy it would be. How easy it would be to get away with it.

He puts his hand on Bess's fur and pulls her gently away. She's been in a trance, almost, and starts into action, galloping up the slope past Rachel. He turns away from the loch and follows.

Rachel is waiting for him halfway up the slope. She has turned to look down at the loch below them. 'That looks deep,' she says, barely out of breath, as he joins her.

'I guess,' he says, not looking. 'I'd best get back to the tern terrace, anyway.'

'Oh, sure,' she says.

He does not particularly want to end up discussing the black water. He has felt the pull of it too many times. Does not want her to start to feel the same attraction to it.

Once, in his first year on the island, there had been a group of ecologists studying the grey seals that arrived in the autumn, with the first pups usually born in October; thousands of them return to the island every year to breed. One of the group, a Swedish woman called Anne, was studying the seals and had wished she had an intact seal skeleton to work with. As it turned out there were occasional seal corpses washed up – killed through fighting, malnutrition or old age – but she could not see how to get the bones bare without a damaging process of boiling and scraping. He had suggested taking one of the carcasses and dropping it, in a net bag, into the loch. It was an experiment of sorts but he had read about how the lighthouse-keepers had had to fence off the loch after sheep had fallen in there and been reduced to bones very quickly through the action of whatever bacteria, or flesh-eating creatures, lurked within.

The seal bones had been white and clean within a few months, and Anne had been overjoyed to have a complete seal skeleton of her own.

He stands, now, and looks back down into the blackness. He thinks it would be easy to tip forward, to roll down the slope and fall the metre or so into the water. You would be instantly stunned by the cold, and unable to breathe. Cold water shock, it's called. And, if you did manage to override your instinct to panic and drown, it would not be possible to pull yourself up and out.

He wonders what's living in the loch, if anything. There might be huge fish in there, or it might be dead and empty. It feels dangerous. Fraser does not like the way that, between the two walls of rock which form the ravine, nothing reflects in the smooth blackness of the water. He has no idea how deep it is but, judging by the near-vertical granite surfaces either side of it, if you fell in it you would find it very difficult to get out again.

Rachel turns and keeps walking, and quickly she's ahead of him again, heading for the lighthouse.

'Come on, slowcoach,' she says, over her shoulder. 'I thought you were in a rush to get back to your terns?'

'Fuck off,' he says, 'I'm an old man.'

In the afternoon the weather takes a turn for the worse and Fraser has to give up on the tern terrace.

They have done a good amount, anyway, and they should be able to finish laying the rest of the membrane tomorrow – then they will be all set for when the gravel is delivered on Tuesday. Assuming the weather is good enough for the helicopter to fly. The bi-annual collection of the island's shit has been postponed three times already because of high winds.

Besides, Lefty is on the verge of collapse.

He has been like this from the start. It's hard to get him to work, but once he starts a task he will carry on until he's about to drop. If Fraser sets him on a job that is physically demanding, or doesn't have a recognisable conclusion, he has to watch him, look for the signs.

'That'll do for today,' he calls across.

Lefty stops, the shovel waving precariously. Staggers a little.

'Put it down. That's enough.'

The shovel drops. Lefty goes to take a step, and then abruptly sits on the step he's created by cutting away the turf. The ground is wet through, but there's no point telling him off. Fraser goes over to him and realises that he's overdone it, the pale face and the vacant expression telling him everything.

'Up you get,' he says, offering a hand.

Lefty looks up at the hand and ignores it, struggling to his feet. He tries to lift the shovel.

'I've got it. You get yourself back to the lighthouse.'

They walk back at the same time but not together. Fraser pushes the wheelbarrow with the tools in it, rattling over the bumps. Lefty is walking like a Glasgow drunk, sometimes veering to the side, leaning back, but somehow always remaining upright.

At least he's in no fit state to talk to Rachel, if she's there. Fraser will tell him to get in the shower and then he will probably have a sandwich and get on his bed and fall asleep for a few hours. Then he'll get up around dinnertime and Fraser might offer him dinner and he will refuse, will instead make himself something involving chips, and will eat it in his room. Then he'll watch TV or play some stupid war game into the early hours. And tomorrow everything will start again.

This has been their life for the past year.

Rachel

Rachel is back in the kitchen with her laptop open in front of her. She has been staring at her email inbox for the past ten minutes and her eyes have stopped focusing on Lucy's latest email. Her intention had been to write to Marion, but now she's here she can't think of the words.

There was something overwhelmingly awful about the cottages. It wasn't just the condition of them, the damp and the smell of rotting wood and mould, the graffiti, the stale, cold air inside. It was the way the atmosphere had changed as they had gone down the hill, the fresh breeze becoming a rank chilliness, as if the ravine were a pit in which a miasma had settled. It felt like a trap, despite the rocky path that curved away, presumably towards the jetty. And the loch – that dark, still water in which nothing reflected but the black granite walls – it was horrible.

She had thought it was her. That she'd brought it with her, carried it down the hill getting heavier with each step, her shame and humiliation and self-loathing; but it wasn't her at all. Whatever it was, it had been waiting for her down there. When they came back up the hill, Fraser following, she could feel it draining away again with every step. She had been so pleased to be out of there that she had almost run up the hill, steep as it was.

I can't stay down there, she thinks.

Aside from the fact that the cottages are derelict, there's no way she would stay in them even if they were renovated. She can't imagine how Marion will ever be able to market them as holiday cottages, given that there is no view of the sea, not to mention the hazard of that slippery slope, the danger posed by the loch.

She closes her laptop. If Marion asks, she will give her honest opinion. But this isn't her job; she is just here to take care of things until Julia can take over. Really it's none of her business.

In any case, she has to make the best of things. She is stuck here with Fraser and Lefty. She has been here for two nights. So far she hasn't been murdered, or assaulted, or threatened. If they were going to do any of those things, probably there would have been some sign of it by now. The presence of a knife, general grumpiness and odd behaviour are not sufficient grounds for bailing out and running back to Norwich, are they?

She is just going to have to stick at it.

At four she heads out to the bird observatory. Ahead of her on the path she meets a curious procession: Lefty, trudging vaguely, head down so that he barely sees her and she has to stand aside; and then, when he catches sight of her out of the corner of his eye, he startles comically, staggers a bit.

'You okay?' she asks, alarmed, but he ignores her and carries on.

A few paces behind him is Fraser, pushing a barrow, shaking his head.

'What's up with him?' she asks him.

'Overdone it a bit.'

'Oh. Right.'

He keeps walking without a further word. She watches him go.

The birdwatchers should all still be out there somewhere, doing counting or ringing or taking photos with their long-lens cameras, or whatever it is they do each day.

She takes the load of bedlinen that she washed yesterday out of the dryer, folds it, and takes it inside to put in the airing cupboard. By the time changeover day comes around she will have washed and dried a complete set of linen, so that the next load of happy campers can have fresh sheets instead of starchy ones straight out of the packet.

The kitchen is a complete state.

She stands in the doorway, folded bedclothes in her arms, and looks with horror at the mess. There are plates and cups all over the table, crumbs and bits of toast on the floor, a spoon with what looks like jam on it on the rug. There is mud on the rug, and footprints all the way through to the bedroom where someone has casually forgotten to take their boots off. The sink is piled high with dishes, and a pan which might, this morning, have been used to make porridge has been left on the hot stove to form a gluey baked-on crust. There are eggshells in a pile, egg white trailed all over the work surface, crumbs, jam, spilled tomato soup in blobs all over the top of the hob, mingled with splattered bacon grease. The kitchen bin is overflowing, a juice carton left on the floor next to it, on its side, orange juice leaking from it.

If someone told her that it had been a week since she was last in here, she would not be surprised.

Shock gives way to dismay which leads to pain, and tiredness, and horror at it. She has no choice – she will have to clean it all. She can't start cooking anyway, can she? Most of the pans have been used.

She takes the sheets through to the airing cupboard and glances in at the bedrooms on the way. They are similarly bad: duvets on the floor, muddy footprints. One of them – the double – is surprisingly neat and she wonders which of them is sleeping in there, and how on earth the rest of them manage to exist as fully grown adult males when they're out in the normal world.

The bathroom is a mess too. One of the taps has been left dripping, wasting the precious water from the well. She will have to do a dip to make sure there is enough – if they have to ration showers the birdwatchers might complain. The towels – the ones she went to the effort of washing and drying – have been left in piles on the wet floor. She picks them up and takes them straight out to the washing machine, loads it and turns it on, two minutes later thinking that actually she should just have stuck them in the dryer and not bothered to wash them again.

Clearing up the kitchen and the main room takes three-quarters of an hour, time she had planned to spend cooking and then getting the hell out of there. While she is putting the vacuum away in the storage cupboard, she hears the door opening and three of them pour in. Her mind has gone blank: the tall one? Roger? She is too distracted, too upset. The one with the beard walks straight through the lounge and sits on the sofa to unlace his boots. Fresh mud marks the floor she has just cleaned.

'Ah, it's you,' Roger says. 'What's cooking?'

Had the greeting been different, she might not have said anything. If it had been nice. If he had apparently remembered her name.

'Nothing, yet,' she says tartly. 'I've just spent the last half-hour clearing up.'

'She's talking to you, Eugene,' Roger says.

Eugene looks up from the sofa and actually rolls his eyes.

'Would it be possible to take your boots off by the door?' she asks politely, using the dustpan and brush to get the mud off.

The young one, who hasn't spoken to her at all yet, loiters by the door looking alarmed.

Eugene gives a dramatic sigh and carries his boots over to where the others have left them. He is a grown man, she thinks, possibly in his fifties, and he's behaving like a toddler. Roger heads for the bedrooms and Eugene returns to the sofa, where he's joined by the younger one.

Rachel starts on dinner.

A few minutes later the door opens again and the remaining two come in. Before they're over the threshold Roger says, 'Boots off, boys. We've been told off.'

Hugh and Steve – she remembers their names all right – come in, *sans* boots, looking from Eugene to her as if they've missed something interesting. She smiles at them, not wishing to make everything worse, and goes back to peeling potatoes. Eugene says, pointedly, 'Remind me what it is we're paying for again?'

Something is muttered in reply, but she can't hear it. Someone laughs.

Rachel bites her tongue, holds her breath, tries hard to keep calm. But her hands are shaking. She hates confrontation, hates herself for being so pathetic, wishes she could stand up for herself. Are they all like this? she wonders. Would it be better if they had regular holidaymakers, couples, and families? Then she would just clean at changeover, wouldn't have to see them every day. Somehow this sounds more appealing. But, for now, she's stuck with this lot.

'Isn't the food ready?' Hugh says, to nobody in particular. 'I thought we were supposed to eat at six. We could have stayed out.'

Fraser

Rachel is late getting back from the bird observatory. He's almost at the point of going to look for her on the quad, wondering if she's actually expecting a lift and whether she's waiting for him there; and then he starts thinking about whether she has her torch, or if she's wandering about outside in the dark, getting too close to the cliff edge.

And then he hears the door, and a few moments later she's in the kitchen with him. Socked feet, pink cheeks, eyes too bright.

'What's wrong?' he asks.

'Nothing. I'm okay.'

'Don't tell me you fell over again,' he says, stirring the gravy. Proper gravy, made with the meat juices in the roasting pan.

'That lot,' she says. 'They're a complete load of arseholes. Sorry.'

He smirks at the novelty of her swearing and at her apologising for it. 'What did they do?'

She bites her lip at him, as if she's still not sure whether she can trust him with her opinions of things. He takes the plates over. Roast beef, rump, done pink. Yorkshire puds like mountains. Carrots, parsnips, peas from the veg patch last year, frozen, but tastier than shop ones.

'God,' she says. 'You did a roast.'

He watches her eat. She's picking at it, though, her head down. Something's wrong with it. Maybe she likes meat well done? Some people are really fussy about that kind of thing. Then she comes to a complete stop, lowers her knife and fork.

'Something wrong?' he asks, trying to keep the edge out of his voice. He's been cooking for hours. He's given up most of his Sunday afternoon.

'No. I'm just a bit…you know.'

'What the fuck did they say to you?'

She looks up. He can see her pale face and the pink spots under her eyes.

'It's not that. It's Sunday, isn't it? You did a roast. I should have done them a roast. That's probably why—'

'Did you have a joint of meat in your provisions?'

She frowns. 'I don't think so.'

'I don't think so either. So, nobody's expecting you to do a roast. Especially not on your first bloody weekend. So that's not it, is it? What's really wrong?'

107

'The place was a complete mess,' she says miserably. 'Crap everywhere. Towels on the floor. Taps not turned off properly. Dirty plates and crumbs and piles of washing-up.'

'Is that right?' he says, concentrating.

'Mud all over the floor. And then they came back when I was still cleaning up after them, and they were just—' She searches for the right word, looking off towards Bess, who's sitting in her bed, head on paws, listening to every word. 'Rude,' she says. 'Just really rude.'

'Did you tell them off?'

'No! Of course not. I asked one of them politely to take his boots off by the door, and he muttered something about what are they paying us for? They were laughing, and not in a nice way. I thought it was rude.'

'And then?'

'I just got on with their bloody bangers and mash.'

He watches her, chewing. Then adds, 'Did you spit in it?'

'Maybe.'

He laughs at her.

'No, of course I didn't,' she adds.

Now she's looking at him, right at him. He thinks she looks … brittle. 'This food is amazing,' she says. 'Thank you.'

'Nae trouble.'

'When I get the next load of shopping, I'll ask them to get us a couple of nice bottles of wine.'

'Aye,' he says. 'I don't bother usually. Too easy to drink the whole thing.'

'We can keep an eye on each other's drinking,' she says, then stops, as if she's worried that she's said the wrong thing.

'Do you need me to have a word with them?' he asks, calmly.

'No!' she says sharply, clattering her fork down. 'Can you imagine? They'd think that was hilarious.'

'I can assure you they wouldn't.'

She sniffs and picks up her fork again. 'Well, maybe, but they certainly wouldn't have any respect at all for me after that, would they?'

'They'll be gone on Friday,' he says. 'You won't have to see them again.'

'Please tell me all birders aren't like that.'

'Mostly they're fine.'

'Shit.'

Fraser finds all this amusing, although he does feel a bit sorry for her.

'And you can stop laughing, it's not funny.'

He raises his eyes to her and knits his brows in a frown. He's not used to being challenged, not in his kitchen, not by a wee ginger who's barely unpacked. He expects her to see his face and back down – most people do. He only has to look at people and they realise that he's not someone to mess with.

To his surprise, her stormy face breaks into a wide smile. 'Okay. Maybe it is. A bit funny, at least. I shouldn't be saying this, it's unprofessional.'

'You know I don't actually have any contact with Marion or any of them,' he says. 'I only speak to them at the Trust when I actually have to.'

'Oh,' she says. And then a little pause before she adds, 'What's she like?'

'Who, Marion? Have you not met her?'

'No. She interviewed me over the phone.'

'Ah, well, you've a treat in store, then.'

'I might never meet her – I mean, Julia will take over and I'll just go back, I guess.'

There is another little pause. He's going to say it, then he stops himself, because it's not something he has ever said before, never even thought it, never mind said it. And then he thinks, fuck it.

'You can talk to me about anything,' he says. Casual as fuck. 'Not like there's anyone I can tell, in any case.'

Rachel looks at him, not in the least bit startled. It's something women say to each other all the time, of course, isn't it? Inviting confidences. Waiting for gossip.

She has finished eating, leans back in her chair.

'What about Lefty?' she asks.

'What about him?'

'You could tell him. If I told you anything, I mean.'

'You can see for yourself,' he says, pointing his knife in the direction of the door, 'we don't exactly talk.'

'And Robert?'

'I only see him for five minutes twice a week. Usually got more important things to discuss.'

'He's a friend, though?'

'He's about the closest thing I've got to a friend, aye. I guess he is.'

'What about on the mainland?'

He gets up, goes to the cupboard, retrieves the bottle of whisky and the two glasses. Uncorks it – this is a proper whisky with a cork; none of that screw-top rubbish here. He thinks about buying two or three bottles of the same stuff. Thinks about answering her question. Thinks about what she's really asking.

'Why do you think I'm out here?'

'I don't know. Don't you like people?'

'Not really.'

'Why not?'

'Are you interrogating me?' he asks, looking at her over the rim of his glass, one eyebrow raised. He can feel the warmth of the fiery liquid sinking down to meet the rising fire from his belly.

'You're the one who said I could tell you anything.'

'*Tell* me anything. Tell. You seem to be asking.'

'Well – same thing.'

'Not the same thing at all.'

'So I can tell you anything, but not ask anything?'

He shrugs, the first two mouthfuls of the whisky making him care just a tiny bit less.

She finishes off her glass. 'How about I tell you things, and you tell me things. Like a conversation, you know. You ask me something, I'll ask you something.'

'You're assuming that I actually want a conversation.' He's getting antsy about it now. He wants to get up and walk away but he's made the mistake of bringing out the whisky – in essence it was to give himself something to do, to give himself time to think – but now that it's here, between them, the suggestion is that he wants to sit and talk to her. As he did last night.

'I'm not much good at chit-chat,' he says. An attempt to shut her down.

She watches him, half-smiling, then the smile slips and her eyes drop to the table. 'Fine, whatever. Whatever you like.'

She pushes her seat back and stands, collecting his plate and hers and taking them both to the sink. He listens to the activity behind him, running water, the clanking of cutlery and crockery, while he rolls the base of his glass on the table in slow circles, the light running through the last of his drink and making kaleidoscope patterns on the pale wood. After three minutes he can't stand it any more, swills the last of his drink down, grimacing at the bite of it, and goes to help. He takes up the tea towel and starts to dry the dishes, putting them away.

'You can have one more question,' he says, 'and then I'm done.'

'Fair enough,' she says. 'I'll have to think about it, if I'm only allowed one. Am I never allowed to ask you anything else, ever?'

He looks at her. 'That your question, is it?'

'No. Don't answer it. I'm still thinking.'

He watches her wiping round the sink with the dishcloth, frowning in concentration. One of his stupider fucking ideas, giving her one free pass. Of course, he doesn't have to answer, whatever it is. She's going to ask something about family, about his life, about why he's on the fucking island, isn't she? And he'll have to think of some clever answer that will just get her off his back for a bit.

'What's your favourite bird?' she asks.

111

The question takes him by surprise, and then he has to think about it. He thinks about it for a long time, long enough to consider having another glass of whisky, although she's wiped down the table and put the mats away, and is leaning against the sink with her arms crossed, waiting for him to decide.

'That's a tough one,' he says, nodding.

'I know,' she says.

'I thought you were going to ask me something else,' he says.

'Well, I thought I'd go in with something less confrontational, since you've obviously got a problem with it. I thought I'd give you something nice to think about instead.'

'Very kind.'

'Well? Have you got an answer?'

'Chicken,' he says.

'A chicken?'

'Aye, a chicken. They lay nice eggs and they're sweet wee things, most of the time. And they're nice roasted.'

Rachel's mouth drops open.

'What? You're a vegetarian all of a sudden?'

'Do you eat your chickens?'

'No, course not. Not while they're still laying.'

'What about when they stop laying?'

'Then they're old and tough and not very nice to eat anyway. I get my chicken from the supermarket, same as everyone else.'

'It's a bit weird, though, liking them and making friends with them and then eating their relatives.'

'The eternal dilemma of the animal-loving meat eater.'

'Like the birdwatchers, having eggs for breakfast and then getting all excited by the eggs and the chicks in the nest. Why are those eggs edible, just because they've come out of the arse of this bird rather than that bird?'

'Eggs don't actually come out of arses,' he says.

'I know that.'

Rachel

They have moved into the living room. It smells vaguely musty, underused.

She watches as Fraser lights the woodburner, and now it smells of salt, wood, hot metal, burning dust.

Rachel is a little bit drunk and she knows she should go to bed. She should have gone an hour ago. But she checks her watch, and sees that it's actually only half-past ten. It's been a hell of a day, in fact it's been a hellish few days, and Dad's whisky has rubbed the edge off it. She will regret this in the morning, probably, but the morning is still hours away, and she doesn't have to get up early.

'What are you smiling about?' he asks, moving back to the sofa.

'Nothing.'

He doesn't press it. Pours whisky into both of their glasses.

'Cheers,' she says, clinking his.

'Cheers. I'm going to have to get Craig to bring us some wine. Not that I trust him to bring anything decent. Maybe I can get him to bring us more of this stuff.'

Of course, he would be a wine snob, she thinks. Just as he's a coffee snob and a foodie. What the hell's he doing out here on an island? He should be living in a Victorian terrace somewhere just off the Earlham Road.

'Something's tickled you,' he says. 'Spit it out.'

Caught out, she says, 'You're just – not what I expected.'

'What?'

'The cooking. The coffee. Being choosy about your wine. How do you manage, being out here on your own all this time?'

'I manage just fine. It's other people's opinions I can do without.'

The smile drops from her face – she's offended him. And he's right, it is a bit judgemental of her, making assumptions about him. 'I'm sorry,' she says.

'I don't mean you.'

He still says it brusquely, and she wants to change the subject.

'What were you doing before this?' she asks.

'Various things. Worked on the rigs for a long time.'

'Oil rigs? Wow. I bet that was interesting.'

He barks a laugh. 'Now I know you're winding me up.'

'I'm not, at all,' she says hotly. 'I guess ... it got you used to the isolation?'

'No, the opposite. Being isolated with hundreds of other people – I guess it's like being in prison.'

He lifts his glass, not looking at her. His hand is shaking, just a tiny bit, so she's not even sure if she saw it or not. What's that all about? And then she thinks: he's been in prison. Or – maybe not that – but something about it. Claustrophobia, perhaps. Maybe that's why he's here. Maybe he can't stand being trapped.

'What about you?' he asks.

He's asked her very little still. The fact that he's chosen this moment to come out with a question makes her realise how keen he is for the subject to move on. And, of course, it's on to a topic that she'd really rather avoid.

'I was just temping,' she says, at last. Her cheeks are hot, her head swimmy.

'Doing what?'

'Just admin, for a pharmaceutical company. Nothing exciting.'

She watches him, thinking. He sips his whisky – he's only halfway through his; she'll have to take it easy. She thinks of the water in the loch, the sinking blackness, depth.

'Things didn't work out,' she says, out of nowhere. And then, without warning, she carries on. 'I had a – a thing – I don't know. I had a relationship with my boss. And it went a bit wrong.'

'Ah,' he says. He lifts the bottle and adds a dribble more to her glass. 'How did it go wrong?'

'Amarjit,' she says. 'His name is Amarjit.'

He waits for her to continue, already thinking that Amarjit sounds like a right arse, despite knowing nothing at all about him other than his name and that he's Rachel's ex-boss, ex-whatever.

'He was lovely…and interesting, and clever, and just basically charming. And I completely fell for it, idiot that I am.'

She stops for a moment, drinks some more of the whisky. Dutch courage. He'll remember this, remember that maybe it'll take a drink to get her to open up. There's more of it in there. He wants to know. He wants to see the cause of her pain, because then she might start to feel better, and, for some reason he can't quite fathom, he wants to help. There's only so much he can do with food, after all.

'We got together – I mean – it was quite quick.'

She won't look at him now, twisting the glass and looking at the liquid swirling, as if she wants to dive in. She takes a big breath in. 'Turns out he was also sleeping with several other women, including his wife, who I thought he'd separated from.'

'Ah,' he said. 'He sounds like a right cunt.'

Her shocked little face, he thinks. And then she manages a stifled little snort.

'Besides anything else, it's unprofessional. You've not just had a relationship end, you've left your job, too, presumably because of this twat. Did you complain about him? I mean, that sort of predatory behaviour…he took advantage. Right?'

'It's not that simple,' she says. 'You've got basically no rights, when you're temping. And how it happened, when I found out – well. It was at a conference, in front of everyone. I'd had too much to drink. I made a scene. People were laughing. Also, can you please stop using derogatory terms for the female anatomy? I don't mind you swearing, just not those words. I like to use them for other things. Nice things. Well, cunt. Not twat, so much. That one sounds too comical.'

Jesus, he thinks. 'Is that so?' he says.

'Yes.'

'Fair enough. I'll call him a prick, then.'

She smiles into her glass. 'That one works for me. You can add "little". Suits him.'

'Ha.'

'You know,' she says, 'I know it sounds like nothing. But I felt so ashamed of what I'd done. It was – it was…I don't know. Like the absolute end of the world.'

Fraser nods. He knows that feeling, right enough. The sharp stab of pain, the numbness, the months where you can think of nothing else, and then afterwards, when something else happens, you look back and think – what? That you should have coped better? That, if only you'd known what was ahead, you'd have managed your feelings properly?

Something's happened, he thinks. Her cheeks are pink.

'I'd better go to bed,' she says, and gets to her feet quickly.

'You okay?'

'I just—' she says, and doesn't continue.

And she turns and goes towards the hallway and the stairs.

'Rachel…' he says, and he has no idea what to say to her.

She stops, a hand on the door frame. Doesn't look round. When he doesn't say anything else, she leaves.

And he hates himself, because he can't help feeling that he's somehow made it worse.

Rachel

Rachel cries for a long time, and then ends up with the worst sort of headache, one that won't go away on its own. She is empty of tears, at least: dry and shrivelled and hurting. So that was a complete bloody waste of time.

She gets out of bed again and goes to the bathroom to get some water. Fraser is still downstairs. It's late, for him, and she wonders if he has fallen asleep down there. *Such a fuck-up*, she thinks. Then: *Pull yourself together, Rachel. How much longer are you going to do this? How much longer are you going to wallow in your misery? Enough, already. Enough.*

But she can't help them, these unexpected waves of overwhelming emotion. And it's changed, since she's been here. Now she's afraid, too, this horrible crushing fear that she'll somehow never manage to be happy again. That she'll just keep making the same mistakes, over and over again. That the next mistake she makes – for it feels inevitable, that she'll fuck things up again – will be even worse. That maybe she won't survive it.

She thinks of Mel and how far away she is. How, actually, she was beginning to feel better – feel that maybe being here, being in a place that was so very different from the city, with the noise and cars and people everywhere, might somehow heal her. Make her realise that other lives exist, other places exist. That she can move on. That she can move away.

She drinks water from the tap with her cupped hand, cold and delicious and making her head hurt even harder. She needs a cup or something to be able to take a couple of painkillers, but there's nothing up here. In the end she takes the blister pack of paracetamol downstairs with her.

The door to the lounge is open, lights on in there, the sound of the TV playing some sort of loud action movie.

At least the kitchen is empty, she thinks. Empty and clean. It was only a couple of hours ago that they were standing here washing up, and Fraser has wiped down the kitchen table and everything is neat and tidy. She is still drunk but she has passed the happy swimmy stage; now she is entering the deep, soaking regret. She must have drunk several glasses, she thinks, before she made such a fucking spectacle of herself. And the crazy part of it was, she wasn't even really upset about Amarjit any more. It was Lucy, and Emily, and—

Enough.

She takes the glass with her, glances at the door to the lounge. From the hallway she can see the rug, the edge of the armchair, Bess lying with her head on her paws, watching. Her tail thumps the rug.

She should apologise, she thinks. It will be more awkward if she leaves it till tomorrow.

With one hand she pushes open the door. Fraser is sprawled on the sofa, his long legs crossed on its far arm, his head resting on the other. He's awake, but he hasn't heard her, or maybe he has and is ignoring her. Maybe he's engrossed in the television – a car chase through a city at night. Could be anything.

'Hey,' she says.

He jumps up from the sofa as if she's electrocuted him, tipping over the glass – thankfully empty – that's balanced on his chest.

'Sorry. Made you jump.'

'That's okay,' he says. 'Come sit down. How are you feeling?'

'You're up late,' she says.

He sniffs. 'Got me started,' he says, lifting the glass. 'It's a bad idea, really, drinking.'

'Yes, it probably is.'

'I drank quite a lot my first year here. Then I stopped.'

'Why did you stop?'

'Just realised if I carried on it was going to get … unhealthy.'

She knows that feeling. She has felt it herself. 'I'm sorry,' she said. 'I guess I should have checked it was an appropriate present to bring you. I couldn't think of anything else.'

'No, you're all right. Drinking with someone else is different.'

'And drinking with good food.'

'Aye, right enough.'

'Perhaps we should just have a pact,' she says. 'One glass with dinner.'

'Sounds good.'

'I used to be a really happy drunk,' she says. 'I know you'd probably think the opposite, given my behaviour earlier. But honestly – I'm usually quite a laugh.'

His eyes crinkle at the corners and he smiles down into his empty glass. 'I bet you are.' Then he adds, 'You'll get back there.'

She looks at him, trying to smile.

'You'll get your happy back. You just need a wee bit of time.'

She tips her head back, breathes in. 'Solitude, fresh air, something to do…'

'Aye,' he says. 'It works like magic, this place. And it's your home now.'

5

Maggie

Rachel

Rachel wakes early despite the late night. It's still dark, and it's chilly.

It's your home now.

He'd said it so casually. She'd wanted to come back with something equally casual. *I'm only here for a few weeks.*

She has always thought of Norwich as home, but it feels like a million miles away. And this place, cold, windy, raining most of the time, bird poop and screaming seabirds and mud – weird how it feels as though she's been here forever. She probes the thought, tries to work out why. A thought comes to her, out of nowhere: I like it here. Despite everything. She likes being away from people, from traffic. It's as though she can think, or at least have the space to think or not think, if she chooses. There is light and air and room to breathe.

She thinks about going back to Norwich, which will be happening soon enough; tries to think of Must as some sort of weird, rainy holiday. Tries to think about wandering down Elm Hill, eating chips from the Grosvenor Fish Bar, wandering around the Jarrold book department. Can't imagine any of it.

It feels as if the whole world consists of this island. Her beating heart is contained in the solid, soaring walls of the lighthouse; her entire life is circled by the sea.

How will she ever go back?

Now she's awake there's no point staying in bed. She washes in the bathroom, shivering, then dresses quickly in jeans and as many layers as she can find until she begins to feel warm.

The kitchen is empty. Coffee and porridge, still hot. She's glad Fraser has clearly already gone out, presumably taking Lefty with him. She's not quite ready to face him just yet. All that stuff she told him about Amarjit.

Oh, God.

Nobody ever asked her if she consented, it wasn't that sort of issue, but, now Fraser has suggested it, she realises that what Amarjit did was very definitely out of order. And Fraser's suggestion has her going over it in detail – the first time, the second time, the third time and just about every time after that – to try to find the moment when it all went wrong. The moment she made the mistake. Because it had to be her that had fucked up, didn't it? It always was.

She had been drunk enough to feel queasy, that first time. Drunk enough to worry that she might be sick on his pristine white sheets, especially when she went down on him and gagged. She remembered him laughing at that – not in a nasty way; she remembered him saying *careful* or maybe it was *easy, tiger* or maybe something else.

His body had been beautiful, smooth and hairless, gym-sculpted. On a subsequent occasion she'd seen him shaving his chest in the shower and, despite it being a thing that guys did, she'd thought that she'd probably prefer him with hair. Although she would never have voiced that opinion out loud.

She remembered being in his flat and looking at the clock and realising it was two in the morning, and closing her eyes and starting to drift off to sleep, only for him to turn on the light in the bedroom as he went for a shower. When he came back, wearing nothing but a pair of grey joggers, she'd been dozing. She'd heard the chink of crockery as he placed a cup and saucer – who even has cups and saucers these days? – on the bedside table. He'd sat on the edge of the bed and shaken her shoulder to wake her up, and said something about how much he'd enjoyed it.

No, not that. *It's been fun.*

The lights were all on, searingly bright, making her wonder what on earth she must look like, so exposed, hair mussed, make-up smudged.

She'd sat up and drunk the coffee and he'd said he'd call her a cab. He'd got up and gone to the living room, presumably leaving her to get dressed in privacy. She had sat there for a moment, hollow, hearing the sudden noise of the TV from the room next door. She'd gathered up her clothes and taken them into the bathroom, looking at her forlorn, pale face in the mirror and instantly regretting what she'd done. Not the act itself, but the stupidity of sleeping with her boss. He liked her, sure, but not enough to have her stay the night. Not enough to want to wake up next to her.

At work after that he was strictly professional. As if it had never happened. So that's how it was going to be, she had thought. Fine. She could do professional.

Then after a few days he had called her into his office and said how sorry he was that she hadn't been able to stay the night. As if it had been her decision. Making her frown and wonder if she'd misremembered it. *I would have liked waking up with you*, he said. *I would have enjoyed fucking you all over again in the morning*.

He closed the door and she ended up on her knees, sucking him off. There was something so deliciously naughty about it, so illicit, that she almost got off on the act itself, never mind that he didn't reciprocate.

Not then, not ever. That should have set off alarm bells, shouldn't it?

And then, one Sunday, he had turned up at the flat. She'd invited him in. Mel, thankfully, happened to be out. He looked as out of place as anyone could possibly ever be, but he was making an effort not to look at the kitchen that had seen better days, the threadbare carpet in the hall. She wanted to take him to her room, but he was stalling. As if he wanted to be here with her really badly but was trying to hold off. Was trying to do the right thing. She made him a coffee, which to his credit he sipped without commenting, although he placed it carefully on the counter and didn't finish it. He didn't have the chance to, because, once he'd finished talking, she took him by the hand and led him to her bedroom just the same.

He said lots of things about *probably we shouldn't be doing this* and *if they knew* and *professional relationship*. And then he said even more about thinking about her all the time, not being able to concentrate, wanting her badly and needing her because life seemed to make sense now that he had her.

He hadn't been thinking about her every minute, of course he hadn't. That was ridiculous. If that were true, he would have come round a lot sooner. She has thought about the logistics of it since, how to think about someone constantly, and it just doesn't happen like that. Which means that he was lying, and, if he was lying about that, then he could have been lying about everything else, too. Every single non-work-related thing that he said to her was probably a lie.

But even now she doesn't hate him. She hates herself instead, for being so thoroughly fooled by a man. For allowing herself to be used. She can't blame him for any of it, because she should have been able to tell. She should have seen through him. She should have never been tempted in the first place.

Get a grip, Rachel.

She eats a small amount of the porridge. Her stomach is still feeling iffy. The alcohol went to her head and then to her heart and then to her stomach.

She is sitting at the kitchen table with her laptop, trying to muster up the enthusiasm to look at her emails. The outside world seems very remote. It's only been a few days, and already she feels Norwich is like somewhere she's imagined.

The laptop pings. It's an email from Lucy. And the subject line is 'Christening???'.

Fraser

Fraser has spent the entire morning battling a headache. In reality he is probably still a bit drunk, and, despite drinking pints of water and coffee before leaving the kitchen this morning, he can feel that the transition from drunk to hungover has begun. He has no energy to do any shovelling. He can't even be bothered to yell at Lefty, despite him doing stupid things like bringing the shovel down on his own foot. Thank God for the steel toecaps, even if the boots don't fit him properly.

His mind fidgets back and forth and, inevitably, frustration and his sore head make him even grouchier than usual. He has an urge to hit something, and if he stays here much longer Lefty is going to find himself launched off the cliff for no valid reason other than that he's breathing.

At about eleven he gives up, leaves Lefty working and walks back to the bird observatory. On a whim.

On a mission.

Two of the birdwatchers are inside, sitting on the sofa with laptops and piles of notes, no doubt collating yesterday's data. He thought they usually did that in the evenings, but Eugene and Hugh have apparently stayed behind.

'Fraser! How're you doing?'

He knows them from previous visits, has never exactly made friends with any of them, although they greet him with enthusiasm whenever he sees them. They see Fraser as the expert, which he is: the one who can tell them the best place to see the birds they're here for. If anyone's in charge here, it's him.

'Good,' he says. 'How's it going?'

'You want a coffee?' Eugene asks. Fraser has always thought he's a bit up himself.

The living room is untidy but not beyond what he might expect. He casts a casual eye over it, taking off his boots at the door (which he always does) and going to get himself a drink of water from the kitchen. The kitchen surfaces are full of dirty plates and dishes, a bottle of milk left out, cornflakes scattered. Crumbs on the floor.

The grouchiness coalesces into something harder. He goes back to the living area.

'We logged purple sandpipers yesterday,' Eugene says. 'We thought they should all have gone by now.'

'Aye, they're leaving every day.'

'D'you want to sit down?'

He's standing there, with his glass of water. Has no intention of lowering himself to their level. 'How are you finding it, having your evening meals cooked?'

'Oh, fine,' Hugh says. 'She's not a bad cook really.'

They exchange glances.

'Anything not meeting your expectations?' he asks.

They don't detect anything in his tone, which is just as well.

'She had a bit of a go at Eugene yesterday,' Hugh says, 'would you believe.'

'Oh, aye?'

'Told me off for leaving mud on the floor!' Eugene adds, chortling.

'And did you?'

'Did I what?'

'Tread mud over the floor. Or did you take your boots off at the door, like any normal adult would? Like I just did?'

Eugene frowns. He's caught up. The stance, the stare, the folded arms, the tone of Fraser's voice.

'We're not used to having someone here during the week,' Hugh says, with an uneasy little laugh, his tone placatory.

'I can see that,' Fraser says, looking round at the kitchen.

Hugh puts his laptop on the table, gets to his feet.

'I'll just do these dishes,' he says.

'Aye, pal, you do that,' Fraser says. 'Not wishing to interfere with your holiday an' all, but perhaps have a wee bit of respect for Rachel's hard work, aye?'

Eugene is looking at his laptop. Fraser takes a step towards him. 'Have I made things nice and clear? Eugene?'

'Sure,' Eugene says, not looking up.

Honestly, Fraser thinks, heading back up the hill, relieved at least that he managed to get through that without taking a swipe at anyone, it's like dealing with fucking children. What will it be like if they have actual fucking children, staying in the bird observatory for holidays instead of birdwatching? What if they get big families staying in there?

He sees the younger one, the gangly youth who to his knowledge has never actually spoken, on the headland. Dressed all in green with a camo hat and a pair of binoculars, looking out over the cliffs. Fuck knows where the other two are. He doesn't want to know.

Rachel

Rachel can't quite bring herself to read Lucy's email, so she types a quick generic reply, hoping that will keep her sister satisfied for a while.

Hey,

All good here. Loving the fresh air and the big skies. I get lots of time to myself in between trips down to the bird observatory. First set of birders are a bit of a nightmare but I've decided there's no point trying to clean up after them during the week, so I'm going to leave it until they fuck off back to the mainland and then I'll get on with it.

She pauses. It's no good. She had better read Lucy's actual email, in case something has happened.

Hi, sis,

All good here. Emily is sleeping off and on and doing really well. We went to the health visitor yesterday for the first time to get her weighed. There's like a little clinic for mums and babies and you just turn up and can chat to the HVs about anything you're worried about. Waiting room full of mums with babies of various sizes. Funny how huge some of them look – Emily's going to be there before I know it but at the moment she looks just tiny compared to most of them. There's another mum who had her little boy the week before Emily, and she's from Castle Drive, so I ended up talking to her for most of it. There's one little girl who must be nearly a year old who has the most amazing hair, with like a blond quiff with darker ends. Like she's had a reverse balayage. Apparently she was born with black hair and then it started growing through blonde. Such a cutie! Emily's getting a bit more hair too now but not at the back yet.

I'm sleeping when I can and when Ian gets in from work he takes over for a bit so I can have a bath or a nap or something – Ian does bottle, bath and bed which is nice, although I don't often get to sleep at that time. Then it's all systems go again about 12ish for the first wake-up.

We are busy planning Emily's christening – looks like we're going to have it on 27th July. Ian's parents are coming over; makes sense to do it while they're here. I'm hoping you'll be there – can you keep the date free? We will have a meal out afterwards so I need to know if you're coming, but perhaps not just yet.

Mum and Dad send love.

Lucy xxx

Lucy has not asked her anything about the island, particularly, and there is nothing Rachel can ask about Emily, although her heart burns with questions. July feels like a long way away. She will worry about that when she gets to it.

She puts off going to the bird observatory until later in the afternoon, but when she eventually goes she's pleasantly surprised. The kitchen is not exactly spotless, but some attempt has been made at least to clear up from breakfast, and the floor needs a vacuum but there are no muddy footprints. The bathroom smells of damp towels and the bedclothes are all over the place, but it's better than she expected.

Hugh and Steve are on the sofa, feet up on the table, ignoring her beyond an initial hello.

Tonight it's a pasta bake, easy enough to do. She makes the heel of the loaf from this morning into garlic bread, sets up the breadmaker ready for tomorrow. Gradually the others return, poring over the day's logs and talking about short-eared owls and tern terraces and all of them ignoring her.

Once they're eating she wipes over the surfaces and leaves them to it, vaguely hoping that they will do their own washing-up.

For a change she makes it back to the lighthouse early, and there is no sign of Fraser or Lefty. Finding the kitchen empty, despite her tiredness she decides to make cheese scones – something she is reasonably confident of not fucking up – as a way of saying thank you to Fraser for all the cooking. She doesn't know if he likes cheese scones, but if they don't go down well she can take them down to the bird observatory tomorrow. Once they are in the oven, she has a momentary panic that Fraser has been saving the flour and the cheese for something in particular – although there is plenty – and is washing up, half-wishing she had not started, when the door opens and Fraser and Lefty come in.

'Sorry,' she says immediately, aware of her face pink from the oven and now getting suddenly even redder. 'Taking over in your kitchen. But these are my favourites.'

'Smells good,' Fraser says, hanging up his coat.

Bess thinks so too. She came racing in as soon as the door opened, and now she's sitting at Rachel's feet, huge brown eyes giving her her full undivided attention.

'Can I give her a bit of cheese?'

'Aye, well, she'll follow you around for the rest of your life,' he says.

Lefty is standing in the doorway, pulling off his boots and watching her.

'How about you, Lefty?' she asks, determined to build bridges. 'You like cheese scones?'

'Aye,' he says, 'right enough.'

She can smell them beginning to catch, opens the oven door and rescues them just as the ones on the edge of the baking sheet are looking a bit on the brown side. Fraser has disappeared. Lefty is watching her warily.

'Get the butter out,' she tells him. 'They're best while they're still hot, I think.'

The domestic goddess apron does not sit comfortably around her neck, especially in someone else's kitchen. The only way she can make it work is to bluster her way through it. Lefty has got the tub of butter out of the fridge and is standing next to her, looking hungrily at the scones. Rachel hoofs the biggest one on to a piece of kitchen towel, holds it awkwardly and slices into it, revealing a steaming yellow interior. Thankfully it's cooked through. She passes it to Lefty. 'I'll leave you to butter it.'

She watches as Lefty slathers each side in butter.

'So,' she says brightly. 'What have you been up to today?'

He looks up at her, startled.

'Making tern boxes.'

'What are they?'

'Boxes, for the tern chicks.'

'Oh.' She's at a loss for a moment. 'Are there terns here already?'

'Not for another few weeks.'

'They breed here?'

'Aye. They migrate from the Antarctic. Longest migration of any bird.'

'Really?'

'Aye.' He takes a mouthful of scone. 'S'good,' he says.

Fraser comes back into the room and something happens between them. Rachel misses it – the glance, or whatever it is, or maybe it's just something that stirs in the air. Lefty shrinks, and takes his scone, and scoots out of the door and across the hallway.

'Wow,' Rachel says. 'That's weird. It's like he's scared of you.'

Fraser ignores her, leans against the kitchen counter, arms folded across his massive chest. She has the strangest feeling of having transgressed. She is in his kitchen. She has taken over, and he clearly doesn't like it.

'How's your day been?' she asks, as cheerfully as she can manage.

'Okay.'

'Want a cheese scone?'

If he says no, she will know she has pissed him off beyond all repair. He doesn't say yes, but with what sounds like a resigned sigh he collects a side plate from the cupboard and takes one delicately from the wire rack, breaking off a chunk and chewing it thoughtfully, watching her with inscrutable dark eyes.

'Lefty was telling me about the tern boxes. Were you both doing that?'

'Aye. Counted some shorebirds just now. They're on the way out.'

'Don't they stay?'

'Some of them. Most of them are heading north now for the summer.' He takes a second big mouthful of scone, chews. 'This is not bad,' he says, after a moment.

'Thanks,' she says. The relief is overwhelming.

'The birdwatchers were telling me what a good cook you are,' he says.

'Really?' She's surprised at this. First that he's been talking to them at all, and secondly that they have actually said something nice.

'Oh, aye. They think you're doing a grand job.'

She narrows her eyes. 'Did they actually say that?'

'More or less. Definitely they like the food.'

'Hmm.'

Fraser

After dinner Fraser and Rachel stay in the kitchen and, because he's been thinking about it most of the day, though it's probably the worst idea in the world, he gets the whisky and the glasses out again.

'Really?' she says, looking at the bottle.

'You don't want any?'

'After last night?'

That's how it is, then. 'Hangover?'

She's deliberately not meeting his eye.

'Not as such,' she says. 'I'd better not, anyway. Thanks, though.'

They move back to more formal topics of conversation, staying well clear of anything personal. There are things she's quite happy to talk about: books, popular culture (which he genuinely has no clue about; there is a TV in the lounge with an intermittent satellite connection but it's regularly blown off course by the wind and he can never be bothered to keep resetting it); food.

She also seems happy to listen when he tells her about the birds, about the island's schedule, how it operates by season.

'April is when everything comes to life,' he tells her.

She's resting her chin on her hand and she's looking at him, either concentrating intently, or taking the piss.

'The puffins will be landing over the next week or so. They'll stay for the summer, and leave again towards the end of August.'

'I've never seen a puffin,' she says. 'I'm looking forward to meeting them.'

'Aye, they're great wee birds,' he says. 'We don't get as many here as they get on May, but there are still so many in the season that you'll have to watch where you're walking.'

'I know they use the same burrows every year.'

'They do. The adults mate for life, and they live for thirty-odd years. That's why it's such a big deal when you step on one accidentally and collapse it. I mean, sometimes they recycle a rabbit hole if they need to, but it's a pain for them to have to dig a new burrow. It's bad enough if you were to step on one now, before they arrive, but bear in mind it's much worse if you step on one while there's pufflings inside. Or eggs.'

'Pufflings?' She is delighted at the word, incredulous almost.

'Aye, that's what the chicks are called. Wee black fluffy things. They'll be all over the place soon enough.'

'I can't wait. I guess all the birdwatchers are waiting for them too.'

'They're not so bothered about the puffins.'

'No? Why not?'

'It's not the seabirds they're so interested in. They come here and help with the counts, but really what they're looking forward to is the migration later in the year. We're a stopping-off point for hundreds of birds, most of them just brief visitors. You get a chance to see birds here that you'd never usually see on the British Isles.'

'And that happens when?'

'Varies. Depends on the birds. But September, October. That's when your bird observatory will be fully booked.'

'Julia will be here by then,' she says.

'Aye. Probably.'

'Hopefully it will all be fully booked for her for the rest of the year,' she says.

'I'd be surprised if it is, for all they fancy duvets and home-cooked meals,' he says. 'Sorry to disappoint.'

'You don't think people will come?'

'We're too far out for tourists. People can go to May if they want seabirds and pretty skies – why come an extra hour on a boat in the rain to see a smaller island with fewer birds?'

'But people won't just come for the birds, surely – they'll come for the solitude and the peace.'

'You can get solitude and peace on the mainland, along with tourist shops and pubs and places to visit if you get bored. You get bored out here, you're stuck. You can't just call for a taxi and head off.'

'I did think that. But when I spoke to Marion—'

'Oh, Marion's full of it,' he says, then bites his tongue. He should be careful. Not that he cares one bit what Marion thinks of him, but he still doesn't want Rachel to think he's talking about someone behind their back. And he'd far rather have the enjoyment of telling Marion off to her face.

'She seemed all right on the phone,' Rachel says solemnly.

'She's got no clue about the practicalities. You know she's never even been here?'

Rachel raises a startled eyebrow.

'Oh, aye. I met her at the offices in Edinburgh a few times, but she's never come all the way out here. All her schemes are based on what she's seen in photographs.'

Rachel shakes her head. 'I did wonder. About those cottages – they're going to take a lot of work.'

'Not gonnae happen.'

'I can't imagine staying there. I can't see the appeal. There isn't even a view. But she's expecting me to sort them out, somehow, isn't she? Or Julia, when she gets here.'

'I wouldnae worry about it. You've got enough to do with your bird observatory, and if you get bored you can help me with ringing and counting. And,' he says, almost as an afterthought, although it's something he's been thinking about a lot since she arrived, 'they're always on at me to start doing a fancy blog about the island, like they do for May and the others. I've managed to dodge that so far, but, if you fancy doing a bit of it, that would be grand.'

He wonders if he's overstepped it, asking her to do his work for him, but Rachel smiles.

'It'd make me feel a bit better about eating all your delicious food.'

'You good at all that stuff, then? Blogging and suchlike?'

'I'm probably better than you.'

'Well, that wouldn't be difficult, to be fair.'

'What sort of things do they want you to blog about?'

'Have a look at May's website,' he says. 'That kind of thing. I mean, don't just blatantly copy them, no? But it should give you some ideas.'

She leans back in her chair, sighs. 'I'll go and get my laptop.'

Rachel

She twists the laptop round so he can see it, but they're both craning. 'Come and sit this side,' she says.

He does, and his presence is suddenly huge, and close. He's really enormous, she thinks. A great wall of a man.

She searches for 'isle of may blog' and finds it quickly. It's good. Lots of pictures, regular entries – every couple of days, even this early in the season.

'That's what you want me to do?'

'Aye, well,' he says, sitting back in the chair, 'you probably won't find quite so much to write about as they've got.'

'But you want me to take pictures? How will I know what to say?'

'Well, I could tell you. You know. Interesting things. The helicopter's supposed to be coming tomorrow.'

'The helicopter?'

'To pick up the tanks. And drop off the gravel for the tern terraces.'

'The guys were talking about the tern terraces in the observatory earlier. And Lefty said he was making boxes. So what's the terrace?'

'It's a big nesting site we're creating for the terns, past the observatory. May has one. You'll see their blog entry. They built it ready for the season last year.'

'Oh,' she says. She's thinking about following him around every day, waiting for something interesting to happen. It would take her mind off things.

'You got a camera?'

'Only on my phone.'

'Aye, well, that's what they use on May, just their phones, I think.'

'So I'll just take random pictures of birds, and scenery, and show you – and you can tell me interesting things to write about? In the evenings.'

'I'm going to need more alcohol,' he says drily.

For a moment she feels a catch of something in her chest, as though he's taking the piss, and she tries to catch his eye to see if he's having a go at her.

'You don't want to be worrying about them down there in the bird observatory,' he says.

'I wasn't, actually.'

'No?'

'No. Not right this second, anyway.'

'You not worrying about what they think?'

'No. Well... It's not that so much as wanting to do a good job. Performance pressure. You know? I don't want to let anyone down.' She is about to add, *I have a tendency to make a habit of it.*

He laughs, just a snort, but stops. He's not laughing at her. 'You're here right enough, aren't you?'

'But Marion has – expectations. Doesn't she?'

'Aye, she may well have, but she's gonnae have to get used to disappointment. And none of that will be your fault.'

'Look, I'm actually trying to be professional about it,' she says, suddenly fed up with feeling like an imminent failure. At some objective level she knows it's not her fault, but she's got used to blaming herself for everything – why stop now? But she can do without him noticing.

'To be fair,' he continues, 'she's got used to me refusing her requests, so her expectations of this island are really quite low.'

The thought of Fraser continually and deliberately disappointing Marion in her office in Edinburgh makes her smile, and then laugh, and he does too.

'I could do some social media generally,' she says.

'Like Facebook?' He says it like he's never even seen Facebook, never mind set up an account.

'Probably better to do Insta, and Twitter. Better for pictures.'

'Right. If you say so.'

'I'll give you the passwords,' she says.

He laughs hollowly.

Fraser

The next day Fraser is heading out to check on the west cliff just as Rachel is going for a walk.

She has her phone in her hand, which he thought was one of those city things, the security blanket, until she stops for the third time to take a picture. 'What's that?'

'A cormorant.'

'Are there lots of them?'

'Aye, it's pretty common. They don't usually breed here, though.'

'And this?'

'That's a herring gull.'

'And this?'

'A shag.'

She gives a little snort. 'Seriously?'

'Aye.'

A little pause. She is behind him, so he can't tell if she's laughing or if she's looking for something else to photograph.

'It's beautiful,' she says then.

'I think so.'

'So stylish. Like – couture.'

'You gonnae put that in the blog?'

'Maybe. I've got to differentiate it from the Isle of May's blog, haven't I? Otherwise, as you said, they'll think

I'm copying. Besides, there's probably a degree of interest for a…what's the word?…a laywoman's approach.'

He doesn't answer, wondering if he's going to live to regret asking her to put her thoughts – and her pictures – on public display.

'It looks like…have you ever seen *How to Train Your Dragon?*'

'What's that?'

'It's a film, an animation. Well, more importantly it's a series of books by Cressida Cowell, but what I'm talking about right now is the film.'

'No, I haven't seen it.'

'Well, there's a dragon in it – actually there are lots of dragons, but this one in particular is called Toothless, and—'

'A toothless dragon?'

'He's still really fierce and dangerous; he's a Night Fury. That's the type of dragon he is. Anyway, he's black and has black scales, and he looks a bit like that…shag.'

He stops, looks at her. 'You should really get to know all these birds, right?'

'I know. I mean, I can recognise some of them. You need to give me a list, or something.'

'You need to do anything down there?' he asks, nodding towards the observatory.

'Not really,' she says. 'Not until later. I was just going to give it a quick tidy.'

'Right,' he says. 'Come with me, then. Let's go and look at some birds.'

Rachel

Rachel spends most of the morning with a notebook, writing down bird names and descriptions as Fraser stands on the clifftop with a pair of binoculars, showing her as many different

137

birds as he can find. 'Razorbills, there, look – black backs, white bellies. Thin white line over the beak and eye.'

'Oh, I've seen those. They look so cool, don't they? Like – I don't know – like master criminals in disguise.'

She knows this probably sounds ridiculous, but she's cheered up a lot being out in the fresh air, and it's amusing her writing things like 'razorbill = master criminals!!' in her notebook with a very rough drawing of one.

'They're auks. Same family as guillemots, and puffins.'

'Orcs? Like in *Lord of the Rings*?'

He looks baffled for a moment, then says sourly, 'Different spelling.'

There is a long pause. Fraser is looking out to sea, or looking at the cliff, and then, with his head perfectly still, he'll whip the binoculars up to his eyes in a swift, precise movement that shows he does this pretty much every day of his life. It reminds her of something – a predator, a kestrel hovering over a roadside, head utterly fixed and wings beating. Fraser hands the binoculars to her to show her something, getting close enough to loop the neoprene strap around her neck (because clearly he doesn't trust her not to drop his binoculars over the cliff) and it takes her ages wobbling around to find what he's pointed out to her, then focus the lenses, and by that time mostly she's missed whatever it was he wanted her to see. But she likes the feel of them, unexpectedly heavy considering how small they are, warm where his hands have held them; she likes the sudden crystal clarity of the view, the movement of the birds and how suddenly they are close enough for her to touch, feathers bright, eyes bright, beaks and feet tucked under them in flight, so many of them, so many. Clouds of bright whites and greys and blacks, all of them getting on with their lives and doing their thing.

'What's Lefty up to this morning?'

He acts like he hasn't heard, and she is about to repeat the question when he replies, 'Up at the tern terrace, I hope.'

'You're pretty hard on him, you know.'

She's not setting out to piss him off, but it feels sometimes as if she can't help herself. She watches his shoulders stiffen.

'Kittiwakes on the cliff,' he says, some minutes later. 'They have nests on the ledges – razorbills and guillemots just incubate their eggs on the rock; they don't have actual nests as such. Shags construct nests, but they tend to use bits of plastic and other rubbish as nesting material. That's partly why we do such a lot of beach cleaning.'

'Sorry. Those ones – the kittiwakes? – they just look like normal seagulls to me.'

'They're smaller than a herring gull. Prettier. And they have black legs, black wingtips. You'll get to see the difference soon enough.'

'How do they stop the eggs falling off the edge, if they don't have nests?'

'The eggs are more pointed than hen's eggs. So if they roll, they roll round in a circle.'

'That's so clever!'

The sun has come out and at one point she thinks about taking her jacket off, but the wind is keen and she doesn't want to get cold.

They move in stages along the cliffs. From the chaos of whirling birds Rachel now realises there are colonies, groups of black birds and white birds and other ones lower down. Rachel can see a couple of the birdwatchers in the distance, apparently doing the same thing as they are – looking down at the cliff face, writing things down. Birds wheel and soar everywhere. The side of the cliff is absolutely teeming with birds, all of them moving. It feels like chaos, but apparently this is all perfectly normal.

At lunchtime they go back to the lighthouse. Fraser heats soup for them both while Rachel butters the last couple of cheese scones. She has only eaten one but the twelve she made yesterday have been depleted, suggesting Lefty has been helping himself. The bowl of soup is huge, chunky vegetables like jewels in a clear broth, small pearls of barley, chopped chives, bright green, floating on the top. Every meal makes her think, *I can't possibly eat all that*, and then she eats it, hungrily.

The helicopter is due at two, and, by a quarter to, everyone's out on the clifftop, trying to find the best place to watch the action. Rachel stays near the lighthouse; the bird observatory's residents are all grouped on the clifftop one hill further off, cameras on tripods. Fraser is down below, near the tanks, waiting. There is no sign of Lefty. She gets some pictures of the helicopter coming towards the island, films a short video of the winchman dropping out of the side of it. He lands on the top above the harbour, not that far away from her. The noise is deafening and the downdraft from the chopper is blowing her hair all over the place – she ties it firmly into a tight bun, sitting cross-legged on the grass. Bright sunshine, noise, wind. Something utterly thrilling about it.

Fraser, who has been sheltering from the downdraft halfway up the track from the harbour, approaches and shakes hands with the winchman, engages in a bit of discussion that involves shouting in each other's ears, waving and gesturing towards the clifftop. Then Fraser starts up towards her. Before he notices, she takes another picture, and another. Something to send to Mel, later.

'You okay up here?' he shouts. It's still noisy.

'Sure. I've got a good view. Have you been sent away?'

'Aye. Best let them get on with it.'

He stands next to her for a while, the solid bulk of his legs next to her head, and then eventually, because there's clearly nothing he can do, he sits down, knees up, leaning back on his hands. The line has emerged from the helicopter again and the winchman is guiding it towards the tank, preparing to attach it to the top.

'Where's Lefty?' she asks.

He looks at her, cups his ear. She leans closer and repeats it.

'Staying inside.'

'Can't he come out to watch? Surely this is a bit of an exciting event?'

Fraser doesn't respond. Fair enough, she thinks. None of her business.

'They don't need you to help?'

'Don't want anyone anywhere near,' he shouts. 'Health and safety.' Eventually, though, he points across to the clifftop. 'They've all got their cameras out. So have you.'

'And?'

'Lefty's camera-shy. Right?'

'Oh. Right.'

What he means is, of course, that he doesn't want to risk Lefty appearing on some blog – theirs, or a birdwatcher's.

The first tank lifts up into the air and the breeze brings with it a gust of raw sewage that makes her gag. The helicopter flies off towards the mainland, the tank hanging beneath it, and the winchman heads up the path towards them.

'First lot,' the winchman shouts, as he gets closer.

Fraser scrambles to his feet. 'Tea?'

'Oh, aye, that'd be grand.'

'This is Rachel,' Fraser says, waving vaguely at her.

Rachel gets to her feet and holds out her hand to the winchman, who's dressed in a bright orange boiler suit and various harnesses that look uncomfortable. Beneath the helmet is a tanned, wrinkled face, a broad smile. 'James,' he says, pulling off a glove and shaking her hand. 'Nice to meet you.'

She follows them to the lighthouse for something to do – clearly the helicopter's going to be a while.

In the kitchen Fraser is actually boiling the kettle – James clearly isn't favoured enough for Fraser's precious coffee – and they are talking about rugby. After a few minutes of standing there feeling like a spare part, Rachel goes out into the hallway, closing the kitchen door behind her. She crosses to Lefty's room. The door's shut; from behind she can hear the sounds of drum 'n' bass playing unexpectedly quietly. She knocks.

There's no reply, but the music shuts off abruptly.

She knocks again. 'Lefty?' she calls quietly. 'It's me, Rachel.'

The door opens a crack. A pale blue eye, a slice of pale face. This close, she can see a scar across his eyebrow where there was probably once a piercing.

'Just thought I'd see how you're doing, cooped up in here.'

'I'm okay.'

'You need anything?'

'Nah.' He's not shut the door, though.

'Can I come in?' she asks.

His eyebrow squats into a frown, but then the door opens wider, and he steps back to let her in.

She looks around. There's nowhere to sit, apart from the bed. She shuts the door. He jumps back on the bed and sits at the head end, giving her plenty of room.

'Can I sit down?'

He nods, watching her warily.

'What are you listening to?'

'Mohican Sun,' he says.

She nods, as if she knows who that is. 'Do you mind not being out watching the helicopter?' she asks.

'Nah.'

'Not bothered?'

'Nah.'

On the windowsill a glint of colour catches her eye. He has a collection of objects, presumably things he has found on the beach. A green plastic toy soldier. A plastic star with the remnants of silver paint and a hole at the top, through which a ribbon was once threaded, to hang it on a Christmas tree. And then, even prettier, scattered pieces of sea glass: various shades of green, white, frosted from the actions of the sand and the shingle, worn smooth by the waves. There is one blue piece, sapphire-blue. It makes her think of the Harveys Bristol Cream sherry that her gran used to bring out on special occasions.

'Pretty,' she says, looking back at him.

He's chewing at his thumb.

'You can talk to me, you know,' she says, sitting down again. Smiling. It's like talking to a scared child. 'I'm not going to tell on you.'

He shrugs. 'Tell whoever you want.'

'I told Fraser I wouldn't let anyone know you're here, and I meant it. He's really tough on you, isn't he?'

He shrugs, picks at the duvet cover with bitten nails. On the back of his right hand is a tattoo that looks like something someone did at a kitchen table with a needle and a bottle of ink. It's a blurred shape that might be a dagger, oversized blood dripping from it. *Fuk dis* underneath it.

Over the sound of the frantic beat she can hear a distant thudding. She pushes herself up from the edge of the bed. 'Want me to bring you something? Next time it flies off?'

He looks up. 'Can of pop would be good,' he says.

'From the fridge?'

'Aye.'

She leaves him to it, shuts the door behind her. The air in the hallway is fresh after the fug of his closed-up little den. The kitchen is empty, the back door wide open. From outside, the deep thud-thud of the helicopter's rotors.

Fraser

The helicopter has returned with two builder's bags of gravel. He stays out of the way as James detaches them from the line and then reattaches the line to the second tank. Fraser is still fed up that the gravel has to be dropped a quarter of a mile from the tern terrace, but it can't be helped. He will have to cart it all up there in several trips. Thankfully he has the quad.

Rachel comes back out just as the second set of gravel bags are landing.

'Where did you go?' he shouts across to her.

'Just went to see Lefty.'

He's standing next to her so she's not looking at his face, which is just as well. What the fuck? He manages a strangled single word: 'Why?'

Now she turns to him. He keeps his eyes on James, who's busy detaching the line. Watching it being done, knowing he could probably do it better and quicker, is making him itchy with tension.

'Just felt a bit sorry for him. Missing all the fun.' She hasn't turned back. 'Why? Am I not supposed to be talking to him now?'

It's way too fucking noisy to be having this conversation. They're having to shout above the noise of the rotors.

'Fraser?'

'You're better off leaving him alone,' he shouts, eventually.

'Why?'

He ignores the question completely because he can feel the fury in him rising up like a tide and if this carries on he's going to explode and yell at her.

'Sorry,' she says. 'It's none of my business. I forgot that for a moment.'

And she smiles.

She pulls her camera out of her back pocket, and walks a few steps towards the cliff so that she can get a different angle of the helicopter hovering.

Rachel

Rachel lies still, trying to sleep, and failing.

It's not the excitement of the helicopter visiting the island. It's not as though she's never seen a helicopter before, and after the initial interest of watching the line being attached and detached, and seeing James or whatever his name was descending the line and then being taken back up again, what she was left with was the lingering smell of shit, and the birdwatchers waiting for their jacket potatoes and soup. From Fraser's room she can hear nothing at all: no snoring, no talking, no nightmarish shouts.

He had been mad, earlier. She had felt it, like a solidifying of his body as she stood next to him. She knew straight away that she had said the wrong thing. That going to see Lefty had been the wrong thing to do. She had been thinking it over in the observatory while she was making dinner, wondering if Lefty is actually a real threat to her – maybe he has some sort of mental illness that makes him dangerous? And that's why he's here, where he can't do any damage, can't hurt anyone?

But she hadn't felt that. She knows what anxiety looks like, has lived with it long enough. Lefty is way more scared of her than she is of him.

And yet Fraser wants to keep her away from him. And, when he knew she had gone to talk to the lad, he'd been absolutely furious. He'd barely spoken to her over dinner. Answering her chatty questions about birds with one-word answers, not looking up, clattering his fork at his plate. Then she'd asked about the helicopter and the septic tanks and he'd stopped talking at all, ignored her completely, got up the second he'd cleared his plate – she was still halfway through – washed up at the sink, then whistled for Bess and taken her out, leaving her sitting there on her own.

No whisky tonight, then, she had thought.

She was surprised by it more than anything. When she'd finished eating, she'd washed up and wiped the surfaces down, trying to work out if she wanted him to come back or whether she'd rather scoot off to bed and avoid him completely until his mood had improved. She had wiped the kitchen spotless and there was still no sign of him, so she came to bed, and only when she closed her door did she hear him coming up the stairs.

This afternoon, before dinner, she had WhatsApped the two pictures of Fraser to Mel, for her opinion. They're not especially flattering, and, given that she was uphill from him, they don't give a fair impression of his height, which Rachel

– being taller than most herself – finds particularly appealing. But they are indisputably Fraser, complete with the frown, and the right hand curled into a fist as if he's about to thump someone.

Wow was all that Mel said in reply. In response to that, Rachel had merely sent three letters: *IKR?*

He has walls, she thinks. He has built up walls over the years, big as you could possibly imagine, and now he's trapped himself behind them and he can't see out.

The island is like a wall in itself, a wall without bricks. Of course he doesn't want a visitors' centre. He doesn't want tourists, he doesn't want holiday cottages; why does anyone imagine he's here? He looks after the wildlife on the island and, yes, he clearly has some affinity for helpless creatures – she's including Lefty in this category, for reasons that she doesn't quite understand – but he's not here for the birds, he's here because of the solitude; that's what's important to him. He's not here because he's the only person willing to do this job. He *wants* to be here, even if it isn't good for his mental health.

She wonders if Marion ever asked him to look after the bird observatory.

She pictures that conversation for a moment, Marion (whatever she looks like; Rachel imagines a large, authoritative lady in a navy suit, rather like the Governess from *The Chase*) sitting at a desk smiling sweetly but forcefully; Fraser, feet planted, arms folded across his massive chest, chin up, jaw twitching.

Captain Haddock with a face like thunder – exactly how he'd been this afternoon.

Well, if that conversation had ever taken place, in real life or over the phone, it had not gone Marion's way. But then it has backfired on Fraser, hasn't it? Rachel is the living, breathing proof of that. He doesn't want more people on the island – and now he's got someone permanently living under the same roof. Sleeping with just a wall between them. No wonder he's struggling.

She thinks, *you're not the only one who needs to brick yourself in.*

She thinks, *maybe you're not the only one who needs an island to hide on.*

Rachel feels the edges of tiredness, fluffy, cloud-like, a blurring of her thoughts. The island is like a prison for him, she thinks again, a prison made of fresh air and sea. And yet it's joined to the land just the same, connected underneath the water. She pictures the sea draining away like something Biblical; she imagines walking across the salty granite from the rocky beach, downhill, sliding over glistening seaweed and looking at rock pools full of fish, and crabs; downhill, then flat and sandy for a while, her toes digging in … and she can see the shore, the houses and the strange black spire of the church on the hill, and she's walking but it doesn't seem to be getting any closer; and she never, ever, quite makes it all the way across.

Fraser

Fraser wakes up with a jump, heaving huge breaths in, sitting straight up in bed. Sweat cools on his skin as he comes back to consciousness.

It's a dream, he says to himself. *It's not real. It's just a dream.*

'Fraser?'

Someone is with him.

'Are you okay?'

'What? Fuck.'

It takes him several seconds to shake free of the confusion. He's in bed, and Rachel is sitting there next to him. Perched on the edge. Her hand on his shoulder, which he shakes off as he reaches for the light switch.

'What?' he says again, squinting at her. Then the anger rises, pushed up by the shame. 'What the fuck are you doing in here?'

She's sitting next to him, against his thigh, in a grey T-shirt with a sheep on it, her hair over her shoulders.

'You were shouting!' she says, eyes widening at his tone. 'I thought something had happened.'

'What? Nothing. Everything's … fine. Get out, will you?'

'Well, yes, of course.' She gets quickly to her feet. 'Clearly you're okay.'

He can't look at her. 'Maybe you could have knocked before, you know, just walking in.'

'I did knock!' She's at the door now. 'Anyway. Goodnight.'

He sighs dramatically and switches off the light again as the door closes behind her. His heart is still pounding with the residue of the dream, not helped by the shock of waking up to find someone in his room. He lies still for some time, not wanting to sleep, considering whether he can get away with never mentioning this again, and knowing with every possible certainty that she will bring it up as a topic for conversation the next time he sees her.

And in his heart, still, fresh, is Maggie: half-alive, holding on. Her face is a swollen mess of bruises and grazes, although he never saw her like that. He thinks maybe he's looking at Maggie, and then he's looking at Rachel, lying in Maggie's hospital bed, and then he looks closer and it's Maggie again. And he is shouting at her to stay with him, knowing that she is already slipping away.

Meanwhile in the dark, cold bedroom his heart is pounding so hard he can hear it, the blood pulsing and squeaking through his ears.

He slows his breathing by timing it with the dim illumination from the lamp as it passes overhead, sweeping round the island and the sea, reflected off the clouds and skimming the chilly black air. He turns on his bedside light because the images stay with him until the light chases them away; twists up slowly like an old man to sit on the edge of the bed, head in his hands.

Usually when he wakes like this he goes downstairs, drinks water, sits in the brightness of the kitchen and gets himself back to normal before he tries to sleep again; but Rachel might come downstairs, and then he will have to apologise for his behaviour. Late-night chats are dangerous. They go to unexpected places.

And still the nightmares keep happening.

He thinks her being here is what's triggering them.

He suspects this, because he is dreaming of her now as well as of Maggie. Of bad things happening to Rachel. Of not being able to get to her in time. He couldn't save Maggie, but now his brain is telling him to save Rachel instead.

After twenty minutes he is still wide awake, the sweat cooling on his naked back. He has been sitting on the edge of his bed, thinking through all the conversations he had with his sister and how he could have handled things differently, how he might have stopped it, and all that's happening is that he is getting more angry at himself. He always tries to fix things and there's no point, no point to it at all. In the end he gets up, puts on a T-shirt and some socks, and goes downstairs.

Bess is in her bed beside the range. The kitchen is warm and the lights, when he's able to open his eyes, are bright. He puts on a pan of milk and rubs Bess's soft ears.

A couple of minutes later he hears a movement, and Rachel comes in, wrapped in a faded blue dressing gown. He sighs heavily at the predicted interruption, yet is strangely glad to see her at the same time. She feels like an anchor. Real Rachel, in his kitchen, alive and well and yawning.

'Cocoa?' he asks her.

'Only if there's enough.'

He adds more milk to the pan, rubs at his face.

'Sorry,' he says.

'What for?'

'Waking you up. Telling you to piss off.'

'Oh, that. I shouldn't have just come into your room, though.'

'Aye,' he says. 'Well.'

'Look, if you'd rather be on your own...'

'You're here now.'

Fraser can feel her watching him as he stirs in the cocoa powder and the sugar and whisks it into the milk. *Say something*, he wants to yell at her. *Out with it, whatever it is.* But she's sitting there quietly, waiting for him to bring the mugs over, and then she sips at the drink, and then, without warning, he's started talking.

'Maggie was my sister,' he says. It comes out of nowhere, as if some unfamiliar part of him has just decided to speak up.

There is a long pause.

Then her hand is on the table over his, her thumb rubbing the back of it, and then it's still, warm on his. He feels a sudden rush of emotion, unexpected, and it's so gut-churning that he thinks for a minute he might vomit. The room spins sickeningly and he drops his head, pulls his hand away.

'She died,' he says. And then adds, 'No – she was killed. Murdered.'

Her eyes widen. 'When?' she asks.

'Six years ago. She was eighteen.'

'I'm so sorry,' she says.

If he looks at her, if he meets her eye, he will lose it. He has heard those words many times, from all sorts of people, and each time he's thought, *Aye, you might be, but you don't understand, how can you?* And he dismisses people because of it, he dismisses their kindness and their empathy. But something about the way she says it – the force of the feeling behind it, the quiet words – catches him by surprise and he feels that vast surge of anger and grief and pain rising in him again. He wants to get up and run away.

'Can you tell me what happened?'

He shoves the feelings back down again, and he's on safer ground because he can trot out these sentences without emotion; he's done it often enough. Those people that asked. The people that read the local papers; everyone he knew back then, all the people in the town, his ma's friends, Uncle Jack's friends from the pub, the guys at work. That's partly why he moved away. Because he got so sick of telling.

'She was in a car with a piece-of-shit drug dealer she'd been seeing, called Jimmy Wright. He was off his face. Drove into a tree. Got away with a few scratches and Maggie was – killed. Not instantly. She died in hospital.'

He looks at his hand, the way it's shaking, closes it into a fist.

'You dream about her?' she asks.

This is unfamiliar territory, of course. Nobody has asked him that question before.

'I guess I do. I don't always remember.'

She lifts the mug and drinks her cocoa and it recalls him back to the kitchen, the drink, the middle of the night. For a moment he'd been back there, looking down at the skinny scrap of life that was his baby sister, tubes in her mouth and the smell of death in the room, and the sick feeling was back. He picks up his mug. The sugar in the cocoa gives his stomach something else to churn over.

'I should have stopped her getting into the car. I should have been there, then it might not have happened.'

'You blame yourself,' she says. 'I mean, I don't know, but I'm pretty sure it wasn't your fault.'

He can't respond to that. How can she even say something like that? She wasn't there. Eventually he says, 'Yeah. It was all a very long time ago.'

'Six years isn't all that long.'

There is a long pause. When he can stand it no longer he looks up and meets her eyes. Smudges of tiredness under them, the bright blue of her irises, regarding him steadily.

'You don't have to say anything,' he says, and shrugs, trying to make it better for her. 'It is what it is.'

They sit in silence for a while.

He's finished his cocoa, and she has too. Now he wishes he'd never told her. Now it feels as though she has something to hold over him, and there will be consequences. But there's no way to take it back. He picks up his mug and hers and takes them to the sink, rinsing them with the pan.

'Will you be able to sleep now?' she asks.

He looks round. She's leaning against the worktop.

'Probably,' he says.

There is a long moment where she's watching him and he can feel the weight of it; not quite judging, not that. He has not talked about Maggie, since he moved away. He has never had to. There is a weird sort of relief in it, as well as the pain of thinking about her, which never seems to get any better. The weight of the guilt he feels, stones in his pockets.

She comes to stand next to him and with no warning slips an arm under his, curving around his waist, and he realises she's giving him a hug. He moves slightly, puts his arms around her back because that's what you're expected to do and it feels strange and soft and when he breathes out he feels her arms tighten a little bit.

He didn't want this. Didn't think he needed it. Feels a surge of some hot, bright pain, as if it's passing through, as if it's leaving his body. And now he thinks he doesn't want to let go. He feels heavy with weariness.

She moves her head and he releases her quickly. He can't bring himself to look at her. Feels a cool hand on his hot cheek, then her breath, and then she plants a quick kiss on his mouth. And then another.

the fuck is this

And he is about to respond and she's gone.

'Goodnight, then,' she says, from the doorway.

'Goodnight.'

He leaves it an hour. Then another thirty minutes. He watches the clock on the wall drag round to half-past two.

There's no point going to bed anyway; he's not going to sleep.

At last he gets up, sighing heavily. Bess isn't keen to go out – it's raining – but he waits with the door open until she trots out into the darkness. He watches the light sweep across the low cloud, soothed by the rhythm of it, the constancy, and after a minute he goes outside in his socked feet, not caring about the rain. Stands there on the grass, taking deep lungfuls of the cold, wet air.

When Bess scampers back in he turns off the lights and goes up the stairs as quietly as he can.

In the bathroom he uses the toilet and brushes his teeth, not quite able to meet his own eyes in the mirror. And then he looks. Studies his face. He feels old, and looks it. It has never mattered to him before, because that's what life is, isn't it? Time passing. He can no more control his own face's ageing than he can bring Maggie back to life. He has lines around his eyes; his brows are rough and unkempt and growing in every direction; his beard is overdue a trim. He's never bothered shaping it. It grows up his cheeks in patches, down his neck and under his collar, merging almost seamlessly with his chest hair. Bits of his beard, his hair, are threaded with grey.

You fucked that up, right enough, he tells himself.

In bed he finds himself lying awake for what feels like hours. The wind has picked up outside, he can hear it, the rain hammering on the window. If it had been like this earlier the helicopter wouldn't have flown. He thinks about that for a while, about the shit, the detritus of the last few years and how it's been lifted off the island. He could have a fresh start. And he thinks of all the things he should have got rid of a long time ago and how they're still here. Stones in his pockets. Maggie's picture, staring at him from the chest of drawers.

Fraser sighs, turns on to his side.

6

Amarjit

Rachel

In the morning Rachel sits at the kitchen table, working up to opening the laptop and doing today's blog. There is something in the slow cooker already that smells amazing – meat and garlic and a rich sauce – and she finds she has something of an appetite, for a change. Which is just as well, because Fraser has gone out, already, and left her a full cooked breakfast on the top of the range, tin foil over it. The eggs have gone a wee bit rubbery but everything tastes amazing, as always. Mushrooms, tomatoes, sausage, bacon, a hash brown, and a little ramekin with baked beans in it.

She senses this is some kind of weird thank-you for her sympathetic ear last night, which is a good thing, because this morning she feels low. The shouting in the night, the desperation in his voice – she had rushed in there almost without thinking about it. And then, the minute he'd woken up and stared at her in his room, sitting on his bed, she'd had the sudden draining horror of having overstepped the mark in a particularly hideous way, invaded his space when he was at his most... vulnerable. How would she feel, if he'd just come into her room when she was asleep? At least she had got to apologise to him directly, over the cocoa. Although there was such a depth of sorrow there. He hadn't wanted to talk about Maggie, not really. She'd sort of forced him into it. And they'd both had another night of disturbed sleep. As a result she had slept late, and now he isn't here to apologise to again.

And to make matters worse, she had hugged him and given him a peck on the cheek when he clearly didn't want her to do anything of the kind.

The embarrassment of it is tempered only by the fact that surely it didn't mean anything; he can't imagine for one moment that it means something. It was the middle of the night and she'd felt this overwhelming sadness for him and she'd given him a hug and then, because it's the way she'd probably comfort Mel or anyone else who was unhappy, she'd given him a little kiss and it was only in the seconds afterwards that she'd thought that this wasn't the right thing to do, they are not actually friends even though it feels a bit like it's heading that way. He is her colleague. She is working with him. And she's not going to be here for very long, which in the cold light of day is some comfort.

But he's left her breakfast. That's a good sign.

When she's finished eating she lifts the plate to take it to the sink and hears a chink and a clatter, as if something small has fallen from the table. She looks underneath and spots something on the grey flagstones: small, pale blue, neatly rounded. It's a piece of Lefty's sea glass. She touches it and holds it to the light. It's quite beautiful. She slips it into her pocket and washes up her plate, wondering how it got there and whether Lefty has mislaid it.

She opens up her laptop and tackles her emails – firstly to Marion and Craig, about her first week on the island, the problem she's been having with the first set of birders. She tries to point out that she's fully aware of her responsibilities here, it's not that she's shirking on cleaning, but that there seemed to be an issue with that one guy in particular from the off. And there are things that are needed for the bird observatory, if they want to make it more of a holiday let. Matching glasses and tableware. Wine glasses, come to that – there are pint glasses and various tumblers which, judging by the beers and ciders they're advertising, came free with some promotion – but nothing for wine, let alone anything else.

Marion replies a few minutes later. Rachel stares at the email, scared to open it in case it contains some sort of disciplinary warning. Or says that they've reconsidered the job offer altogether. She helps herself to Fraser's coffee and opens it with a big breath.

Dear Rachel,

Thank you for your email. Please don't worry. Fraser already emailed to explain - I had heard from the customer in question but I suspected it was more to do with the increased cost of the holiday accommodation in comparison to previous years when the service was a hostel, as he had already complained to me about this at the time of booking. By the sound of it you're doing a good job.

I'll be in touch again soon, as I'm trying to arrange for a builder and an architect to come over on the boat to assess the cottages. It would be great if you could meet with them and discuss requirements. I'll try to come over with them too and bring you some things for the observatory but I can't guarantee it.

Best wishes,

Marion

The reply from Marion prompts five minutes' worth of staring into space and thinking about Fraser.

Fraser already emailed to explain.

The laptop pops up another email notification: this one from Craig, not commenting on the birders but asking her for Friday's shopping list. Wine, she thinks. Maybe gin. Her first thought. But this is the shopping list for the observatory, not for the lighthouse – Fraser's in charge of that.

Her phone pings with a WhatsApp from Lucy – two pictures that she'd rather not see.

> Hey did you get my email re the christening? That date okay for you? Looking at pics again today and thought I'd send you these - they're my favourites. Love from Emily and me xxxx

One of the pictures is from about six months ago. It's of Lucy and Rachel, a selfie with Lucy's arm outstretched, holding her phone, her other arm around Rachel's shoulders. She has seen this picture before; she saw it immediately it was taken, remembers thinking how bloody pale she looked, how wide-eyed and terrified, but she had been smiling and that was why Lucy had loved it. She had had a print of it made, framed it, given a copy to Rachel, which had gone into a drawer. She remembers that day clearly enough. Doesn't necessarily want to be reminded of it. But there are very few photos of Lucy and Rachel together, before Emily.

The other one was taken just after Emily was born, when she was placed in Rachel's arms. Rachel is looking up at the camera, smiling. And Emily's tiny, red, scrunched-up little face, the only part of her not swaddled in towels.

She has to reply, or else Lucy will just keep on.

> Ta for the info re the christening, might still be on island, will let you know. Fingers crossed! xxxx

She shuts the app down. She doesn't want to see the pictures any more.

Fraser

Sometimes he thinks he shouts at Lefty to give himself something to do. It doesn't make any difference, anyway, because he carries on regardless. The lad barely flinches any more. He is used to Fraser's dark moods, used to being shouted at. Unlike the early days when he used to cower every time Fraser came near, now he seems to have realised that he's not actually going to get beaten up. Sometimes he even answers back, although never very loudly.

'Aye, well, I'm going as fast as I can,' he mutters under his breath now.

Fraser hears it clearly because of the wind direction.

He thinks about going over there but in reality he's not got the energy left, not after a day of hauling gravel about, and especially not now the weather has turned. They have maybe half an hour, judging by the clouds gathering over the Firth.

And besides, he's just seen Rachel heading for the bird observatory, pulling that stupid flimsy jacket around herself and lifting the hood over her flying hair, only for it to blow off again. He has decided that he won't have a go at Lefty in front of her. He doesn't want her to be unnecessarily scared.

He doesn't want her to think badly of him.

All the anger from yesterday, from last night, has gone. He has been thinking about her all day. When he tries to take his mind off it by shifting gravel, it's still there. Instead he thinks about Maggie, and Lefty, and all the other things that usually make the grinding fury rise up and choke him, but even that doesn't seem to be working. It keeps coming back, the weight of her pressing down into his mattress, the feel of her hand on his shoulder, the concern in her voice. *Are you okay?*

And then that really fucking awkward hug in the kitchen.

He is not in any way fooled by it, by that kiss. Rachel is twenty-whatever-the-fuck-she-is, pretty and sweet and kind, and he is an ugly old bastard, arteries clogged with anger and shame. He does not believe for one minute that she is attracted to him. She feels sorry for him, which is far worse. He doesn't want anyone's pity. He does not have the time or the energy to care about what anyone else thinks of him.

He looks across at Lefty, who's being blown about in the wind as if he weighs nothing, still gamely wielding the shovel, even if the gravel is half falling off it before he gets it to where it needs to be.

Rachel

Rachel is just leaving the observatory, having tidied up a bit and made a casserole for later. She feels she is ahead of the game now, pleased with herself. Fraser and Lefty are still working on the tern terrace although it's starting to rain and the wind has picked up.

She can hear Fraser yelling at Lefty, the roar of *Not like that you fucking imbecile* floating across on the wind.

Despite the rain she heads up the hill towards them, sees Fraser straighten as she approaches, slowly easing himself to his full height as if his back is hurting. Lefty hasn't noticed or doesn't care, keeps going, and is still shovelling when she reaches them.

'All right?' she asks, holding her hair back from the wind, for the want of something better to say. Now she's here she's aware of interrupting them.

'All okay here,' Fraser says.

'I could make you a coffee, bring it up in a flask or something?'

'We're nearly done.'

'Right. Anything I can do to help?'

Now Lefty stops, and Rachel looks across to see him stagger a little bit in the wind, right himself, putting his weight on the shovel. He's not looking at her. His head drops, and for a minute she thinks he's actually going to keel over.

Fraser mutters something and tosses the rake he's holding to one side, taking three huge strides to Lefty and taking him by the shoulders. 'Sit down, you idiot.'

'Ach, I'm all right,' Lefty says.

'I'll take him back,' Rachel says.

'He'll be fine,' Fraser says, quickly. 'We're nearly finished.'

She has a sudden urgent desire to intervene. Whatever's going on here does not feel comfortable, and for all of his protests she has the strong sense that Lefty is not okay.

'Come back with me, Lefty. Fraser can finish up.'

Even as she says it, she can feel Fraser bristling. Lefty looks up at her briefly and she's struck by the pale skin and the dark shadows, and a spark of injustice – the only time she ever really feels angry – lights up inside her and she takes him firmly by the arm.

'You can manage on your own, can't you, Fraser?'

She doesn't wait for a response. Lefty resists for the briefest second and then goes along with her, stumbling a little across the gravel, glancing over his shoulder at Fraser.

'Come on,' she says, quietly, when they're almost back to the path, 'don't you worry about him.'

It's not easy walking side by side on the rutted path. Lefty is marching along on autopilot but she can't let go of him. She can feel how unsteady he is. She can feel the hard wiriness of his physique, muscle over bone, not an ounce of softness.

At the last hill he says, 'I can manage,' and almost pushes her away.

She follows him up the hill and into the lighthouse, peeling off her jacket. Lefty kicks off his boots and heads straight for his room.

'Lefty?'

In the doorway he turns. Not looking at her. 'Aye?'

She fishes in her pocket for the sea glass. 'I found this. This morning. In the kitchen. Is it yours?'

It lies in her palm. She brings it closer so he can see. Briefly he reaches out, his hand a mess of dark tattoos, a red scar like

an old burn. He touches the sea glass with one bony finger –
bitten, mud-rimmed nails, shredded cuticles.

'I left it for you,' he says.

'You did?'

'Aye. Like a ... you know.'

'It's a present?'

'Aye.'

'Well, thank you. It's lovely.'

'It's my best one,' he says.

Before she can say anything else, he goes inside and shuts
the door firmly. Rachel can hear the motor of the quad bike as
it reverses into the workshop. Fraser's back.

Fraser

Rachel is sitting in the kitchen drinking coffee and looking at
things on her phone. He's relieved to see she's alone, which
means Lefty is in his room. He can't have missed much; they
got back just minutes before he did.

He has half a mind to go straight back out again. The rain
has stopped, of course, which is inevitable as soon as you give
up on a job. But he's had enough of shovelling gravel, they've
made good progress, and he's tired. He's too tired to argue with
her, tempting as it is. The way she just strolled up and took
Lefty's arm and carted him off with her, without waiting to ask!
When he had expressly told her to leave him alone. The only
positive as far as he can see is that Lefty was past the point of
conversation, so it's not likely that anything was said.

'You're tough on him,' Rachel says. 'There's coffee in the
pot.'

He wants to tell her to mind her own business, but then he
remembers her sitting on the edge of his bed in the middle of
the night. He has only just stopped kicking himself for telling
her to go away.

'He's a lazy wee fucker,' he mumbles instead.

'You don't seem to like him very much.'

He thinks about this for a while, as he pours himself a coffee. 'Does that matter?'

'Well, if you're trying to work with him. Surely it would be easier if you—'

'I don't like anyone very much.'

Right. He sees the way her mouth shuts quickly. She doesn't ask anything else, and that's something, even if he does think that he's done it again, just at the point where he was starting to make things better with her. He sits still, warming his hands around the mug, trying not to look at her and not quite able to stop himself.

'How're the birders?'

'I've done a casserole,' she says defensively. 'I'll go back later. Just didn't want to hang around down there.'

There's a strange sort of hollowness to her voice, and he thinks that she's still worrying about the bloody idiots in the observatory. As though they count for anything. As though any of it matters. He finishes his coffee, gets to his feet.

'I was going to check on the shorebirds,' he says, reaching for his binoculars.

'Right.'

He slams the door behind him, stupidly, because now she'll think he's angry at her – which he is, because she's doing exactly what he told her not to do, talking to Lefty, but more importantly he's angry at himself because he can't concentrate on work, can't stop thinking about things.

He changes his mind about the shorebirds and heads instead towards the cottages, stopping halfway down the hill and looking down towards the loch. There are eiders displaying on the surface of the black water, elaborate pairing rituals that happen every year. He watches them for a while, only half-paying attention.

Lefty has been here for a year. A year of being yelled at, and threatened, and grabbed unexpectedly; a year of being called

162

imbecile and *wee piece of shite* and all the other names he's been landed with. And he's still here.

Says something, that being stuck on an island with a man who hates you is somehow less awful than being stuck in the city where you grew up, surrounded by the people you grew up with.

Rachel

Lefty emerges from his room at six, comes into the kitchen and almost jumps out of his skin when he sees Rachel sitting at the kitchen table.

She has been contemplating making a start on dinner, since Fraser isn't back yet. Wondering if it would make him happy, or annoy him even more, to come back and find her prepping vegetables to go with whatever is in the slow cooker.

'Hi, Lefty,' she says, glad to see him on his feet at least. 'How are you feeling?'

'Grand, aye,' he says, moving quickly to the freezer and pulling a box from it. It's a frozen burger, complete with bun. Microwaveable.

'Why don't you eat with us? You know Fraser's a really good cook.'

He mumbles something in response, expertly hitting the microwave's buttons and jolting it into life.

'I'm sure he wouldn't mind the three of us eating together.'

'He would mind.'

'Shall I ask?'

He doesn't respond. His back is towards her, shoulderblades sharp through the thin fabric of his T-shirt, the neck of it frayed. The microwave pings just at the minute the door opens from the outside, and Fraser fills the doorway, Bess scampering past him. Lefty grabs at the box and practically runs back to his room.

They both hear the door shutting firmly.

Fraser looks rough, she thinks. He's not looking at her. As if something bad happened. As if he's trying to pretend she isn't there.

'Hey,' she says, gently. 'You okay?'

'What was he wanting?'

'Just his dinner. I didn't get two words out of him.'

'Right.' He's unlacing his boots, pulling them off, leaving them on the mat by the door.

'I was going to start doing some veg,' she says. 'Only I didn't want to piss you off any more than I have already. So, you know, if you want me to do anything to help, I'm here.'

She notes that he does not deny being pissed off. Instead he washes his hands, gets out the chopping board. She looks at his fierce, hard back, the fight in his shoulders, and turns away. In the time it takes him to get the vegetables on, she has written a whole blog entry about the helicopter and has started a second one about kittiwakes.

'Tell me again the difference between kittiwakes and gulls?' she asks.

At that point he's washing up the chopping board, wiping the surfaces, his back still to her, but then he turns and leans back and actually looks at her for the first time. 'They're completely different birds,' he says.

'Well, obviously. To an expert. But I'm trying to appeal to the non-birdwatcher here, right?'

He expends a heavy sigh. 'Kittiwakes are gentle wee things. They have a very distinctive call, nothing like a gull. The young have very specific markings, also nothing like a gull. If you saw them side by side you'd see the difference straight away.'

Rachel shuts her laptop. This isn't working.

She watches as he gets the whisky glasses out of the cupboard, brings them over to the table. A peace offering, she thinks.

'Sorry,' he says.

'What for?'

He doesn't reply.

She clears the laptop away and lays the table and by the time she's done that dinner is ready and for some reason she can't help herself. He has apologised and it's almost as if it's given her free rein to push him, to find those buttons and jab at them hard, and she doesn't know why but she would rather have angry Fraser than anything else right now. Because he wrote to Marion. Because of Lefty, staggering back from the tern terrace. Because of all the shouting and swearing.

'Do you actually *want* me to do a blog?'

He shrugs vaguely. 'Thought it would keep you out of mischief,' says, and raises his eyes to her.

She doesn't know quite how to respond to that, so she changes the subject. 'Marion seems to think she's going to come over for a visit. With a builder and an architect.'

'Is that so?'

'She emailed earlier. Which reminds me – she said you'd been in touch with her about the arseholes down at the bird observatory.'

In response to this he makes a non-committal humph and shovels some food in.

'Thanks, anyway. I appreciate it.'

'Nae bother. They're not all arseholes, you know. You just got unlucky with the first lot.'

'Right. Do you ever get women, or is it going to be grey beards and camo gear every week?'

'We sometimes get women. Some of them don't have beards.'

This makes her laugh, properly laugh, so she has to put her fork down, and then he's looking at her, amused. Thank goodness.

'I guess this isn't the best job for meeting women,' she says.

'That's true enough.'

She wonders if a line has been crossed. Not enough whisky has been consumed for this conversation to be happening. But, now it's started, he can't just be allowed to leave it there. She thinks about it, trying to get her head around what he could possibly mean, and then she just comes out with it, because she is not able to just leave things.

'So – what? You just go without?'

He doesn't answer. Spends several minutes eating without looking at her.

'You're full of the personal questions tonight,' he says.

'Well,' she says, 'sorry.'

'You go for it, I don't care.'

'But you're not going to answer. Why not? Are you worried I'm going to judge you?'

Now he looks at her, full on. 'I'm not worried about any-thing,' he says. 'Least of all what you think of me.'

She raises an eyebrow at him, because this feels like a challenge. 'Really?'

'Really.'

'Are you actually interested in what I think of you?'

'Not especially. But I think you're going to tell me anyway. Aren't you?'

It's very tempting to disabuse him of that and shut up. For several minutes she manages it. When she looks away she can feel his eyes on her. When she looks at him directly, he goes back to eating. There's a weird atmosphere now, as if he's testing her. And she's testing him, too. Would he get angry at her, properly angry, the way he does with Lefty? She doesn't think so. She can't imagine him yelling at her. It feels a little bit dangerous, this – poking the bear. Seeing how far she can go.

'How about what *you* think of *me*?' she asks.

'That's a difficult question.'

'Why?'

'You might not like the answer.'

'I'm willing to risk it if you are.'

He's finished eating. Somewhere in there she stopped, and now he's pushed his plate to one side and he's regarding her with something in his eye that she thinks is amusement, though perhaps it's annoyance.

'Fair enough,' he says. 'I think you're out of your depth.'

'Well, duh. I've said as much.'

'I think you're capable of much more than you think you are. I think you're spending too much time worrying about the past.'

'Well, thank you.'

'I like you better like this.'

'Like what?'

'Arsey. Challenging. Brave.'

She has no response to that, so she carries on eating. She would absolutely not describe herself as brave. Or indeed arsey, or for that matter challenging. She is, actually, a little bit offended.

'Go on, then,' he says after a few minutes.

'What?'

'You were going to tell me what you think of me. Fair's fair.'

She narrows her eyes at him, as if she's trying to psychically connect. Wondering what words she could choose out of the many that have been floating around inside her head.

'Sure?'

'Go for it.'

'Um … well. Arsey. Challenging. Vulnerable.'

He throws back his head and laughs, a proper meaty guffaw. 'Vulnerable?'

Rachel stares him out. 'That level of arsiness only comes from a place of true vulnerability.'

'That so?'

'Absolutely. Why else are you so opposed to relationships?'

She sees some sort of shutter come down at that, thinks for a minute she has poked the bear a little bit too hard. There is a long pause and then he collects the plates and goes to wash up. She follows him, picks up a tea towel, waits for him to come round.

'How's the blog?' he asks, eventually.

She has the impression he said it for want of something neutral to say. She fishes out her phone and brings up the first entry, a general one introducing the island, written yesterday evening. So far it has thirty-one hits. Her new Twitter account has forty-three followers, thanks to her following pretty much everyone who follows the Isle of May's Twitter account. One of these days she will hunt down every seabird enthusiast and follow them. As she checks it, three notifications pop up with new followers. On the blog is one comment, from someone called SteelySeabirder. It says, *Nice.*

'Thirty-one people saw it? Since yesterday?'

'That's right.'

'Good going.'

He seems to have forgiven her for her interrogation of him earlier, but she hasn't forgiven herself. This is what she does, she thinks – she oversteps the mark. She fails to see when she's pissing people off. She gets too close to people too quickly. It's as if she hasn't learned anything, anything at all.

Before things get any worse, she takes herself off to bed, leaving Fraser downstairs with Bess.

Mel sent a message earlier this afternoon:

At the birdcage

wish u were here

everything ok?

She hasn't replied yet. And now, because she feels the darkening shadow of an imminent Rachel fuck-up, her mind keeps going back to the conference. The thing that ruined everything with Amarjit, the thing that precipitated her fall into depression.

In the days and weeks after it happened, when she was staying up all night and sometimes sleeping in until four or five in the afternoon, not getting dressed, not showering for several days at a time, she would think about it all, every conversation, every encounter, everything he'd said to her and what it might have meant, right back to that meeting room and Amarjit strolling in late.

She had never been paid attention like that. She had never been listened to before, never been seen in the way he saw her. It wasn't inevitable. If she had known, if she'd had hindsight, of course she wouldn't have fallen for him quite as hard as she had. But she didn't know how to stop herself. She didn't even want to stop herself.

Fast forward all the way to that conference.

That first night…everyone drunk. She was looking for Amarjit everywhere and whenever she found him he was drinking with a group of people, and she was thinking, *oh, that's fine*, and waiting for the moment when he would come and look for her and tell her his room number. She knew it anyway, of course. She had done all the room bookings. He would come and find her and tell her to come up in five minutes. And then what actually happened was, she went looking, after midnight, and couldn't find him. She was absolutely exhausted by this point because she had been working without a break since seven a.m. She decided to go to her room and send him a text, just a little reminder. Something cheeky. And he'd reply with something like *yeah sweetheart come over I'm waiting*. She had organised it so her room was just three doors along from his. This would make it easier for her to go to his room, or for him to come to hers; lower the risk of someone seeing.

And she stepped out of the lift just in time to see Cheryl, one of the PAs, someone Rachel thought of as a friend, standing outside his door. Then the door opening, and Cheryl smiling and walking in. And the door closing behind her.

It hit Rachel hard enough to jolt through the alcohol into cold reality. She thought maybe she had made a mistake. Maybe she was on the wrong floor. Maybe that wasn't his door after all. She went to check. Walked right up to it. Eventually put her ear to the door, heard Cheryl's shrieking laugh, briefly, then a squeal, then Amarjit's voice saying, 'Take this off.'

169

She went back to her own room and drank her way through the contents of the minibar. Since Amarjit would eventually be signing off her hotel bill, she thought it unlikely he would complain when she told him what she'd seen, what she'd heard. She went through all the conversations that would take place back in the office, next week. He would challenge her about her bar bill, which was already huge, given that she'd been buying drinks for everyone, even without the extortionate expense of the minibar. She would tell him what she'd seen. She would be hurt, resentful, but ultimately dignified about it. He would be apologetic, devastated; he would tell her that Cheryl had come on to him, that he was so drunk he'd barely known what he was doing. That she had knocked on his door. That he had – could it be possible? – thought it was Rachel, opened the door, and then maybe he'd felt unable to say no.

How could she even have thought any of those things? she thinks now. How could she have instantly hated Cheryl, who had been nothing but kind to her and at that point had known nothing – as far as Rachel was aware – about her feelings for Amarjit? And how could she have casually absolved him of any blame in it?

Well, it felt dazzlingly obvious now. Because the alternative – that he was an arsehole who was using her for sex and actually did not care for her feelings at all – had been just too painful.

And then – because it had to get worse, didn't it? – the last night of the conference. And now, finally, she's going to take herself back there and confront it.

Saturday night. A five-star hotel in Manchester. Rachel can't even think of its name now without feeling sick.

She has been busy photocopying a document three hundred times because one of the marketing managers had changed his mind about including it. Couriering some promo booklets from the printer to the hotel. Arranging a hire car for someone whose company Merc had had a sideswipe from a lorry on the M6 on the way up. The only way she is coping is by staying very slightly drunk. A shared bottle of wine with lunch keeps her going until the evening. Two vodkas and a gin from the freshly restocked minibar while she is getting ready for the gala dinner. She has been thinking about resigning, worrying how hard it might be to find another job. Recruitment agencies don't like it when you walk out of temporary contracts; it makes them look bad. She has been thinking about what she will say to Cheryl in the car on that long drive back to Norwich, and she has changed the table seating plan, moved herself from Amarjit's table to one not too far away.

At the last minute she swaps the place-markers so that she won't have her back to him. She is wearing a dark blue dress, short, and high heels. She spends a lot of time on her hair and her make-up. If she can't tempt him away from Cheryl and back into her bed tonight, looking like this, then she has lost him and nothing will work.

The meal is fine. She doesn't eat it.

At that point in her life she is measuring her value wholly in terms of how much attention Amarjit pays her. A little over a year later, on an island in the North Sea, lying awake in bed with tears dripping down her temples, she will feel ashamed of that. But now, in the conference hotel, despite feeling vulnerable and alone, she wears her short dress like a kind of armour, strides comfortably in heels down the thickly carpeted corridor.

The change to the seating plan means that she has a full view of him when he steps up to the podium to give his speech. He's looking relaxed, sleeves folded up over his forearms, heavy expensive watch, the dark hairs, the way his muscles work under the skin. She wants to run her tongue up the inside of his forearm more badly than she's wanted anything in her life. He talks about the conference and makes people laugh. He talks about the prospects for Caleril and how they are going to make a genuine difference to people's lives by promoting it to GPs and to cardiovascular physicians in hospitals.

At that point, he says he has a special guest.

Rachel has had three double gin and tonics in the bar before dinner, plus most of the bottle of house wine on the table that nobody else wanted to touch. She is watching Amarjit and thinking of what she would like to do with him, later. She is visualising how she is going to approach him, what she's going to say, how his eyes are going to flick down to her cleavage and back to her face.

At that moment the special guest comes to the podium. Applause, whistles. Most of the people in the room seem to know who she is. Amarjit introduces her as an associate professor of cardiothoracic surgery. And he says he is proud to add that she happens to be his wife.

He kisses her and applauds as he backs away to his seat, his chair fully turned so he can take her in. She is beautiful, poised, fluent, clearly brilliant. Rachel finds she cannot breathe properly. She hears almost nothing of the speech. The room, suddenly airless, swims.

Afterwards, to make everything worse, Amarjit brings her over to Rachel's table – most people have gone to the bar and she is still sitting there, hollowed out and dark – and introduces her – 'Darling, this is Rachel; she's the one who's been looking after me so well in the office' – and Rachel has to stand and try to smile and shake a cool, delicate hand that feels like a baby bird but which has opened ribcages and restarted stopped hearts. Her own heart sputters, broken into pieces.

It would have been easier if she hadn't been so lovely. 'I understand he must be a complete pain in the arse to work for,' she says. 'I couldn't do it.'

Amarjit's wife says, 'Are you okay?' seconds before Rachel crashes sideways against the table and throws up. It keeps coming, and coming, all the liquid pouring out of her, barely a second in between to gasp a breath, almost choking on it. Amarjit's wife holds her hair. Rachel passes out, and when she comes round a few moments later she is in the recovery position, the carpet against her face, her nostrils stinging. Lots of people are crowded round. An ambulance is called, but it doesn't take her to hospital. She spends nearly an hour sitting in the ambulance in the car park, crying, and retching into a cardboard hat. Later, Cheryl takes her to her room and ends up staying the night in case she's sick again.

The next morning Rachel is driven home by Cheryl and Louise. She pretends to sleep in the back of the car the whole way home. She listens to them talking about Amarjit, about what happened on Friday night. Cheryl says that he was just okay, she wouldn't bother again. She says that his wife knows that he shags around, that she doesn't care. Cheryl says, 'You know that if they were happy with their wives they wouldn't be fucking other women, would they?' There is a long pause and then Louise asks if Amarjit said that and Cheryl does not reply.

A while later Cheryl turns in her seat to check on her. Rachel's eyes are closed. She has been dozing, but now she is fully awake. She listens while Cheryl and Louise talk about her quietly. They use words like *unstable* and *unreliable*. Louise says it's a shame. Cheryl says that she feels sorry for her and everyone makes mistakes, don't they?

Rachel takes Monday as a sick day. She has a phone call from the HR manager asking her to come in at five p.m. on the Tuesday, to stay home until then. She sounds sympathetic on the phone. When she gets to the office her pass doesn't work. She has to wait in reception to be called up to the sales director's office. Carrie, the HR manager, collects her. Amarjit is in there, unsmiling, not meeting her eyes. Louise is in there too, Rachel isn't sure why. She has had half a bottle of gin over the course of the day to prepare for this, and, as a result, afterwards her memories of it are patchy.

She remembers breaking down in tears. She remembers them not moving, watching her from their chairs. She remembers Carrie saying it might be best to do this another time. Then herself shouting, screaming at Amarjit, begging him to stand up for her and knowing he won't, he can't, and then the fat security guard who'd always smiled at her coming to escort her from the building.

In the end, once her temporary contract was terminated, there wasn't much to it from Evans Pharma's point of view.

Someone emptied all the personal crap out of her desk and left it on Mel's doorstep in a cardboard box. There was a note from Cheryl in there.

Hope you're ok babe. Call me if you feel up to it xx

Meanwhile Amarjit had carried on as normal, and Rachel had fallen apart. It had taken three weeks before he emailed her from a Hotmail account, asking if she wanted to come over to the flat. He wanted to check she was okay. He wanted to show her he had no hard feelings. Rachel had not replied, and an hour and a half later he had turned up at her doorstep, drunkish, having driven there from Cambridge. She hadn't wanted him to drive home again in case he had an accident. The sex wasn't very good and she had hated herself afterwards, cried a lot. After that he had messaged her, emailed her, almost every day.

She hadn't replied to any of them, and eventually he'd given up.

She had felt as if her world was ending. She had genuinely thought that she would never get over the humiliation of it.

And then the conversation with her sister, with Lucy, had happened when she was at her lowest moment, and she had lurched off into another, completely different disaster.

The best that could be said about it was that it had taken her mind off Amarjit. It had taken away the sting of the humiliation.

For a while, at least.

Fraser

Thursday.

Fraser manages to avoid Rachel for most of the day. He comes back to the lighthouse at two, having seen her heading for the bird observatory an hour earlier, but unexpectedly she's sitting in the kitchen.

'Oh, hey,' she says brightly, looking at her laptop.

'How's it going?'

'Sixty views. I'm writing another one.'

'Right.'

'Lefty with you?'

Why she's so fucking concerned with Lefty, he has no idea.

'He's up at the north end. Strimming the path.'

'Oh, right.'

'You want a sandwich?'

She's eaten already so he makes himself one, eats it leaning back against the sink, watching her as she types, moves the mouse, clicks.

'What have you been up to this morning?' she asks, without looking up.

'Counting shorebirds.'

'Uh huh.' She's not really listening. 'You going back out?'

'Aye, in a minute.'

He finishes eating. Thinks about making a coffee, about sitting down opposite her. Or not sitting down at all. Maybe he could just walk over there and stand next to her and she might stand up and while he's thinking this he says, 'Want to come? It's sunny out there now. Get more pictures for your blog, or whatever.'

'Sure?'

'Of course.'

Her face breaks into a huge smile and it cuts through him like a blade, the relief in it. He's not exactly in the mood for company, he never is, but her sudden enthusiasm for a walk to the beach with him lifts his spirits.

Ten minutes later they're on the jetty, and she hasn't stopped talking, and he's on the verge of changing his mind and suggesting they go back. But then she's here, next to him, and something about that is making him feel good.

'What's that one?' she asks, in a hushed whisper that's still pretty loud.

'That's a turnstone.'

'But it looks different from the other one.'

'That's because it's getting summer plumage,' he says. 'They're greyer in the winter.'

'I know how they feel.'

Yet again he has passed her his binoculars, and he's watching her with some amusement as she struggles to focus on this bird and that bird. He could do this job in half the time on his own, and if he had to do this all the time no doubt it would be frustrating, but for now he's managing. Actually, it's almost entertaining: perhaps because the sun is shining and the water is calm, and on this side of the island, sheltered from the prevailing wind, it feels warm. He can smell summer.

'B408,' she says.

'Which one?'

'That one. The grey thing.'

'The turnstone?'

'The first one, the one you said wasn't summer plumage.'

He notes it down. Actually he recognises that bird anyway: it has a slight twist to its bill where it had some long-healed injury. It's been here every year for the past three years.

'And this one is rare?'

'No.'

'Common?' She looks round at him in surprise. 'But it looks really weird. I've never seen one.'

'It's common around the coast. Worldwide, in fact. Slightly different variations on the species, I guess. But it's not threatened.'

'Why are you counting it, if it's common?'

'I count bloody everything, along with everyone else. That's how we know if they *become* threatened.'

'B442,' she says, back at the binoculars. 'That one that's brownish. It's got the same bill.'

'Ah,' he says. 'Hello again, B442.'

'You know that one?'

'I ringed it, last year.'

'So it lives here?'

'It's been to the north of Finland since I ringed it. And it's been here all winter, and now it's just about to head back to Finland, I expect.'

'How do you know it's been to Finland?'

'Because it was spotted on a nature reserve by someone like you with a pair of binoculars, who looked up the number and reported back.'

There is a pause. From here he can see, even without binoculars, several knots and a few purple sandpipers as well as at least fifteen turnstones in various states of plumage. He could probably rattle off the ring numbers of at least half of them. But let her have her fun.

'I could write a blog about B442,' she says.

'Aye, that would be a nice one.'

She hands him the binoculars. 'I'll try and get a picture.'

She skips down on to the beach, crouches, points her phone and swipes with two fingers to zoom in, frames the shot, takes several. He watches B442 doing its thing, stalking the shoreline in the sunshine, looking for crabs and molluscs, nudging at pebbles with its beak.

'Does it have chicks here?' she asks, looking back at him.

'They'll breed after migration,' he says. 'Probably in Finland, this lot. Some of them go south to the Antarctic, but from here they usually go to northern Europe, as far as Russia, sometimes.'

'Does it just lay one egg?'

'Up to five. That's why it's not threatened. It's usually the ones that only manage one egg that are struggling.'

She comes to stand next to him. 'What do you think?'

She holds her phone out to him and shows him the pictures she's just taken, swiping between them. He looks and can't see properly, because the bright sky is reflecting off the screen.

'You do it,' she says, handing over her phone. 'There's other ones I took this morning.'

She goes back to the beach and peels a carrier bag out of the wet sand, regarding it with a wrinkled nose as he swipes inexpertly between what feels like three hundred identical pictures of various sea- and shorebirds. Some of the pictures look okay; some of them the bird has turned away and all she's got is its snooty wee backside.

He looks up from the screen for a moment to see her walking the tide mark, picking up scraps of plastic.

'Look at this!' she calls. 'Another bloody toothbrush. How do they end up here, for God's sake?'

Fraser scrolls on. She has captured a nice shot of a fulmar in flight, a shaft of sunlight catching it, looking apparently straight at her camera. Some more fulmars, on the cliff, already on their nests. Two razorbills, displaying.

He flicks through. More razorbills. A couple of guillemots. Herring gulls, hanging in the air, barely visible against the roiling waves below them. Then, suddenly, after all the birds and sea and sky, he's got to a picture of two women. He's gone too far.

The breath catches in his throat. He doesn't want to see, but it's too late. He's taken in everything, all at once. It's a picture of Rachel and another woman, whose outstretched arm indicates that she's taking the photo. There is enough of a similarity in their faces for him to realise they must be related, although the other woman is dark-haired, shorter, curvy – they have the same eyes, the same smile. Rachel is wearing a short blue dress and leggings, and she looks pale, and thinner.

Apart from the round bump swelling the front of her dress.

He has not much idea about pregnancy, has never been around a pregnant woman apart from Kelly and that was only briefly, and seven years ago. But even he knows that there's no doubting it – this isn't just a wee bump.

Fraser looks up. She is away at the other end of the beach, the carrier bag hanging from a finger, now heavy with items she's picked up. Her back to him, hips swaying, she's absorbed in it, looking into the sand.

He swipes left, again, and then there's the next picture and there's no doubt at all.

Rachel, eyes bright, ghost-pale, tendrils of hair sticking to her forehead, looking up at the camera. Bare shoulders, light freckles on the creamy skin. On her chest is a wee scrap of pink baby, nestling in towels.

And he looks up at her again, and thinks, *where's her baby?* And his breath catches in his throat. Because she's here, and her baby isn't – so something has happened.

Something terrible.

Part Two

May

7

Emily

Rachel

Rachel is cleaning the kitchen in the bird observatory when she hears the door go.

She knows, without looking, that it's Lefty.

'You want a squash?' she asks, but she has already got the pint glass out of the cupboard and is pouring thick blackcurrant cordial into the bottom of it.

'Aye, ta.'

It's sunny outside, almost warm, and Lefty has been doing his usual Friday afternoon task of gathering driftwood for the woodburner. They are all settling into a routine now, Rachel included.

It's been five weeks. She has seen five lots of birdwatchers come and go; the latest group left an hour ago. They were nice. In fact, the groups of birdwatchers have all been very different – the rude ones at the start were the worst of all, and ever since then she has had friendlier ones, some who've tidied up after themselves and invited her to eat with them (which she declines), or offered her a beer while she's cooking (which she usually gratefully accepts). The second week there were four of them, then there was a full house including two married couples and two teenage girls. The couples were Dec and Susie, and Cristina and Enrique; the first time she'd seen women since leaving the mainland. The fourth week it was just three older men, who barely spoke. The most recent lot, the ones she saw off today, were a family group of three lads ranging in age from fourteen to twenty-one, plus their dad. The dad had been a bit flirty. Not unpleasantly so. Bizarrely, it had made Fraser twitchy.

Anyway – this lot have even managed to strip the beds and wash up their breakfast dishes, so she has raced through the cleaning in record time. The washing machine is rumbling away in the outbuilding and sunlight is flooding the main room.

Yesterday there was an email from Julia.

Hey Rachel!

How's the island? I've been keeping track of the weather up there and it seems like you've had a good spell, I hope it continues! I've been really enjoying the blog and all the pictures you've posted. I hope I can keep it up to your standards when I get there and not lose too many followers.

My mum is doing well, we had a check-up yesterday and her kidney is functioning brilliantly. You know she was so much better from the minute she came round from the op, it was just amazing to see. She had been so poorly for so long. It's just a case of waiting to see how she recovers from the operation itself - she had a little infection last week which has set things back a bit, but she's getting over that. As soon as she can get about more easily I should be good to go. She's not allowed to drive yet but she has friends locally who will take her out, get shopping etc. I think if I wasn't going so far away, to a place that's so cut off, I could probably come sooner - but I don't want to leave her and then have to come back again. I hope you understand.

I must admit I'm quite looking forward to getting away - all that fresh air! Although it must be a real shock to the system when you first start. I don't think I've said this to you but I am SO SO grateful for you taking the job on temporarily and at

184

such short notice. It feels like I'll get there with you having done all the hard work to start things off - I don't want you to think I'm not really appreciative of that.

Anyway - hopefully I might get to meet you at some sort of handover point and I can thank you properly. I'll keep you updated so at least you have a bit of warning as to when I'll be able to start.

Best wishes,

Julia xx

Rachel had noticed it wasn't copied to Fraser or Marion, which might have been an oversight, although it feels a bit more personal than the previous emails she's seen. She had given little thought to Julia, other than as an abstract person who's going to come here and take over, but when she read the email she realised that coming from a situation as stressful as caring for her mum following a life-changing operation might be actually quite difficult for her.

A real shock to the system when you first start.

Rachel had almost forgotten what it was like, but it was only five weeks ago. She recalled that constant, low-level panic she had felt about getting things wrong. The wind and the rain and the mud and the birds, the sense of being a million miles away from everything she knew and understood. It makes her realise how far she's come. She noticed something else, too – the fact that Julia was expressing gratitude for her taking on the job *temporarily*, as if maybe she was worried about feet being under the table and Rachel being reluctant to leave.

She had sent an immediate, cheerful, reassuring reply. *Everything on the island is fine, the sun's shining, don't worry about it, it's nothing.*

So much else she could have said, but didn't. *Watch out for the grumpy bastard you're going to be living with. By the way, there's a semi-feral fugitive on the island, you'll feel a bit better when you get to know him, he's really not that bad. Fraser has a massive knife hidden somewhere but I've stopped worrying about that. Here's a recipe for chicken curry, they all seem to like it. Get yourself a proper jacket.*

I like it here but I'm not staying.

Lefty finishes stacking the driftwood in the wood store next to the burner, perches at the breakfast bar on one of the two bar stools, takes the pint glass and gulps the squash down. He fishes in his pocket and finds something, slaps it on to the kitchen counter and slides it, under his palm, across to her.

She meets his eyes.

This is the new Lefty. The one who brings her presents. They are, in a manner of speaking, friends. He watches for her reaction, his hand still firmly over whatever it is.

'What have you brought me?' she asks.

He grins. 'Close your eyes.'

Here we go, she thinks, but she obliges him.

'Right, now you can open them.'

He's found her a good one today, dark green, perfectly smooth, an almost-triangle, large enough for the curve of the bottle it came from to still be evident. She picks it up and turns it over in her hands, assessing it. The curve of it hugs her middle finger. European lager, she thinks. Maybe a Stella. Judging by the gentle slope, more probably a Kronenbourg.

'Wow,' she says. 'That's nice. Has a nice feel to it.'

'Right?' he says, leaning forward on his elbows, fidgety with the excitement of it.

In exchange, she reaches up to the top cupboard and fetches the biscuit tin, the one that she keeps stocked with chocolate biscuits, and passes it over. Lefty lifts the lid like a kid at Christmas, smiles wide enough to reveal his missing teeth, picks out two chocolate Hobnobs and a little stack of Bourbons.

'Seriously? I'm not sure it's a five-biscuiter.'

'At least a five-biscuiter. You don't get triangles every day.'

They have developed a completely arbitrary system of grading the sea glass that Lefty finds. Triangles are worth more than random polygons, although the most valuable one was an almost-perfect square. Ovals and circles are nice but they are common. Green glass is the commonest, then white – still common, but harder to find in the pale sand. Brown glass is never pretty – sometimes he leaves it where it is – but the best of all is the blue glass, the darker the better.

He has found six pieces of blue glass in the past four weeks. Three of them he has given to her. They are sharing.

She pretends not to notice that he always gives her the best ones.

'Fair enough, then. Are you going to eat with us tonight?'

'Nah.'

She puts the Bourbons back in the tin and closes the lid and he looks up at her, mouthful of Hobnob crumbs, bereft.

'No dinner, no biscuits.'

'Ah, fucksake.'

'Come on, you know you want to. I think it's steak night. You like steak, don't you? Everyone likes steak.'

'There won't be enough,' he ventures.

'That's bollocks. There's always enough.'

'Not steak. He only gets the fancy stuff for you and him.'

'I bet you he's got three.'

'What you gonnae bet?'

'Brownies tomorrow?'

His eyes light up at that.

Now that she's got a routine, Rachel has been doing some baking in the bird observatory. She makes things in the morning on Saturdays before the boat comes, leaves them in the oven while she cleans. When she has enough ingredients she makes two batches, one for the lighthouse, one for the new lot of visitors as a welcome gift. Muffins, cakes, brownies.

To take her mind off other things, her new challenge is to fix Fraser and Lefty. As part of this plan, she has decided she needs to get them at the table together every evening. So far she has only managed it twice, and both times ended somewhat disastrously. But she is nothing if not determined.

187

Fraser

At half-past five Fraser takes the quad up to the bird observatory.
It has taken him most of the day to think of an excuse. Having
spent half an hour standing in the workshop looking vaguely at
the tools and the equipment, he loads the trailer with some half-
full tins of white paint, a ladder, and brushes. He can always
plan to whitewash the exterior, in fact he has been talking
about doing it for at least the past two years. The weather or
something else has always got in the way.

He has no actual intention of painting anything, of course.
Although that may change.

The weather has been beautiful for the past three days –
warm sunshine, the evenings stretching out into glorious sunsets
across the water – and today is no exception. The island is full of
nesting birds. Terns have just begun to arrive from the southern
hemisphere and a couple of them have been seen inspecting the
newly constructed tern terrace. It crosses his mind to go further
up the hill on the quad and have a look, just in case there are
nesting pairs, but he has checked already today, twice, and he
doesn't want to disturb them any more than necessary.

It's good, though. It's keeping him busy.

At the bird observatory he unloads the tins of paint and
carries them into the store. The washing machine and the
tumble dryer are both going, the air warm and fragrant. When
he comes out again, Rachel is leaning against the doorpost.
Sunlight and blue sky and her, and he takes a deep breath.

'Hello,' she says.

'Hello yourself.'

'What are you up to?'

'Just brought some paint up here.'

'You want a coffee or something?'

'What, that shit stuff? No way.'

'Suit yourself.'

She retreats inside and he stands in the porch for a minute,
then takes his boots off and comes in. The main room smells of
lavender floor cleaner, strong enough to make his eyes water.

'You want a ride back?' he asks.

'I don't mind walking. The sun's shining.'

'I've got the quad here.'

'Well, thanks, then. If you can wait a few minutes.'

He shrugs, as if it's no bother to him either way. Watches Rachel moving around the kitchen, wiping the surfaces, putting things away.

'I've asked Lefty to have dinner with us,' she says, chirpily. No warning. Not even looking at him when she says it.

'That so?' he says, colourless.

'I said you'd probably got plenty. I told him you wouldn't mind. You don't mind, do you?'

There is a pause.

'He's not keen on green stuff.'

She folds a tea towel briskly and slides it over the guard rail of the stove, looks up at him, meets his eyes. 'I'm sure he'll eat something.' And then she does that huge bright smile out of nowhere. 'And I'll be grateful enough for the both of us, as usual.'

Minutes later, Rachel is climbing on to the quad behind him, and he's still prickly with it. She's getting much more confident sitting on the back of the quad and doesn't quite cling to him in the way she did the first few times, but now he can't stop thinking about dinner, how it's ruined before he's even cooked it.

Today is his birthday, not that either of them have a clue about that. Not that he's celebrated it any time in the last five years.

He had a text earlier, from Kelly.

Happy birthday fella. Hope you're having a good one. Give us a call some time? We miss u xxx

He might phone her. He's overdue a visit, really, but his trips to the mainland are usually dictated by other errands that need to be run and he doesn't have any of those right now. He sends her a quick reply:

Almost immediately she's back with another:

What u up to?

He doesn't respond to that. If she ever asks, he will say he lost the signal and then forgot about it. He hates texting. If pressed, he would tell you that he would far rather call someone, but actually he hates talking on the phone too.

Steak, salad, a good bottle of wine. He's even made cheesecake, a rare dessert but today he was worried that the meal wasn't going to be hearty enough. And last week he made apple crumble and she clearly enjoyed it very much indeed.

That was the day before Lefty sat down to dinner with them for the first time since Rachel arrived.

No, not the first time, he thinks, as the quad bumps round towards the workshop. She had persuaded him to sit down with his plate of chips the week before. Fraser remembered him standing in the doorway, looking from one of them to the other, eyes wide. 'Come on,' Rachel had said. 'You don't have to talk, if you don't want to. Just sit.' Then she'd glanced across at him and seen the expression on his face and said, 'Fraser...'

He had looked at her and then down at his food. Duck stir fry. Suddenly his appetite had evaporated.

Lefty had come and sat on the spare chair, tension making him rigid, picking at his chips. Fraser had kept his head down. After a few minutes, the chips half-eaten, the boy had skulked away.

'What's going on?' she'd asked Fraser then, but gently. 'Are you ever going to tell me?'

'Nothing's going on,' he'd said. In that moment it had been true.

Then, a week later, she had warned him in advance that Lefty was going to eat with them. Roast chicken. Apparently Rachel had asked, and he had said that he liked roast chicken, and she had invited him to dinner. What could Fraser say? He couldn't very well say no. Meanwhile Lefty has gone soft on Rachel, which is another thing that makes him seethe. He can see the way the lad straightens whenever Rachel approaches. And by the smell of him he's even washing more, wearing clean clothes every other day instead of every other week.

So he came to dinner, wordless, awkward. Lefty sat, Lefty ate, both of them silent and unmoving like blocks of concrete in their chairs while Rachel smiled and chatted away as if nothing was wrong. Neither of them spoke to each other however hard Rachel tried. She asked questions – puffins, seals, what's the weirdest thing you've found on the beach – and Lefty would answer, and she would say, 'Fraser?' to prompt him to respond, and the best he could manage was a miserable shrug.

Now he's got that ordeal to come tonight, all over again, and he had been looking forward to tonight because steak and salad is his absolute best meal, his favourite, and it's his birthday, and now it's ruined.

Rachel

Lefty has had a shower and washed his hair, and combed it. He's hovering in the doorway when Rachel comes down the stairs, and jumps out of his skin when she nudges him gently.

Fraser is at the kitchen counter. The table is set for three. Two wine glasses and a can of pop, a bottle of wine already opened. He has made an effort. She thinks this is really rather lovely of him.

'Anything I can do?' Rachel asks, brightly.

'Sit,' Fraser says, bringing plates to the table. 'It's done.'

His effort doesn't extend to actually being cheerful about it, though. His face betrays the very darkest of Fraser's moods. There's nothing wrong with the dinner, nothing at all – a beautiful green salad, pink radishes, yellow pepper and ripe tomatoes nestling in the leaves like treasures; steaks for each of them, no evidence that two steaks have been hacked about to serve three. Additionally there's a coleslaw, beetroot, fresh bread in chunks. He's taken care with it. The dinner is amazing as always. But Fraser is hunched, not meeting her eye, certainly not looking at Lefty; just as he was the last time she attempted to get them all together.

Maybe, if she does this often enough, he'll come round, she thinks. If she just chips away at it.

'So,' Rachel says, pouring wine into her glass and Fraser's, 'apparently I've got a university professor coming tomorrow.'

Nobody says anything. Lefty has taken a small, wary slice out of his steak and is chewing it as if it might be laced with rat poison. He's helped himself to two salad leaves and a few bits of tomato.

'Craig emailed me. Apparently this guy's an expert on guillemots?'

Rachel likes the black guillemots. She has just written a blogpost about them, which she might still delete, or amend, because she thinks it doesn't sound scientific enough. She likes that there is another name for them, the Norse word, tystie, which sounds ridiculously cute for such a serious-looking bird. Fraser had pointed out one that had white markings on its black face – like elegant little spectacles. Apparently about five per cent of the birds, randomly, have these markings. She wasn't quick enough with the binoculars and missed it; she is determined to get a picture of one before she leaves the island. She has been looking ever since, but only seen the ones with a pure black head.

Now Fraser looks up for a fraction of a second, then back to his plate. There's a bottle of wine on the kitchen counter that looks empty; Rachel wonders if he drank it all while he was cooking.

'Craig said he's been before. And there's a couple of others.'
'Two women?'
'Yes, I think so.'
Fraser snorts at that.

'What? What's funny?'

'You'll see.'

Rachel drinks her wine, taking advantage of his refusal to look at either of them to drink him in. The way he's holding himself, the amount of energy it must be taking to just not relax, is astounding. His huge hands, holding the cutlery tightly, the way he's stabbing at each bit of meat.

Is it a mistake, to try to make things better? At the moment it feels as if she's making it all worse. She takes a deep breath in. *Don't say it, Rachel, don't say it.*

'How come you two can spend all day together and get on with it, but when you sit down at the dinner table it's like you can't stand each other?'

Lefty looks up, startled.

Fraser's knife clatters on to the plate. He looks up, at last, meets her eyes, chewing.

'We manage just fine,' he says.

His eyes are calm, focused entirely on her. Something about the stillness feels dangerous. As if he's about to blow.

Her heart thuds, suddenly feeling exposed. She does what she always does when she's possibly fucked up – paints on her best smile. 'I know you do. I know you're managing. But it would be nice if you actually spoke to each other like civilised adults instead of shouting all the time.'

'I don't shout,' Lefty points out.

Fraser carries on staring.

'I know what this is about,' he says to her. As if Lefty's not there.

'Me?'

'You want to fix things. Make everything nice, make it all pretty and happy. Sometimes things just can't be fixed, aye?'

Her voice all but disappears. 'Doesn't mean you shouldn't try.'

He takes a deep breath in, lifts the wine bottle, fills his glass. And hers. 'Well, you've tried.'

'These things take time.'

The wine bottle slams on to the table, hard enough to make Fraser's fork fall off the side of the plate. Lefty flinches, scrapes back his chair, and without another word he leaves the room. Rachel stares Fraser out, listening for the sound of Lefty's door closing and, a few minutes later, the sound of the TV turned up high.

'There,' Fraser says coldly. 'Happy now?'

She shakes her head, gulps the wine, which is, she realises, very alcoholic and really very good. Lefty's steak lies abandoned and half-eaten. Fraser tuts and spears it, adding what's left to his own plate. Bess, watching everything from her bed, gives a little whine of protest.

Rachel looks at him, determined not to cry. All she wants is to try to make things better, and each time she tries she just makes it worse. And now she has made Fraser angry, which is the very last thing she wants to do. He may be grumpy, but he's been nothing but kind to her, helping her with the bird observatory, giving her lifts on the quad, even when it isn't raining. And cooking all the time, not just chips and beans and basic food but proper fresh, elaborate meals that taste fantastic and make her feel...

Hm. She thinks about it. Special? No, not quite. Wanted? Not that either. Valuable? It doesn't work in the way she wants the word to work, but the alcohol is beginning to affect her brain, making everything just a bit less important.

Deep, slow, breaths. Sips of wine. *Don't get pissed*, she thinks. If she has too much of it, she'll make a tit of herself, even more than she has already. She's baffled by most of this, frankly, but one thing she's sure of is that she wants to stay here, sit this out, not run off like Lefty. That would feel too much like giving in. She has a strong desire to not give in.

Mel has developed a theory about Fraser. Well, not so much a theory, of course, since he exists for Melanie only in the descriptions Rachel has sent to her, plus those two photos she passed on, the ones of him striding up the hill. After the last abortive Team Dinner attempt, last week, Rachel had messaged Mel with the results, which were broadly similar to this evening's, only with less wine-bottle-slamming and no actual raised voices.

Mel had said in reply:

> Anger is never really just anger tho is it?

> What do you mean?

> I mean there's always something else behind it. Like, I dunno, hurt. Or fear. Or something.

Rachel has been thinking about that ever since, about Fraser's anger. It's pretty much the only emotion she's seen him display, and he seems comfortable displaying it all the time, especially in Lefty's direction. Tonight is the first time she's had any of it directed at her – except it wasn't, really, even though the thing that's making him angry – being forced to share his table with Lefty – is entirely her doing.

Fraser tips the wine bottle up into his glass. It's empty. Rachel has had a couple, no more than that, and she can feel the deep red glow of it inside her.

'Fuck,' he mutters.

'Have we run out?' she asks.

The shopping runs in the past few weeks have included several bottles, and one bottle of whisky per week. Robert must think she's got a serious drinking problem, since the alcohol portion of the shopping list only started once she arrived. Now Fraser is clearly the worse for wear and she is a good bottle or so behind him. She thinks about opening another one, seeing if a bit more wine will loosen him up further, but there's something so sad in the hunched shoulders, the way he seems utterly exhausted all of a sudden, and she doesn't want to make it worse.

His hand on the table. Something makes her reach out and put her hand over it. He flinches, leaves it there for a moment, and then pulls his hand away. He collects the plates, begins to wash up.

'Fraser,' she says.

He doesn't answer.

She gets up, takes the bowl of coleslaw and finds clingfilm to fit over the top of it, and she's aware of him the whole time, the physicality of him, the tension in his shoulders and the attitude, whatever it is.

She listens to him shouting in his sleep. Maybe once or twice a week. She has not gone into his room again, although each time she has thought about it. Once, she thought she heard him yell her name, *Rachel*, just once. She sat up in bed, heart thumping, listening in case something had happened, in case it was an actual emergency and he needed her, listening for him to call out again. And she'd heard a groan, like a … like a self-disgust kind of thing. And silence.

And now here they are again. Fraser with his back to her, solid muscle and tension and looking as though he'd really like to punch something. She wants to touch him again, but she fights the urge. She's not afraid of his anger, not put off by it. Not worried about it, not really, all the way to the moment when he says, 'Here's the thing I want to know—' and then stops himself.

'Yes?' she says, waiting. Suddenly it feels bad.

He turns, points a soapy finger. 'What happened to your baby?'

Her world falls apart, right then. Like the floor falling away beneath her.

'What?'

'Where's your baby, Rachel?'

Anger is never really just anger tho

is it?

Fraser

Where's your baby, Rachel?

Man, if he could have taken that back he would have done so in an instant. What on earth was he thinking? What was he playing at, so drunk he was swaying, saying something like that to her?

He had hated himself all over again the second the words were out of his mouth, the smile dying on her face and a flush rising from her chest, shock in her wide eyes. He'd thought she'd run. He'd been counting on it; it was the only way his stupid pissed-up brain could think of to get her out of the kitchen, give himself time to think, to breathe. But she had stayed put, rooted. Staring at him.

'How...what makes you think...'

'Your phone. You got me scrolling through the bird pictures you'd taken. Then there's a picture of you, pregnant. You, with a baby.'

Her eyebrows had shot up. 'Oh!' And then, 'When were you scrolling through my bird pictures?'

'On the beach. When you were picking litter.'

She had looked at him, confused. 'But that was weeks ago.'

'It was, aye.'

'Why didn't you ask me about it at the time?'

He'd had no real answer for that. 'It's none of my business,' he'd said, after a moment.

'No. Not really.'

He was drunk, tired with the anger. Her horrified face...he'd felt sick, hating himself for that. Then she'd left, and he hasn't seen her since.

She's busy today. The new lot of visitors are due at five this evening, the professor and the two women, and she's doing whatever she's doing at the bird observatory. Cooking. Cleaning. Keeping out of his way. Avoiding him at all costs.

He can't blame her, of course, not after last night. His birthday is well and truly over for another year, passed unrecorded, unremarked. If she ever talks to him again he'll consider himself fucking lucky.

He can see what she's trying to do – keep the peace, have everyone playing at happy bunnies – but she has no fucking clue what she's walked into. He told Lefty to keep out of her way. He told her to keep out of Lefty's way. And now suddenly they are best pals, chatting and getting on and who knows what else? He's seen Lefty going in to the bird observatory when he's been told to do something – cutting the grass, beach-cleaning, tidying the workshop, cleaning the hen house; he's stood and watched him going inside.

It's crossed his mind that maybe they're fucking. Although he can't believe it, can't believe Rachel could be that desperate. Also he can't quite believe that if Lefty has got involved with Rachel to that extent he wouldn't know about it. For all the extra washing and the liberal application of Lynx, Lefty is not giving off signs of having got some action.

Fraser is used to the anger, the feel of it rising and falling inside him. It's always there, waiting, ready, swallowed down by his need to remain civilised, choking him sometimes, then pushed up by something much farther down inside, something darker. Shame or hatred or just sheer apathy. Last night it was there, seething: the sight of Lefty's wet hair combed down flat, his pale grubby neck because of course he missed that bit when he got in the shower, the ugly fucking tattoos that someone did for him with a needle when he was off his face on something, back in the day.

Lefty had got out of the kitchen at just the right time. He pushes Fraser's buttons on a daily basis. He knows exactly where they are.

Now Fraser is standing on the east cliff, binoculars in hand, watching for terns. Lefty has been sent to the north beach to clean, but it's not long before he turns up again, swinging the jute bag against his legs, half-full.

'That it?'

'Aye. It's clean.'

'Fucking doubt it.'

'It is!' Lefty's already turned to go.

'Where the fuck are you going now?'

The lad stands stock-still, waiting. He's turned in the direction of the bird observatory.

'You leave her alone,' Fraser says, his voice low. It doesn't matter. Lefty can hear him well enough.

Something is muttered back.

'What did you say?'

He covers the ground between them in two strides. For a change, Lefty is standing his ground.

'I said, she's no' yours.'

Fraser wants to grab him by the neck and shake him like a rat, like prey, but he's here in full view of the observatory and it isn't only that stopping him. It's a weariness, the end of it... this is never going to get better unless he stops.

'She's no' yours either right enough, ya wee shite.'

Lefty, who has been braced for some sort of assault, breathes out and relaxes ever so slightly. Turns to face him. There's no defiance in his eyes, just a sort of quiet resignation. 'She's just doing her best. She's a good person.'

'Which is why I want you to stay the fuck away from her. She doesn't need to be hanging out with the likes of you.'

'She's kind. She's just being kind.'

There is a pause, then Lefty reaches into his pocket, opens his fist to show Fraser what's inside. Nestled in his palm are two pieces of glass, worn smooth by the waves and the sand.

'What the fuck have you got there?'

'She likes them.'

'What?'

'She likes the sea glass. I've been collecting it for her.'

Fraser stares, wanting to summon up the rage now because if there's something to make him angry it's here: the sight of this pathetic wee gift in the grubby hand of this idiot, the person he hates more than anyone or anything; the fact that this little shit has established enough of a relationship with

Rachel that he's bringing her presents like a stray cat bringing a mouse.

And the fact that Lefty has suddenly grown a pair. All the time he's been here, over a year of cowering and running and doing what he's told, and suddenly he's standing up for himself. And instead of roaring in Lefty's face as he should be – instead of taking him by the throat and reminding him that here, on this island, in this place, he is lower than a rat in the pecking order, scarcely fit to clear up birdshit and not fit to be heard, that he has no voice, no say, no rights, no right to even be alive because of who he is and what he's done – there's nothing. No rage. Just a sudden urge to weep.

Fraser takes a stumbling step back, dizzy.

'I'm going tae take them,' Lefty says.

This time, Fraser doesn't stop him. He has a strong sense of fighting the tide, and he's tired. Just for a change, he wants to try swimming the other way.

He thinks of Rachel with the sea glass, pale, silky blue jewels, almost but not quite the colour of her eyes, the nuggets of glass trickling through her long fingers like water. He wishes he had something like that. Something to give. Something to apologise with.

Rachel

Fraser brings the quad at seven.

He usually comes to collect her when it's raining, and it's blowing a gale out there, heavy rain and wind enough to tip her over the cliff if she's not paying attention, but even so when he fills the porch she's suffused with a weird mixture of relief and trepidation. She hasn't spoken to him since the *where's your baby, Rachel?* No whisky last night. No porridge waiting for her this morning, either. He had arrived on the jetty with the quad just in time to help make the boat fast, had ignored her completely then, loading the luggage and the shopping into the trailer and speeding noisily off up the hill. By the time she had walked to the bird observatory with her new guests in tow, the luggage was in the porch and the shopping in the kitchen, and the quad had gone.

Thankfully at five when they'd got here, it hadn't been raining.

Now Fraser looks even more enormous than usual, and the reason for this becomes clear as he peels off his dripping coat and reveals a second hi-vis jacket underneath, which he also removes and holds out to her.

'What's this?' she asks.

'You'll need something better than that,' he says, pointing vaguely at her waterproof jacket, hanging up in the porch.

In the main room the professor – whose name is Brian – stands to greet Fraser.

The two women are chatting on the sofa with bottles of beer. Rachel hasn't quite worked out what their relationship is, because Brian simply introduced them as Carol and Jane. One of them is younger. She thinks maybe Carol is his wife and Jane is their daughter, but the level of affection between Professor Brian and Jane appears to be rather more than just paternal.

There is a bit of casual discussion between Brian and Fraser about guillemots while Rachel finishes putting the casserole in the slow cooker for tomorrow night's dinner. When she's ready, Fraser holds out the huge waterproof for her to slide her arms into. Does it up for her, since the sleeves drape down over her hands. It's like climbing inside a warm padded tent. She feels alarmingly helpless, especially when he lifts the hood for her and it falls over her eyes.

Outside, the wind blows her sideways. He helps her on to the quad and she fastens her arms around his waist as tightly as she can, pressing her face into his wet back.

Lefty is in his room, the thud-thud-thud of his music drowning everything else out. The kitchen smells of oven chips, and yeast.

Fraser has made pizza, from scratch. Rachel goes for a shower while he finishes things off, peels off her wet, cold jeans. Thinks about getting into her pyjamas and decides instead to get dressed again. Leggings and her purple shirt, open over a dark green vest. Twists her hair into a bun. It'll do.

'Here's the thing,' she says, when she's had three gulps of wine. White, cold, goes well with the pizza. 'I don't think you can ask me about personal stuff – like those photos you saw – if you don't like me asking you about personal stuff.'

'Fair enough,' he says.

She eats the pizza, drinks the wine. Several minutes go past.

'You don't have to tell me anything,' he says, eventually.

'Talking about things makes them easier,' she says. 'Didn't you feel better, after you told me about Maggie?'

He raises an eyebrow. 'I guess.'

'Until I made it all awkward by kissing you on the cheek, that is,' she says, and laughs, a bit, to make sure he knows that it didn't mean anything.

He says something that she doesn't quite catch.

'What?'

'Wasn't on the cheek,' he says, looking at her, raising his glass and swigging from it. 'Just saying.'

'It bloody was. You saying I took advantage?'

'Not saying anything of the kind.'

She thinks she is being teased, a bit. Hopes that's the case, because if he's serious then it would be awful. And of course it's her fault for bringing it up again. She had been hoping that he had forgotten all about it.

'Anyway,' he says calmly, 'we're talking about you now, not me.'

He's finished eating, pushes his plate away. Leans back in his chair, long legs stretched out, wine glass cradled against his chest. Just so relaxed.

Where to even start? She takes a deep breath. *Get it out there. Do it, Rachel.*

'I had a baby. Emily. For my sister, and her husband. I was their surrogate.'

He sits up again. Raises one eyebrow. 'Seriously?'

'Yes. Lucy can't have children. They were looking into surrogacy and on the spur of the moment I offered to do it for them.'

'Wow. Okay. On the spur of the moment?'

'Pretty much.'

Putting it so baldly, describing it in such basic terms – as if it were something that happened to someone else ... it's actually easier than she thought it would be. And it's out there now; she can't take it back.

'So there you go,' she says. 'I got pregnant. I had Emily. I handed her over. Now I'm here.'

Her voice had gone, just a little, on the *handed her over*. The wrong phrase, perhaps. She should have left that out completely. She has a sense of having given something away, in more ways than one. And now she can't look at him any more.

He refills her glass. 'When was she born?'

Of all the questions. 'January fourteenth.'

'That's only four months ago.'

'Yes. I know that.'

He sits back in his chair and she risks looking up at him. The way he's looking at her, curiosity, something else.

'That's why you're here?' His voice is gentler than she's ever heard it.

'Don't be kind to me,' she says.

'Why not?'

'If we keep talking about this I'm probably going to start crying. Hormones, right? Just to give you fair warning.'

'Aye, well, I'm not bothered by it. Just – you don't have to keep running off. You can cry on my shoulder, if you want. You've got reason enough, besides the hormones.'

'It wasn't like that. It was my decision.'

'If you say so. But it hurt you, though,' he says, looking right at her. 'Didn't it? Or, if not that, something did.'

Fraser

They go to the living room with the bottle of wine, which is nearly empty anyway, and another that he's already opened. Rachel takes her usual position in the armchair.

Where's your baby, Rachel? Well, now he knows. And he's upset her again, and he feels bad about it.

He has a sudden memory of Kelly telling him she was clean, and then a few moments later adding that the reason she was clean was that she was pregnant. Seven years ago, more or less.

Kelly was not his girlfriend. He has never had a girlfriend, not that he will admit to, but Kelly is probably the closest thing he's had to one. He has known her for nearly fifteen years, seen her through good times and bad times. In the past four years, Kelly is the only woman he has had sex with. Even that has been sporadic.

'So,' Kelly had said, 'yeah. I'm pregnant.'

The baby wasn't his. He had not seen her for five months and she was barely three weeks gone. She was telling him because she needed money, and he would only give her money if he thought she wasn't going to spend it on drugs. Other times she had told him she was clean but her landlord wanted to sell the flat, or she had the promise of a job in Aberdeen and needed to move, or her friend needed money for a sick dog's operation; he'd heard all of them. She'd never told him she was pregnant before, but there was something about the way she said it that told him she was telling the truth.

'How did that happen?' he'd asked. 'You get careless?'

It had been a combination of erratic pill-taking and a split condom, apparently.

'Do you know who the father is?'

She must have had an idea, of course, but she wasn't about to tell him. She had lied to him in the past but that was always the smack talking, not Kelly, and on the rare occasions when she did manage to get help and was clean she was a different person. Truthful.

Kelly asked him, sometimes, that very question that he'd imagined Rachel asking. 'Why aren't you married?' she'd ask, teasing. 'Great big lovely man that you are. Why has no woman snapped you up?'

He'd never answer.

'Someone hurt you, big man?' she'd asked, once. He'd caught her eye by accident and looked away immediately, but she'd seen it. 'Aye, that's it, right enough. Some bitch broke your heart and now you can't trust anyone.'

'Fuck off with your pocket psychology,' he'd said, nudging her knee. She knew nothing about Maggie. He'd never told her.

'There are lots of good women out there, Fraser Sutherland. You'd make one of them very happy.'

'Then I wouldn't be able to come and see you,' he'd said.

'I'd survive – just.'

There had been other conversations like that one, but they'd always ended the same way. He'd thought once or twice about marrying her, just for the convenience of it, to get her out of trouble and to see her right. Sort of a penance, if you would – a life saved for a life lost. When the boy was born he'd thought about it seriously. He had seen her a lot through her pregnancy, because he couldn't imagine how hard it must be, to go through such a life-changing thing all on your own. She was staying off the gear but struggling, despite the help of Social Services and the NHS and any charity that would offer her counselling, support, money, things to keep her busy. She had stopped seeing punters and Fraser had given her as much money as he could afford. Helped her find a flat she wasn't going to get thrown out of. Helped her furnish it. Helped her write a CV.

Eventually Kelly had got back in touch with her family and, troublesome as that had been in the past, now she was apparently doing so well they'd agreed to see her, and the boy, and Fraser had taken a step back with some degree of relief. It had started to get to him. He had started to care.

He knows that feeling well enough, has started to think it might be happening again.

The most dangerous thing of all, this is. Starting to care about someone else.

Rachel

Norwich. 29th April. Just over a year ago.

Mel has arrived back from a fortnight in Tenerife where she had been with her aunt, was dropped off at home in the early hours. At eleven on Sunday morning, Mel is at the kitchen table with Rachel, telling her all about the hotel and this guy from Stockport who jumped in the pool with no trunks on, presumably because the lads he was with dared him to do it.

Mel has brought back vodka, Spanish chewy sweets and some olive oil. Halfway through their discussion Rachel has to go to the bathroom to be sick.

'Pregnant?' Mel says, when Rachel tells her, ten minutes later. 'You're joking, right? Please tell me you're joking.'

'It's not what you think,' Rachel says.

She wishes she'd kept quiet. Telling people, telling your best friend, makes it real. And she's not quite sure if she's ready for it to be real. This is all very new. And Mel's face is just...horrified. She wasn't expecting congratulations, she certainly wasn't expecting Mel to be pleased or anything mad like that, but she wasn't quite expecting this. Mel is absolutely fucking furious.

'I didn't even know you were seeing someone,' Mel says.

'I'm not.'

'So it's that fucker's?'

'No, it's not Amarjit's – will you even let me get a word in?'

And Mel just looks at her, and the words all dry up and she feels hot tears welling up and she can't even really say why. 'Fucking hormones,' she mutters.

Mel passes her a tea towel that has a tomato sauce stain on it, and that makes Rachel hiccup a laugh.

'So, it's my sister's baby,' she says.

Mel's mouth falls open. 'Your – sister's?'

'I'm their surrogate.'

'Since fucking when?' Mel has never shouted at Rachel but her voice is very definitely raised right now. Why? Because Rachel has gone ahead and done something without discussing it with her first? 'I've only been gone a fortnight, for fuck's sake. You decided to do this and got pregnant within the space of fourteen days? Jesus Christ.'

It's been longer than that, of course. She had the discussion with Lucy over a month ago. She didn't tell Mel about it then for the same reason she didn't want to tell her about the results of that discussion, about how it's ended up. Talking about it out loud means it's something that's really happening, not something she's just thinking about. In reality she hasn't thought about it. She has very deliberately been trying not to think about it at all.

'Why are you so angry?' Rachel asks.

Mel leans forward and looks her right in the eye. 'Because you're vulnerable, that's why, and they're fucking taking advantage of you.'

'It was my suggestion,' Rachel says hollowly.

'Doesn't make any difference; you could suggest you're planning to walk up the M11, doesn't mean they should just go, oh, okay then, here, I'll drop you at the slip road, does it?'

'But,' Rachel says, 'they don't know how I've been. I've been hiding it from them, or trying to. It's not their fault. And besides, it's done now, and yes it's really fucking hard and I'd quite like it if you could try and be a bit supportive instead of telling me how fucking stupid I am. I know that already. I know.'

Mel's eyes fill with tears, and that alarms Rachel more than anything else. She has never seen Mel cry before. 'What is it?' she asks, suddenly fearing that something about pregnancy and babies is a trigger for Mel, something she knows nothing about. They have talked about lots of things, but they still haven't plumbed the depths of all the horrible things that led them to that doctor's surgery on that Tuesday morning almost a year ago.

'You're just... you're just too bloody lovely for your own good, Rach. What are we going to do with you?'

'I feel fine about it,' she says, and manages a smile, even though the smell of Mel's burnt toast is making her heave.

Mel wipes the tears away angrily, and calms down a little. 'Bollocks you do.'

'Look,' Rachel says, 'I can't say this to Lucy, but maybe it won't happen. I only just had a positive test. I'm trying not to think about it too much.'

'Yeah,' Mel says, 'maybe. Look, I'm sorry for going off on one like that. I just – I know how far you've come in the last couple of months. I don't want you to end up going downhill again, that's all.'

'Everything's just been a bit of a shock. I'll get used to the idea soon. It just... it happened really quickly.'

'I thought they were doing IVF,' Mel says.

'That's not possible for them. They were considering adoption but Ian's not keen, he wants there to be some biological link. They were on various surrogacy forums and they had a couple of potentials but it didn't come to anything. Lucy told me all this out of the blue. She's normally so... so together, you know? And she was just falling apart over it.'

'So you – what, you offered? Just like that?'

'Kind of.'

'Did she ask you?'

'No. I just said, well, I'm free for the next few months, why don't I do it for you?'

'Jesus Christ, Rach.'

You fucking idiot.

Mel doesn't say it. She doesn't have to. Rachel knows it's what she's thinking. Yes, it's a big deal. She had known it the second those words were out of her mouth. *I'm free for the next few months. Why don't I do it for you?*

Lucy's reaction – the overwhelming relief, exhaustion, hope, gratitude – all there in front of her. What was she going to say? *I was just joking, didn't mean it, whoops, just ignore me.*

Lucy had called Ian straight away, still in tears, so hysterical she could barely get the words out. And Ian had asked to speak to Rachel, and to her shock he was in tears on the phone too – all he kept saying was, 'Are you sure? You mean it? You really mean it?'

And what could she say, then? That afternoon their reaction, their gratitude, had carried her on its shoulders, given her nothing but relief at having finally done something good, something positive. Lucy had taken Rachel into the city and Ian had left work early and they had gone for a drink at the Assembly Rooms, champagne and cocktails to celebrate.

They had already done their homework, of course: they knew, or rather Lucy did, exactly what needed to be done in terms of the legality of having a baby for someone else. She would email it all to Rachel to look over. They were both keen, very keen, for this to be entirely Rachel's decision. In the toilets, Lucy had cried again, and said to Rachel that she would understand if she changed her mind, and she mustn't think that it would spoil their relationship, they would always be sisters, Lucy would always love her no matter what.

Drunk by then, drunk and hollow and a bit numb, Rachel had nodded and said that she would think about it over the weekend, think about all the paperwork and the legal stuff and the practicalities, and then she would give them her final answer on Monday.

Lucy had stopped crying and gone very quiet, and not long after that she had called a cab and dropped Rachel off on the way. As she had got out of the cab, almost as an afterthought because surely this did not need saying, Rachel had looked over her shoulder and said, 'Don't tell Mum.'

And Lucy had replied, 'Course not.' With a huge Lucy smile.

On Saturday morning Lucy had phoned to see how Rachel was. She had a headache, and a weird feeling inside, a kind of emptiness, as if she was already a vessel waiting to be filled. She had been awake for hours, thinking with a mixture of excitement and terror about how it would work and how it would feel. On the one hand she had nothing to do, and this would give her purpose. This would give her a reason to not have to look for a job and not deal with Amarjit. By the time she'd had a baby it would all probably be clearer, what she wanted to do next. It would be a year or so out of her life. A year doing something brilliant, something positive, that would change her family's life for the better. It would make Lucy and Ian happy, her parents happy, and at what cost to her? Probably quite a lot of pain, but women did this every day, had always done it – how hard could it be? The pain wouldn't last for long. And then Lucy and Ian would have a baby, and Rachel could go out into the world and make a fresh start. Again.

On the other hand, it was a fucking big deal. A massive deal. Having a baby for someone? What if it didn't work, whatever they did to get her pregnant? She was envisaging blood tests, IVF, hospitals, drugs to make her fertile. It might take years. What then? Did they give up? At what point would they call it a day? Would she spend the fertile years of her life trying to get pregnant for someone else? What if she met someone? What if she decided she wanted a child herself?

That was a kicker, of course. Rachel had not felt vaguely maternal, not at all: she had friends who'd had babies and she always found herself feeling sorry for them – the lack of sleep and the lack of freedom and the sudden, insane pressure of responsibility. And the babies themselves were tiny and weird-looking and a bit alarming, and Rachel was good at cooing over them and then gratefully handing them back.

Then on Saturday evening she had gone out for a walk – some fresh air to clear her head – and had walked round to her parents' house to see Dad, mainly – not to tell him, but just to absorb some of his quiet wisdom and gentle dadness. And instead she was confronted by her mother, dry-eyed but more emotional than she'd ever seen her, pulling Rachel into a bony embrace.

'You've always been so kind, Rachel. I'm so proud of you for doing this. So, so proud.'

Her mother had, to her sure and certain knowledge, never used the P-word in relation to Rachel before. She'd previously reserved it exclusively to refer to Lucy, whose school reports, first-class maths degree and eventual accountancy partnership had undoubtedly warranted it.

Rachel had looked at her phone a few minutes later to see the text from Lucy, sent an hour before.

Sorry – Mum asked re surrogacy and I had to tell her. Xxxx

Her mother being actually proud of her for the first time added an extra weight on to the pressure on her shoulders. Now it wasn't just Lucy and Ian she'd be letting down if she changed her mind. Not just Lucy and Ian who would think less of her.

Then, on Sunday morning, Lucy had turned up unexpectedly and taken Rachel out for coffee. Mel had still been in bed. She'd been out on a date with Darius the night before and Rachel hadn't seen her; had heard them both come in at threeish. He was probably still in the house.

Rachel had had another sleepless night and was scarcely functioning. But a double espresso and a chocolate brownie had perked her up and she was actually listening when Lucy dropped her next bombshell.

'So, Ian and I were talking. I know you really like sharing with Mel, but we thought you'd need somewhere better to live, so we decided you could move into my old house while you – you know, while you're having the baby. We can't give you money, that's not legal, but we can give you expenses, and we can definitely give you somewhere to live. For free.'

Lucy and Ian had three properties, at the last count – the four-bedroomed cottage they lived in, and both the places they'd had before they married: Ian's flat in the city, currently occupied by a recruitment consultant and his girlfriend; and Lucy's old house, a Victorian terrace not far from the university. It had been a student house for a while but Lucy had recently redecorated it, in the hope of attracting a slightly more careful class of tenant. It was currently empty.

'But … you'd be losing out on the rental,' Rachel had stammered.

Lucy had shaken her head. 'We can afford it,' she said. 'And at least this way we can – you know – help you out a bit. To say thank you.'

Rachel had been overwhelmed by the implications of it, of being beholden to them. What if they needed money suddenly, and turfed her out? What if she didn't get pregnant – at what point would the offer of free accommodation be withdrawn?

She had gone back home to think about it. If Mel had been there, then probably this might have been the moment that she would have told her, and it would undoubtedly be the moment at which Mel would have said something like *what the actual fuck* and *how about fucking no, for a start, you're not a fucking baby machine*. But Mel had gone out for lunch with Darius.

She does not say this to Mel now, of course. It's not her fault.

She had only been home for twenty minutes when her phone started buzzing with messages. One from her mother was warily happy, but with a subtext.

I'm so pleased you're thinking about Lucy's idea. It's a good thing to do. But you know Lucy and Ian have been through such a lot - so you need to be certain about it. I know you'll do the right thing.

She was waiting for Rachel to screw up again and ruin everything, of course. Because Lucy and Ian have *been through such a lot*. And because Rachel always screwed up eventually.

There was, of course, really no choice. There had been no going back, from the moment that the suggestion had left Rachel's mouth, having barely passed through her brain on the way.

She'd looked half-heartedly at the websites Lucy had directed her to, the forms she would have to complete to sign the baby over to her sister. If the child was Ian's, of course, then it was all a whole lot easier and more straightforward. It had looked almost easy.

'Tell me about that picture,' Fraser says.

They are halfway down the second bottle. Rachel finishes her glass, as if fortifying herself. 'Which one?'

'Both, if you like. Only if you want to.'

There is a pause before she speaks again. Then she tells him.

The baby had stopped moving. She had gone to bed the night before, thinking, *she's been quiet today*, and the next morning had got up feeling like something was definitely wrong. She was twenty-six weeks and four days pregnant, her bump well and truly out there, and the baby had a definite sort of routine: she would move a lot when Rachel got up in the night to use the toilet, sometimes a proper little wriggle party that made it hard to go back to sleep; she would move in the mornings when Rachel had breakfast; and she would move regularly throughout the day. She had tried to remember how long it had been since a definite movement had been felt, panicked, and phoned Lucy in tears.

Lucy had been at work about an hour, had a meeting scheduled for 10.45, but immediately cancelled it and came to pick Rachel up from home. Rachel had worked herself up into a terrified silence. Lucy took her to a posh deli and sat her down with a coffee and a piece of artisanal seeded toast with plum jam that came in a little silver dish. Rachel had stared at it, hand on top of her bump.

'It's fine,' Lucy said. 'Honestly, darling, I know you're worried, but I'm not. I'm sure she's fine, and you are too.'

'How do you know?'

'I *don't* know, but fretting about it definitely isn't going to help. So I've made us an appointment to get checked out.'

After the coffee and the toast Lucy took her, not to the maternity unit, but to the private scanning place where they had had a massively expensive 4-D scan done last month. They had fitted them in straight away, Lucy said, and they only had to wait a short while before they were called in.

And, of course, everything was fine. As soon as the gel was applied to Rachel's belly, she could feel the shifting movements inside her again. An elbow, or a knee, some lump pushed Rachel's skin from underneath, and then the scan was just a formality, checking that everything was fine. The baby had changed position and her feet had been towards Rachel's back – any kicking would have been less easy to feel.

Afterwards, out in the bright sunshine of the car park, Lucy had insisted on a selfie to record the moment.

You could see everything on Rachel's face: the exhaustion, the panic, the relief. And Lucy's wide smile – relief too, no doubt, but also a weird kind of triumph at having been vindicated. *See? Everything's fine. I knew it was.*

Fraser

'My sister loves that photo,' she says.

'It's a nice one.'

'You think?'

'Don't you?'

'It's nice of her. I just look – a bit done in.'

'I think you look good.'

She lifts her head and smiles at him. 'You think I look good?'

She's a bit sad and vulnerable and he doesn't want to take advantage. He knows that there will be a 'fuck it' point. In his head he's started calling it that, meaning that he's acknowledged the inevitability that at some point something is going to happen. He can't pinpoint the moment something changed, but there is a dynamic here that feels beyond his control. They've moved from awkwardness to some sort of weird teasing companionship, and beyond that into something else. It simmers inside him every day, while he puts a lid on it and waits. The clock is ticking down on her stay on the island. She will be leaving in a month, maybe less. There is no point in doing anything, and then sometimes he thinks that there is no point not doing anything, either. What's the worst that can happen? She might laugh in his face. And then she'll be gone, and if he really needed to he could go and see Kelly and none of it would matter anyway.

Whichever way he slices it, though, the issue gets complicated.

Rachel isn't some girl in a nightclub. Rachel isn't a sex worker. Rachel is someone he's going to see every day for the next however long, someone he's sharing a house with. And, if he makes an idiot of himself, then the time she's here is going to feel like a fucking eternity.

And besides, he doesn't want to hurt her. Not now, not ever.

And he can feel the slipping of control over his life, already, and nothing's even happened.

'I mean, I don't know. Pregnancy suits you. Is that the wrong thing to say?'

'No…'

He wishes she would come and sit on the sofa next to him, thinks about asking her to do that. Fights the urge.

'What about the other one?'

'The one of me and Emily?'

'Aye, that one.'

'You want to hear about giving birth?' she teases. 'All the gruesome details?'

'Sure.'

215

He doesn't, really. That is to say, he wouldn't if it were anyone else but Rachel. But he wants to keep her talking.

He's not going to tell her this, but he was there when Kelly had her baby. It wasn't planned, she hadn't exactly asked him to be present, but he had been laid off the month before she was due and he had been spending a lot of time round at hers. Helping her out. Fixing things. Not staying over, even though she'd asked. On that day he had come round in the morning with a couple of bags of groceries and found her in considerable pain. Stayed with her long enough to work out that this was it, it wasn't just backache from overdoing things. Then her waters broke. He cleaned it up while she sat on a folded towel at the kitchen table, then he drove her to the birthing unit at the hospital. He had been giving her lifts to her appointments, had been with her at the birthing centre so many times that the staff there undoubtedly thought he was the baby's father. He didn't disabuse them. He didn't care what they thought. He was never going to see any of them again.

He hadn't intended to stay with her, but she had nobody else, and there hadn't seemed to be a good moment to say goodbye and fuck off out of there. Once they arrived at the hospital everything had happened quite fast. Or it hadn't, but it'd felt as though lots of things happened and there wasn't a space in between. Kelly was hooked up to a monitor and then he heard the baby's heartbeat and from then on he didn't really want to leave.

Charlie was born at 8.33 in the evening. Fraser had cut the baby's cord, even though afterwards he'd felt he should have told them all that this wasn't his baby. Nobody seemed to care much, though, and Kelly certainly didn't seem to mind. She'd been absolutely beaming with joy from the minute the pain stopped. When he had seen her with the baby, snuggled up with his wee hat on, he'd felt such a rush of something. It wasn't love. It was just … pride at what she'd done, what she'd achieved. And an overwhelming urge to make sure that nothing bad ever happened to the boy.

216

He can see that same look in Rachel's eyes in that photo. The elation at having done it, at having survived it, at having this little life in front of her. She's not smiling, though, in the picture. He thinks she looks utterly shell-shocked. And really quite beautiful.

'It was okay,' Rachel says. 'I don't know if I'm remembering it differently now. It was quicker than they expected. I was going to have an epidural but there wasn't time. I was shit-scared and that made it all hurt a lot more, but at least it was quick. When I got to the hospital she was already on her way.'

'Was your sister with you? For the birth?'

'Yes, and her husband. Ian. My brother-in-law.'

'No. Seriously? You were okay with that?'

She hesitates.

'Well,' she says, 'it was his baby. I suppose he had a right to be there.'

'I'd say you were the one with all the rights.'

'Hmm.' There is a little pause. 'That's not how my life seems to work out.'

She waits, taking a drink of her wine. Not looking at him. Her thoughts are off somewhere, he thinks, back in that hospital room, the pain and the shock and the stress of it.

'You can ask.'

'Ask what?'

'You want to know how we did it. That seems to be what people want to know.'

'None of my business.'

'Fair enough,' she says.

Her smile, curved around the rim of her wine glass. He's not going to rise to it.

'Put it this way,' she says, eventually, 'I haven't had actual sex with anyone since Amarjit. That feels like a bloody long time ago.'

'Right,' he says, trying to work out the mechanics of it and coming down on the side of IVF.

'Funny, though,' she says. 'One of the hardest things is that it felt as if my insides belonged to them. All the most private bits of my body weren't mine any more.'

'I guess it would feel like that.'

'I don't even like him that much. My brother-in-law, I mean. I didn't really like him in the first place. He's all skinny and accountanty. He's got this laugh – like *heh heh* – sounds really creepy. And his family, well, they're just so weird. All of them. His sister said to me at their wedding that she thought I looked like a face that missed a sneeze.'

'A what?'

'I know. I'm still trying to work out what that means.'

She sits up, then, quite abruptly. Puts her glass firmly down on the table, leans forward, hands between her knees. Her hair sticking up over her ears. He thinks he could look at her for the rest of his life and not get tired of it.

'You want to know something really TMI?'

'Sure,' he says.

'Lucy asked me not to have sex while I was pregnant. I mean, not that I was with anyone. Not that I even felt like it.'

'Hmm.'

'Something to do with alien sperm. She'd read a theory that having multiple partners causes miscarriage.'

'Is that true?'

'I have no idea. It's just Lucy was reading up on everything, you know, totally obsessing about it. For my own benefit, of course, as she was always fond of telling me. Anyway – I didn't. But the weird thing was, I didn't do anything else either.'

'Anything else?'

'I mean, on my own. I didn't have a single orgasm for a whole year.'

'Bloody hell.'

'Is that too much information? Sorry if it is. I never told anyone that before.'

He's concentrating very hard on her lower lip, thinking about the time that's passed since the fourteenth of January.

Thinking about how many orgasms she might have had, on her own, since then. Can't stop thinking about it at all. He's very aware that this feels a lot like the 'fuck it' moment; he's been expecting it, and now here it is, and whatever he says next might as well be those actual words.

Fuck it.

'Your body's not theirs any more, though, is it?' he says, quite calmly.

She takes a sharp breath in. Shakes her head. And looks at him for a long time.

Rachel

She doesn't know where the bravery comes from but perhaps she's just tired of waiting. Perhaps she's just too drunk, or too turned on, or too sad. She gets up, goes to the sofa and straddles him, sitting on his lap and kissing him, no confusion about it this time, straight on the mouth. And to her relief he doesn't hesitate about responding. His hands move up inside her bra, and she has to pull away and breathe and tell him to be gentle because her breasts are still quite tender. He says *sorry* into her mouth and then his touch changes to something else, feather-light, sending bolts of pure heart-stopping desire straight through her. There is an awkward slipping down on the sofa until they are both horizontal. His hand moves from her chest down inside her leggings and grips her backside. She can feel his hardness against her leg as he pulls her tighter against it, and there is something really quite alarming about the size of it and then Rachel feels short of air, because he is half-lying on her and he is big and heavy and his mouth is entirely covering hers.

'Oh, God,' she says.

'We shouldn't do this,' he growls into her hair, breathing hard.

'Don't say that.'

He kisses her again, devours her, for several minutes before answering, as if he needs that in order to think.

'Had too much to drink,' he manages.

'Really?' she says, sliding her hand down the front of his jeans to double-check. *Bloody hell.*

'Fuck, not that. Didn't mean that.'

More kissing. Take a breath. She has forgotten about Lefty, next door in his little den. What if he comes in?

'Consent,' he says. 'You know. I don't want to take advantage.'

'Are you fucking kidding me?' she says, really quite loudly. 'I'm not that bloody pissed, Fraser.'

His hand still on her arse.

'You want to?' he says.

He sounds a bit amazed. Pulls away from her so he can see her face.

'Just sex,' she says, her eyes on his.

'That's what you want?'

She nods emphatically. 'Yes. Do you?'

He's not going to say no. Is he?

Funny to think that in the previous eighteen months she has had no sex, but she's been pregnant and had a baby.

Within a week of the decision, Lucy had been charting Rachel's basal temperature. A week after that, Lucy had decided Rachel was probably ovulating, and, giggling, had suggested 'having a try'. They'd discussed clinics, different methods, discussions that had left Rachel baffled and numb. Those conversations are all a blur, now, because after that conversation about 'giving it a try' there weren't any clinics, any interventions, because there wasn't any need.

Rachel had accepted the syringe full of her brother-in-law's sperm at the door of the spare bedroom, taking it between finger and thumb and trying not to pull a face. Listened to the murmurs of conversation from Lucy and Ian's bedroom next door while she lay on the bed with the syringe next to her, wondering what the fuck she thought she was doing. And just a moment later she'd thought *what the hell, just do it* and had inserted the syringe as far as it would comfortably go, and pushed the plunger down. She had stayed still, nose wrinkled in disgust at the thought of Ian's little swimmers flapping around in confusion next to her cervix, thinking that there was no way it was possible to get pregnant like this, but if it made Lucy happy…

Of course Lucy hadn't been content with one little syringe. They'd done it four times over the next day and a half, and each time Rachel had had to physically stop herself from racing home so she could get in the shower. Meanwhile Ian was beginning to look as if he would vastly prefer the expense and medicalised justification of IVF to the indignity of having to wank into a cup with his sister-in-law within earshot, even if Lucy was there when he was doing it. Rachel didn't want to think about that too much. The whole thing was just insane.

In any case, those four times were all that was required. Two weeks later they'd done the test, and she was pregnant. Rachel had barely had time to think about it.

Fraser follows her up the stairs, Bess trotting after him. On the landing she looks from her room to his, suddenly at a loss.

Then he takes her by the hand, leads her into his room, and shuts the door behind her.

Fraser

He never meant for this to happen. He didn't plan it but here they are: they are in his dark bedroom alone and between them the air is boiling. His heart is absolutely pounding.

He turns on the overhead light.

'Want to see you,' he says, moving towards her, vaguely expecting her to flinch, or turn away, but instead she leans into him a little, anticipating, and he kisses her, intending to be gentle this time but then not managing gentle at all. He hears, feels her give a little squeak into his mouth. His hands are around her, cupping her arse and pulling her against him and then pushing her gently back against the nearest solid surface, the chest of drawers, so that she's higher, and her arms are around his neck, her fingers in his hair, her other hand fisting the fabric of his shirt.

He pulls back, breathless, to look at her. Her pupils are huge, her irises somehow darker, sea-blue, her skin porcelain, flushed with two red spots high on her cheeks.

He is as hard as he has ever been in his life, his crotch pressed against hers, grinding into her like a fucking teenager. His hands push up under her top, the smooth hot skin of her back, the gentle bumps of her ribs and her spine, the planes of her shoulderblades. He feels a further rush of blood, moves back. Deliberately, he moves her towards his bed, turns her round so she is facing away, pushes his hands under the waistband of the tight grey leggings she's wearing, smooths them down, over her arse, down her thighs, crouching as he does so: plants his face against the hot skin and kisses her, nibbling at her, sliding his fingers between her thighs. She is wet, slippery with it, makes a noise in her throat as he pushes one finger inside her: but in the same moment he can feel the tension in her thighs, in her buttocks, and he stops, reluctantly. Lets her go.

She climbs on to the bed. Holds out a hand for him.

He can't help himself: he devours her mouth again, his hands on her waist, pushing against her. He feels her fingers at his belt buckle, pulling at it; hears the clink of her releasing it, her fingers on the buttons of his jeans. *Not yet.* She makes a sound into his mouth, and he lets her go in case she can't breathe, in case she's trying to speak. Instead there is just a little gasp.

He moves down the bed, pushing up her top and planting kisses on her stomach, on the curve of her hip, on her thigh. Sits up, then, and drags her leggings down and off in a purposeful way. Thinks maybe he should check, again, that she's up for this. He looks up at her, half-sitting, her weight on her elbows.

'This okay?' he says.

She nods. 'Yes. I mean…'

'Yes?'

'I just—'

'What?'

'It's been a while.'

'I know.'

He pauses. It's not that she looks scared, exactly.

'If you don't want to…' he says, thinking, *Please don't say you don't want to.*

'I do.'

'Sure?'

'Definitely sure. Will you… have you got condoms?'

He clambers over her to the bedside table, turns on the lamp, then gets up and turns off the overhead light, which is making his bedroom look as if he hasn't cleaned it in weeks.

Although, actually, he hasn't.

He sits on the edge of the bed and rummages around in the drawer, finds nothing, then the sports bag under his bed that he uses when he goes to the mainland. In his washbag he finds the box of condoms. He has had them a while, checks the expiry date on them surreptitiously, wondering in the same moment what the fuck he's going to do if they are out of date. To his immense relief they still have a couple of months left.

'Here we go. All right?'

She nods.

'So, you want me to stop, you just say. Right?'

She nods again.

'Now I'm going to carry on with what I was doing, if that's okay with you.'

He thinks, *I can't believe this is happening.*

He thinks, *this is probably a mistake.*

223

Rachel

'What?' she asks. He has said something, muffled, kissing her side. She pushes a hand through his hair.

'I said, you need to eat more. I can feel ribs here.'

Charming.

'You taste good.'

That's all right, then, she thinks, and then he nudges firmly at her thigh with one huge, warm hand, and she opens her legs and thinks, *don't look down*, because there's always been something so disconcerting about making eye-contact with a man performing oral, but then she thinks maybe he isn't going to after all, because his beard is tickling her inner thigh, as though he's skipped that bit and is going down her legs instead – surely he wouldn't – and she almost drags him back up by his hair, almost gives a little growl, and then he's there, his tongue, and she thinks, *oh*.

For several minutes she doesn't think very much at all. And then his fingers join in and she thinks of his hands, how she finds them somehow the sexiest thing about him because he has huge, beautiful, practical hands. Turns out they're actually quite skilled.

She asks him to stop. *Breathe*, she thinks, because she hasn't been. She feels light-headed, spacey, exhilarated. His fingers are still, but they're right there, waiting. She touches his head again, stroking her fingers down the side of his face, until he catches them, kisses them, bites them. She pulls him back to her, and this time he doesn't build up to it, as if he's hungry, as if he can't wait – and she throws her head back against the pillows and gasps. Something intensely erotic about it, his unfamiliar fingers inside her. She feels close to it but the climax keeps slipping away, and then she starts thinking that he must be getting fed up and at that point she tells him to stop.

He does as she asks, which makes her think that probably he was getting bored. He crawls up the bed to lie next to her, casually wiping his mouth with the back of his hand.

'Will you take these off?' she asks, pulling at his clothes.

'You want me to?'

'I just asked.'

He sits on the edge of the bed, his back to her. Pulls his T-shirt off, over his head.

'No,' she says. 'Stand up. I want to watch you.'

'I'm not a fucking stripper.'

'I'm not asking you to dance.'

He obliges, then. She can tell he's embarrassed, although he has no reason to be. He's actually, she thinks ... what's the word for it? How to describe him?

He's not one of those smooth bronzed vain boys, the ones she's supposed to go for. His chest is covered in dark hair, which extends to his arms – tanned forearms, pale everywhere else – and even his shoulders. His chest and back and shoulders are broad and strong and muscled, his belly rounded, but hard with muscle too. Just before he pulls down his shorts he catches her eye and actually manages a smile, which she thinks is the sexiest thing she's ever seen.

Her vest is rucked up around her chest anyway, so she sits up and pulls it off, discards her bra off the edge of the bed. She is still really quite ridiculously turned on. He looks down at her, hesitates. She sees his eyes travelling from her toes up her legs all the way up to her face.

There is a really long pause where he's just staring at her.

'What?'

'You're in my bed,' he says. 'And you're ... I don't know.'

Out of nowhere, bizarrely given what he's just done, she has that flash of having transgressed, somehow. 'You want me to go?'

'Fucking no. Of course not.'

Then she finds one of the condoms in the tangled duvet, kneels on the bed, kisses him. She hears him take a deep, gasping breath in. She was just going to kiss him once and put the condom on but now she's here, close, and he's really just beautiful and she can't help herself. Cups his balls. Kisses them.

Runs her tongue up and down. His hands thread through her hair. He pulls himself away, takes the condom out of her hand, applies it.

'Okay, then,' he says, and she giggles.

Then he takes her breath away.

8

Deep water

Rachel

Rachel thinks she should really get back to her own room. Fraser is asleep, or dozing at least, his arm heavy on her waist. His hand occasionally moves half-heartedly, as though he's some huge beast succumbing to an anaesthetic.

She is very aware that she is in his bed. Despite what they've spent the last several hours doing, sleeping feels like a different sort of intimacy. And besides, she's absolutely wired, and there's no way she is going to actually sleep.

No man has ever made Rachel come during sex, so the fact that she didn't was really not a surprise, despite the not inconsiderable effort Fraser had put in. Amarjit had never really bothered much about that, once she had admitted that she found it difficult. In all the time she was with him, she'd got there herself maybe a couple of times. This is what is normal to her, but being with Fraser last night has made her question whether it is normal at all. She has no problems on her own, even after a year of abstinence. Maybe she just needs to relax a little bit? Fraser hadn't said anything about it but he'd kept trying until it got awkward and she'd had to say, 'It's fine, I'm just tired'. She had probably been more turned on than ever before, but something about it made it impossible.

She knows it's a bad idea to compare them – Fraser and Amarjit – since they are clearly so different in so many ways, but she can't help herself.

It's not just that Fraser spent so much time over it. All of a sudden it feels important, that she had been in a supposedly loving relationship with someone who was not in any way bothered about her pleasure, and here is someone she isn't in a loving relationship with who seemed to be treating it as a personal mission. It's everything else, all the things she can see as if someone has turned on some sort of light. How did she fail to see that yawning inequality between her and Amarjit? How did she ever think it was okay that he never wanted her to stay the night? That he never took her out anywhere, to the cinema or for a meal? That he never introduced her to his friends outside work and that he never wanted to meet hers? It all seems so very basic now, so fundamentally wrong, and at the time she just had no idea.

She will never let that happen again.

Fraser's breathing has deepened. She eases his arm away from her waist, and he grunts, fidgets, turns on his side away from her, and farts.

Well, she thinks. But now she can get out of bed, at least. She finds her clothes discarded on the floor. She reaches for his bedside lamp and turns it off. The grey square of the window makes her realise that it's later – earlier – than she'd thought it was.

Back in her own bedroom, she lies still, thinking about what's just happened. Out of nowhere, apparently. She'd had no idea he felt like that about her. Perhaps he doesn't. Perhaps it was just a shag, which was, after all, what she had said to him right before it happened. What she had asked for.

The irony of it all, though. All that time she has spent loaded down with the shame of falling for a man she worked with, a man whose circumstances made it more or less impossible for any relationship to have worked. And now what does she think she's doing? Almost exactly the same thing.

The same thing, and yet entirely different at the same time. At least Fraser's being honest. At least he's been upfront about it.

Whatever this is, it's definitely not a relationship.

Fraser

Rachel is sitting in the kitchen with her laptop when he gets downstairs. It's still early – nearly seven – but it's later than usual for him. In fact it was the noise of the shower in the bathroom next door that woke him.

He eyes her warily and then concentrates on making coffee to give himself something to do, the grinder sounding horribly loud in the quiet of the kitchen.

'You okay?' he asks, eventually. His voice sounds hoarse, as if he's spent the entire night talking, or shouting. He hopes he didn't do any of that after he fell asleep. When he woke up this morning she had gone, and he's gutted about that, as he had gone to sleep looking forward to a possible round two. He already has a deep, churning anxiety that he might have done something wrong.

'Yes.'

He risks a glance at her. She looks pale, but perhaps that's just the light from her laptop screen reflecting on her face. And she's probably tired, he thinks. God knows he's pretty worn out himself. Three hours' sleep? Something like that.

'Did I hurt you?' he says.

She looks up, frowning. 'No.'

'Hm, okay, then. You want coffee?'

'I've just had a tea. Thank you, though.'

It's an oddly formal exchange, given that a few hours ago he was buried deep inside her, his face in her hair, thinking himself dreaming or at least just extraordinarily lucky.

While the coffee is brewing he stands with his back to the counter, pretending not to be watching her, when in fact he's finding it quite difficult to look away. He wants to sit down opposite her at the table but he can't quite trust himself not to touch her again and there is something about her this morning, something about her demeanour. As though there is a forcefield. As though she doesn't want him near.

'Last night...' he says, and the sound of his voice takes him by surprise. He'd been thinking it and suddenly it was out there. Clears his throat.

She looks up, focuses on him properly. He thinks maybe she's been crying, but maybe he's imagining that, projecting it on to her.

'So, I wanted to say, just to be clear. Right? This isn't a thing.'

'A thing?' she echoes.

'A whatever you want to call it. A relationship.'

'Fraser, we just had sex.'

He can't help himself, he flicks a glance out to the hallway to Lefty's room, but unsurprisingly the door is shut. Lefty has never voluntarily emerged from his room before late morning, on those rare occasions Fraser hasn't dragged him up and out with him.

'I know that. But I wanted to be clear about where we are.'

'You already said you don't do relationships. I was listening when you said it.'

Her voice isn't hostile. There's just a strange sort of resignation to it.

'Right. Well. As long as that's okay with you.'

She doesn't answer. She has already gone back to her laptop. What's she looking at? He has a sudden burning desire to know.

'I don't want you to get hurt, you know?'

'Don't worry, Fraser. I'm used to not getting things I want. My parents' approval. Amarjit. Emily. You.'

Her words take his breath away. He feels them like a stab. Behind him the coffee machine is gurgling away. The warm rich smell of it; his morning cup of coffee is like the capital letter at the start of every day. Usually it makes him feel better. But today everything just feels slightly wrong.

'It was good,' he says at last. 'Last night, I mean. Really good.'

He can't shake the feeling that somehow he got a lot more out of it than she did. He knows she didn't come. That bothers him.

This time she doesn't even look up. He has forgotten about the porridge, feels oddly exposed, here, as if he can't remember how to operate in his own kitchen. He gets the oats into the pan and adds water to them, sets them on the stove. Then he lets Bess outside, although she gives him the side eye as though she's already been. The fresh air gives him a jolt. It's raining outside, a dull persistent drizzle, the clouds heavy with the promise of not letting up all day. Maybe he'll stay inside. Maybe he'll do the laundry, or run the vacuum round. Change the sheets. Maybe he won't do that.

The oats begin to boil and he turns the hob right down, stirring. Bess comes back in and shakes herself vigorously, droplets of water flying all over the place.

'I fed her,' Rachel says, from the table.

'Did you? Thanks. You'll get no extra from me,' he says, to the dog. 'No point looking at me like that.'

She gives him an affronted look and retreats to her bed, chin on paws, looking from one of them to the other as if she's trying to work it out.

More stirring. He adds a pinch of salt, a glug of cream from the fridge.

'I thought it was good, too,' she says from behind him. 'For the record.'

'You want some porridge?'

'Yes, please.'

It gives him an excuse to sit with her, at least. He brings over the bowls and she shuts her laptop and puts it to one side.

'I was looking at the blog. New entry.'

He blows on his spoon. 'About last night?'

231

'Yeah, sure. I wanted to let the world know about it.'

He looks up and meets her eye and this time they both smile.

'About the terns, actually. Can I get some pictures of them?'

'Sure. They're all still arriving, though. We won't get eggs for another couple of weeks.'

There is a quiet pause. From the corner, Bess lets out a tiny whine.

'Did you get any sleep?' he asks.

'Not really.'

There is a pause while he thinks about asking why she didn't stay. Manages to not say it out loud.

'I was thinking about Amarjit.'

He wonders about the significance, tries not to link it to her dissatisfaction, despite his best efforts. They spent the night fucking and first thing in the morning she's thinking about her previous lover.

'He's been in touch?'

'No, it's not that. And I know I shouldn't compare things, that's just ... bad. I know I told you it was a mistake, you know, one of Rachel's inevitable fuck-ups. And I have the strong sense of being about to do the same thing with you, that I'm going to fuck things up and make a fool of myself again, only I'm not, I'm really not. I'm not going to push you into a relationship because I know that's not what you want, and it might surprise you to learn that it's really not what I want either. Honestly. I've had enough of all of that. I think I can be happy just on my own, especially if there's the option of occasional really good sex with someone I'm attracted to, someone ... kind. I think I need to be happy on my own, and I don't need – I mean I shouldn't need, should I? – I shouldn't need a relationship for that. To be happy. Although I don't think you've really said what you think a relationship is; maybe what you think a relationship looks like is very different from what I think it is, and also I think maybe you're just as confused as I am. But anyway.'

Finally she pauses for breath. He looks at her, eyes narrowed, thinking how she talks a lot when she's nervous. As if all the thoughts become words and it all just comes pouring out, a distraction from what's really going on.

'Sorry,' she says.

'What for?'

'I don't know. Going on about it.'

He heard everything she said but if he's honest his concentration had wavered when he heard the words *the option of occasional really good sex* and his body seems to be hoping that it means what he thinks it means, at the same time as his brain is trying to stay rational.

He's caught now, snagged on her gaze like a fish on a line. Her lips look dark, full, like last night when he'd been kissing her so hard he thought he might have bruised her. The urge to kiss her again hits him like a punch to the throat.

As he always does when he starts to feel caught, he gets up from the table, takes the bowls and washes up.

'No problem,' he says. 'Whatever.'

Rachel

Rachel heads for the bird observatory at five. It's still raining, a slow, quiet drizzle, the clouds overhead dark and low enough to shroud the higher points of the island in a dark grey blanket of damp. It feels more like October than the middle of May.

There are eider ducks everywhere now. They nest in random places, including on the paths, just sitting there. She has to pay attention to where she's walking because the brown females are so still and tucked in that they look like rocks sometimes, especially when the weather is dull, as it is today. She thinks about it, takes a couple of pictures of a female sitting on eggs, although the light's not very good. She'll do a blog about the ducks. They are cute, really, even if she's come close to accidentally booting them once or twice.

She knocks and goes into the bird observatory, hoping that there's nobody there, but Professor Brian is in the living room with Carol. After a moment Jane comes out to say hello. They went out this morning, came back early because of the weather. Brian and Carol are in pyjamas. Jane disappears again and Rachel hears the shower running.

She leaves them to it and begins to prep the veg. They've got casserole this evening, the one that she put in the slow cooker last night. Just a bit of mashed potato and green beans, maybe, to go with it. This lot seem great so far at keeping the place clean; they feel much more like the sort of customers she was expecting, as if they are holidaymakers and this is a holiday let, rather than her running some sort of hostel for people used to roughing it.

Meanwhile Rachel has started to enjoy birdwatching. Especially with Fraser, who is the best sort of expert – patient at explaining things. He has no expectations of her knowing anything at all, but manages to impart his knowledge, somehow, without sounding patronising. Not only does he know what all the birds are, he knows most of them as individuals, can tell you where they've been, how many chicks they've had, how old they are. Most of them were hatched here themselves. She tries to imagine the scale of the migrations that some of them undertake: from Scotland to the Antarctic, in the case of the Arctic terns – every single year, completely under their own steam. Just because that's the way it's always been done; that's what they do. And then flying all the way back again, to here, the place where they first opened their eyes, took their first drink, ate their first mouthful. This tiny island, in a sea of other islands, all looking very similar. It's mind-blowing.

And the puffins – she shouldn't have favourites, but they already are. They are everywhere now. Over the course of a couple of days a week or two ago, they were landing on the turf and marching about shouting at each other, claiming the island back as their own. They are smaller than she'd thought they would be, and bossier, and not at all bothered about her presence. If she gets too close to one it moves away, but complainingly. She thinks of them already like City types, queuing for public transport, or maybe like a huge family at Christmas, everyone talking at once. They all seem to know exactly where they're supposed to be and yet there is no discernible organisation, no pattern to their movements.

And they look so funny in flight, their legs dangling haphazardly underneath them, as if they've forgotten to tuck them away the way other birds do; or they simply can't be arsed.

'In a group, they're called a circus,' Fraser told her, and she can see why. Not so much a circus with a ringmaster and clowns, she thinks, more like Piccadilly Circus, full of noise and bustle and attitude. Everyone moving and somehow not colliding.

Her mind keeps drifting back to last night, to how it felt. All day there has been a delicious sort of ache between her thighs, a soreness from being unexpectedly battered and stretched that has now developed into a sort of longing to have that all over again. She wants it again. She wants more of it, without any stress or debate, preferably without having to talk about sad things first. She tries to imagine that conversation, whether she can ever be that bold; whether she is going to have to wait for him to suggest it, or make a move on her. She thinks that last night she did make the first move, and he did respond, but will two nights in a row make him wary? It's not exactly casual, is it, two nights on the trot? He did seem to be enjoying himself, but he was quiet all the way through it. Amarjit used to talk to her during sex, which even at the time she'd thought was weird but it was quite sexy too, this constant narrative of *yeah baby that's it take it* and *you're so wet for me aren't you you needy little bitch*. Once Fraser got down to it he hadn't said anything. He hadn't guided her or given her instructions when she went down on him, apart from once when he stroked her cheek and

235

she looked up and caught his eye and he closed both of his, as if it was too much.

What does that even mean? she wonders. He said it was good. Not great. Not amazing. Maybe it was just okay, and he's given it a go and he's really not bothered.

And he didn't come until right at the end. She'd thought he would want to come in her mouth or on her face or her breasts. But they were fucking and he lifted her thigh higher so her knee was up to her chest and he went really deep, gasped and swore and that was when.

Was it good, though? Was she good? Is she good enough for him, even just as a casual fuck?

She wasn't good enough for Amarjit.

It hurts now, she thinks, bringing the casserole over to the table and placing it carefully on the trivet, but for some reason it hurts much less than she thought it would. It's as if she is watching it from this distance, seeing Rachel being so wounded and feeling nothing but sorrow for her. There is a strange sort of clarity that has appeared out of nowhere. She used to think, *who am I without him?* – as if she had no definition, no shape, except that which he had given her. She had shaped herself into Amarjit's lover, into something she'd thought he wanted and needed and loved. And without him she had felt inconsequential, half of something, irrelevant. She wants to blame him for that, for making her want him so badly that she lost her sense of self, but it wasn't his fault. He didn't want her to dissolve against him.

He didn't, actually, want her at all.

She thinks that if he had told the truth at any point she would have been okay. It was the lies that did it. Because you will tell yourself lies in order to believe that someone you love is telling the truth.

That's what happens when you're infatuated, she thinks. Your judgment is clouded by it.

Is that what's happening now, too? From outside, she can hear the sound of the quad's engine getting louder. Listens to

236

it idling for a second, and then cutting out. The vibrations of the engine feel suddenly weirdly, intensely erotic. It's a curious thrill that goes through her, almost fear. As if she's afraid of what she might say, what she might do, especially given what she's just been thinking about in detail. She takes a breath in, holds it, squeezes her thighs together.

He's coming for me.

She brings over the vegetables and the serving spoons, and there's a knock at the door. Everyone looks over and Fraser comes in, huge, filling the doorway.

'I'll just be a minute,' she says, not looking at him. Her cheeks are hot from the steam coming off the veg.

'Aren't you lucky?' Jane says, nudging Carol. 'Does he always come to give you a lift back?'

'Only when it's raining,' Fraser says.

But the truth is he's come to get her every evening for quite a while now. Even when it's sunny.

Fraser

Without a word he goes into the outbuilding, out of the rain. If she doesn't follow him, he'll come back out again. Make some excuse.

But she does, and he holds her very tightly and kisses her straight away. He's hard, again, but he's been hard most of the day, thinking about last night. It hasn't felt quite real.

She makes a sound when he kisses her, like a gasp. It takes her a second and then she's kissing him back, and he's so happy about it that he could actually cry with relief.

He has been thinking about this morning's conversation, about the things she said when he was too busy staring at her to pay full attention, thinking she was just wittering on because she was nervous or embarrassed or regretting what had happened. Now he's thought about it, he has decided – although such a thing seems so unlikely as to be almost impossible – that actually she might be willing to do it again.

I can be happy on my own, she had said. And then, again, that thing she said about *the option of occasional good sex* with someone she's attracted to. He thinks she must have been referring to him. So she's okay about them both being single, about there being no commitment, about them just having sex. Occasionally.

He manoeuvres her back until her bottom hits the washing machine, hoists her up on to it. Now she's more on his level, his mouth near hers, her arms around his neck. He unzips her jacket and puts his hands around her waist, tugging at her top, trying to find bare skin. Through the wall he can hear a woman laughing. Not sure which one it is, but he thinks of them as interchangeable, the prof's women. Last time they were here he'd caught them at it, the three of them. He hadn't intended to; he had been up on the cliff and some movement had caught his eye. His binoculars had sought out the movement and he'd found himself looking at one of the back windows of the observatory, the three of them on the bed. Of course he had looked away quickly, laughed at it.

Thought a lot about it since then, mind you.

She pulls back, suddenly. 'Stop,' she says, breathless.

He stops kissing her, stops stroking her. Leaves his hand where it is, though, because he can't quite bring himself to remove it yet.

'What?'

'They'll wonder why they haven't heard the quad.'

'Right.'

He helps her down from her perch and they go outside to the quad. Her arm tight around his waist. He has a vague thought about her hand dropping down lower, thinks that he would crash if she did.

Rachel goes for a shower while he finishes dinner. He's done lamb, slow-roasted, with new potatoes. He's gone easy on the garlic. He's put a bottle of wine on the table, one of the better ones. It's not a seduction attempt; he just thinks he could do with a glass of something alcoholic. There is no whisky left, which is what he really wants. He has added it to the list for Friday, but Friday feels a long way off.

Stop it, he thinks. *Just stop.*

Lefty comes in through the back door into the hallway. He comes into the kitchen, dripping.

'Where the fuck have you been?' Fraser asks, his voice rising.

Lefty looks at him in surprise. 'Chickens,' he says.

Lefty has something of a relationship with the five chickens. He has gradually taken over the care of them, and by and large he has done a good job. He's not so good at tending to injuries and mite infestations – Fraser still gets called on to deal with that – but Lefty is the one who feeds them, cleans the coop, changes the water and makes sure they're locked away. If he isn't in his room, then the first place Fraser always looks for him is outside in the workshop, where probably he will be cradling one of the hens in his lap, talking to her. He thinks he has probably named them all, although he told him not to.

'What's goin' on?' Lefty asks warily. He's standing in the doorway with the can of Coke he's just retrieved from the fridge.

'Nothing,' Fraser says.

'Smells good. What is it?'

'Roast lamb.'

'Ah.'

There is a long pause. Fraser's back is to the doorway but he can sense Lefty is still there. He has developed an acute sense of where he is at all times. He turns his back to Lefty often. It's like a challenge. A dare. He knows that if the lad moved towards him it would be slow. His own reactions are faster. He knows that he can think more quickly than Lefty can move.

'You want some?' he asks, at last.

Now he looks round. Lefty is looking startled. 'Me?'

'Don't see anyone else in here.'

'You mean – I can take some tae ma room?'

'No, you fucker – you eat my food, you sit at my table. You want some, or not?'

'Aye,' he says, eyes wide.

'Right, then. You lay the table.'

Something about Lefty coming in, water dripping off him, has reminded him of the first night.

Fraser had gone back up to the lighthouse, had left the kid down at the harbour with Robert. He had been raging, absolutely raging. In the kitchen he had drunk a glass of vodka and then another one straight after. An hour later he had gone outside to find the lad crouched on the doorstep. It was raining, and he was wet through.

'The fuck are you doing?' he'd said.

No reply. Just a wild shrug.

Fraser had assumed he was on something. He'd marched back down to the harbour, not looking back to see if Lefty was following. If he did, he might just pick the boy up and throw him into the water.

Robert was still there, the motor on the boat idling. He'd been just about to cast off. 'Cannae wait any longer,' he'd said. 'He coming, or what?'

Fraser had looked round at last, and there was no sign. 'He fucking better be. He's not staying here.'

At Fraser's insistence, he and Robert had both gone back up to the lighthouse. But the lad wasn't there any more: he'd disappeared. They had performed a quick search of the lighthouse – the door was never locked, of course, so he might have gone inside – and the outbuildings, but there was no sign of him.

Robert had said, 'I'll miss the tide …'

So the boat had left. Fraser had stood on the jetty, rigid with fury, watching it go. The wind had picked up, it was raining, but he'd barely felt it. When the boat was out of sight around the bay he'd walked back via the cottages, in case he'd decided to hide there, but there was nothing. By then it was getting dark, the rain hard, the wind biting.

He had walked up the hill to the lighthouse, feeling sick with it. Thinking that at any minute a crazed wee figure might jump out at him, push him backwards, that he'd end up in the loch.

Inside he had searched the lighthouse from top to bottom, even those small spaces where a human body couldn't possibly hide, all the time muttering, 'I'll get you, you wee fucker, come out, show yourself.' But there was nothing. He'd known the boy wasn't in the house anyway, because Bess was watching all this, utterly baffled. He had made cheese on toast, fed Bess, drunk vodka. Woken up chilled on the sofa at eleven. Outside, the wind had been blowing a fierce gale, rain hammering at the windows on the eastern side. He'd wondered again where the boy was. Even if he had found shelter somewhere – the cottages, maybe – it would be freezing cold, damp. If he was anywhere at all, other than the bird observatory, then he would probably not survive. There was also the possibility that he'd been on the boat; that he'd got on board while Fraser and Robert were at the lighthouse, that he'd stowed away somewhere. That was the best bet. But somehow Fraser knew in the pit of his stomach, swilling sourly, that that wasn't what had happened.

He had thought about going to look, but he was still staggering drunk and, although the rage had gone, what was left behind was just a sort of dull nausea; he'd known he should care but he absolutely couldn't find the energy to do it. It could wait till morning.

Now, he looks at Lefty, sees him look up and smile as Rachel comes in, hair still damp, like all the colours of autumn. The sour feeling is still there in his stomach. He doesn't touch vodka any more.

'I'm having dinner,' Lefty says brightly.

'So I see. That's brilliant. Anything I can do to help?'

'No,' Fraser says. 'Sit. Eat.'

Rachel

Downstairs, she is surprised to see Lefty sitting at the kitchen table looking pleased with himself. Fraser's expression is giving nothing away. He must have issued some sort of invitation; there's no way Lefty would have taken it upon himself to ask if he could eat with them, for all Rachel's efforts in getting them together.

Fraser pours the wine. To everyone's surprise, he tips the bottle questioningly in Lefty's direction.

'No,' he says, wiggling the can of Coke. 'Thank you.'

Rachel's grateful for it, though. She is bone-tired, thinks that drinking is probably a bad idea, but, like most of her bad ideas, she is going to do it anyway.

'This is cool,' she says.

'What's that?' says Fraser, without looking up.

'Having a meal together. Isn't it?'

Fraser shrugs and says nothing.

'Aye,' says Lefty. He looks from one of them to the other and then back at his plate. He's a noisy eater when he gets going. There is no picking at the meat today. He is going for it as if he hasn't eaten in days.

'What did you do today, Lefty?'

'Checking the trap. Fixing holes.'

'The bird trap, thing? For the passerines?'

'The Heligoland, aye.'

'Anything in it?' Fraser asks.

'No,' says Lefty. 'All empty. There was a big hole in the top netting right enough.'

She watches them eating, the two of them, both heads down. The conversation stalls. Even so, she feels that some massive leap forward has taken place, unexpectedly. There's a silence but, unlike the other day, there doesn't seem to be that tense hostility.

Lefty finishes eating first. Given how he's been inhaling his plateful, this is not a surprise. He sits there awkwardly for a minute, looking up furtively, wondering what's expected of him. This is clearly new territory.

'Go on, then,' Fraser murmurs, 'if that's what you want.'

'Thanks,' Lefty says, takes his plate to the sink, washes it up very quickly and scoots off to his room.

Rachel sips her wine, waiting for Fraser to look up. Eventually he does. She catches herself in his gaze and tries to read his expression. It's completely blank. 'That was nice,' she says.

His mouth twists in a grin. 'If you say so.'

'Nice of you to ask him.'

'Well, he was here. And I thought you'd like it.'

'I did like it. Maybe we could do this more often. Maybe – once a week?'

'Maybe.'

That's as much as she's going to get.

They've both finished eating. Minutes pass. Rachel sips her wine.

'I'd suggest Monopoly,' he says.

That wasn't what she'd been expecting. 'But?'

'You'd beat me. I've no ability to concentrate.'

'Me neither. I'm a bit tired, I think.'

'Aye. Wonder why that is.'

What she wants right now, what she really wants, is to go upstairs and get into bed with him and curl up against his warm, solid human body and sleep. She thinks about how this isn't something she's supposed to ask for, how really she's supposed to wait for him to do the running; that she has made this mistake before. That you shouldn't be too keen. That you shouldn't ask; you should wait, you should take what you're given and you're supposed to be grateful for everything. She wonders if he has any inkling of all this *should* and *supposed to* going on in her head. She wonders if he has ever thought about what *he* should do, or whether he just does what he wants, whenever he wants to do it.

She drinks the rest of her wine in one gulp. 'Can we go to bed?'

Fraser

She says she just wants to be held. There is half an hour or so during which he holds her as requested and is quite happy to do so. But then the holding becomes touching and then long, deep kissing, her hands on his face and then on his body, and then there's a point where he has to ask her to stop.

'I changed my mind. I don't want to be just held,' she says.

'What do you want?' he asks.

'I want to be on top,' she says.

'Right, then. Off you go.'

He prefers to be in control, it has to be said. He has always been in control because that's just the way things have been. But right now he wants her to get exactly what she wants, and he wants to be there to watch her face as she gets it.

There is something intensely sexy about holding her hips loosely as she moves. His hands on her waist, trying hard to concentrate or it'll be over in seconds. Counting kittiwakes in his head. Thinking of the time he drove to Arbroath in the summer and got sick with food poisoning from a supermarket sandwich. The telephone number of his flat in Aberdeen, twelve years ago.

He slips his fingers in between their bodies and times it carefully, watching her face. Tries to hold back, tries to wait for her. Can't. He explodes inside her. He has to grab hold of her to stop her toppling over.

She's on her back, breathing hard. Without looking at her, he mumbles, 'Sorry.'

'What for?'

'That was too quick.'

'Well, that was my fault, not yours.'

He turns on to his side so he can look at her. Rests his hand on her stomach, fingers tracing the patterns. 'I like these,' he says, eventually.

She looks down. 'They're stretch marks.'

'I know what they are. I'm saying I like them.'

'I have a spongy belly,' she says, moving it with the palm of her hand to demonstrate.

'I like that too.'

It's soft, lightly rounded, painted with tiger stripes. He bends to plant a kiss, ends up staying there.

'You're a little bit mad,' she murmurs.

'It's not just that I like it,' he says, moving lower, lifting her knee. 'It's the proof of what you did. Of how brave you were, how selfless. It's like the medal Emily gave you to say thank you for helping to give her life.'

Rachel makes a little 'hmph' which might be agreement. 'Lucy emailed me about Emily's christening a while back,' she says. 'She wants me to RSVP.'

'When is it?'

'The twenty-seventh of July.'

'That's ages away.'

'I know, and there's a chance I might still be here then. I'm sort of counting on it, to be honest – that would be a really good excuse.'

'She wants to know now?'

'That's Lucy for you. She'll be crafting personalised table decorations. Will you come with me, if I get forced into it? I realise I'm not selling it as an exciting prospect.'

'If you want me to,' he says, a little bit distracted.

'Promise?'

He settles himself between her thighs. Uses his tongue. Takes his time with it, edges her for as long as he can. Eventually she grabs at his head, panting, pushing him away. He kisses her thigh, not quite wanting to move away from what he thinks is the best view on the island.

'You're a bit bloody good at that,' she says, when she gets her breath back.

'Well,' he says, 'I'm glad you think so. I could do with more practice.'

'I'm the one who's out of practice. Even for someone who's practically celibate you probably had sex more recently than me.'

He moves up the bed. She snuggles against him. His hand in her hair.

'Who said anything about celibate?'

She looks up at him. 'Oh. I just assumed ...'

'Well, don't assume.'

'So when was the last time you had sex?'

He thinks. Has to think quite hard about whether he really wants to go there. 'Just before Christmas.'

'Seriously? Who with?'

She shifts on to her belly, props herself on to her elbows. Now he can feel the full force of her eyes on the side of his face.

'A friend.'

'A friend?'

'I do have some.'

'A female friend?'

'Aye. I have one or two of those.' Actually, that's probably not entirely true, he thinks. 'Well, one.'

'But not a relationship?'

'No. Just someone I see occasionally.'

'Like a fuck buddy?'

'Jesus, Rachel. So many questions. No. More of a ... whatever you'd call it. Friend with benefits.'

'Oh. Right.'

'Look,' he says, 'while we're talking about it. I'd better tell you something. In the interests of being honest.'

He risks a glance at her, sees the way her eyes look. She's braced herself.

'I used to work on the rigs,' he says, by way of introduction.

'And?'

'You don't meet women on the rigs. Well, not in those days, probably a lot more of them now, but maybe not the sort of women who really want to fuck men, I don't know. Anyway. So there's a certain way you go about things.'

'What are you trying to say? Just spit it out.'

'I had some one-night stands,' he says. 'And, you know, more often than not, I paid for it.'

'You paid for sex?'

'Aye.'

'You mean with sex workers?'

'Right.'

'Oh.'

'So this friend you slept with before Christmas...' she says.

'What about her?'

'Is she a sex worker?'

Man, all the questions. Does he really want to do this? He can't very well just stop the conversation dead, now he's started. Besides, better to get it out of the way. If she wants nothing more to do with him, at least he's been here, with her. In his bed. Done all this.

'Not any more. She was. Years ago.'

'That's how you met her?'

'Aye.'

'What's her name?'

He takes a deep breath in.

'I don't see why you need—'

'Because she's a person, Fraser. I don't want to be thinking of her as a random former sex worker.'

He doesn't want Rachel to be thinking of her at all, really, but he doesn't feel up to arguing the point.

'Kelly. Her name's Kelly.'

He looks at her. Her expression is unreadable.

'I should have told you before, maybe. But it's not something that you can just say.'

'It's really none of my business,' she says.

'No, it's not.'

'It possibly would be my business, if we were going to have a relationship. But since we're not – I don't know why you told me.'

'I don't know either,' he says, hesitant.

'It's called oversharing.'

'It's called being honest.'

Her mouth twitches. He can actually feel himself blushing.

247

'I'll understand if you – you know… If you want to end it there.'

She rolls over on to her back with a sigh. 'I can't think about it. My brain is fried.'

'I know what you mean.'

'Is it all right if I sleep for a bit?'

'All right?'

'I mean, do you want me to go?'

He looks at her shoulder, a little bit horrified. 'No. I don't want you to go.'

'I can sleep here? With you?'

'Why are you even asking?'

'Because we're not in a relationship. Sleeping with someone, it's an intimate thing.'

Her voice is slow, drowsy, as though she's already drifting. He turns on his side towards her, wraps his arm around her waist, pulls her back against him. 'It's a practical thing. Warm. And you're too tired to get up now, anyway, aren't you.'

She doesn't answer. He thinks she might already be asleep.

Rachel

In Fraser's bedroom there is a framed photo of a young woman on the top of his chest of drawers.

Rachel is lying in bed, in warm sunshine, and, although she knows she needs to get up and go and sort out the bird observatory, she's comfortable and happy and doesn't really want to move. Fraser is long gone, out somewhere with Lefty. She remembers hearing him get up but he didn't wake her, and she likes that he seems happy for her to stay here.

She gets up and takes a closer look at the picture. It's a close-up, head and shoulders, of a young woman – maybe a teenager. Eyes squinting against the sunlight, tip of her tongue poking out, head tilted to one side, the expression deliberately

248

cheeky, challenging. Long hair tied in one of those ridiculous buns perched right on the top of her head, two strands of hair loose on either side of her face.

Maggie, she guesses.

She wonders how long it was after the photo was taken that she died. It doesn't seem a particularly flattering photo to have on display, but perhaps Maggie wasn't the sort to pose for photographs. Maybe this is just the best picture there is, or maybe it's the only one. Or maybe it's the last one.

And then her eyes alight on something else, stuck incongruously on the side of the wardrobe. It's a child's picture, roughly crayonned on to a piece of A4. Three stick figures and a small black scribble with four legs. One of the stick figures is very much taller than the other two. With a black squiggle beard and two dots for eyes.

There is no sign of the knife on the bedside table, which is some relief. There is a pile of books – a Dickens; two she recognises as part of last year's Booker shortlist; Sam Warburton's autobiography. The room is painted dark blue, which makes it feel like a cave on the occasions she has looked in from the doorway; but in here, sitting on the edge of the rumpled bed, with the sunshine on the sheets, it's as if the room has been transported to somewhere far warmer and brighter than the Isle of Must; it feels different. Cosy. Sensual. Dramatic.

Strange how this feels comforting and familiar, given that really she doesn't know Fraser at all. Who is responsible for the child's drawing? Did Maggie have a child? Is Fraser an uncle to someone, or is he a father himself? She likes to think he would have told her, but everything he has shared with her has come out reluctantly.

He doesn't do relationships, and yet he has been seeing someone for years. Even if he only sees this Kelly infrequently, even if he thinks of her as a friend, or a friend with benefits, what he has with her is what Rachel would describe as a relationship. She wonders how Kelly would describe it. And what is it about Kelly that has turned her from a one-off visit for the purposes of sex, to someone he has seen regularly for years? Why is he friends with her, and not any of the others?

Later, Fraser comes to the bird observatory. She has emptied the dishwasher and given the rug a vacuum. Now she is about to start cooking.

He blasts in and fills the space the way he usually does, but there is something in the way he's not looking at her.

'You seen that email?' he says at last.

She pulls the phone from her back pocket and checks – there is one from Marion, titled 'Visit Monday'.

'Shit – she's actually coming over?'

'Looks like it.'

Rachel's heart sinks. She had been so looking forward to this week, her first with no birdwatchers booked in. Now she will have to spend the whole weekend after Brian and Carol and Jane leave cleaning, scraping the bird shit off the low wall outside, making things look the way Marion would approve of. She wonders whether Fraser will have time to clear the guttering, which overflows when it rains. And then she sees his face.

'What are we going to do about Lefty?'

He doesn't answer immediately, just takes a deep breath in. Then he says, 'Maybe the weather will turn.'

'Is it supposed to be good for Monday?'

'Bright and sunny.'

'Could he go back on the boat with Robert on Friday?'

'Back? Back where?'

'Um, the mainland? Back to wherever he came from? Isn't that what you want him to do?'

He's silent for so long that she goes to the kitchen and puts the kettle on, thinking that even the crappy instant coffee might help. She half-expects him to leave again but he's still standing there in the doorway, lost in thought. She comes up and touches his arm and he actually starts.

'Take your boots off,' she says. 'Sit down and have a coffee. Don't look like that, it's not that bad.'

He does as she tells him and while she waits for the kettle she thinks he looks utterly defeated, his hands between his knees, his head down. The birders are off somewhere in the sunshine enjoying themselves, thank goodness, although they might come back at any moment. It's an hour till dinner.

She brings two mugs through and sits next to him on the sofa, her hand on his back.

'I can't think straight,' he says, managing a brief grin that disappears as soon as it's landed. 'For some reason my thoughts are all over the place at the moment.'

'Okay,' she says, wondering what that's supposed to mean. Is she responsible for his state of mind? Because she's been keeping him up at night and distracting him?

She drinks her tea and thinks. He is staring at the coffee as if it's poisoned.

'Look, it's the bird observatory and the cottages she's interested in, right?'

'Aye, but—'

'How long between the tides? I mean, how long can she stay before the boat has to go back?'

'A couple of hours,' he says.

'Well, she can't pack that much into a couple of hours. I can do lunch for her here – what time's the boat coming?'

'Early.'

'Well, I can do elevenses or something. We can show her the cottages with her experts, then I'll bring her straight over here, tell her there's no time to be hanging about. And Lefty can stay in his room. I'm sure he has no great desire to see her either, right?'

He shakes his head slowly.

'What is it that's bothering you?' she asks softly.

A long pause. 'Feels like a risk,' he says.

'Well, we just need a Plan B. If she sees him, then we'll just say he's your nephew, over for a visit because there are no birders next week. Or something like that.'

'My nephew?' he says, snorting.

'Well, we need to agree on something just in case. Yes?'

At last he looks up at her, touches her cheek. 'He's right, what he said about you.'

'What did he say?'

But he doesn't answer. Just kisses her.

There's a sound from outside and she pulls away from him awkwardly just seconds before the door opens.

'Ah, Fraser! Good to see you!'

Rachel picks up the mugs – Fraser hasn't touched his, of course – and heads to the kitchen to get the dinner ready. Brian is on his own. Carol and Jane are still photographing puffins, apparently. Outside the sun is low and everything is golden and bright.

It feels as though nothing bad could happen, and yet at the same time Rachel has an ominous feeling in her stomach.

Fraser

Against his better judgment he lets Rachel invite Lefty to eat with them again. He casts a suspicious glance from one of them to the other, sensing that something is up.

He's done salmon, poached with lemon, and salad. Lefty isn't keen on any sort of fish that doesn't come wrapped in batter but he sits with them and Fraser lets him have some bread and butter and fucking ketchup with it as a compromise. He listens while Rachel talks about Marion coming, phrasing it carefully as if it's no big deal. If it were down to him he wouldn't have said anything until Monday in case it doesn't happen – Marion has been threatening to come for a visit since she first started, after all – and he can see the alarm spreading across Lefty's face as Rachel mentions the visit.

'She's comin' here?' he asks, his voice high. 'Is that definite?'

'No,' Rachel says, gently, 'but it looks quite likely. So we need to be prepared for it.'

He looks at Fraser, eyes wide. 'You gonnae send me away on the boat?'

Fraser doesn't look up from his meal. He feels morose and pissed off and can't quite manage to articulate what exactly he's worried about.

'He's not going to send you away,' Rachel says firmly.

I fucking would, though, he thinks. It would be the ideal solution: send the fucker back where he came from, get rid of him. Then it would just be him and Rachel and—

'I cannae go back,' Lefty says, almost rising to a wail.

'Look,' Rachel says, 'it's fine, honestly. She won't come to the lighthouse, she doesn't need to. You just need to stay in your room for a couple of hours. Lock the door, if you want to.'

'I don't, I can't,' he says, looking panicked.

Fraser lifts his eyes wearily. 'He doesn't like locked doors.'

'Don't lock me in!'

'Of course we won't lock you in,' she says, soothing. 'It'll be fine. Really it will. And if the weather turns, she might not come at all.'

'What if she does? What if she wants a tour of the lighthouse? What if she comes in?'

Rachel looks at Fraser. He shrugs and looks away. He senses her exasperation but this is all utterly beyond him just now. He doesn't want to even think about it.

'If that happens,' Rachel says, 'and, look, it's really unlikely…but, if it does, then we'll just introduce you as Fraser's nephew. Say you're over for a visit.'

'What?' If anything, he looks even more panicked than before. 'But I'm no' his nephew!'

'It won't come to that. It's just a back-up plan, right? You won't have to say anything to her. It'll be fine.'

'Told you we should have left it,' Fraser mutters.

Lefty takes another two slices of bread and legs it to his bedroom. His piece of salmon is largely untouched, despite a bloody smear of ketchup. Fraser gets up and scrapes it into Bess's bowl, where it is despatched in a matter of seconds.

'I'm sure it'll be fine,' she says. 'Why is he so scared of going back?'

He thought this might happen: that this would lead on to a discussion about Lefty. He is no better equipped to explain things than he was when she first arrived, because he doesn't understand it himself. He has not even managed to think everything through, because he has very deliberately not thought about it. Now he gives a non-committal shrug.

'This is all really frustrating, you know,' she says.

'I know.'

'Do you think she'll like cheese scones?'

'Aye, of course she will. I'll make veg soup over the week-end if you like; you can heat that up for her.'

'Really? Thanks. That would make me feel better. Although—'

'What?'

'Feels like cheating.'

'For fuck's sake don't tell her I made it, even if she asks. I don't want to get lumbered with cooking if that Julia woman doesn't work out.'

'You have my word,' she says solemnly.

He catches her eye, then, and he's lost. He still can't quite believe that he's had her in his bed and just a few hours ago he was kissing her. He feels that surge of hot desire again and for a moment it's all gone – Marion, Lefty, the birds, all of it. Just her. Just that desperate desire to get inside her again, the place where he's suddenly decided everything is all right, even if it's just temporary.

'You,' she says, and smiles.

'Me?'

'The way you're looking at me.'

'Sorry.'

'Don't be. I like it. You look like you want something.'

'Aye. Of course I do.'

Her gaze is unrelenting. 'I'll be honest, I'm still getting my head around it.'

'Me too.'

'You really want me?'

'Jesus, Rachel. Are you kidding?'

'I mean, I feel a bit competitive about it.'

'What do you mean?'

'I don't know if I've met anyone who's been with a sex worker before.'

Not for the first time, he wishes he hadn't told her. She would probably never have found out, and in a few weeks' time she will be gone and he will never see her again. But he had that desperate need to be honest with her, felt she deserved it. His truth.

Besides, he's not ashamed of it.

'You probably have and you just don't know it. It's more common than you think it is. Why? Is it bothering you?'

'I wouldn't say that. I just ... I think I'd like to know more about it. Why you do it.'

'Because it's easy,' he says.

'Easier than going on dates?'

'Going on a date implies you'll be wanting a second date. It's not a good thing to lead people on, is it? It's not fair. It's disrespectful.'

She considers this. 'But what about the women? Aren't they trafficked, vulnerable? Isn't it disrespectful to just use them for sex?'

'I'll admit it's not ideal. But I was always careful about things like consent. I never went with anyone who was drunk, or drugged up.'

'And it was ... good?' she asks.

Of all the questions, he thinks. Probably what she's really asking is if she is enough. The thought of this, that she feels as if she's being compared to the women he paid, hurts his head a bit.

'Sometimes,' he says.

'Is that why you keep going back to Kelly? Because she's really good at it?'

He has already been thinking of Kelly, of course; from the minute the idea of comparison was brought up he has been thinking of her, the stress of seeing her and the stress of not seeing her, the way he hates himself because if he pays he feels like shit about it and if he doesn't pay he feels even worse. He still finds Kelly attractive, but the hot, fizzing desire he felt for her years ago is no longer there. In truth he still sleeps with her sometimes because he can, and if she won't let him pay in cash then he pays in other ways. Fixing things. Buying things that she needs, or Charlie needs. The fierce lust that he feels when he looks at Rachel – he thinks about Kelly and it's not like that at all.

But he can't tell her that. Can he?

'When you want to stop,' he says, deliberately not answering her question, 'you just say, right?'

'I don't want to stop.'

'You will,' he says.

Rachel

Friday.

Rachel is waiting on the jetty for the boat. She's done a cursory beach clean while she's been waiting, and after a few minutes of collecting – crisp packets, bits of nylon rope, a tangled ball of fishing wire – she hears the quad up on the cliff. A minute later Fraser is coming down the slope, the trailer full of luggage and empty plastic crates. When he kills the engine she can hear the diesel chugging of the boat.

It's a nice day today, hazy sunshine and complete stillness, the first day she thinks she has felt no wind at all. The water in the harbour is still, huge mats of seaweed rising and falling gently.

Carol and Jane and Brian are going home today. Rachel will miss them; they've been her favourite guests so far. They've talked to her more than anyone else, thanked her more than anyone else, asked her how she is every time they've seen her. After a week she has almost begun to think of them as friends, although now they're leaving and the chances are she'll never see them again.

Fraser comes to stand next to her on the jetty.

'Hello,' she says.

'Hello yourself.'

She has been back in her own bed for the past few nights. No reason in particular, although if she's honest she has been thinking a lot about Kelly. Despite the fact that there has been a mild sort of flirting going on, Rachel has gone to bed early in an attempt to catch up on sleep; she hasn't heard him come upstairs. He has been out with Lefty before she's got up in the morning.

A moment later the *Island Princess* chugs around the corner, bright and cheerful in the sunshine. Behind her, the Prof and Carol and Jane come down the hill, chattering and laughing.

Fraser helps to make the boat fast, and then there's the ritual handing over of crates of shopping, the return of the empty crates, the brief exchange of news between Fraser and Robert, since he won't be coming back tomorrow; there are no new guests this week. Then the passengers are helped aboard, goodbyes are said. And they're off.

'Better get on with it, I suppose,' Rachel says.

'I'll give you a ride back.'

At the bird observatory he offers to help, but she has a system now and, besides, he has a million other jobs to do.

The cleaning doesn't take her long at all. She will give it a second going-over at the weekend, make everything look super-smart for Marion on Monday. And it turns out she only has one set of bedding to launder.

She thinks about Brian and Carol and Jane, the three of them in their relationship, how it works, whether it works. They all seemed happy enough, didn't they? And they've been coming here for years, in that same relationship, so it's lasted a long time. There are religions that allow polygamy. Rachel thinks they all seem to be about enabling men to have multiple partners while still remaining virtuous in their particular faiths; she wonders if there are any religions that allow women to have multiple husbands.

Not that she wants more than one.

Not that she wants a husband at all.

Fraser

Tonight's wine is a good rioja. Should go well with the tagliatelle he's made from scratch, with tomato and olive sauce.

The boat has brought a veritable cellarful of wine. Despite that, Fraser is wondering how long he can make it last. It's not that he wants to drink. It's not that he needs to drink. Perhaps what the bottles represent is a reason to sit in the kitchen or in the lounge for an hour or so after they've finished eating.

When he'd emailed the order through, Craig had actually phoned him to discuss it, the nosy bastard.

'She there with you?'

'No. She's upstairs. Why?'

'How youse two getting on, then?'

'Fine.'

'Aye?'

'Aye. Why d'you ask?'

'No problems with her?'

'If there were, I'd say so.'

'Ah. The wine for her, is it?'

'No.'

'Jesus, Fraser, could you be any more cagey?'

'Everything's fine,' he'd said, with a heavy sigh.

Craig had made a hmm noise and Fraser could hear the smirk in his voice and he thought he was being laughed at. He'd felt the anger rise in his throat, swallowed it down.

'You got me decent bottles, I hope?'

'Ha! You expecting vintage stuff?'

'I'm expecting something I can actually drink.'

'You going to manage five bottles in a week? Plus whisky?'

'I'm paying you the extra, it's none of your fucking business.'

'I'm assuming you're sharing it.'

'I'll pass you the empties; you can think all you fucking like.'

He'd ended the call. Craig was fishing for gossip. What was he expecting? That he and Rachel were best pals? Or did he want to hear that suddenly Fraser was drinking himself to oblivion every night?

After dinner they take the bottle into the lounge. From Lefty's room next door comes the sound of some loud movie with car chases and machine guns. He thinks about suggesting a game of Scrabble or something but instead he finds himself kissing her, and she's kissing him back hard enough for him to realise that this is going somewhere. The condoms – a dwindling supply – are upstairs. He can't bring himself to go upstairs and get them and he doesn't want to interrupt things to suggest they move, so he contents himself with his hand inside her jeans, his fingers slipping inside her while she fidgets and squirms and he kisses her harder.

'Lie down,' he says, after a while.

She is flushed, breathing hard. 'What if Lefty hears?' she says.

He is pulling her jeans down, easing her bum up on to the arm of the sofa so she is just at the right height. 'You'll just have to try hard to keep quiet,' he murmurs against her.

Her fingers tangle through his hair as he lifts her thigh over his shoulder. He's going to make her wait a while, but not too long – even he has no desire to be confronted with Lefty at the door, although once he's in his room Lefty rarely comes out again. But he's decided this is almost his favourite thing, his mouth on her, besides which, he is learning what works and what doesn't. He's been paying attention.

259

After a while he feels her hand on his cheek.

'Hey,' she says. 'Stop.'

He moves up to her and kisses her. 'You okay?'

'I just – I don't know. Thinking too much.'

'Hm. What about?'

She doesn't answer straight away. Pulls up her jeans, finds her glass of wine, discarded on the coffee table. 'Nothing important. I think it's just too hard to relax with Lefty next door.'

Fucking Lefty.

'And Marion coming on Monday.'

Oh aye, fucking Marion.

'I was thinking about the cottages,' she says.

'What about them?'

'Do you think we need to clean them up a bit?'

'What, for her visit? No, fuck that. She should see them exactly as they are.'

'I guess you're right. Anyway, it's not my job to worry about all of that, is it?'

'Oh, aye,' he says, 'you're going to bugger off soon and I'll get Julia. I'd forgotten about her.'

'She'll be good with the birdwatchers,' she says.

'Aye, maybe. Bit different from lichens, though. At least lichens don't shit on you from a great height.'

'Although neither do birdwatchers, generally.'

It's not even particularly funny but for some reason it tickles her; she laughs and then she can't stop laughing.

'I don't want you to think…' he says, and then stops.

'What?' she asks. 'You don't want me to think what?'

'That I'm using you. For sex.'

A slow smile spreads across her mouth. He can't take his eyes off her. She sips at the wine, looking at him over the rim of her glass. 'Maybe *I'm* using *you* for sex,' she says. 'After all, I keep ending up in your bed.'

'Well,' he says, 'whatever.'

There is a long pause, in which he thinks about just taking her by the hand and going upstairs.

'This isn't a relationship, though,' she says, and the way she says it feels like cold water.

'No,' he answers, slowly. 'Does that matter?'

'No,' she says. She leans forward, takes the wine bottle off the table and fills his glass, and hers. The bottle's empty now. 'I think the issue is that you and I have very different ideas of what a relationship is. And the main point is … it's just a word.'

He doesn't answer that.

'Why don't you do relationships?'

She's going to keep at it, he thinks. They were always going to have this conversation. The trick is to allow it to happen, allow her to ask. The trick is to get through the next few minutes without getting angry. He focuses on her mouth, the shape of it, the fact that he wants to kiss her again but she would think he was just doing it to shut her up.

'Because I don't want to be responsible for someone else's happiness.'

'What about your happiness?'

He can't respond to that. It's never even crossed his mind.

'Your head is too full of feelings to let anything else in,' she says.

He barks a laugh. 'I can assure you there is nothing swimming around in my head, feelings or anything else. Other than maybe wine.'

'That's because they've all gone hard and solid, like a brick, weighing you down. You've got no room for anything else.'

stones in my pockets

'Is that a problem?'

'Well, it isn't, it's fine. But it doesn't seem very healthy. Human beings are designed to be in pairs, and—'

Man, it comes from nowhere. Surges up, pushed up from his gut by the shame and the knowledge that she's right and he hates himself more than he hates anyone else right now. 'What is it you want? You want the two of us to fall in love and get married and have babies?'

It's as if he wants her to flinch. But she doesn't.

261

'I just want you to be a bit more open to yourself. Not sitting there like … like … a padlocked cupboard, or something.'

'What the fuck? Why do you even care? You'll be away to your family soon enough.'

'Yes, I will. Which proves my point. This isn't anything to do with me. It's about you being kinder to yourself.'

He's looking at the bottom of the wine glass, the last of the wine spiralling as he twists the glass in his fingers.

'There's no point in committing,' he says. 'I can't commit to anything. To anyone. Ever.'

'Why not?' she asks.

He looks at the door. Thinks about getting up. Thinks about walking out, right now, walking away.

'Fraser? Why not?'

'Because of him,' he says.

Stop it, he thinks. *Stop it now stop it right now.*

'Because of Lefty? Why? Because you're looking after him?'

stop it don't say it don't say another word

He drinks the last of the wine.

'Because I'm going to kill him.'

9

Marion

Rachel

I'm going to kill him.

She's spent most of the day thinking about it. As soon as he said it, she could see that he was desperate to take back the words.

'What do you mean?' she'd asked.

'Nothing. Don't worry about it.'

Moments later into the subdued silence he'd announced he was tired and going to bed. She'd called his name, asked if he was okay, and he had just said goodnight.

Today he has been avoiding her as much as he can. He's been quiet over dinner and, although she's tried – more than once – to coax him into talking, he has retreated into himself.

'It was nothing,' he says, now. 'I had too much to drink, mouthing off as usual.'

They're eating a chicken stir fry, delicious as always but not as elaborate a meal as she's been used to. Fraser does look tired. Last night she slept in her own room again, listening out for him shouting, didn't hear anything. She wonders if he has slept at all.

'But it's got something to do with Lefty. What's going on between you, Fraser? Why is he here, if you hate him so much?'

'He's just an annoying little runt. I know I push him, but if I didn't he wouldn't do anything at all, just sit in there playing games all day.'

'But you said you're going to *kill* him.'

'Would you just leave it?'

He poured her wine over dinner, had half a glass himself, and no more. As soon as he finishes eating he gets up to wash up. She watches him. She can't pretend it wasn't just a little bit scary, hearing him say those words. It's not just the words themselves, it's the way he said them. There was no venom behind them, no real anger; it was just a statement of fact. Baldly put. He meant it. She knows he meant it.

And then there's the knife she saw, on her first night here. She had been wondering if maybe she imagined it, maybe had been seeing things, since she has been in Fraser's room quite a lot since then and has never seen it since. But she knows it exists, and she doesn't know where it is, and that bothers her. She'd rather it were there, in plain view, so she could keep an eye on it.

She brings her plate and the two glasses, leaves them on the counter and picks up a tea towel.

'You know I'll never hurt you,' he says. 'Right?'

That he even needs to say this adds a whole new level of concern. 'But you'd hurt him?'

'That's got nothing to do with you.'

'Does he deserve it?' she asks, shocked.

He's not going to answer that one. She can see that he's shut down again.

When the dishes are dry and put away he stands in the open doorway while Bess races out into the darkness. Rachel comes to stand next to him, her hand on his back in a gesture that's meant, somehow, to be soothing.

'I might go to the mainland,' he says. 'Once the visit from Her Majesty is out of the way.'

She frowns, confused. 'Why do you want to go to the mainland?'

She feels the muscles working under her hand as he tenses, then he moves as Bess scampers back through the door. Moves away from her, deliberately.

'I just have some things I need to do. Admin stuff.' After a moment he adds, 'You can come with me, if you like.'

She has the strongest sense that he would rather she didn't. There's nothing in what he actually says, just a feeling.

'Would you like me to?' she asks, testing him.

'It'll be boring,' he says. 'I need to do a few jobs. Get a haircut, buy some things. I'm only going for one night, maybe two.'

That's it, she thinks. To confirm, she says, 'Where are you going to stay?'

He smiles, a little, a grim sort of smile that doesn't make it up to his eyes. 'I do have a house in Anstruther. Just a wee terrace. It's where I spend most of the winter.'

She had been half-expecting him to say that he was going to stay at Kelly's house, so this makes her feel marginally better. There is no reason why he couldn't have Kelly over, of course. And, the more she thinks about it, it's entirely possible that Kelly actually lives in his house – maybe she is his tenant? After all, would you really have a house sitting empty for nine months or more of the year, without letting it out? Maybe she's actually a lot more than his tenant. Maybe they are even married, or something.

She thinks he is being deliberately evasive. She also thinks she is being suddenly, inexplicably needy, not to mention ridiculously imaginative. What he does is none of her business, as he is just stopping short of telling her. And she doesn't think he's ever lied to her, so he probably isn't now. She bites her cheek and stops herself asking him anything else.

She takes a step back from him at the exact moment that he moves towards her. His hand brushes her arm and she stops and looks at him in surprise, just as he wraps his arms around her and pulls her into a hug. 'I'm sorry,' he says, into her hair.

265

'What for?' she asks. A small pit of anxiety opens up inside her, the feeling that he's about to tell her something really awful.

'There's just some stuff I can't talk about.'

'Oh. Are you ever going to tell me about it?'

'Possibly not.'

He kisses the top of her head firmly, and releases her.

Two hours later, she is in bed when she hears him call out. A cry of alarm, as if someone has jumped on him. She has not slept yet, still thinking about the knife and the *I'm going to kill him*. Despite this, her heart thumps wildly as she waits and listens. It's all quiet. After a moment she hears him getting up, going to the bathroom. Hears his footsteps on the landing outside. A moment later there is a very soft knock at her door.

'Rachel?'

She gets up to let him in. Doesn't say anything. Just lets him.

Fraser

It's just sex, he thinks, watching her sleep.

She's turned to face him, her cheek resting on her hand, and her cool breath is faintly scented with garlic, and he wonders how, at the same time, it's a little bit unpleasant and yet he finds it utterly impossible to turn away from her.

Maybe that means it's not just sex, after all. Who knows?

He keeps staring at her just the same.

In the morning he gets up without waking her, makes porridge and coffee, collects a few things in a carrier bag, and then takes Bess down to the cottages. A thick fog is blanketing the island, a heavy stillness with the calls of the birds echoing through it. A weird sort of day. Fog sometimes settles on the Firth and stays for a long time. Fog won't stop the boat, though. They need strong winds and heavy seas for that. And the forecast for tomorrow is still fine.

He has left Lefty in bed. Today is usually the day Lefty cleans out the chickens, but, even so, he has no desire for company this morning.

The steep path disappears into the fog below him and he's aware of the loch the whole time even though he can't see it, thinking of the flat black surface and what might happen if he took a wrong turn. He's grateful when he sees the looming white shape of the terrace coming into view, and a minute later he's there.

Rachel had seen the cottages, seen what was in the second cottage, and had not commented. Maybe she hadn't noticed. Maybe she had seen it and, coming from a bustling city, had not thought it odd. But Marion will be here tomorrow and she will be looking at everything very closely, and if there's something to be noticed Marion will notice it. He cannot take the risk of leaving things as they are.

The cottages, the ravine, always make him think of Lefty. There is always a chill here, even on the warmest days of summer. Usually it is still, the walls of the ravine providing shelter from the wind, apart from on those odd days when the wind is blowing directly from the southeast, when the ravine becomes a wind tunnel and emits a sour, hollow moan that can be heard all over the island.

I'm going to kill him.

He shouldn't have said it. But the words were out before he had time to think – too much wine in his head and not enough self-control. He knows it's damaged things with Rachel. When she opened the door to him last night he could see it in her eyes, a weird sort of wariness, as if she's not sure she can trust him.

But she still let him in. Still took him in her arms and touched him and kissed him, even though he knows he doesn't deserve it.

The fact that he regrets it is only slightly worse than the fact that he can't, actually, take it back. It's not that he was exaggerating, or making a point. He absolutely means it. It has been in his head for the past five years. He is going to kill Lefty. The only decision is how, and when, and the only thing playing on his mind is that he hasn't done it yet, because he is a fucking coward and the longer he leaves it the more ashamed he is of himself.

He might have died in those first few days, and then he wouldn't still be here thinking about it.

Even now he has no idea how Lefty survived it.

Saturday, 7th April, 2018.

It has been raining hard all night, the wind howling. Despite all the vodka he drank last night, Fraser has had little sleep. He has been lying fully awake since four, watching it get as light as it's going to get, which owing to the weather is unnaturally dark for April. At six he gets up and dresses, makes coffee and thinks about what to do. He has more or less convinced himself that the wee scrote must have stowed away on the *Island Princess*, but when he checks his phone there is no message from Robert to say he's been found hiding in one of the storage compartments.

In the end he puts his jacket on, and then he opens the door and closes it again and goes to fetch the full storm gear, the heavy hi-vis and the waterproof trousers and the boots. And a torch, because it is barely light enough to see.

Outside, the wind is roaring, and above it he can hear the sound of the waves thundering against the cliffs. The rain on his face is salt-heavy. Even if Robert hasn't found the lad stowed away, even if he is still on the island, there's no way the boat is coming back today. Fraser wonders at what point he should call the coastguard. Probably he should have done that yesterday. Probably Robert should have done it. He might still have done so, but Fraser thinks it must be unlikely as there has been no alert, no message from them to demand to know the status of the search on the island. The radio has been chattering to itself with various warnings and problems with the storm, all of it too far away to be any concern of his.

As he trudges towards the bird observatory, the wind strong enough to make him stagger at the exposed parts of the cliff, he thinks that maybe at some point in the future when a body has been found there will be an enquiry. He will have to try to talk to Robert, get some sort of agreement. It doesn't need to be complicated – Fraser can say he thought Robert would have done it; Robert would have thought the same about Fraser. Just a simple miscommunication. A tragic case. All down to the weather, really, because if it hadn't been for that…

He has reached the bird observatory. Knocks on the door, but he's made enough racket crashing into the storm porch; they know he's there. He stands on the mat inside, water streaming from his gear. Inside it's warm from the woodburner, the air damp and thick with the smell of socks and burning driftwood and something else, sausages maybe. There are four of them, including Andy, the reserve manager from the Western Isles.

'Just checking you're all safe and well,' Fraser says.

They are. He doesn't need to ask if they've taken in a stray overnight; there is no sign of anything unusual, other than the fact that it's nearly ten in the morning and they're all indoors. They are waiting out the storm, ready to go out there and count nests once it's all over with. The Must birds are resilient, but there will be many casualties after a storm like this one.

He heads north, although now he's looking for a body rather than someone sheltering. There is no shelter here, and it's exposed enough for the wind to make him feel vulnerable. He bends low against it, gets as far as the ruins, and then turns back. He reaches the lighthouse after another half-hour, the wind behind him now blowing him almost into a trot. Thinks about going inside, drying off, having a rest for a while, then coming out again. In the shelter of the workshop he checks his phone again for messages from Robert, but the signal has gone. He lets the chickens out of their coop but keeps them inside the workshop. They won't like it much, but if he let them outside they would disappear. As it is they sit in the doorway and stare at him.

He eventually finds the lad just before eleven.

He's in the second cottage, where he had searched yesterday. He must have been hiding somewhere else then. Fraser sees that the door is ajar, forces it open and something makes him check the room at the back, shining his torch around the bare, damp walls. In the corner of the room is an old bedstead, a rotten mattress on it. The boy is crouched on it, his back to the wall. A bone-white face looking back at him. He is wet through and shaking. Fraser roars at him, swears, calls him every name he can think of, while the boy cowers. Whatever swagger he had brought with him is long gone.

He leaves the cottage and shuts the door firmly behind him. The door is rotten and warped and takes some effort to open and close. He doesn't lock it because there is no key, but later Lefty will tell him that he tried the door and couldn't open it, thought himself locked in.

Fraser is sick with fury. He will not have the boy in the lighthouse. He does not want him on the island at all, but here he is and the boat's not coming, so there is no choice. Back at the lighthouse he fills a bottle with tap water, fetches the old blanket that Bess sleeps on sometimes, a bag of crisps and an apple. Takes it back out in the rain, heaves open the door and launches his way inside.

The boy is waiting for him. Standing there with a big fuck-off hunting knife, pointed at him. The fact that he is so cold and weak that he can barely stand up does not seem to occur to him. He thrusts the knife vaguely in Fraser's direction. Fraser has never been threatened with a knife before, though he's had occasional encounters with bullies and idiots at school and work since, and he has not learned the lesson that a knife, even wielded by someone who is lacking in strength, adds a new layer of danger to the mix. He doesn't think about that. Within a few seconds he has disarmed the boy and stripped him of the soaked jacket he's wearing. Now that Fraser has the knife the boy is crying, scoots back over to the bed and cowers beneath it like a scalded cat. In the pockets of the jacket Fraser finds a bag

270

of weed and a bag containing three tablets, a pack of fags and a lighter. A wallet with five pounds and various bits of paper. Three phones. He confiscates all of that and throws the jacket towards the bed. At the door, he leaves the carrier bag with the water and the food and the blanket.

'As soon as the boat comes, you're fucking leaving,' he growls. 'Until then, you can stay in here.'

Rachel

Rachel can hear sounds in the kitchen, but when she gets in there it's Lefty, making toast.

'Fraser's gone out,' he says, a tone of surprise.

'Oh. Did he say where he was going?'

'No. He's gone wi'out me. I'll do the chickens in a minute.'

Lefty eats his toast without a plate, lifting it straight from the toaster, buttering it, and eating it while leaning against the counter. A blob of butter slides from it and on to the front of his ragged T-shirt, but he doesn't seem to notice.

There is some porridge left; Rachel spoons it into a bowl and sits at the table. 'You going to sit with me?' she asks him.

He obliges, although he's finished his toast. He sits with his chin in his cupped hands and watches her.

'At least you get a morning without being shouted at,' she says.

'Aye. But I don't mind it so much any more.'

'Really?'

'It's no' the shouting. That's no' so bad. It's when he goes quiet that you've to worry.'

Rachel looks at him with concern. 'When he goes quiet?'

'Aye. He goes all sorta – calm. Like he's just all so casual, right? And if you push it then he just – well. Just don't push it.'

There is a long pause while Rachel digests this information.

'Has he ever hurt you, Lefty? I mean – really hurt you?'

271

Lefty thinks about this for a long time.

She adds, 'I know you've got this weird sort of loyalty thing going on, despite the way he treats you. But you know I'm not going to take sides.'

He looks up, then, looks at her directly for the first time. She's noticed that Lefty has a hard time holding eye contact. He glances at her sometimes and catches her eye briefly, then immediately looks away. But now he looks right at her, holds her attention. 'You are, though,' he says. 'I know there's stuff going on.'

Rachel feels her cheeks flushing.

'It don't matter to me. See, I used to think he needed someone to shout at. Get all o' that anger out, no? So I thought, well, if that's what he needs, let him shout. I deserve it. But he's been shoutin' all this time and he's no' feelin' any better. Then you turn up and now I'm wondering if that isn't what he needed after all.'

'What do you mean?'

He thinks about it, watching her. 'When his wee sister died he lost the only person he had to care about. And he cared about her a lot. So maybe that's what he needs.'

'Look,' she says, 'I'm only here for a few weeks, you know? This – it's not serious.'

'That's up to you, an' him. Just, you know, don't be saying about no' takin' sides. I know what would happen to me if it came to it. I know what you think of me.'

'Lefty—'

But he gets to his feet. At the doorway he turns and adds, 'It don't matter. You'd be right, anyway. I am all of those things you think. All of the things he accuses me of.'

It takes her an hour to find Fraser. He's not in the workshop, and the quad is inside. The fog that she woke up to this morning is clearing, and, while she can't see the whole of the island from the top of the hill, she can see all the way to the bird observatory, and down to the harbour. There's no sign of him, no bulky shape in his dark waxed coat. From somewhere behind her she can hear a tinny clinking, like someone chiselling at rock.

She takes the steep path down to the cottages, hearing the noise getting louder. The fog is lingering in the ravine, and out of nowhere Bess scampers up the path to meet her, fur damp and cold, tail wagging.

Fraser is in the second cottage.

She already knows what he's doing.

'Fraser?'

He comes out to meet her, wiping his hands on a rag. Something about his movements tells her he's not pleased to see her.

'Just clearing up a bit,' he says.

'You're chiselling it out? Really?'

His eyes widen but he doesn't reply. She goes past him into the cottage, into the back room where on that first visit she'd noticed the old iron bedstead, the rotten, stinking mattress. That day she'd been thinking of somewhere to move to, some way of getting out of staying in the lighthouse with a man she didn't know. She had looked at the room and been overwhelmed with the misery of it, even before she'd taken a step closer to the back wall and seen the graffiti etched into the grimy remains of the whitewash that covered the interior.

fuck dis shit
let me out
Ima gonna die here

And, underneath it, a single word, a name.

Mags

She hadn't said anything at the time. In fairness she hadn't even thought about it. It's only in the last few days, with Marion coming, that she has remembered and wondered who the hell has put graffiti in the island's derelict cottages. The birders? No. Previous inhabitants? Of course not. The cottages haven't been occupied for years, have they? And then she realised that they must have been.

Fraser comes up behind her.

The wall where the graffiti had been is a mess of chiselled plaster. There is no sign of the words any more.

'Well,' she says. 'You made a right mess of that.'

'I couldn't just leave it, could I?' he says.

'Better to have scrubbed it off?'

'It was deeper than it looked.'

Rachel glances at the floor, which is littered with bits of broken glass and the odd rusty screw. She goes to the wall, rubs at the bare plaster and the slimy, mould-speckled wall next to it. 'We could just rub some muck into it. It'll be dark enough in here. We could push the bed over to this wall?'

'What are you talking about, "we"? You don't have to do anything,' he says. 'Go back to the lighthouse.'

'Give me the bucket,' she says. 'I'll go and collect some grass, find some mud.'

'I said go back. This is my problem, not yours.'

There's an edge to his voice she has not heard before. She thinks of what Lefty said, about that dangerous calmness. She thinks he is not like that now. What she senses instead is something else. Sadness, maybe. Guilt. Unbearable pain.

'Will you just go?'

Fraser

Fraser scrapes up the plaster he's chiselled, scoops it into the bucket. She's right, of course. When he goes outside a few minutes later he can see her, nearly at the top of the hill.

'Rachel!' he shouts.

She doesn't turn round. He thinks she must have heard.

He collects handfuls of grass, moss, dark mud from beside the loch. Inside he rubs it into the exposed plaster, a child's finger painting that looks anything but natural. He hadn't meant to bodge it. His intention had been to just chip over the words, make it so that they were just random scratches in the wall, but, once he started, the memories of those three days came hurtling back and his blows became more forceful and by the time he heard her say his name outside there was a massive shapeless hole in the wall.

You made a right mess of that.

If only she knew the truth of it.

For three days the storm rages outside. He sits up listening to the radio traffic, waiting for a call from the coastguard or a message from Robert. His mind skims through all the possibilities. More than once he pulls on his jacket and is about to go down there with the knife. To finish it. To be done. Something stops him each time.

When he'd got back from the cottage he had flushed the pills down the toilet, smoked the lad's weed and slept for a day, then spent the following night in a paranoid frenzy thinking that the police would be on the next boat. All the while the rain and the wind and the darkness outside, and the boy down there in the cottage with no light or heating or food.

He should have just done it, got it over with. Put the body in the loch and left it. They could have denied all knowledge, him and Robert. They could have said the lad went back on the boat and got off at Anstruther and disappeared into the night. If anyone had asked.

The longer he leaves it, the worse it gets – the paranoia, the self-loathing, carried along by memories of Maggie in the hospital bed; Maggie phoning him up thirteen times in a single day to ask him for money, a different excuse every time. She had no money for food. Her purse had been stolen. She'd had to pay a debt, had nothing left until the crisis loan was approved. Had been short-changed in the corner shop. Had left her last twenty quid at a mate's house. Maggie crying on his doorstep when he wouldn't let her in because she'd broken in the day before and stolen fifty pounds out of his wallet. His mum swearing at him on the phone and then bursting into tears because she expected every time the phone rang that someone would be telling her Maggie was dead from an overdose. If the boy hadn't killed her with his car, he would have killed her some other way, eventually.

On the third day, the weather still wild, his curiosity drives him mad enough to go down there and look.

The door to the cottage is open.

The fury rises in a wave and chokes him: he has done a runner again. He is probably cosy in the bird observatory, feet up, telling them all about it.

But, as it turns out, he hasn't gone far. Fraser finds him a few minutes later, hiding next to the loch, crouched behind a metal container. Fraser thinks at first that it's just an old tarp that's blown in from somewhere and snagged, but the shape of it is wrong and then he sees the white trainers and he knows.

Afterwards, when he tells himself this story in his head, he thinks he hesitated, stared for a moment and thought about going back up the hill, pretending he hadn't seen. In his fantasy version of these events he builds in time to think about what he's doing, allows himself that. He remembers that the dark water beside him is choppy and there is a smell coming off it, rotting seaweed, rotting something else, carried on the wind that down here is less strong but still swirling in gusts fierce enough to make you stagger.

Afterwards, he remembers thinking that it would take a second and a little nudge to tip the boy into the water. He was barely conscious anyway, might have easily fallen in on his own. He's always thought of the loch as an accident waiting to happen. It felt as though minutes passed, while he constructed the story he'd tell, the way he'd absolve himself of responsibility. Maybe he'd get away with it, maybe not.

In reality, there is no time at all between realising what he's looking at, and grabbing at the lad's jacket, hauling him up.

He is a dead weight but he is not dead.

Fraser shouts at him and yells and looks into the chalk-white, wet face, the dark tattoos like Sharpie on white paper, the shaved scalp dripping. He tries to get him to stand. The eyes flicker but do not open. Fraser roars at him in frustration, swears, calls him names that will stick.

Eventually he bends and hauls the body over his shoulder, stands, staggers, looks up at the hill and begins the ascent.

He doesn't remember the climb. He doesn't remember stopping or resting because he probably doesn't stop once. He doesn't remember slipping, losing his footing as the wind gusts and swirls. He doesn't remember the pain of carrying an adult male on his shoulder up a slope that he struggles with on a warm, still day in summer. He just remembers the body sliding from his shoulder to the floor of the lighthouse kitchen, the numb shaking of his hands as he peels off his waterproofs and leaves them where they fall. He remembers fetching towels and heating soup and stripping off the boy's clothes – designer jeans that he's probably stolen from somewhere and a T-shirt from a supermarket, no underwear – his skinny tattooed body horribly like a child's, bones visible through white skin, ribs and hips and shoulderblades, a weird little distended belly and old scars that he doesn't want to know about, livid red marks on his chest and his back and arms that even now he can see, burned on his memory. Small circular dots on his back, bright red, as if someone's dabbed him with a bingo marker. Huge bruises on his back and side, yellowing, as if someone gave him a bad kicking several days ago. Seems like he's not the only person who wants the little shite dead.

He finds a T-shirt and a hoodie and a pair of joggers that only just stay up, two pairs of thick socks, dresses him like a doll. Now the boy has started shaking, fear or cold, one or the other. Shaking too hard to be able to speak. Eyes wide. Can't hold the cup of soup so Fraser gives him water, holds it to his mouth and he spills it everywhere but takes a bit at a time.

This is all wrong, all wrong. He should have left him. What's he supposed to do with him now?

He knows he should have called the coastguard. The logical course of events would be that they would have sent the all-weather lifeboat. With great difficulty, expense and risk to life they would have stretchered him off and taken him to hospital, and he would have been fine, and maybe Fraser would have never seen him again.

But Fraser did not call the coastguard. It would have put lives at risk in rough seas, with no guarantee that the lifeboat's RIB would have been able to get to the jetty. In the pit of his belly the whole time was a raging fury that this idiot who had already caused such immeasurable damage might potentially end up being responsible for good people putting themselves in danger, and he was not going to let that happen. Let the fucker die; it was his own fault. And, besides that, he'd turned up here and made Fraser responsible for him, and the wee shite had now ruined his life all over again. Although he has a chance to do something about that. He has the object of his hatred here in his kitchen, barely alive, at his mercy. It's entirely his decision what he does next.

The lad sitting in his kitchen, eyes now wide and then closing slowly as though he's too exhausted to keep them open, shaking as if he's having some sort of fit. He wants to punch him in the face over and over again until he's a bloody mess.

Instead he makes toast.

That's devoured so quickly the lad chokes on it. And then eventually he manages soup, and more toast with cheese on it, and he says, 'Got ketchup?'

Fraser makes up a bed on the sofa where he can keep an eye on him, check he's still breathing, although he still thinks it would be so much better and easier if he weren't. He's past the point of caring what happens to him – he almost relishes the idea of being interviewed by the police. *Yes, officer. I killed him. I'm glad I did it. I'd do it again.*

But he doesn't kill him. Instead he checks on him every twenty minutes. Makes him more toast and soup and then, later on, a full dinner of shepherd's pie with fresh vegetables and gravy. And fucking ketchup.

He wants to kill him. But what he does instead is keep him alive.

Rachel

Rachel makes her cheese scones and a coffee and walnut loaf cake, and cleans the kitchen. She takes the cake and half of the scones down to the bird observatory for tomorrow and checks that everything is still spotless. Later she writes a half-hearted blog entry about the weather, and deletes it again. She emails Lucy and Mel. Lefty stays in his room playing loud music.

At a little after six Fraser comes through the door. He pulls off his boots and his jacket wearily and carefully.

'You okay?' she asks.

'I need a shower.' He walks past her, doesn't even look.

Half an hour later he comes downstairs again, starts getting things out of cupboards, as if she isn't there.

'Anything I can do to help?'

'I've got it,' he says.

She watches him for a while, and then something about the way he is holding himself, the hardness of his back turned towards her – she wants to put her hand there, the small of his back. Imagines it. Pictures herself doing it.

She's on her feet and there, next to him, and it's only later that she thinks really this was probably quite stupid given that he was holding a kitchen knife at the time. He might have reacted suddenly. He might have turned, with the knife, not realising she was there, and caught her with it. He might have pushed her away, hard. He might not even have moved.

This is what happens.

Rachel finds herself next to him. Her hand on his back. She can feel the tension in him, all his muscles hard. She moves her hand a little bit higher, leans into him, rests her forehead very gently against his bicep.

The knife clatters into the sink.

'I wanted to kiss you back,' he says. 'That night. When we were talking about Maggie.'

She can't say anything, at first. Why he has brought this up now, after all this time?

Then, 'Well, why didn't you?'

'Took me by surprise, is all.'

He turns towards her and she catches sight of his right hand. The knuckles are swollen, red, a cut across the middle one. She takes a sharp breath in and reaches for his hand just as he pulls it away, goes back to the chopping board.

'What have you done?' she asks.

'It's fine,' he says.

He hasn't punched Lefty, and there are no birders here he could have got into a fight with, even supposing he would do something like that. And his hands were fine earlier. So down there, in the cottages, probably, in the intervening hours, he has punched a door or a wall hard enough to break the skin.

He's not going to let her look; there's no point in her asking, or making a fuss. Instead she goes to the freezer and finds a half-full bag of sweetcorn, wraps it in a clean tea towel. She doesn't ask. She just stands really close to him until he goes still. Takes his hand gently, places the makeshift ice pack against it. Holds his hand in both of hers. He lets her do it, although she feels him wince.

'You might have broken something,' she says, very quietly, looking sadly at the tea towel. It has a selection of lifeboats on it. She thinks there is one the same in her parents' kitchen.

She feels the fingers of his left hand skimming her cheek. She doesn't want to look up because she thinks she might cry if she sees his eyes. Doesn't want him to see that.

'Can I kiss you now?' he asks.

'Will it make you feel better?'

'Worth a try.'

Fraser

Later he asks her if she will spend the night with him. He wants to be clear, because he knows he has behaved badly today. She has every right to be scared of him, the way he spoke to her at the cottages, the way he came back in with his hand in a mess. Like a teenager, with too much emotion and not enough self-control.

In answer to him she says, 'Of course,' although to his mind there is no 'of course' about it. Every time they do this it's as though she's giving him a gift. He can't get used to it. He can't take any of this for granted.

In the darkness of his bedroom she holds his hand and kisses it gently, although he would prefer it if she just left it the hell alone. He doesn't want to be reminded.

Down there in the ravine, the dank air had seemed poisoned, making him feel worse and worse. He'd sorted the wall out quick enough and moved the bedstead, and then he'd noticed that the floor had scrape marks through the algae, showing that it had been moved – so he had scuffed at the ground with the soles of his boots, and the longer he'd spent in there the less it had looked unoccupied for decades and the more it'd looked as if someone had been in here fucking about with things for no apparent reason, and in his head he was going round and round with the conversations he'd inevitably be having with Marion tomorrow. With what he'd say if Lefty put in an appearance. With what Robert might say to her on the way over.

That place is bad for him, the cottages: the air seethes with it, making his thoughts spiral into paranoia and self-loathing.

The feel of her soft warmth under his hands brings him back to the present, her kisses getting harder and fiercer and he wants to be gentle, needs to be, fears hurting her if he loses control and he feels as if that might actually happen tonight. Everything he has felt today is still there, just under the surface, all the pain of what he's done and what he's failed to do.

it's just sex

If she were gentle too it might have reminded him, might have been easier to hold back. Instead she grips his polo shirt with so much force he's surprised it doesn't rip. As he uses his body weight to hold her up against the door, she pushes his jeans down over his arse with her socked foot, grips him hard. Her mouth crashes against his and his teeth graze her lip and he can taste blood and it stops everything in its tracks.

'Fuck,' he gasps, 'you're bleeding.'

She doesn't answer but turns to the bed, pulling off the rest of her clothes as she goes, and he watches her rooting around in his bedside drawer for the condoms and by the time he has pulled off his jeans she is there at the edge of the bed and after that it's very quick.

The room feels airless. For a moment he can't catch his breath; lying next to her, it's as though he's forgotten how. He turns on to his side to face her, watching her breasts rise and fall. Her eyes, closed, so he can look without worrying that she'll think he's perving. Strokes his hand down her body, over her thigh, curving in to touch her. She opens her legs, a little. She is wet and his fingers slide easily inside. Did she come? He likes to think he'd be able to tell. He doesn't want to ask. And then he goes down on her because if he doesn't keep his tongue occupied he's going to say something stupid and ruin everything. She parts her thighs and he can hear her breathing quicken again, her hand brushing his hair. He knows how this goes. He knows every woman likes it a bit different, knows to pay attention to the signs, fast or slow, up and down or circles, varying it, letting her edge, letting her escape and breathe and then coming back just a tiny bit harder, a tiny bit faster.

He thinks she is nearly there, thinks about slowing down again because he's not ready to stop doing this yet. The feel of her, the taste of her, the little sounds she's making, all of it is making him hard again and if he's going to fuck her again he wants it to be slow this time, wants it to last a bit longer than five minutes.

Then she pushes him away.

'Stop for a minute,' she says.

He lifts his head, his fingers still buried. Keeps them still.

'Come here,' she says.

He moves up the bed, into her arms. She kisses him.

'Your beard's a bit damp,' she says.

'Funny that.'

'You taste of me.'

'Best taste ever.'

Her hand reaches down for him. 'Wow,' she says.

'Yeah, well. That's gonnae happen.'

He lets her play. 'You haven't come yet,' he says. 'With me.'

'No.'

Her head is nuzzled into his shoulder. He looks down and kisses her hair, dark red; it smells like something. Mango.

'Will you show me how to make you come?' he asks.

'It's not that you're doing it wrong. I get really close.'

'But you can come when you're on your own?'

There is a little pause. He senses that this is making her embarrassed.

'Sure,' she says.

'What about with other men?'

The pause this time stretches. Her fingers around him move more slowly.

'Never happened,' she says eventually.

'You're fucking kidding me.'

'Look, it's not a problem. This is … it's really good. I mean, *really* good.'

She sits up and looks down at him; her breasts swing and he cups one of them, the skin so soft, feeling the weight. She reaches for the condoms. 'May I?'

'Be my guest,' he says.

She straddles him, and holds him so that she can sink down slowly. He watches her face, the concentration of her finding her rhythm, the heat of her. His hands on her hips, the right one such a fucking mess but it only hurts when he looks at it. When his fingers were inside her a few minutes ago he never felt a thing.

Her fingers stray to her sex. Then she stops. Her hand moves away.

'Why d'you stop?'

She's out of breath now, the exertion of it, and that in itself is so fucking sexy that he struggles to contain himself.

'Can't concentrate with you watching,' she says.

'Close your eyes, then,' he says, 'because I'm sure as hell not closing mine.'

It's just sex, he thinks, again.

A while later he sees it in her face, feels it in the force that grips him and pushes at him. *Yeah*, he thinks. *That's better. About bloody time.* Next time he'll get her there and she won't have to help.

Rachel

Mixed in with the familiar yelling of the seabirds outside, Rachel can hear something else that doesn't fit. A low droning, coming from a long way off. Getting louder.

'Fuck. Fuck!'

The bed suddenly lurches and she opens her eyes to see Fraser hopping across the bedroom, pulling up his jeans.

'What is it?'

'The fucking boat's here.'

'Shit!'

It takes her less than five minutes to dress, tie up her hair and race down to the jetty, panicking the whole time. Fraser has made it before her, thankfully. He's doing his best intimidating stance, full height, head up, arms crossed. A woman is there who can only be Marion, plus three men of varying ages. Bess is sniffing Marion's crotch, and only moves when a manicured hand swipes at her head. After that she moves away and watches suspiciously.

'Hi,' Rachel says brightly, drawing level with them.

'Ah – Rachel?'

Everyone is introduced. A builder called John and his son Damian. Someone else called Phil who she expects should be an architect but his job description was more long-winded than that and involved the word 'advisor'. Rachel's mind is clouded with the stress of waking up so suddenly.

Marion is shorter than Rachel had imagined her to be, but with a voice loud and forceful enough to dominate everything. It makes the whole island feel different, suddenly, having her on it. The three men, who've had a two-hour boat crossing with her, seem subdued by comparison.

'I thought maybe you'd like to see the bird observatory first?' Rachel says, thinking about the cheese scones. It's barely nine, but the thought of skipping breakfast entirely is making her feel light-headed.

'Later,' says Marion. 'Let's get the important stuff out of the way first.'

Fraser leads them up the slope from the harbour, taking huge, effortless strides and ending up at the top before everyone else. Rachel's pleased to see she has got fitter in the last few weeks, because she manages the climb without getting out of breath.

The path at the top divides into three – to the right, the path that leads along the side of the cliff to the bird observatory. Straight on would take them to the lighthouse. But Fraser wordlessly takes the left path, sloping downwards almost immediately through a rocky outcrop.

'Watch for birds,' he says.

The puffins are everywhere, complaining about the interruption, grunting and moaning and sounding like so many doors creaking open. Over their heads terns circle, screaming at them. John the builder stumbles on the overgrown path but manages to keep to his feet. Marion had gone quiet on the climb, but now she is making up for it.

'Well, this will have to be cut back – really no good at all – can you even imagine? Why's it not in better condition, really?'

'Don't use this path much,' Fraser says. 'No reason to. Best to leave it to the birds.'

'Well, really, but even so … oh.'

At the bottom they have rounded the corner and got their first sight of the cottages.

Rachel wonders why Marion didn't ever just email Fraser and ask him to send her some photos. Maybe she did. Maybe he just ignored her.

'Good heavens. John?'

All three men have been standing at the bottom of the slope looking at the sorry state of the buildings in front of them, but at the sound of Marion's bark they scoot into action. She watches them go. Rachel comes to stand next to Fraser. He's perfectly still, perfectly silent, but the tension is palpable. She hopes she's imagining it, or, if she isn't, that Marion isn't overly intuitive.

'I mean,' Rachel says, filling a silence, 'clearly they are going to take a prohibitive amount of work to get into a reasonable condition—'

'Prohibitive?' Marion says, turning sharply. 'I don't think that's your place to say, is it?'

'Rachel's right,' Fraser says. And, under his breath, 'And you should fucking wind your neck in.'

'I beg your pardon, Fraser? Did you say something?'

She comes over to them. She has wellies on over a pair of dark jeans, a pink shirt, collar up, with a padded bodywarmer over the top. She looks as if she's come to spectate at a gymkhana.

'You can see for yourself,' he says, not raising his voice. 'They're a mess.'

'Nothing a bit of hard work won't fix, I'm sure,' she says, sniffing. 'And I must say I'm very disappointed, given how long you've been here. I know you have other things to do, but part of your responsibility here is maintaining the fixtures and fittings.'

'They were in this state when I got here,' he says.

'And you put in a request,' Rachel pipes up, 'didn't you? You were telling me about it. When you first started, you asked them for materials…'

Fraser clears his throat. Rachel doesn't look at him.

'That was before my time, I'm afraid,' Marion remarks. 'You should know by now that I'm the sort of person who gets things done. We could have been well on the way to opening the cottages this season. And now we will probably miss it. That's quite some considerable loss, not to mention the cost of the repairs themselves.'

Rachel wonders if she's leading up to announcing some sort of pay cut. She isn't earning very much at all, given that her board and lodging are included, but she had been hoping to save money to be able to afford a rental deposit when she gets out of here. Once more she finds herself thinking of the state of the bird observatory, hoping that the work she's done in cleaning it will meet Marion's standards. She has a horrible feeling it won't.

She has been chewing her nail, and Fraser nudges her so her hand is knocked away from her teeth. Gives her a tiny shake of the head. The tiniest of smiles.

She is reassured, a little bit. There is something about the glint in his eye. As though he absolutely doesn't give a shit about any of this. As though he's almost enjoying it. And then she remembers again that she's only here for few weeks; none of this has anything to do with her. Why is she even worrying about it? If Fraser isn't, then she shouldn't either.

Marion has gone into the first cottage, following John and Phil and Damian. She can hear them talking, snatched edges of the conversation.

'Aye, well, that's a fairly major settlement in the west elevation – probably caused by saturation.'

'And the crack to the party wall and at the gable end – the whole of the cement render will have to be replaced.'

And Marion's voice, rising above the others. 'Never mind a structural engineer. I just want to know what it might look like and how much it'll cost to fix.'

Someone – possibly Phil, almost apologetic, adds, 'It's going to be a real challenge to get planning passed. I just want to make that clear.'

Rachel keeps glancing towards the second cottage. Marion hasn't been inside yet.

'Will you stop?' Fraser says to her.

'Stop what?'

'You're fidgeting like crazy.'

'I can't help it,' she says, but she takes some deep breaths and feels a bit better.

Marion emerges. 'Right,' she says. 'Let's go. I'm going to leave them to it.'

'Great,' says Rachel, smiling her brightest smile, which fades as Marion makes for the slope that leads to the lighthouse.

'Not that way,' says Fraser sharply.

'Why not?' Marion asks, turning.

'The path is really dangerous,' Rachel says. 'It's slippery and very steep and there's nothing to break your fall if you lose your footing.'

Marion sighs dramatically, looking up the hill. 'What? It's worse than the way we came?'

'Much worse.'

They go the long way round, back towards the jetty. At the point where the paths converge, Marion makes determined strides towards the lighthouse.

'Marion!' Rachel calls, trying to keep the panic out of her voice. 'It's this way!'

Once again Marion turns, with a small, impatient flick of her head. 'I've come all this way,' she says. 'I want to see everything. So show me round the lighthouse.'

Rachel tries again. 'Can we not do that after we've visited the bird observatory? We don't have a lot of time before the boat has to leave.'

'I'm sure the bird observatory is just fine, Rachel. And we have nearly two hours; it won't take long, will it?'

'Fucksake,' Fraser mutters.

The pair of them exchange glances and follow. Rachel thinks of the messy bed, the bathroom that probably could do with a clean, but most importantly Lefty. They hadn't been expecting Marion to want to see anything apart from the cottages and the bird observatory. But she is already making her way purposefully towards the lighthouse. There is no getting out of it.

Fraser

The kitchen is clean. Marion frowns and stares pointedly at Fraser's coffee machine, then wrinkles her nose at the dog bed next to the oven.

Fraser steers her deliberately towards the rear, the same way he had done when he gave Rachel the tour. He notices that Rachel can't help casting a glance at Lefty's door. All is quiet. Fraser opens the door to the workshop and Marion steps inside. He watches her scanning the room. His tools, the quad, the chickens. 'You have them inside?'

'Only when the weather's bad.'

'But you can't have livestock indoors, it's a filthy idea. A proper health hazard.'

'They're cleaned regularly. And if we had the coops outside they wouldn't survive.'

'Even so, we shan't have them inside. It won't do at all. You'll have to move them.'

Rachel goes to say something and Fraser reaches out a hand to stop her, behind Marion's retreating form. Marion is already making her way up the curved staircase to the lamp room.

'Of course,' Marion calls, her voice deafening in the echoing space, 'we can offer tours of the lighthouse, can't we?' Very quickly she has to pause for breath. 'It's a historic building… People will come to the island… just for that… never mind the wildlife.'

'It's also my home,' Fraser growls at her, two steps behind.

'It's not yours, Fraser… as I keep telling you… it belongs to the Trust… you're just a guest here… the same as everyone else.'

She has reached the first landing, the grimy window giving a limited view of green and sea and sky. If she's embarrassed at her comparative lack of fitness, she's not going to show it.

'Can we not clean these windows?'

'They don't open,' Fraser says. Tries not very hard to sound as if he's never heard anything so patently stupid in his whole life.

'From outside?' Marion says, biting sarcasm.

'We're around sixty feet off the ground,' he says. 'I don't have a ladder that reaches that high.'

Marion throws him a look and sets off again. For a moment he allows himself a brief fantasy of flipping her by the ankles over the balustrade and watching her smacking into the tiled floor below.

But she would probably bounce.

They spend no more than ten minutes at the top of the tower, while Fraser delays things by blocking the hatch with his body, and leaves Rachel to carry out the chitchat. Rachel is at her perky best, talking about the whales (which she hasn't seen) and the weather, which of course she knows all about. She is veering awkwardly from excitement at having a new person to talk to, even a belligerent old jobsworth like Marion Scargill, to remembering that the idea is for Marion to be put off the whole notion of inviting holidaymakers.

'Of course, you'd need to do a full health-and-safety risk assessment,' she says now, uncertainly enough to make him think she probably doesn't possess any clear concept of what one is and whether it is, actually, required. 'The whole island is one big hazard, really. The clifftops are very dangerous, you have to stay well away from them, especially when it's windy, which it is most of the time – you'll see what I mean in a minute. And the puffin burrows are a real trip hazard.'

'Don't forget the terns,' Fraser mutters.

'Oh, yes! The terns. They dive-bomb you. When they're nesting.'

Rachel hasn't experienced this yet, but Fraser has warned her. She is going to need a hat, or else she'll get pecked every time she gets near the terrace.

'And we're a very long way away from a hospital,' she adds.

Marion is looking at the view. Fraser wonders if she's even listening. The whole thing has a terrible sense of inevitability about it. He knew this was going to happen. And it's not going to get any better. To take his mind off it he reaches out his hand and skims Rachel's backside and she looks round at him sharply. Holds her gaze. Raises a single eyebrow.

'You seem to be assuming I've never done something like this before,' Marion says. 'And you'd be wrong. I think you should both bear that in mind.' And she stands right in Fraser's face, until he moves out of her way.

A few minutes later they are back downstairs, in the hallway. Rachel is a few steps behind him. Marion is ahead and he can see it before it happens. He thinks about shouting at her, thinks about pushing her out of the way, but what's the point?

She is at Lefty's door. 'And what's in here?' Her hand on the doorknob.

Rachel says, 'Oh, that's just storage, it's not—'

And Fraser is just standing there, watching. Closes his eyes slowly and opens them again. Breathes in.

The door opens. His view of the inside is blocked by the door and by Marion's body. Marion gives a shocked little gasp. Fraser hears something from inside the room, some noise. He can't see, but he can imagine Lefty sitting on his bed, shrinking back, his startled face.

'And just who is this?'

Rachel

Rachel and Marion are sitting at the table in the bird observatory. The very best that can be said about things is that there is less than an hour to go before the boat has to leave.

Marion doesn't like cheese scones, as it turns out, but she accepted a slice of coffee and walnut cake and a cup of tea, and then picked at the former and hasn't bothered to drink the latter.

'It just isn't appropriate,' Marion says for what feels like the fifth time. 'He clearly knows what's expected of him. He signed an employment contract that was very clear.'

Fraser had parted company with them on the headland. Marion at that point had been red in the face and uncommonly silent, as if she was about to actually explode. Fraser had taken advantage of the break in the conversation, saying he had to go and see to things with Robert, and, although Rachel was momentarily terrified at the prospect of being left on her own with Marion, actually a lot of the tension seems to have dissipated. Perhaps Marion has a problem with men, she thinks, or tall, arsey ones at least. Now, having listened to a good half-hour of Marion's vitriol, she desperately wants to defend Fraser against this ongoing character assassination, but has the strongest sense that whatever she says probably won't do the blindest bit of good. Besides, the less she speaks, the fewer times she will have to tell blatant lies.

'And you said he's been here – how long?'

'I don't know exactly. Not long.'

Fraser hadn't stuck to the plan. He hadn't introduced Lefty as his nephew. Hadn't introduced him at all. Just turned away and walked out, Bess at his heels.

'He's just visiting,' Rachel had said.

'Visiting?' Marion had said, looking aghast. She had cast her gaze once more into the room, at the Xbox and the tatty bedlinen and the bathroom beyond.

Now Marion has thought of something else. 'He's subletting,' she says, lips pursed.

'No, of course not,' Rachel says, almost amused at the very idea that Lefty has any money to pay rent. Not to mention the idea of the housing crisis being so acute that a casual tenant might decide to house-share on an island two hours out in the North Sea.

'He wouldn't tell you about it, of course, but I bet that's what he's doing.'

On the bright side, Marion has not commented negatively on the bird observatory. She hasn't said anything complimentary either. She is too busy laying into Fraser.

'Look, I know he probably should have said something,' Rachel offers. 'But it really isn't a big deal. He's just staying for a little while and then I'm sure he'll be gone.'

'What's he eating? Drinking? We're not providing you with provisions so you can share it among all and sundry.'

'Robert also brings stuff that Fraser pays for,' she says. 'Other things he needs. So that's probably what's happening with the extra food.'

As she says it, Rachel feels Marion's gimlet eyes focus on her. 'Other things?' she echoes. 'What other things?'

Is this something else that's going to get him into even more trouble? Rachel hopes not. 'You know – coffee beans, the odd bottle of wine. Stuff like that.'

Marion lets out a little snort of disgust. Outside the bird observatory, the sun comes out, bathing the room in warm light. Even viewing it through Marion's hyper-critical eyes, she thinks the place looks very appealing. The picture window shows birds and sea and sky, the very best of the island. Rachel makes another desperate attempt at changing the subject.

'What about Julia?' she asks. 'Have you heard anything more from her?'

'She's doing well, I gather – the mother, that is.'

'Any more news on how long I'll be needed?'

'No. Of course, she might decide not to come after all.'

'I'm sorry?' There have been no further emails from Julia, which makes Rachel wonder if she's missed something. Last she'd heard, Julia was really looking forward to it.

'Well, I don't know. But you'll be all right to carry on, won't you? I mean, if she decides not to take up the position?'

Rachel frowns. 'I guess so...' she says, wondering how Fraser would take that news. 'I don't know, I'd need to think.'

'Oh, come on. You wouldn't let me down as well, would you? Nobody seems to be reliable any more, it's an appalling state of affairs. Clearly I need someone on the island who's going to take things seriously. What a complete pantomime this whole thing is.'

Rachel thinks Marion is just hedging her bets. The older woman casts a glance around the room and Rachel braces herself for the inevitable critical assault.

'What about your food hygiene certificate?' Marion asks. 'When's that due for renewal?'

'My – what?'

'Your food hygiene certificate. To permit you to prepare and serve food.'

Rachel feels the blood drain away from her face. 'Um,' she says, 'am I supposed to have one of those?'

Marion's expression changes from sour to thunderous. 'Yes, indeed you are. Are you telling me you don't have one?'

'Nobody told me I needed one, I—'

'Good God, Rachel. You should have thought of it before you accepted the job. Of course you need a certificate! You're preparing food illegally, then, making you personally liable if you poison someone, right? I'm hoping you've got public liability insurance, at least?'

Rachel can feel the panic rising. She is going to be sacked, she thinks, right here and now. She is going to have to go back on the boat with Marion and the builders. She won't even have time to pack.

But Marion purses her lips firmly. 'Well, there's nothing to be done about it now, is there? You'll have to get yourself certified if we employ you permanently, although given your casual attitude to the safety and wellbeing of your guests that really will be a matter of some consideration. In the meantime, thank God we haven't had any comments or complaints about it. Other than that first week, of course.'

'That wasn't about the food, though,' Rachel says, as if that makes anything better.

'Indeed,' Marion concedes, seemingly reluctantly. There is a little pause. She looks around the room, at the painted breeze-block walls, the rough table and chairs, the cracked linoleum and the mismatched cushions on the shapeless sofa, and sighs heavily. 'The whole thing is a joke,' she says wearily. 'An absolute joke.'

Rachel glances surreptitiously at the clock. Wonders if Fraser would be pissed off if she were to bring Marion to the harbour half an hour early.

Fraser

'Well,' Rachel says, 'that was fun.'

They are sitting in the kitchen, which is flooded with sunlight from the open back door. It's turned out to be the warmest day of the year so far, which is typical when he had been hoping for a storm. Bess is sitting in the doorway, watching the birds, the light breeze stirring her fur.

It's just over an hour since the boat sailed. Back at the lighthouse Rachel had gone to see Lefty, coaxed him out with the promise of warmed cheese scones, although he'd been reluctant.

'Wasnae ma fault,' was the first thing he said when he saw Fraser.

He's not sure if he would have shouted even if Rachel hadn't been here. He's too tired for any of it. Three hours' sleep followed by three hours with Marion Fucking Scargill – he was done in. And Rachel looks tired now too, as though the effort of maintaining the chirpiness for Marion's benefit has finished her off. Lefty's head is down; he's picking at his food and saying nothing.

'Nobody's blaming you, Lefty. She was just a bit of a nightmare all round.'

Fraser has made coffee because if ever a situation called for coffee, this is it.

'What's gonnae happen,' Lefty asks.

'We don't know,' Rachel says. 'I'm sure it'll be okay, though. Everything will work out.'

Fraser can't help himself.

'Sure about that?'

'Well, I might get chucked off the island before anyone else,' she says hollowly.

'Can I go?' Lefty says.

'Go where?'

'I wannae see tae the chickens.'

'Aye, go on, then.'

Fraser watches him depart. He's left his plate of crumbs behind. Then he turns his attention back to what Rachel's just said.

'How'd you figure that out?'

'Apparently I'm supposed to have some sort of food hygiene certificate.'

Fraser throws back his head and barks a laugh. 'Not the fucking food hygiene certificate! Christ on a bus.'

'I don't see what's funny but I'd love to find out,' she says.

'She threaten you with it?'

'She said I was serving food illegally and if anyone gets food poisoning then I was going to be liable.'

'Oh, aye. I've heard that one before.'

'And she asked if I had public liability insurance, too. Which of course I haven't.'

Fraser knits his brows and nods. 'You realise this is all complete bollocks.'

'How can it be?'

'Firstly, she'll be liable if anyone is, not you. Did you have training?'

'No.'

'Did anyone ask you if you've got a certificate, or insurance for that matter?'

'No, of course not.'

'Then the whole thing is dodgy as fuck and she knows it, so don't you worry about it.'

'But clearly I do need a food hygiene certificate, otherwise why would she say that? I'm guessing that means she wants me off the island before anything bad happens.'

'No, she doesn't. And what she was doing, Rachel, was just taking out her frustrations about me, on you. Which makes her an even bigger arsehole, as far as I'm concerned.'

Rachel thinks about this for a second or two. 'She really does seem to have a bit of a problem with you.'

'Was she complaining about me, then? You do surprise me.'

'I mean, it was good in that she didn't have enough time or breath to criticise the bird observatory. But I had to give up trying to defend you in the end.'

'You were defending me, were you?'

'I was trying my hardest.'

'Hm. Well, that was sweet of you but really there's no need. I don't give a flying fuck what Marion thinks of me. In fact it's almost entertaining how much she hates me.'

'You don't think she'll use Lefty to try to make things difficult for you? She might try to sack you, Fraser.'

He genuinely hasn't given this a moment's thought. For all her complaining, Marion recognises that Fraser can be left to carry out his duties with minimal supervision. If he's left alone, he gets on with it. That in itself makes him valuable. The cost of recruiting a replacement will probably prevent her trying to get him out.

On the other hand, now she's mentioned it, the thought of it has a strange sort of appeal. He loves the island but right now, if someone told him he had to leave, he thinks he might just do it without complaint. Something about Marion's visit has soured the place for him in a way that a whole year of Lefty's presence never did.

It will do him good to get away for a while. A day or two with the traffic and the people everywhere will remind him that what he actually likes is the solitude and the salt, the crash of the sea and the roar of the wind.

'She won't,' he says.

'Let's hope not. In the meantime, I guess I have to just wait to hear from her?'

'Or you could be a bit proactive.'

'How?'

If left to his own devices, Fraser's attitude towards Marion is to ignore her totally unless absolutely boxed into a corner. She tried the same thing with him, not long after she started – back in the days when she was trying to assert herself with him and get him to jump through the very precise and utterly arbitrary hoops she had set up for no discernible reason other than to make their respective positions clear. He had, of course, jumped through no hoops. He had strolled around them, feigning interest for a wee while, before kicking them over and going on his merry way.

Since then, his professional relationship with Marion has veered from awkward to frustrating, with brief moments of triumph and despair. Still, it isn't all doom and gloom. He had taken the employment of a person to manage the bird observatory as some sort of defeat for him and a victory for her, but that had turned out surprisingly well so far.

'We can ring the council's Environmental Health Officer.'

'What?'

'And they can provide appropriate advice for you.'

'Really? But what if they say yes, you do need a certificate and we're going to close you down until you have one?'

'They won't say that.'

'How do you know?'

'Because I phoned them last year when Marion joined the Trust, when she tried the exact same scare tactics on me. In fact – hold on a sec.'

He goes to the drawer in the kitchen into which random objects are tossed, ferrets around inside it until he comes up with a business card. 'Here you go.'

Ellie Griffiths, it says. *Senior Environmental Health Officer.*
An office number and a mobile, and an email address. He passes
it over to Rachel, who studies it.

'I spoke to this very nice lady last year,' he says. 'Why don't
you call her – or, better still, send her an email so you've got
a paper trail? Explain the situation and be honest, and let's see
what she says.'

'I'm not sure,' Rachel says. 'I don't want to make things worse.'

'I have a feeling you'll find it reassuring.'

There is a chance it could backfire, he thinks, but he's not
going to tell Rachel that. Really, in the ongoing war between
him and Marion, this is another chance to get a shot fired over
her proverbial bows. Because last year the very nice lady at
the council had informed him that Marion was responsible,
and liable, and that if he wasn't serving food to anyone then
he didn't need a food hygiene certificate. A letter had been
sent to Marion to make that position very clear. She had been
fully informed of the legislation and given plenty of guidance
regarding the practical and legal requirements of opening the
business to the general public rather than guests, which was
what the birders had been up to that point. He knows this,
because the nice lady had kept him informed. And clearly
Marion has ignored all of that guidance.

He feels positively buoyant at the thought of it.

Rachel

Thursday.

They have heard nothing from Marion.

Rachel has been corresponding with Ellie Griffiths by
email. The Environmental Health Officer was reassuring,
explaining that this was definitely Marion's responsibility.
But then things took an alarming turn when she also said she
would be communicating with Marion about it and ensuring

that action was taken to ensure that no members of the public were put at risk.

Rachel is hoping that Marion will not think she has been telling tales. She points this out to Fraser, who gives her an amused smirk and says something like, 'Serves her bloody right,' which doesn't help at all.

Fraser is going to the mainland tomorrow.

Rachel has deliberately not commented on this because she doesn't want to seem needy or desperate. Or jealous.

She wants to know if Fraser is going to see Kelly, and at the same time she wants to know nothing about it. There are moments when she almost asks, and then she changes her mind and bites her lip and tries to think about something else. And of course the whole thing is pointless anyway, because he is not hers, she is not with him, they are not a couple.

He is going tomorrow when the boat comes with their provisions, and he is coming back on the boat with the new lot of birders, on Saturday. He made the mistake of asking her if there is anything she needs, and she has issued him with a shopping list of items she doesn't feel comfortable asking Robert to get. She tried to give him money, but he insisted they should settle up when he gets back, when he knows how much it costs.

He asked her again – in bed, just as she was falling asleep – if she wanted to come with him.

She didn't think he meant it then, either. If he was serious, he'd ask her properly, when she's wide awake.

Fraser

This is just sex.

He thinks it on Tuesday, when they have recovered from the horrors of Marion's visit and are sleeping together again. He watches her sleep and can't quite believe it, still can't fully fathom how this came to happen, this girl in his bed, this girl and how she makes him feel.

This is just sex, he thinks on Wednesday, as he watches her picking up her clothes which are scattered around the floor of the main room in the bird observatory. She is strolling around casually naked, glancing at him over her shoulder and laughing.

He came to see what she was doing because he was bored and thinking about her, thinking about the boat ride on Friday and the mainland and whether he's going to see Kelly, and so he came over to the bird observatory and found her wiping down the cupboards, which to his mind are perfectly clean; he kissed her hard and lifted her on to one of the high stools at the breakfast bar and let her unbutton his jeans. Fucked her there until the stool felt as though it was going to topple, and then on the sofa, and then on the rug on the floor. And then he watches her dress and thinks how impossible the whole thing is.

This is just sex.

He repeats it like a mantra, as if the act of repeating it will make it true.

It's just sex, fucking her against the sheltered wall of the lighthouse, the sun warming his bare arse as he penetrates her, concentrating on her hand splayed against the stone, the bones under the pale skin, the tiny golden freckles, trying to hold on, trying to make it last. Every time, in case it's the last time, for surely his luck is going to run out soon.

It's just sex, nothing else, he thinks, as he glances down at her fellating him in the living room on Wednesday night, the TV on for a change, the ten o'clock news showing the prime minister making a tit of himself outside a hospital, a placard being held up behind him by a fierce-looking woman which says, *This too will pass*. It's only the fact that he's muted the sound – lest he misses the sound of Lefty's door opening – that makes it possible for him to stand it. And then Rachel looks up at him, meets his eyes, her mouth full – and winks.

It's just sex.

'It's just sex,' he says aloud, on Thursday night.

She's straddling him on the bed. They started in the bathroom, maybe half an hour ago. She looks down at him, breathless, brows knitted.

'What?'

And he backtracks. 'Nothing,' he says. 'Nothing.'

The more he says it, the less it is true. It's as though he's diluting it. But he keeps saying it, keeps thinking it, until Friday morning, early, when he's watching her sleep, her hair all over the place, her eyes closed. The boat is coming at eleven. He has hours yet, and although he should get up and feed Bess and take her round the island, checking the trap and searching for injured birds and migrant birds, he has no desire to move. He has been looking forward to getting off the island for a while, because, whenever he does, he always misses it and wants to come back. He has also been looking forward to seeing Kelly, although he hasn't called her, hasn't told her he's coming, just in case he changes his mind.

It's not that he feels he owes Kelly anything. It's not that he thinks what he's doing with Rachel is somehow cheating on her – he and Kelly have no commitment to each other; he's made that clear and she understands it. She is undoubtedly sleeping with other men and he neither cares nor wants to hear about it. It's not that. He just feels a strange sort of trepidation about what he might say to her.

In the half-light, hypnotised by the sound of Rachel breathing, he explores that thought, intersperses it with a brief fantasy about what he's going to do with Rachel when he comes back – absence making the heart fonder and all that – and, while thinking *it's just sex* for the hundredth time, he realises that he's kept himself so distracted with his own mantra that he seems to have backed into something else entirely.

Something a wee bit life-changing.

10

Kelly

Rachel

Rachel stands on the jetty and watches as the *Island Princess* roars noisily backwards, doing its awkward three-point turn in the harbour.

She had been in two minds as to whether to see him off, thinking of what she would look like, all forlorn on the concrete jetty like a tragic soul waving goodbye to her lover. In the end she comes down to watch because she always does, and seeing the boat is like a little reminder that the real world still exists beyond the grey-green waves.

On the jetty she is bright, chirpy, having issued him with a list of things to get her while he's near some shops. Shampoo. Some gossip magazines. Thick socks. Bess sits by her feet, looking anxiously at Fraser's sports bag.

'We'll be okay, won't we, Bess? And he'll be back tomorrow. I'll give you extra cheese.'

There is no awkward hug or anything. Robert ties the boat up loosely and the boxes of shopping are handed over. Lefty is going to bring the quad later, and take them up to the bird observatory. Fraser casts off and steps across on to the deck.

Robert waves at Rachel from the little bridge on the upper deck, then they're off.

As soon as the boat has chugged out of sight Rachel heads back to the lighthouse and climbs the tower. She has done this a couple of times, usually in the mornings, watching for whales, although she has not been up here since Marion's visit. It would make such a good blogpost, although the likelihood of her phone's camera zooming in well enough to take a picture is quite slim.

She likes being up here. She likes looking out for Fraser, and Lefty, and the birders, mapping their presence on the island, little dots moving on the green slopes, the seething mass of birds in the sky making it difficult to spot them.

From here she can see the boat, looking as though it's barely moving, heading towards the Isle of May. They have to pick someone up on the way back. This is why Fraser chose today to go to the mainland; with no birders to collect this week, Robert would have brought the shopping on Saturday otherwise.

There is still radio silence from Marion. Rachel has spent the past few days helping Fraser, sometimes with Lefty present. They have counted terns from a distance, although whatever the distance they still risk being pecked on the head, as the birds have started laying eggs. They have counted eider pairs and noted the positions of this year's nests. They have ringed a short-eared owl, which Rachel found slightly terrifying. They had one brilliant day – Wednesday – when an easterly wind blew a whole load of migrating warblers on to the island for shelter. They ringed several that ended up in the Heligoland trap, and Rachel had her first sighting of several birds – chiffchaffs and willow warblers, whitethroats, and a blackcap that Fraser told her was a rare visitor. Lefty was with them when they were ringing, passing over the correct-sized ring while Rachel noted down the number and the bird's weight.

She thinks that Fraser is shouting at Lefty less often. Maybe he feels sorry for him after Marion's terrifying appearance at the door of his room – although this seems unlikely. It might be just when she is there, because yesterday she was walking back towards the east cliff and she heard the familiar sound of Fraser's roaring: 'You stupid arse, get down here now!' Whatever Lefty was doing, he had stopped doing it by the time she reached them, and everything was calm.

It still surprises her that Lefty does not seem upset by Fraser's outbursts. She has seen him flinch, without a doubt; she has actually seen him cowering while Fraser stands over him, barking obscenities. But once it's out of the way they just seem to carry on as if nothing's happened.

Now she looks north towards the low, rocky end of the island, the ruins; sees Lefty trudging back towards the lighthouse, trailing a plastic sack behind him which is probably full of beach litter.

She thinks, again, of the knife on the bedside table.

Because I'm going to kill him.

Rachel

Lefty is in the kitchen when she gets down the stairs, making himself a huge breakfast sandwich full of microwaved bacon, crisps, cheese and ketchup. He grins at her.

'Big man wouldnae let me have something like this,' he says, cheerfully.

'Well, don't worry. I won't tell him.'

She leans against the counter, watching as he puts the cheese away. Bess sits up, staring hopefully.

'You found lots of litter?'

'Aye. All be back again tomorrow, though.'

He looks at his fingers, licks off a smear of ketchup. She can see him thinking. Waits for the thought to come, waits for him to say it. If he doesn't speak soon, she's going to ask.

And then he looks at her, clear blue eyes, straight at her.

'You an' Fraser,' he says.

'Yes?'

'Just to say you should be careful o' him, though, right? You know?'

'What do you mean, careful?'

'It's no' that he's got a temper, I mean you can see that for yersel', right? And he's no' shoutin' at you, right, not like... It's just that he's ...'

'He's what?'

'He's no' right in the head,' he says, tapping his fingers on his temple.

Rachel frowns at this assessment, thinking that on more than one occasion Fraser has said almost exactly the same thing about Lefty, and, while it has been easy to believe of the wild-looking, scrappy-haired youth, perhaps it doesn't sit quite as well on Fraser's calm, solid shoulders. But maybe it should.

'You mean with his anger?'

'That, and depression.'

'He's depressed?'

'Aye, he has been – well, before you turned up, anyway. He wouldnae admit tae it. Or talk about it, if you asked him. But that's what I'd call it.'

He goes to the fridge and retrieves one of his cans, pops the ring, takes a deep swig. Lets out a not very subtle bubble-cheeked belch.

'What was it like here before, just the two of you?'

Lefty looks at her, eyes narrowed. She has the sense that he's getting near the point where he's going to scarper. This is probably the longest conversation they've ever had.

'Sometimes went days wi'out sayin' a word. No' like we have big conversations, mind.'

'Does he – did he ever hit you?'

He looks at her, swigs, belches again. 'Nah,' he says, eventually. 'Threatens to, most days. Never actually has.'

'I've seen him grab you, push you.'

'That's no' what you asked.'

'It's still violence.'

He explodes with a big 'Ha!' then, as if she's said something hilarious. 'That what you call violence? Fuck me.'

He leans against the counter, a shorter, skinnier version of Fraser, regarding her casually. 'Go on, then, hen. Ask me. I can feel it. All they burning questions. He's no' here, is he, so you can ask.'

'Are you going to answer?'

'Might do, might not,' he says.

She is starting to wonder if she prefers Lefty silent and a bit scared. He has suddenly become quite a lot more casual, a bit more laddish, and she's here all on her own with him. Tonight they are going to be alone together in the lighthouse.

'How come you're here?' she asks.

Eyes never leaving hers, he swigs the last of the can, swallows, and thunks it down on the counter behind him.

'I came tae apologise. Tae make things right or, if not, take what was coming to me, fair 'n' square. Would've been no worse than what would've happened back home. And then I just kinda stayed, because he wasnae listenin', but he wasnae beatin' the shit outta me either.'

'Apologise?'

There is a pause. Rachel can see him thinking, deciding whether he's going to say any more.

'For killing his wee sister. For what happencd wi' Mags.'

Fraser

Saturday morning.

Inevitably she has moved house since the last time he saw her, the fourth or fifth time over the course of the past year. Just about every time he's visited her, she's been somewhere new.

This is the nicest place she's had for a while, he thinks – a neat row of terraced houses, hers somewhere in the middle of them. Front doors that give directly on to the street. A single step up to the front door, a gentle curve showing the passage of thousands of footsteps over, probably, the past couple of centuries. He is two streets back from the main road and although cars are parked either side, giving a very narrow channel down the centre to drive down, there is not a soul to be seen. Good. He has no desire to be seen either, although he wouldn't be surprised to learn that a few curtain-twitchers would have watched his progress from the end of the row.

She opens the door as soon as he knocks.

Kelly.

He hasn't seen her in five months, and despite his misgivings she is looking well. He only called her an hour ago.

'Hey,' she says. 'Come in.'

The front room is tiny, made more so by a comfy-looking two-seater sofa and two matching armchairs that would suit a much larger room, facing each other across a coffee table. There are brackets on the wall above the blocked-up fireplace that show where a flat-screen TV used to be.

He takes all this in in a matter of seconds. Already she is through the back to the galley kitchen.

'You want coffee?' she asks. 'I've got they wee coffee pod things. They make a nice cup.'

'Sure,' he says. 'Thanks.'

In his wallet he has five hundred pounds for her, in cash. It might be that he doesn't give her all of the money. He hasn't decided yet. Hasn't decided what's going to happen here.

'Where's Charlie?' he asks, following her into the second room, which is half dining room and half kitchen. There isn't room in the kitchen for a fridge-freezer, so it's in the dining area.

'At his friend's house,' she says, getting milk from the fridge and pointing to the certificates that are attached to it with letter magnets in primary colours. 'He's doing pure dead brilliant at school, you know. Really proud of him.'

Fraser manages a smile. 'Glad to hear it. You've done well with him.'

'Aye, I have, right enough.'

'And you're doing okay?'

'Aye,' she says again. 'I'm still having a wee drink every now and again, but not too bad. I cannae afford it. School uniform, books, they all cost so much money. But aye, I'm still clean. No worries about that.'

He believes her. She looks very different from the girl he knew years ago, the beauty she was back then, and the terrible state she got into, and then the long, slow process getting out of it. It was getting pregnant with Charlie that had done it, finally. She'd never thought the pregnancy would last – she had lost others – but it had, and she'd managed to get off the gear.

And now here she is. Close up, her dark hair is threaded with silver at the roots, and there are lines at the corners of her eyes that tell something of the journey she has been on, but her complexion is clear.

'You looking at me, Fraser Sutherland?' she teases, coming towards him and slipping her arms around his waist.

He hugs her back, appreciating the familiarity of her body against his. She slides a hand down the front of his jeans, cupping him.

'Kelly ...' he says, and moves away.

'No strings,' she says. 'I'll even make you another coffee afterwards, if you want one.'

'It's no' that,' he says. 'I didn't come here for that.'

'I know, big man. You came to check up on me, to see I wasnae in trouble again.' She pulls away, one cheeky glance down at him and back up to his eyes.

'Aren't you?' he says, looking back at the front room. 'Only I can't help noticing that it looks like your telly's gone.'

'Aye, well,' she says, 'you always were observant.'

'You sold it?'

'It got broken. It's nothing to worry about.'

She goes back to the kitchen, which means it is something to worry about. She gets the coffee from the machine and hands him the mug.

'Want to go upstairs? It's warmer up there. And I want to show you my room, it's really pretty.'

He relents and follows her up the narrow stairs, ducking his head under the low ceiling. There are two rooms up here – one for Charlie, with a pile of books and toys and a small bed with a Spider-Man duvet cover on it. And then her room, painted pale blue. What some people might call minimalist but probably has more to do with a lack of spare cash: just the bed and a single wardrobe set in the alcove beside the fireplace, bare floorboards, a single white cotton rug, an IKEA chair.

'Very nice,' he says.

'Thanks.' She sits on the bed, cross-legged. He goes to the window, looks out over a small concrete yard.

'Have you met someone?' she asks, out of nowhere. How she knows this, he has no idea. She's never asked him that question before, not once.

It takes him a moment to respond.

'Aye.'

'Really? How on earth?'

He manages a smile. 'Long story.'

'Is she good to you?'

'Aye, I guess she is.'

'And she likes you?'

'Don't sound so bloody surprised about it. I think she does. Maybe. If I'm lucky.'

'So it's early days? Ach, well, I'm very happy for you.'

He had been kidding himself, thinking that he might end up here in her bed. It was never actually going to happen, even if he'd been pretending to himself that it wouldn't matter, that he wouldn't be bothered by it, why should he be? Turns out right now his thoughts are full of a certain redhead, and if he were to do anything with Kelly it would feel wrong. It would *be* wrong. He has never felt like this about a woman before. Everything about it feels strange.

'I like your house,' he says. Then he looks round at her. 'Is it safe?'

Her face clouds and he knows it, then.

'Who broke your telly?'

'Just some guy,' she says.

'A punter?'

'No!'

He believes her, but almost immediately she adds, 'I'm no' doing that any more, Fraser, I told you that. I'm clean and just living for me and the wean now. I need money but it doesn't matter how bad it gets, I'm no' doing that again.'

'So who's this guy?'

'Someone I was seeing. Turns out he's a bastard, same as everyone else. Apart from you,' she adds. 'You're about the only decent man in the whole of Scotland. Probably the world.'

'Thanks for the compliment. I can be a bastard just like the rest.'

'Not that I've seen. You've only ever been kind to me.'

He drinks the coffee, tries not to wince at it. It tastes like gravy. He comes to sit on the side of the bed. He can see the grey sky outside, hear the rain as it starts and gets heavy almost immediately, rivulets chasing their way down the window.

'Tell me about your girl,' she says.

He lets her ask, knowing that if he pushes her for information about the arsehole who's broken her telly she will clam up.

'She's working on the island with me.'

'That's handy.'

'Aye. It's only temporary.'

'What, the job is temporary?'

'Aye. Someone else is supposed to be doing it, she's just … filling in. What?'

'So what's gonnae happen when she leaves?'

He's been trying not to think about that. Looks at her. Shrugs.

'Nothing's gonnae happen.'

'What's her name, your girlfriend?'

'She's no' my girlfriend.'

'What is she, then, big man?'

She's teasing him. And what's with their insistence on knowing each other's names? It's not as though they are ever going to meet. He has a sudden image of it, of them shaking hands and having a chat about him over a cup of tea, and shudders.

'Her name's Rachel,' he says, reluctantly.

'So you an' Rachel, who's not your girlfriend, she's just a temporary thing too?'

'Aye.'

'She know that?'

'She does. Are you trying to get at something?'

He's trying to work out what that expression on Kelly's face is all about. There's a weird sort of concentration, as though she can't quite join the dots.

'So … what you're doing basically is using her as a temporary fuck?'

'Nobody's using anybody. We both know what's going on. It's good. It's fun. I don't need a bloody lecture, all right?'

'What's she like?'

He has to think about this for a few moments, trying to summarise what it is about Rachel that is different from every woman he's ever met.

'She's kind.'

'And gorgeous?'

He looks back at her, still a bit suspicious as to where this might be leading. 'I think so.'

'Prettier than me?' she pouts.

What's he supposed to say in answer to that?

'Kelly, I'm always going to look out for you. I promised, right enough. But maybe you could give her a bit of room?'

'Temporary, huh?' She smiles back at him. 'Can I give you a wee cuddle, then, if I'm not allowed to get you naked any more?'

He puts the empty coffee cup on the floor and lies down next to her, folding his arms around her. She nestles her head into his shoulder.

'You need to find somewhere else to live,' he says.

'I'm sick of running away. I've done it too many times. And Charlie likes his school. I don't want tae make him go through what I went through at his age. I moved around so much, I never finished a school year in the same place I started it. He's smart, Fraser, really clever. Much cleverer than me. He deserves a proper education.'

'So what about this guy?'

'He's gone. I telt him to piss off.'

'And has he?'

She's silent. Here we go, he thinks.

'Maybe you could have a wee word,' she says.

'A wee word?'

'Not even that. If you just telt him to leave us alone, maybe?'

Later, he gets her to write the guy's name and phone number down on a piece of paper. He takes it and folds it and sticks it in his wallet. At the same time he gets the envelope out of his jacket pocket and places it on the dining room table, next to the pile of maths books.

'What's that?' she asks.

'That is your insurance,' he says. 'Use some of it to get a new telly, maybe. And keep some in case you need to move.'

'You don't have to—'

'I know I don't. I'll do it anyway.'

'Fraser,' she says. But there's no end to her sentence. She puts her arms around him and buries her face in his chest.

His hand, on her shoulder. She's shaking.

'Come on, now,' he says.

'I'm okay, big man,' she says, her voice high. 'We'll be okay.'

He wipes her tears. 'Enough of that,' he says.

'Will Rachel mind, do you think, if you visit us sometimes?'

'Not up to her, is it,' he says. He's about to make some comment about her not being around for much longer and then changes his mind. 'Maybe I'll introduce you to her. If you want.'

'I'd like that,' she says, smiling, wiping under her eyes with a finger. 'You cannae keep giving us money, though.'

'If you need it, I can.'

'Rachel won't like it. Your not-girlfriend, that you came all the way over here to tell me about.'

He wants to tell her not to talk about Rachel any more. Something about it is making him uncomfortable: that sense of past and present colliding, something happening that is beyond his control. Probably he will visit Kelly again in a month or two, to tell her that Rachel's gone, that Rachel never really happened in the first place, and he'll bring her another couple of hundred and sleep with her again and it will be like old times.

Except he will have Rachel in his head, won't he? Temporary or not, he thinks Rachel will always be in his head.

Rachel

Rachel gets up early to let Bess out and feed her. She's used to being fed at some ungodly hour of the morning but when Rachel emerges from her bedroom Bess is lying on the landing, stretched out and comfortable, where she had been last night. There is much tail-wagging when breakfast is produced.

Lefty's door is still firmly shut and the lighthouse is silent. It's possible he's already up and out somewhere, but Rachel thinks it's unlikely. If the weather holds today and it's not too windy she and Lefty are going to clear the guttering on the bird observatory's roof.

There has been no further discussion about what he's doing here.

She's been thinking about it a lot. Lefty. Maggie. Fraser. Has decided that Fraser has probably told him not to say anything. All that insistence that they should keep out of each other's way – no wonder he didn't want Rachel talking to Lefty. None of it really makes sense, that Lefty is – what was the guy's name?

Lefty is Jimmy Wright, the drug dealer who was driving the car when Maggie was killed. What she would dearly like is to talk it all over with Mel, but she promised not to tell anyone about Lefty and Rachel is someone who takes her promises very seriously. And now she has been here all this time, now that she and Lefty have this weird sort of friendship, even if it's based on a mutual love of sea glass – it feels as if Lefty's presence on the island is a glaring omission.

Besides, it's been nearly a fortnight since she last communicated with Mel. That's not deliberate. It's just that the island is another world, a different place. As if Island Rachel is a different person from Norwich Rachel. She doesn't want to be reminded of her old self any more, the fuck-ups that probably weren't really her fault, the endless trying to do the right thing and getting it wrong, the way she hated herself and her failure to get things right. The way she couldn't let herself be happy.

She makes a coffee using Fraser's beans. It feels illicit, but she needs something to stop her head spinning.

And then, she opens up her laptop, sees her emails and her stomach falls to the floor.

From: Julia Jones
To: Rachel Long

Hey Rachel,

I hope you're well. Just wanted to let you know some really great news - that my mum is much better. She has lots of friends who can help her with day to-day errands, and her mobility has improved a lot in the last few weeks. She's insisting that she doesn't need me here any more, so I'm hoping that I can start work, maybe at the beginning of the month? I've written to Marion to ask if I could get the boat over on Friday 7th June, then we could maybe have a handover and you could get the boat back on Saturday when the birders arrive? Would that work for you? I think Marion should be pretty flexible about it.

I hope this might be okay with you. Marion says she thinks it will.

Anyway, thanks so much for what you've done. I'm looking forward to meeting you and saying thank you properly, and also to seeing the island.

Julia xx

She can't quite manage to open the other email, which is from Marion. She shuts the laptop and looks at Bess, who is fast asleep in her bed. The dog has been subdued without Fraser but she has succumbed to tummy rubs and treats, and has behaved herself impeccably.

Just under two weeks left! She feels a sudden clammy grasp, as if Norwich Rachel is clutching at her. This new life is temporary after all; she might love the island, all of it, the rain and the mud, the pecking terns and the puffins and the wind, but it's not hers. It's not her life. She's going to have to go back.

She needs to clear her head. And Fraser will be here later.

Fraser

It's late afternoon when the *Island Princess* sails. Two hours spent staring across the grey, choppy sea. The sea matches the sky matches his mood, and, although Fraser is never seasick, there is a queasiness rolling around inside him at the thought of going back.

There are no new birders. The lot that were supposed to be coming today cancelled at the last minute. It was Craig who messaged him, not Marion, so he has no idea if it has anything to do with Environmental Health. Craig was vague about it, said something about costs, and that he's already told Rachel.

Fraser has other things on his mind.

He has more or less decided that he needs to finish things with Rachel.

He has been thinking back to all the times they fucked, all those times he was inside her thinking *it's just sex* and *it doesn't mean anything* because of course it does. You don't fuck someone regularly without it meaning something; that's why he used sex workers and why he only saw Kelly every few months. He needs to finish it, now, before she gets too attached to him. Before she gets hurt.

Added to which, he has received an email from Marion, and another one from Julia herself. Rachel will be going sooner than he thought. Of course this was always on the cards. But the past couple of months have gone by much faster than he had anticipated. He remembers that first day, thinking she wouldn't last. He remembers her coming into the hallway covered in mud where she'd slipped on her way back from the bird observatory. But she'd stuck it out, and now he can't quite imagine the island without her. Can't imagine someone else coming here in her place.

He is full of good intentions, here on the boat, watching the horizon swinging up and down and the island getting closer and closer. But who knows what will happen when he gets there?

This, he thinks, is exactly why it's easier to not get involved with anyone.

Meanwhile he is thinking of the man he had a word with a couple of hours ago, in a bar near the harbour. He'd been easy enough to track down, easy enough to recognise from Kelly's description. There hadn't been a need for any actual violence, or any actual threats, or even a raised voice. Fraser had realised long ago that people are most scared of him when he's quiet, when he's calm. It's as though they recognise the look in his eyes, and that, coupled with the sheer size of him, is enough. They can see in his eyes that look, the one that says that he genuinely does not give a fuck about anything. That he has absolutely nothing to lose, and would explode just for the hell of it if he needed to, and that he wouldn't regret it afterwards.

Nobody likes to challenge a man like that. And wee Kevin Murray didn't, either, even with three of his friends. The only thing left to think about as he left the bar was to wonder what the hell Kelly had seen in the guy, even for a brief moment. Even in the fucking dark. Even with a drink inside her.

Afterwards he'd sent a text to Kelly, telling her to call him immediately if she had any more trouble, although what he thinks he can do about it when he's two hours offshore, he couldn't say. It's not that he enjoys hurting people. But if it's going to happen, he'd rather do it to someone who deserves it, like Kevin Murray, or Lefty, than someone who doesn't – like Kelly. Or Rachel.

Robert shouts down from the wheelhouse, something about a flask. In the cabin Fraser finds a canvas bag that has a stainless steel flask inside it, an old ice-cream tub with what looks like two rounds of sandwiches inside. He takes the whole bag up the narrow metal stairs.

'Ta,' Robert says. 'You want coffee?'

Fraser thinks about it for a moment and declines, although his stomach is rumbling. 'What's in your sandwich?'

'Sausage. Want one? Help yoursel'.'

He opens the tub, catches a whiff of the cooked sausage. The sandwiches are a little clammy from having been put in the tub still warm, but the bread is fresh and they taste good.

'How's things going over there wi'out you?' Robert shouts over the noise of the churning engine. 'You heard?'

'Not heard anything,' Fraser replies, mouthful of sausage.

'You reckon the lassie's been okay over there wi' him?'

'She can look after herself,' he says. 'Besides, they're best friends.'

'Seriously?'

'Don't look at me like that. I feel shit enough about it.'

'He been behavin' himself, though?'

'Aye. More or less.'

There is a pause.

'Cannae quite believe he's still alive, if I'm honest.'

Fraser thinks. 'Me neither. Given the state he was in.'

'Did you ever think about just leaving him where he was?'

They have made this boat journey together a few times since Lefty arrived on the island. Fraser has had dinners at Robert's house, with his wife, and his daughter Annie and her boyfriend and their wee baby. He has had plenty of nights drinking with Robert in the Dreel Tavern and has worked his way through a bottle of single malt in his own front room with him. But, every time this subject has come up, one or the other of them has shut it back down again.

'Aye,' he says. 'I think about it all the time.'

'But you didnae, though, did you.'

'Hate myself for it, mostly.'

'You couldnae win. Whatever you did, you would end up doing the wrong thing, right?'

'I thought you would phone the coastguard.'

Fraser thinks he detects a fleeting, wry grin before Robert replies. 'Why would I want tae do that, eh? Far as I was concerned, he never got on the boat in the first place.'

When Maggie was just a baby, Robert's eldest daughter Rosemary had been just about to finish school. She'd been getting good grades, looking likely to get a place at university – the first in his family to go. There had been no real event, no point at which things had started to go wrong, although Robert had told Fraser he'd been through it in his head many times. She just started hanging out with the wrong people, he'd said. She was stressed over grades. Started smoking weed to relax, then other stuff, then crack. Then she'd left home and they'd lost touch for a while. Two years later she was dead, an overdose of heroin in a squat in Edinburgh.

So Robert has his own issues with Lefty. Perhaps not with Lefty specifically, but with drug dealers in general. The dealers who supplied Rosie were never identified. Lefty has provided him with someone to hate.

'Do you ever blame yourself,' Fraser says, 'for Rosie?'

'Aye, it would be easy to do that. Jeannie does. She's had counselling, you know, I told you. But I figure lots of girls get through schools and exams and life wi'out drugs. They tell 'em all about it in schools. She was a clever girl. She made her choices. But if it wasnae for the dealers, right, there wouldnae be the availability. They're the bad guys, Fraser, no? Not us.'

Fraser thinks it isn't quite so black and white. If it were that easy, he would have tipped Lefty over into the loch that night. He'd had the anger right enough, but something had stopped him doing that, the same thing that's still stopping him today. He thinks it has something to do with that skinny white child's body, marked all over with ink and bruises and scars.

Rachel

Rachel can see the boat coming from her position at the top of the ladder. It's still a long way off, about an hour, maybe more. She has been looking for it all afternoon and now she's seen it she is finding it hard to concentrate on scooping the crap out of the bird observatory's gutters.

She is out here in a T-shirt with a fleece over the top, a pair of rubber gloves, two buckets. Lefty started off holding the ladder but there is no wind to speak of, just a warm breeze. Now his job is emptying one bucket of the mess of moss and dirt and crud while she fills the other, taking the mess who knows where but hopefully somewhere downwind of the bird observatory's windows, because it stinks of rotten fish and slimy vegetation.

Unsure how to bring it up, eventually she just comes straight out with it.

'So,' she says, 'I'll be going in a couple of weeks.'

'Going where?'

'You know I'm just temporary, right?' Even as she says it she wonders if Fraser has ever actually told him, ever bothered to explain about Julia coming and how come she's here instead.

'Do you no' like it?' Lefty says, holding up the bucket of fermented seabird shit as if it's pirate treasure.

'I do like it. But this isn't my job. I'm not allowed to stay, even if I want to.'

Lefty shrugs as if he's not bothered either way, but when the bucket's still half-full he takes himself away to empty it, leaving her with a handful that she has to drop back into the gutter.

A cloud crosses the sun and Rachel has a sense of time slipping, of all the things she could do, meant to do, all the things that need fixing and now she probably won't get to fix them. Lefty being one of them.

'Tell me about Maggie,' she says, when he comes back.

He looks at her, startled by the abrupt change of subject. 'I'm no' supposed to.'

'He's not here, though. And I want to hear about the Maggie you knew. Not his sister. She was your friend, wasn't she?'

'Aye.'

He says she was a pain in the arse a lot of the time. He says she was unreliable and vague and was never answering her phone or turning up when you needed her. She was funny and bright and pretty. She argued with her mother a lot, hated school, hated teachers and losers. And she idolised her big brother.

'She talked about him?'

'All the time. But he was different wi' me.'

There is a pause while Rachel lets this sink in. She scans the horizon, and locates the boat again. She has a sudden sense of urgency, of this being an opportunity for Lefty to talk freely, that might not come again.

'How do you mean?'

'She always said he was soft as shite, and all I saw was this huge fucking arsehole of a big brother.'

'You knew him then?'

'Only through her. But I met him loads of times, aye. Met him in the pub. Sometimes he was all right, but most of the time he was – well, you know … I telt him I'd look after her. That was my mistake, maybe.'

She looks across at him, standing there swinging the empty bucket against his knee. 'What do you mean?'

'Couldnae look after mysel', let alone a wee girl.'

'He blames you for it,' she prompts.

'Aye. He does. He's right to.'

'It was an accident, though,' she says, 'wasn't it?'

He doesn't say anything for a long time and she wonders if he's heard her. He just stands there, holding the bucket. She looks across to the horizon – the boat is getting closer.

'Aye, right,' he says, at last.

'You want to tell me what happened? Here.' She passes him the full bucket and he hands her the empty one. For several minutes there have been three puffins sitting on the roof, watching her efforts critically. One of them has a beakful of sand eels and a moment later a razorbill flaps up and tries to grab at the silvery haul. The puffin lurches off and the other two soon follow, barking their disapproval.

Without another word Lefty walks off with the bucket. She watches him go and glances again at the boat, wonders where Fraser has been and what he has done and who with. Wonders about Kelly.

A few minutes later Lefty comes back. She's not going to press him, she thinks. Besides, this part of the operation is requiring all her attention because the ladder is now just at the edge of a flight of three stone steps and it's not completely level.

'Anyway, I don't remember what happened,' he says.

'Lefty,' she says, 'will you just hold the ladder again?'

He comes up behind her and puts a foot on the bottom rung, which causes a distinct wobble. She grips the top and sucks in a sudden breath.

'They said I was going too fast, lost control on the bend. Hit a tree.'

'Were you unconscious?'

'I don't remember,' he says.

There is a long pause, punctuated by slops of muck dropping into the bucket. The smell of it makes her gag. She blames the puffins – the smell on the island has worsened considerably since they came back. Out on the sea, the boat is closer. Maybe half an hour left, she thinks.

'I remember her crying,' he says, quietly. 'I remember telling her it was going to be okay.'

She looks over her shoulder at him, but he's looking at his foot on the ladder, his fingers still tight around the empty bucket. They are nearly at the end of the gutter. She stretches to reach for the last handful.

'Wasnae okay, though. Was it?'

Rachel climbs down the ladder carefully. He puts the bucket down and grips the sides of it until she descends lower, and he moves to one side.

'Are you still taking drugs?' she asks.

'No,' he says, looking startled. 'Course not – where would I even get them?'

'When did you get clean?'

A pause. 'Here,' he says vaguely.

'Here?'

He shrugs. 'No drugs here, is there? Didnae have a choice.'

'You could have gone back.'

'The weather was bad, you know. The boat couldnae come back. At first when I thought he'd locked me in that cottage and taken ma gear I was sure I was gonnae die. I was sick wi' it, ravin'. And then I got out and it was peltin' down and I didnae have a fucking clue where I was and then I woke up in the lighthouse, fuck knows how long after that. By the time the boat came back I thought about going through that all again and I wanted tae gi' it a try, you know, see if I could stand it. Not many places in this country where you physically cannae get drugs if you want them. If I was gonnae get clean anywhere, it was here.'

'And Fraser let you stay?'

'He didnae want me here really.'

'I know. But – I mean, he could have got you back on the boat, couldn't he?'

'Aye.'

'But he didn't.'

'No. And—'

'And what?'

'And he fed me food wi' vegetables, and gave me a bed. And an Xbox.'

'So he must actually want you here, right?'

'Aye. It's like he wants me here as a reminder.'

'Of Maggie?'

'Aye.'

He wants to keep hurting, she thinks. *He's punishing himself for letting her down.*

'Still, even with Fraser looking after you, I can imagine that getting clear of drugs must have been awful,' she says. Pretty much everything she knows about drugs and drug addiction comes from *Trainspotting*.

He says nothing to that.

'What about now?'

He looks at her, brows furrowed.

'I mean, you could leave now, couldn't you? If you wanted to.'

'If I wanted to?'

She goes back to the gutter, unable to bear the look in his eyes. Trying to keep it casual. Even as she says it, she wonders what the hell she thinks she's doing. It's the frustration of wanting to help, wanting to make things better for both of them, and not being sure of the best way to go about it. *If you fling enough solutions at a problem*, she thinks, *maybe one of them will stick.*

'Where would I go?' he asks.

'You could come back with me.'

'Where?'

'To Norwich.'

He makes a noise, like an incredulous *pfft*, as if she's just asked him to move to the moon. *Worth a try*, she thinks.

'Will you empty this and then fill the buckets with clean water? I just want to swill it through, check it's all clear.'

She passes him the last one, and he trots off willingly enough.

The boat is rounding the south side of the island, skirting the coast. She can see it clearly enough to see the two figures in the wheelhouse. Thinks about waving.

Fraser is nearly home.

Fraser

The sun comes out just as the boat comes in to the harbour. Must in all its glory, emerald-green and screaming with birdlife.

He had not expected a welcoming committee, but as he throws his bag on to the jetty and steps across he notices Rachel at the top of the slope, wiping her hands on something. She sees him looking and waves.

Robert passes across the two crates of extra stuff Fraser has acquired on the mainland and then says goodbye. By the time Rachel has joined him on the jetty the *Island Princess* is already manoeuvring her way out of the harbour.

'Fuck me,' he says. 'What's that smell?'

She smiles at him, a bright, white, happy smile. 'Well, hello to you, too,' she says. 'The smell is probably me. I've been clearing the guttering on the bird observatory.'

'I was supposed to do that. It's on my list.'

'Well, now you don't have to. Anyway, the bird observatory is my territory for the time being. Although not for much longer.'

'Aye, so I heard. How's it been here?'

He means Lefty, of course. She doesn't answer for a moment, as if she's thinking about it.

'Fine. How was your trip?'

'Good. Got things done. You know.'

He's not hugged her – she stinks, and her fleece is spattered with God knows what – or kissed her. Lefty knows to keep out of Robert's way when the boat comes. As soon as the boat

325

rounds the headland, he's entirely alone with her. But she's already started heading back up the hill.

'I need a shower,' she calls.

Rachel

Lefty stays for dinner.

He doesn't want to, but Rachel asks Fraser while he's standing in the kitchen, one hand on the door of the freezer, about to remove one of his frozen ready-burgers.

Fraser has brought asparagus back with him and he's adding it to a risotto. Rachel's not entirely sure Lefty will eat that, but when she says, 'It's just like extra-tasty rice,' he nods and looks at Fraser for his approval. Maybe Fraser can be persuaded to put peas in it, and get the ketchup out. That'll help.

While he was on the mainland Fraser has found the time to get a haircut and his beard has been newly trimmed. He looks very different. Smarter. Less wild. It's taking her a while to get used to it.

The whole thing – interacting with the two of them – is getting easier, and harder at the same time. Lefty goes out to put the chickens away for the night. Fraser has his back to her.

She wants to get this out of the way early, so that she can get used to whatever he says in response. She's been thinking about how to approach it, how to ask, whether to try and lead him into the topic gradually or whether to skirt around it, and as always she ends up just blurting it out.

'Did you see Kelly?'

He doesn't look round. For about five seconds he stops snapping the asparagus stalks. Then he says, 'I did, aye.'

'She okay?'

'She's fine.'

There is a long, hollow pause. Waiting for him to say something else, wondering if he's going to elaborate. There is no sign of Lefty and Rachel suddenly wishes he were here, because she is better at keeping her emotions in check when Lefty's around.

Then there is a weird rollercoaster moment, a quick one-two in which suddenly everything is brilliant, and then everything is not very good at all.

'I was telling her about you,' he says, really quite cheerfully.

'Oh?' She wants to ask him to elaborate, but she doesn't get a chance. He turns around, leans back against the counter, looks at her. There's something going on behind his eyes. Either she's got better at seeing it, or he is being less careful about what he gives away.

'Thing is,' he says, 'we shouldn't be doing this.'

She feels her stomach drop. 'Doing what?'

He makes a vague circle with his finger. 'This,' he says. 'This whatever it is that you want to call it. This having sex all the time.'

She raises an eyebrow that she hopes suggests a vague *what the fuck* that she can't quite bring herself to express.

'I don't want you to get hurt,' he says.

'I'm doing just fine,' she says, really quite coldly. 'But, you know. Whatever you think. Given that I'll be leaving on the eighth. I guess you're just getting it out of the way now, right?'

'Rachel...' he says.

She stares at him. She is absolutely not going to cry. Not now, not later when she's alone. She is not going to let him see anything – no disappointment, no hurt, no anger. He has been absolutely clear about everything all the way through. He has been fair.

She wants to yell at him, in truth. She wants to remind him that he's been as enthusiastic about what happened between them as she has. She has wanted him fiercely because the pleasure he's given her has been like nothing she's had before, but even so she has not pressured him, she has not asked him for anything, and still this same thing is happening, and it feels a lot like rejection. And even when there is no fucking relationship, she wants to shout, it still fucking hurts.

But it's too late to take it back now. It's already done.

'Yes?' she says, smiling.

'I'm sorry. I'm giving you mixed messages. I just wanted to make things clear. Right?'

'No more sex,' she says, her voice tight and cold. 'I got it.'

In the doorway, Lefty gives a little cough.

'Ah, fuck's sake, you wee scrote,' Fraser says. 'You been listening?'

'No,' Lefty says, alarmed. 'I just got here.'

'Fucking sit down, then.'

'There's no need for that,' Rachel says. 'It's not his fault you're in a bad mood, is it?'

Lefty's eyes widen, staring at her, then he looks over to Fraser as if he's ready to leap in between them. Fraser brings over two of the plates, puts them down on the table with a tiny bit more force than might be required, but thankfully not enough to break anything.

'It usually is his fucking fault,' he growls. 'Pardon me if I got it wrong for a change.'

Here we go, she thinks. *Another man who always has to have the last word.*

Fraser

Before dinner Fraser had retrieved his bag from the hallway. He has bought her, as requested, some ridiculously expensive shampoo, three pairs of thick wool socks size 4–7, and four of the worst-looking gossip magazines he's ever seen in his life, one of which includes a photo-exposé extending to six pages that mainly consists of two celebrities he's never heard of going for a walk in a park in London. He had stared at all the magazines for ages before finally just picking some at random. They all looked as bad as each other, and the expression on the cashier's face as she scanned the contents of his basket – the magazines, plus dark chocolate, four bottles of single malt and a box of condoms – said a lot.

He left the rest of it and brought out one of the whiskies, the Balvenie, and the magazines. He does not exactly regret buying the condoms, as he had only one left, but he's wondering now whether they are going to be left to go out of date. He had a large slug of whisky while he was cooking.

The conversation over dinner has been pretty much non-existent, although she has expressed some gratitude for what he'd bought her, insisted on paying him back, even for the socks, which now aren't going to get a lot of wear.

As soon as he's finished eating, Lefty mumbles his thanks, washes up his plate and scarpers.

Rachel is sipping her wine – a beautiful cold Orvieto that went well with the risotto. 'This is lovely,' she says, 'as always. Thanks.'

'Nae bother,' he says, glad that she is apparently talking to him after all.

'It's not that I don't care about you,' he ventures, after a pause. 'I don't want you to think that.'

'Oh, please,' she says. 'We both knew it was coming. Don't go all soft on me.'

He doesn't want to get drunk but it feels as if that's what's going to happen and he doesn't have the energy to get out of the way. He's already halfway there, or more than halfway, because he has had more of the wine than Rachel has. The bottle's empty and she's still on her first glass. He's going to need to rely on her to be strong, he thinks, and that's a bit fucking unfair of him, given what he's just done.

While he washes up she tells him about the guttering, and the puffins, and he listens, or rather he doesn't, because he's thinking about Rachel leaving and someone else coming and how the hell he's going to cope with that. He doesn't *want* anyone else. He wants her. He wants her to stay forever. He wants Julia to cease to exist. But it's fine. It's all fine. Rachel will probably forgive him, and maybe she has already, if she even

329

had a problem with it in the first place, which he's suddenly not sure about.

It would have been easier if she'd cried, or if he'd seen some sort of upset on her face. Then he could feel like a shit but at the same time know that he had absolutely done the right thing at the right time because she is vulnerable and lonely and she has begun to get – he searches in his fogged brain for the right word – attached. But instead she had just looked at him, maybe a little surprised, maybe a little bit disappointed, but with something resolute and casual about the expression on her face. As though she's okay either way.

Which means, he realises with a jolt that makes him want to pour another glass of the Balvenie, which *means* that he's the one with the feelings, and she's the one that's mastered the casual thing. Fuck. And to make matters worse the whisky has loosened his tongue and, where she had always been the one nervously filling the silence with chatter, to his utter horror and confusion he's doing it himself.

'She's got herself a new place,' he says, 'yet again. Kelly. A nice wee house right enough, but she's going to end up moving on again before too long, I can see it, aye. Like she cannae stay anywhere longer than a few months and it's not good for the boy. He's good at school, she says, and yet she cannae stay in one place long enough for him to get settled.'

'How old is he?' she asks.

He wonders vaguely at what point he told her about Charlie. He can't remember telling her but he must have done, and he can't even really remember coming into the living room but he must have done that, too, because he is on the sofa and she is curled up in the armchair, the woodburner is lit – she did that, he remembers her crouching – and the bottle of Balvenie is looking like it's about half-full. That can't be right. He looks at the clock. It's nearly eleven.

'Six,' he says. 'Seven on the twenty-fifth of July.' There is a little pause, then he adds, out of the blue, 'Two days before your niece's christening.'

'Oh. I'd forgotten about that. I guess I won't have the excuse of being on the island any more.'

'Your sister will be delighted. You'd better RSVP, though, or she might not have space for you.'

'Don't. She'll be all huffy as it is.'

'Still want me to come with you?'

'Of course. If you can stand it.'

'I've never been to Norwich.'

He's not even sure if she's joking, but she leaves the silence to stretch, sipping at her wine. He thinks he has drunk too much. Then he opens his mouth to confirm it.

'She wanted to know all about you,' he says. 'She was all over it. I don't know what it is wi' you women, wanting to know everything about each other.'

'We all have this need to compare notes,' Rachel says evenly.

'I told her you were gorgeous.' He goes to say more, stops himself. Something at the back of his brain is firing off, some sort of drunken defence mechanism.

'Well, that's nice. Anything else?'

'Just that you're good to me. She said she'd like to meet you.'

He sees her eyes widen, thinks maybe that she finds the idea alarming. 'Och, don't worry. She's never met anyone before, I mean, not that there's been anyone before. Nobody's met anybody. Whatever.'

More whisky, he thinks. It will help him gather his thoughts.

'You're a bit drunk, Fraser, I think.'

'Aye, well. Drowning my sorrows, right enough. Aye.'

'What sorrows would those be?'

'The *losing you* ones.'

'Losing me? How are you losing me?'

'You're going and that other woman's coming instead. And I don't want you to go.'

'You seem to be having trouble deciding what you want,' she says.

Ah, fuck, he thinks. Somewhere in his brain the defences are ringing an alarm bell and some sort of siren alongside it. But he's made the mistake of looking at her, curled up there with her hair in a long plait over her shoulder, and he can remember combing his fingers through her hair when she was asleep on him, and he's never going to get to do that again, is he? And the loss of it is just, for a moment, a bit devastating.

He feels the cold, dawning horror of having made a massive fucking mistake.

'I think I'd best go to bed,' he says, and struggles to his feet.

He makes it to the door and then upstairs, somehow aware that she's following behind him, as if she's going to be able to stop him if he falls. If he falls backwards he will tumble straight into her and push her all the way down the stairs, and that's why he's holding on to the banister with both hands very tightly indeed. And now he feels like a fucking idiot and he goes into the bathroom, attempts to lock the door and fails, and gives up and goes for a piss. Pisses all over the floor and makes a half-hearted attempt to clean it up because he's not a fucking barbarian and then he gives up on that too because when he bends over he nearly falls head-first into the pan.

When he leaves the bathroom the landing light is on but there is no sign of her. Bess is at the top of the stairs, as if she's standing guard to stop him falling down them. She shoots him a look that says just about everything he's feeling about himself.

'Don't you start,' he says to her, and snorts.

She looks at him in disgust and turns to scratch her neck, flicking black hairs in his direction.

There is no sign of Rachel, but the light is on under her bedroom door.

'Rachel,' he says, outside. And then again, louder. 'Rachel.'

'You okay?' comes the voice from inside.

'Oh, aye. I'm just…' he says, and forgets what he was going to say.

She opens the door. She looks so tiny, all that gorgeous red hair and the blue eyes and she used to kiss him, and he would do anything for one of those kisses right now. He reaches out a clumsy hand and tries to stroke her cheek, misses, catches her ear and then lands on her shoulder rather heavily. 'I'm sorry,' he says vaguely, breathing loudly through his nose. It sounds weird.

'For what?'

'All of it, all of the shite. You deserve better. Will you come to bed, Rachel?'

'No,' she says.

'Why no?'

'Because you're drunk.'

'Is that the only reason?'

She smiles at him, and he knows deep down that she thinks he is an absolute fucking loser.

'You should get some sleep,' she says. 'Have you got a bucket?'

'What for?'

'Go to bed,' she says. 'I'll get you one.'

Rachel

Rachel had not been expecting Drunk Fraser to put in quite such a dramatic appearance, nor for him to be quite so revealingly honest.

It takes a while, but eventually she finds a bucket in the workshop, removes the old rags and scrubbing brush and rinses it in the kitchen.

'Fraser?' She pushes open his bedroom door with some degree of trepidation.

He's already asleep, or perhaps passed out, face-down and diagonally across his bed. He's managed to get his jeans down to his ankles but other than that he's still dressed. She pulls them off, turns them the right way out and folds them, leaving them on his chair. He has not moved a muscle. There's no way on earth she is going to be able to wake him or move him. She puts the bucket at the side of the bed nearest to his head, turns on the bedside lamp so he can see it if he needs to, folds the duvet over him as much as she can, although he's lying on it. Then she turns off the main light and pulls the door to. It's very tempting to stay with him, in case he's sick, in case he needs help, but she will hear, anyway, if he wakes up in the night.

And besides, she thinks, it's entirely possible that he's been at least this drunk before, and survived it.

Fraser

The weather worsens throughout the day.

Fraser sends Rachel a text message but gets no reply; after half an hour he takes the quad out in the driving rain and heads to the bird observatory.

When he opens the door the scent of a curry hits him. He is simultaneously ravenously hungry and very slightly nauseous. And also really quite ashamed of his behaviour last night, which he can scarcely remember. Which means it was bad.

'Smells good,' he says.

Rachel looks up from the hob and smiles. 'Hope it tastes good. How are you doing?'

'Not bad. How come you're cooking?'

'I ordered all the food for this week before they cancelled, can't let it go off. So I'm doing some batch cooking for the freezer. It might help Julia out, who knows? Or maybe she'll have to bin it because of the food safety issue.'

'Can we have some of it for dinner?'

'Sure, if you trust my cooking. Does Lefty like curry?'

'Does he fuck. Is it beige and tasteless? No, then. Well, he doesn't eat my curry, anyway.'

The bird observatory is spotless, warm, fragrant; welcoming and ready for the guests that didn't come.

'Might as well stay here for a bit, then,' she says.

He's been thinking the same. The cliff path is grim in this

sort of weather, and he has no idea how to transport a pan full of curry back over the bumpy terrain. If they're going to eat it, they might as well eat it here.

'It'll be twenty minutes or so for the rice. Did you bring anything to drink?' she asks, bringing plates and cutlery over to the table where he's parked himself.

'You fucking kidding me?'

'Well, there are some beers in the fridge. One of the previous lot left them behind.'

'Aye, well, I can manage a beer if there's one going.'

He watches her in the kitchen, thinking how weird it is, like being in her house. She's got the radio on low, some classical station, not his sort of thing at all but somehow it feels soothing and civilised.

'I guess I owe you an apology,' he says eventually.

'What for?'

'I woke up to find a bucket by the bed. Was I that bad?'

'You were pretty wasted.'

He has very little memory of it. Just the feeling of having absolutely ruined everything, drinking too fast in an attempt to escape from it.

'Was I an arsehole?'

'You were … honest. It was quite refreshing.'

He feels a flare of annoyance at that. 'What d'you mean? I'm always honest.'

'Open, then. Which you're not, usually.'

'What's that mean?'

'It means I ask you things, and if you don't want to answer them you change the subject or you walk away.'

'What's wrong with that? Some things I just don't like talking about.'

'Like Maggie,' she says. 'And Lefty.'

Oh, aye, he thinks. *Here we go.*

'Look,' she continues, popping the lids of two beer bottles and bringing them to the table, 'I don't want to pry into your business, yours or Lefty's. But what you've got going on here

– it's just… it doesn't feel right. I just think things would be so much better if you could manage to talk to each other.'

Outside, the wind has picked up and is blowing hard against the side of the building. She looks up as the window rattles slightly in its frame. He starts to wish he had left it at the text message, that he'd never come.

'I'm not much good at talking,' he says. 'You've seen that for yourself.'

Because he can't meet her eyes he looks at her hand on her knee, at the tiny freckles on the back of it, the framework of the bones. Has a sudden vision of it clutching his shoulder. How that feels.

'He's hurting. You're hurting. Isn't that true? Isn't it time you did something about it?'

'Ah, give over. Talking isn't going to bring Maggie back, is it?'

'Nothing is going to bring Maggie back.'

That's the bald truth of it, right there.

'Fraser?'

He drags his gaze up from her delicate fingers to her face, finally meets her eyes.

'It wasn't your fault,' she says. 'And it wasn't his, either. You can't keep living through all this blame. It's just making everything worse.'

'How d'you figure that out?' he says dully.

'You're not taking responsibility for yourself. You're so busy blaming yourself for not being there when Maggie went out that night, blaming Lefty for being off his face and crashing the car. Blaming Maggie for, I don't know, for not being able to get herself clean. And it's horrible, but it's nobody's fault, is it? It just *happened*.'

He waits for several moments, not sure of the right words.

'You make it sound so simple,' he says.

'It's not simple. But you've been complicating things for years. It's not easy to fix. But it's not impossible, either.'

'Feels impossible right now,' he says. 'I don't know where to start.'

'By talking,' she says. 'Maybe just by getting it out there?'

'Maybe,' he says. 'Maybe.'

Rachel

At about eight in the evening the wind drops a little. They have been sitting in the living room in front of the woodburner, the radio still on in the background.

Fraser has been talking. They both have. There have been moments of depth, but mostly he is paddling round in the shallows, talking about Maggie as a baby, Maggie at school, their mother. How things were when he was younger.

Now Rachel goes to the porch and opens the door. It's still windy outside but it looks brighter; on the horizon the clouds are very black. Behind them the sky has patches of broken cloud and blue sky, the evening sun throwing shafts of light on to the stormy black sea.

'It's not so bad,' she says. 'If we're going back, we probably need to do it now.' Tempting as it is, she has no real desire to spend the night in the bird observatory, even with Fraser. Besides anything else, the linen is all clean and on the beds ready for the next lot of visitors; she doesn't want to be stripping beds and doing laundry if she doesn't have to.

The ride back to the lighthouse is bumpy and blustery, the quad splashing through deep puddles. Fraser drives round to the workshop and she opens the double doors so he can drive it inside. The chickens have already been tucked away for the night. Inside the hallway, the sound of Lefty's television is blaring from his open door. Rachel goes to see him.

'Thought you two had blown off the cliff,' he says cheerfully.

'We were waiting it out at the bird obs,' she says. 'Are you okay?'

'Aye,' he says. 'Tell Fraser the coastguard have been calling him.'

But Fraser is already in the living room, calling the coast-guard on the radio. Eventually he comes through to the kitchen. Rachel feeds Bess, although she has a strong feeling that the dog has already had something to eat, given that there is a bit of gherkin and a crust of ketchup-smeared burger bun remaining as evidence in her bowl.

'Everything okay?' she asks.

'Aye, so far. Lots of boats struggling out there.'

'Anything we need to do?'

'No. We're on alert.'

He stands in the kitchen, watching her. He is stone-cold sober and there is something going on with him, she thinks, something major. She remembers what Lefty said, yesterday, about Fraser being depressed. Is that true? Has she made things worse, by pushing him?

'You said something once,' he says. 'I've been thinking about it a lot.'

'What's that?'

'You said you thought I don't know what a relationship is.'

She nods. Where is this going?

'What is it, then? What's your definition?'

Deep breath in, Rachel. 'I think it's about allowing yourself to be happy, and wanting to make someone else happy.'

'So happiness is your definition? What if you're perfectly happy on your own?'

'Are you?'

'I'm fine, thanks very much. I just don't think I could make someone else happy. I think I could make someone else very unhappy, without meaning to. And anyway, if you're happy you're just waiting for the next disaster to come along and ruin things. It's better to stay where you are. It's easier to stay ... balanced.'

'The absence of happiness isn't balance, though, is it? It's misery. That's what you're feeling, all the time. It's been so long since you've been happy you've forgotten what it feels like. You're scared of it.'

Fraser

He has no energy left, no concentration whatsoever. His brain cells are pickled and yet his body is still wide awake.

Maybe he needed to get drunk last night to see it, to see what a complete arse he's been. He has ruined everything, he thinks, ruined his one chance at escape, his chance at happiness.

Rachel went to bed ten minutes ago. He lets Bess out, although the door nearly flies off its hinges and she casts a glance up at him as if he's insane. She is out less than fifteen seconds and then back inside, shaking the rain off her coat and then huddling next to the range.

He knows he should wait until she's asleep. He knows he should leave her in peace. He knows he wants more than anything to spend the night with her warm soft body pressed up against him. He wants to spend as much of the night as possible between her thighs. He wants to make her come, as many times as she can before she falls asleep. He wants to do this every night for the rest of his fucking life. Would she say yes, if he just came out with it and asked?

Fuck it, he thinks. She should be in bed by now.

But when he climbs the stairs she is just coming out of the bathroom and he can't help himself – he looks. Black pyjamas with wee stars on, her pretty little feet, the hair loose over one shoulder, and he's turned on by her as he always is. Can't help himself. She could just say a quick goodnight; she could go into her room and shut the door and that would be that. But she stands there on the landing, as if she's caught. Her eyes flicker down his body and back up to his mouth.

His self-imposed abstinence has lasted a day. What he's feeling is some kind of serious withdrawal.

He takes a deliberate step towards her. She doesn't move. His hand slides around her cheek to her neck, fingers stroking into her hair. He has to stop this, he thinks, vaguely. And then he kisses her.

Her hand comes up, falters, grips his bicep. His hand around her waist, pulling her up against him. She makes a sound and he lets her go.

'You said—' she says, breathing hard.

'I know what I said,' he admits, and into her mouth he says it again, for good measure. 'I know.'

'You need to go to bed,' she says, softly.

'Come with me,' he says. It sounds like begging, even to him. He can hear the desperation in his voice as keenly as he feels it.

'No,' she says. 'This isn't what you want.'

'Fuck that,' he says, his voice harsh, 'I've never wanted anyone more in my whole life.'

There is a moment where he thinks she's going to give in. And then he feels her pushing him away.

She can't quite meet his eyes. 'It's okay. It'll be okay. Just go to bed,' she says.

The weather is wild outside. He can hear the wind and the rain against the windows, the noise of a rising storm.

It's not the sex, he thinks, lying in bed and staring at the ceiling. It's not even what he wants, particularly, although obviously he wants that if she does; obviously he would give anything to have her here with him right now. It should be just about that, but it isn't.

She's leaving in less than two weeks. What's he going to do when she's gone? How is he going to carry on?

For years he has survived on his anger. It's the only thing he has let himself feel. Now alongside the anger suddenly there is desperation, desire, the fear of Rachel leaving, all of it rising up, sour and choking and terrible.

Something is going to happen. Something has to happen, or he'll explode.

11

Death wish

Fraser

At four-thirty, as it's beginning to get light, Fraser gets out of bed, dresses, and goes downstairs.

He has barely slept, and has the gritty eyes and dry mouth of someone who has lain awake for hours, brain belting out scenarios and suggestions without ever managing to rest. He has spent the last two hours with Lefty's knife in his hand, the one he had hidden under the bed – not really a very effective hiding place, but he couldn't seem to manage to get rid of it entirely. And now he's glad he didn't.

Bess is surprised to see him. She sleeps downstairs in the kitchen when she can't decide whose room to guard. He doesn't blame her, he thinks, as she eyes him reproachfully. He's a bad man, and, worse than that, he's a fool. Dogs may be faithful but Bess can see right through him.

He pulls on his jacket and his boots and Bess scampers to the door. 'Not now,' he says to the dog. 'You stay here.'

She lets out a long whine. This is not usual. She knows something's wrong.

In the end he relents and takes her with him.

The wind is violent and there are thick clouds scudding overhead, promising more rain. He walks to the cliffs, Bess a black ghost shadowing him, overtaking him and looping round, while the birds wheel and soar like angels overhead.

The bird observatory is in darkness and he skirts past it, heading for the north shore. It's only after a while that he realises he can no longer see Bess, and he stands and turns in a slow circle, taking in the roiling white waves, the grey-green turf, the leaden sky and the black stones, rain-soaked, of the ruined abbey. Something about the stones looks odd, unfamiliar, and he detours to the ruins, picking his way carefully between the burrows.

It starts to rain, a determined, soaking drizzle which develops into a downpour, heavy rain blasting into him horizontally, the wind making it hard to keep to a straight path, buffeting him off his feet.

From the ruins comes a strange sound, a moaning, a wailing; at first he thinks it's Bess and he hurries, tripping on a tussock of grass and catching himself just in time, his ankle twisting painfully.

The Victorian lighthouse-keepers had believed this place haunted, and this was why: the wind blowing from a particular direction whistled in a certain way through cracks and fissures in the stones, sounding like a child crying, sounding like a woman screaming. It's a horrible sound, calling to mind unbearable misery and desolation.

He finds Bess eventually, cowering under the altar stone, barely visible in the driving rain. He crouches down with her, the wind momentarily abating as he reaches the shelter, reaches his hand to her head. She licks his cold hand with a hot, dry tongue. If she's whining, he'd never hear it.

People came here for solace, he thinks, shocked by the thought as if he's just realised it. Once there was a building – the only building, the first building, before the lighthouse and before the cottages and before the bird observatory. Older than time, this place. And it was a place of sanctuary, a place of healing, a place of peace.

The emotion he's been holding back all this time rises in him and he gasps at it, gasps for breath against the buffeting wind. He thinks he's going to vomit and he pitches forwards on to his hands and knees, saliva running. His stomach lurches, and is still.

Gulping, he sits back on his haunches, feels something soft behind him. Bess pushes back against him and he hears a whine, another soft lick on his cheek. He wraps his arms around her, buries his face in her neck, the black fur wet and cold on his skin, warmer as he threads his fingers through to the drier, denser fur beneath the surface. The unmistakable stink of wet dog. It feels like something inescapably real, something he can hold on to to stop the madness of the storm, the madness that's raging even more fiercely inside his head.

'Make it stop,' he cries, not sure if he's talking about the madness or the wind or the wailing or the storm… but it doesn't matter. There's nobody to hear.

He feels the weight of the knife bumping against his chest. Thinks about it. He could die here, without too much trouble. He could use the knife. Or even take off his jacket, move out to the middle of the ruins where the wind and the rain are so fierce he can see nothing but swirling grey – he'd be dead within a few hours. Long before Rachel wakes up. She and Lefty probably won't even go outside today; why would they? She would think he was still asleep, in his room. She probably wouldn't even check till late morning, maybe even lunchtime.

And it would be peaceful, he thinks, despite the raging storm, because he's already tired, exhausted even, and he's not even feeling the cold any more. It's just the island, his island. He's seen fiercer weather than this, and the weather will continue and get worse and get better the way it always does, on and on, for the centuries to come. Long after the lighthouse has gone, the birds will still be here and the storms will come, and the island will stay, a granite rock upon the sea, the place where the pilgrims came and the sick got better, the place where Fraser Sutherland lay down and gave up.

He thinks, *I don't deserve to live.*

After all this, he recognises it for what it is. He's not angry at Lefty, he doesn't blame him. Not any more.

It's what Rachel said: the utter, bald truth of it. It's nobody's fault. So what's left, then, to explain it? It's not anger. It's something worse, something filthy, degrading, unforgivable: the shame of it. He's ashamed of Maggie. He was ashamed of her addiction, of her inability to fight, of the easy way she slipped from one phase of self-destruction to the next. How she went from weed to MDMA to cocaine to heroin and crack with barely a pause. How she said she was trying, and yet she never quite managed. And he'd loved her so much despite it all; it was easier to look for somewhere else to focus all of that emotion. Make it anger. Make it blame. Anything but the shame of having a drug addict for a sister; the shame of failing to protect her. The shame of failing to look out for his ma. The shame of failing to take his revenge for Maggie's death, when the opportunity had literally walked up to his door and waved in his face.

How do you ever recover from that? You don't, he thinks. You can't. He has spent the last six years ignoring it, pushing the guilt and the self-loathing down, using Lefty to explain the fury that keeps rising, and rising, and won't go away.

It took Rachel to make him see it. And now he's losing her, too.

His life, my life, he thinks. *It's right. I should have done this years ago.*

Beside him, Bess shivers and growls and then whines. He feels the muscles of her shoulder and her back tense, and then she springs out of his grasp. He looks up, looks for her, but, with a single bark that sounds as if it's come from a long, long way away, she is gone.

And then there's an inexplicable slow warmth, as if the sun's come out; but it's coming from inside, spreading outwards. He feels it flooding through him, emptying him, draining away and leaving nothing behind but exhaustion.

This is it, he thinks, his hand on the knife in his pocket. *This is it.*

He looks out into the swirling gloom, and waits.

Rachel

Rachel sits at the kitchen table. Outside, the storm is raging, howling against the lighthouse. The building should be solid as anything, but she is sure she can feel it moving, buffeted by the wind. It's been here for two hundred years, she thinks. Surely, if it was going to fall down, it would have done it by now.

Bess and Fraser are out there, somewhere. She tried to open the door but the pressure of the wind from the other side was too strong. She went the back way, through the back hall, and through the passage into the workshop. It was empty, the chickens still in their coop. She considered letting them out, at least into the workshop, but the wooden doors were rattling and the rainwater was coming in under the door. If the door went, the chickens would be blown away. So she left them where they were.

This morning when she got up there had been no coffee, no porridge, no sign that Fraser has had breakfast. She had gone upstairs and knocked, lightly, on his door, and when there was no answer she'd opened it a crack, and it was empty. She considers the possibilities, her hands cradling a mug of tea. Perhaps he went out early and the storm got worse suddenly, and he had to take shelter in the bird observatory? That must be it. Except, he wouldn't have taken Bess out in this weather, surely? She'd be at risk of flying off the cliff.

An hour passes. She fires up her laptop but there is no internet connection – the signal booster on the side of the lighthouse must have blown over. Lefty emerges after a while, stops in the doorway when he sees she is alone.

'All right?' she asks.

'Aye. Blowin' out there.'

'I don't suppose you know where Fraser's gone?'

He shakes his head. 'Taken Bess?'

'I'm worried.' Now she's said it out loud it has become true. It has become a thing.

'Ach, he'll be fine.'

'In this weather?'

'You should try it in winter.'

'But the wind—'

Lefty pushes some bread into the toaster.

Something's wrong, she thinks. Last night, wide awake, rattled by the kiss on the landing, her decision to say no, Rachel had lain listening to the storm for a long time before she fell asleep. Fraser has come back from the mainland different somehow, and not just because he's been smartened up. Something happened to him; it's as if he's broken, as if the depression that Lefty had named has come back. She has seen the effort of keeping himself together, the tension he holds in himself the whole time, has seen it seeping from him as if she'd pulled out a plug somewhere.

She gets up from the table and heads for the back hall and the staircase leading to the lamp room. From the top she might be able to see where he is – there's a view of the whole island, after all. But she's halfway up the stairs when, above the roaring of the wind, she hears the whirring and clicking of the light, which is still illuminated. She can't get up there until it switches itself off. She hears Lefty go back to his room and shut the door.

Halfway up the stairs, she stops at the window. It gives her a vertical letterbox view of a tiny bit of green and sky – but now it's just dark grey with low cloud and rain. Like being in a washing machine, she thinks. The view from the top will be the same. She won't see anything at all, much less a wee black speck of a dog and a man dressed in dark green waterproofs.

In that moment an enormous crash comes from the kitchen. Rachel jumps to her feet from her place on the stone steps and races down the spiral, through the hallway and into the kitchen. She's expecting the door to have blown in, not thinking that, actually, the wind could only blow it shut, because it opens outwards.

By the time she gets there, the door is closed. Fraser is standing there, soaked to the skin despite his enormous bulky jacket, which he has opened to reveal Bess, cowering in his arms.

Fraser

'Thank God,' she says, and throws her arms around his middle, even though she's warm and dry and he's freezing and wet. 'I was so worried about you!'

'I'm fine,' he replies, his voice hoarse, although he isn't. He is far from fine. But what else can he say?

I thought about dying…

and then I chickened out of that, too.

Bess has shaken herself all over the kitchen tiles, but right now he doesn't care. In the cupboard that houses the coats, which has a radiator inside it, is the old towel he uses occasionally for drying the dog; he retrieves it once Rachel has let him go, wraps Bess in it and rubs at her fur. She's shaking. Or perhaps he is. It's hard to tell.

He wants to be alone, and at the same time he thinks that being on his own might be a bad idea.

He is aware that he has somehow been at the edge of something. That he could have jumped, and for some reason he chose to turn back. At the moment he feels… nothing. Numb.

'Where were you?'

'Got caught in the storm.'

'But where? You've been gone hours. Were you at the bird observatory?'

'The ruins,' he says.

'The ruins? But there's no shelter there.'

He can't answer any more. He's weary, bone-tired; all he wants to do is get in the shower and then go back to bed, to sleep forever. If he doesn't wake up, it won't even matter.

'Fraser? Are you okay?'

'Sure,' he says.

'Why don't you go and get dried off? I'll make some porridge, shall I? Or soup – it's nearly lunchtime.'

'I don't want anything,' he says.

He turns away because he doesn't want to see the way she's looking at him any more, the way she's studying his face, her brows knitted in a frown. As if she's waiting for him to say something, or do something. Nothing makes sense. He has no idea where to begin.

Rachel

Rachel is dozing in her room, a book abandoned on the floor next to the bed, and she wakes, startled by a loud alarm. She gropes for her phone, but it's not that that's making the noise. Then she hears the thundering footsteps of Fraser emerging from his bedroom, thumping his way downstairs, and Lefty in the hallway.

'What is it? Is it a boat?'

She follows Fraser down the stairs. Finds him in the living room. Eventually the noise shuts off.

'Jesus Christ,' he says, and reaches for his phone.

'Signal's dead,' she says.

'Of course it is.' He makes for the radio. 'It's the coastguard,' he says to her. 'They page us if something's happening nearby.'

'Is it a boat?' Lefty says again, fidgeting with excitement.

Fraser ignores him and rubs a hand over his scalp, over his forehead. He's been asleep for hours, with the wind raging outside. The storm is still fierce, and the sky is dark, even though it's only just after six.

The radio connects.

'Anstruther Coastguard,' Fraser says, 'this is the Isle of Must. We had a page, over.'

She watches his face, trying to determine what's happening. The voice coming out of the radio is loud, but heavily accented and indistinct. Wherever they are, the wind is blowing wild too.

'Coastguard, roger that,' he says. 'Stand by.'

They wait for a moment and then Rachel goes to the kitchen to make some coffee. Fraser looks as if he needs it. She can hear voices: the radio and Fraser's reply. By the time she goes back in with a mug he is ending the call.

'A yacht's in trouble,' he says. 'Last location was halfway between May and here. The wind will likely blow her towards us. The lifeboat is searching, but we're going to look too. It's hard to see boats when the waves are high; the more eyes, the better.'

He takes the mug and downs the coffee, grimacing.

'Right,' Rachel says, her heart thudding. 'Do we split up?'

He looks at her. 'You don't have to come out,' he says. 'You can stay with the radio. Lefty and I can do it.'

'Stuff that,' she says. 'You literally just said the more eyes the better.'

He stares at her for a moment, as if he's readying himself to tell her in no uncertain terms that she's staying put, but then he seems to give up. 'Right,' he says. 'Whatever.'

He takes her to a cupboard in the hallway, pulling out thick waterproof jackets and trousers. They are all miles too big for her but he finds the hi-vis waterproof that he made her wear on the quad that time and hands it across to her. When she and Lefty are all kitted up, they stand in the hallway waiting for Fraser.

'Lefty, you go down to the south end. Stay away from the cliff, look for lights. Radio me if you see anything. I'll stay near the western shore. Rachel, you head for the north.'

He hands her a heavy-duty torch, and a smaller, hand-held walkie-talkie. 'We can't use these to contact the coastguard, only each other. You press this button to talk, and then release it to listen. If you see anything, contact me and I'll relay to the main radio to contact the coastguard. Right?'

'What if we don't see anything?' Lefty asks.

'Stick it out as long as you can. Come and find me, or radio if you need to. Is that clear?'

Fraser

The storm has abated considerably over the course of the day, something Fraser is glad about. His memories of the early morning spent in the screaming wind and the drenching rain have taken on a vague, surreal quality, not helped by having spent most of the day asleep. It feels as if, if it happened at all, it happened years ago.

Nevertheless, he thinks, as he walks unsteadily over the lesser-used paths to the west of the island, he is still here and he is glad of it, now. He came close this morning, closer than he's been for a long time, probably since Maggie's death, when all he'd wanted to do was follow her into the darkness. And now he's left with a headache and a sense of shame, his old companion, the wind no longer screaming at him but now just moaning, a vibrant sort of complaint that he's still standing.

The island has tried to claim him, has chewed him up a bit and spat him back out.

He looks up to see the bright neon bundle through the gloom, heading towards the bird observatory. She is being buffeted by the wind so she's actually walking at a diagonal, trying to keep her face to it so it doesn't knock her off her feet.

Then he looks back at the sea. The waves are monstrous.

He's seen it like this before, swirling grey and white, the foam and the surging waves crashing up the side of the cliffs, the roiling seas beyond. He can see no yacht, nothing but the waves rising and falling, white birds dotting the tops and hanging in the wind above them. The cliffs below him are full of nests, plenty of them already with eggs. Many of these will be gone by the time the storm passes, either blown off the side of the cliff or washed off by a wave. With luck, some of the birds will rebuild and start again – but many of them will not.

He looks to his left, along the ragged black coastline past the lighthouse to the southern tip of the island. He can see a glimpse of a hi-vis jacket there, too – Lefty. He is, for perhaps the first time, glad he is here. Who would have thought that the lad would be capable of so much? That he could want to risk his own comfort and safety for the good of others? That he would do it not just when asked, but willingly?

You gonnae kill me, big man? Here I am...

For a brief moment, the rain pauses, then starts again. He looks again to his right. He can just about see Rachel, a small, bright dot. She is past the ruins, nearly at the top end of the island. He is glad he can still see her. It's getting dark, difficult to pick out the rise and fall of the waves, only the contrast of the white as a wave breaks.

He concentrates on the horizon. He can see the line of light from the mainland. He can just see the dark, humped shape of the Isle of May. A moving light distracts him for a moment but he can tell from the beams that it's the lifeboat, a searchlight sweeping the waves. It appears, and disappears, rising and falling in the rough seas. He is glad his feet are on the springy turf of the island and not on the rollercoaster deck of the boat. And definitely not on the deck of the missing yacht, wherever it is.

They have probably made it to port somewhere.

In his experience as a veteran of coastguard searches, missing people usually turn up having a cup of tea in someone's kitchen, oblivious to the men and women who were out scouring land and sea in the dark and foul weather, their lives at risk. But no one minds, because that isn't always the case. None of the lifeboat crew he's met have ever felt anything but relief when a missing person turns up safe and well.

The weather is definitely easing. The seas are still furious, but the wetness on his face is the salty spray rising from the cliffs now, and not rain. He looks to his left, where Lefty, slightly closer, is still near the cliff edge. To his right, he cannot see Rachel at all. She is much further away.

It's a second before he sees it that he thinks: something's wrong. He is already making his way north, breaking into a perilous run on the uneven ground, when he hears the crackle of the walkie-talkie in his pocket, and sees the light of Rachel's torch, frantically waving to him in great wobbly circles.

Rachel

It appears from nowhere.

For a long time all she can see is the surf crashing over the black rocks, surging towards her. She has never seen the water come this high over the long, rocky beach before, and for a little while she thinks that maybe it will keep rising and will come to meet her, to snatch her away.

After half an hour this is beginning to feel like a distinct possibility, and so she scrambles up the slope a little to where there is a low cliff, the start of the hill that will rise around the west coast of the island and eventually get to the place where Fraser's standing.

The light is on in the lamp room and the beams sweep the grey sea, churning and roaring. Huge waves. No boat.

But up here, higher up, it feels at least possible that she'll see something, if it's out there.

And then, unexpectedly, as a wave falls, there it is.

The yacht has a dark hull, but she can see the white deck and the broken mast, snapped and dragging in the water. The yacht is listing badly, the waves breaking over the deck, because it is side-on to the waves and completely helpless. It's close, unexpectedly close, and each wave is driving it closer to the rocks.

She gasps in shock. On the deck is a person, clinging on to the broken mast.

'Oh, my God,' she says, and then, to the person, her hands cupped around her mouth, 'Hold on!'

Then she switches on the torch, the powerful beam searing through the darkness, and turns it in what she hopes is Fraser's direction, and waves, and waves, tears choking her because suddenly this has become very serious, potentially horrific.

'Fraser!' she screams into the walkie-talkie, pressing the button and hoping for the best. 'It's here, it's on the rocks!'

The wind snatches her words away. She thinks, now, that shouting 'hold on' in the direction of the yacht is really silly; instead she yells, 'We're coming to help! Don't worry! We'll get you!' which of course is also silly. She can promise nothing of the kind.

But Fraser is coming, and he will know what to do. She can see the beam of his torch bouncing in her direction.

He is coming.

He is running, fast.

Fraser

He can see her hi-vis jacket. She has stopped waving the torch around and instead is pointing it at the waves, near the shore; and he sees it as soon as he gets closer, breathless and on legs made wobbly by the rough yomp across the island.

He has already shouted into the walkie-talkie, instructing Lefty to go back to the lighthouse and call the coastguard. Lefty knows how to use the radio, even if he's never used it in a real emergency. With luck nobody will bother to ask who he is.

'Stop!'

He's yelling at Rachel now, because she's clambering over the rocks towards the boat. There's a sickening crunch as the keel hits a rock and shears off. The yacht stops moving abruptly, throwing the figure on the boat to the deck. Then a wave comes and crashes into it from the side, it rises and falls and lands with a horrible tearing sound that rises above the roar of the sea, rammed between two razor-sharp granite rocks.

It's wedged.

He has a moment to think, *thank fuck for that*. Then another wave crashes, and turns it on to its side. The hull splinters. Another two waves, maybe three, and it will be in pieces.

Maybe Rachel hasn't heard him, or maybe she's just not listening. What the fuck is she doing?

'Rachel! Fucking stop, will you! Get out of the water!'

His words are snatched on the wind. He keeps his torch trained on her back, following her as best he can, thinking that if he loses sight of the hi-vis he has no idea what to do. The surf surges forward over the smaller rocks as a wave breaks again against the boat. The water rushes up to Rachel's knees and he sees her stumble.

Fucking hell. She's still going. It's still a good ten metres, fifteen, between her and the yacht. It will get deep very quickly, and then the water will take her.

'Rachel!'

He thinks about running back to the bird observatory, where there's rope in the outhouse. But there's no point doing that unless she stops and waits.

He sees her pause. She's waiting for a break in the waves. As one surges back, she runs forward, slipping on the rocks, her arms wheeling to keep her balance. She's going to fall in.

please God, no

'Rachel! Stop!'

He's followed her up to his knees, hoping to clutch her back, but she's ahead of him still, the water surging around her waist, her arms outstretched, her red hair whipping wildly in the wind over her jacket.

Now he can see a person wearing black or navy waterproofs, clambering down from what's left of the boat on to the rocks towards Rachel. Below, the waters churn.

'No!' Fraser roars. 'Stay where you are!'

Then everything happens at once. A huge wave, the biggest he's ever seen, comes crashing, booming over the rocks. The wave is bigger than the yacht; it's going to swamp it, and it does. For a terrible few seconds everything disappears – the yacht, the casualty, Rachel.

They're just... gone.

The water surges towards him, nothing but white foam picked out in the light of his torch. It hits him up to his chest and snatches his breath from his lungs. And something knocks into him under the water, and he reaches down and grabs it, and finds it's the sailor's life-vest, with him still inside it. Fraser heaves him upright, grasps him tightly, hauls him up the beach towards the turf. The man is a dead weight but mercifully still alive, stumbling, coughing.

where is Rachel where is she?

The yachtsman looks round and Fraser does too, and Rachel is there, Rachel is just a few feet away as the water subsides again, on her hands and knees in the water, a wee hi-vis drowned rat, gasping and choking, hair trailing. He throws the torch up the beach and strides towards her, grabs at the back of her jacket, numb fingers clenching down like a vice, heaving her along.

Rachel manages to get to her feet too, staggering back to the shore.

'Are you okay?' he yells, and repeats it. 'Rachel, are you okay? Talk to me.'

'Fine,' she gasps, choking hoarsely, retching.

'Did you swallow any water?'

'No,' she says.

Fraser drags them both further up out of reach of the waves. He thinks it's still not safe here with the water so high but suddenly he can't go any further; he has to look and see. He lets go of the man's lifejacket first and he tumbles face down on to the grass, groaning.

Then a light brighter than his torch picks them out and it takes a second for him to realise that it's coming from the sea. Rachel has managed to get to her feet and she's waving with both arms, her hair long, dark rat's tails stuck to the hi-vis.

'How many casualties?' comes a voice over a loudhailer.

'Two,' Fraser roars back.

'I'm not a casualty,' Rachel says indignantly, her teeth chattering like bones.

'Stay where you are,' the loudhailer calls.

From overhead, above the wind, they can hear a deeper thudding – a helicopter.

'Can you walk?' Fraser asks the sailor, who has managed to twist round to a sitting position. Now he can actually see, he realises with shock that it's a woman: short greying hair, ashen face. She nods, shaking. Fraser helps her to her feet. 'Were you alone on the boat?'

'Yes,' comes the response.

'What's your name? Can you tell me your name?'

'Shona Carter.' Her voice is just a gasp.

She's looking at what's left of her yacht, split in two and glistening, shredded and terrible, picked out by the lifeboat's searchlight.

Fraser helps her to her feet. From overhead someone is being winched down on to the headland. Rachel is heading towards the helicopter already, holding her hood futilely over her head. The paramedic runs towards them as the helicopter takes off again. It looks as though it's going to try and land on the helipad, which is past the ruins, towards the bird observatory.

'Who's been in the water?' the paramedic yells.

'These two,' Fraser yells back.

'And you?'

'Only my feet,' he fibs.

'I'm fine,' Rachel yells. 'This is the lady from the boat.'

'Any other casualties?'

'No,' Fraser shouts.

'If you can walk, make your way up to the helipad; I'll assist here.'

Fraser leaves the paramedic with Shona and wraps his arm around Rachel's waist, supporting her along the path, lighting the way with his torch. The helicopter has landed and the engine quiets, and suddenly it's just the wind and the waves again.

'Are you okay?' he asks her. Through the wet hi-vis he can feel her trembling.

'I'm fine, stop asking.'

'Jesus Christ,' he says again. And, quieter, more to himself, 'I thought you were dead.'

He's shaking too.

Rachel

The paramedics let Fraser take Rachel back to the lighthouse. She's blue with cold, but what she really needs is dry clothes and to warm up, slowly. They only let him do this when he explains that he's a first-aider.

Lefty comes into the hallway when he hears them come in. He's wide-eyed with shock when he sees her.

'I'm okay,' she says, to fend off the inevitable questions.

'What happened?'

'The yacht broke up,' Fraser says. 'Rachel was in the water. She went in after the sailor.'

'Fucking hell,' Lefty says.

Rachel detects that tone in Fraser's voice, dangerously calm. As if he's beyond angry with her. She can see why: he shouted for her to stop. He told her to stay put. He kept shouting at her and she ignored him and went ahead anyway. But what else was she supposed to do? She could see the woman clinging to the broken mast. She could see what he probably couldn't: the huge split in the hull that meant the boat was about to break up. What she'd missed, of course, from her position in the water, was the massive wave that had lifted her off her feet and hurled her back towards the shore.

'We need to get her warmed up,' Fraser says to Lefty. 'You stay near the radio.'

He peels the hi-vis jacket off her and leaves it in a heap on the stone floor of the hallway.

'I'm sorry about getting everything wet,' she says.

He ignores her. 'Upstairs,' he growls.

'You got wet too,' she says, teeth chattering.

Her legs feel unbelievably heavy, as if she's run a half-marathon, and her hip is hurting where the wave hurled her against the rocks. The ice-cold water had been a shock at first, had made it difficult to breathe. She had paused and calmed herself, despite the roaring of the sea, the darkness, the tug of the water around her knees. Forced herself to breathe deeply. Then she'd heard Fraser yelling at her and she had moved forward again. If she looked round, she'd thought, she would have to stop, turn back, and she wouldn't be able to live with herself if the person on the deck of the yacht had ended up in the water.

After that the cold had been just cold. She was numb and moving automatically, trying to stay on her feet, until the wave came and she saw it and knew she was going to go under – the panic of holding her breath, gasping in just as it hit, bowling her over and her head smacking against the rocky ground and then her feet, and then her hip, and then the wave pulled back again and she found the shingle rolling under her hands and dug in.

'You're shaking like anything,' Fraser says, gentler now, but still clearly furious. He is peeling clothes off her in the bathroom. She has tried to do it herself but her fingers are completely numb. 'You really need to go to hospital.'

'No, I really don't. What are they going to do?'

'Warm you up with one of those special blankets – I don't know. Jesus Christ, Rachel, what the fuck did you think you were doing?'

He has tugged down the waterproof trousers and her jeans underneath them, finally, and he sees the huge red mark on her hip, livid against the mottled bluish whiteness of the rest of her.

'Fucking hell,' he says.

'I must've hit a rock,' she stammers. 'It's fine.'

He turns on the shower, his mouth set in a grim line.

She gets in, still wearing her bra and knickers and one sock. According to the dial the water is barely above lukewarm but it feels boiling, searing her cold skin and making her gasp. Her nostrils are sore with the salt water. She told him she hadn't swallowed any but of course that was a lie.

A hand reaches into the shower and turns the temperature dial up slightly. Searing heat, again.

'Is this how you're supposed to warm someone up?' she calls.

'Body heat is better,' he says. 'But the only warm person here is Lefty.'

'Right.'

Then the shower curtain is pulled back and Fraser gets in with her. He might think he's cold but she feels warmth from his body, watches the water running down through the dense dark hair on his chest and shoulders, forming dark rivulets. She reaches out a hand and presses it against the hard muscle of his chest. His arms are holding her up, under the spray.

'I thought you'd died,' he says.

'I promise you I'm very much not dead.'

His eyes are searching her face, his brows knitted, his breath fast.

I'm not going to do this again, she thinks, and then she leans forward and kisses him anyway. Cold mouth, hot mouth.

Fraser

He was careful of her hip. He found other injuries too: a graze on her forehead that she insisted was just a scratch; marks on her back. He kissed them in turn, first in the shower and then afterwards in bed, dry and warmer now, moving quickly because at any minute the paramedic was going to be back to check them over.

He had brought her up here and undressed her, and fucking her had been the very last thing on his mind, but somehow it'd happened anyway. She was wrapped up in her towelling dressing gown, had pushed him on to his back and straddled him, and they had forgotten to use a condom, and immediately afterwards he had apologised and she had too, and said something about bigger things to worry about.

And they had both heard the knock at the door.

He pulled on dry jeans as she limped to her room to find clean clothes. He came downstairs first.

It's not the helicopter paramedic but two of the lifeboat crew. They have managed to dock at the jetty, which privately Fraser thinks is little short of miraculous given the narrow channel to the harbour and the high seas outside. They are, of course, used to performing difficult manoeuvres in dangerous conditions.

Lefty has boiled the kettle and left them to it, and the crew are helping themselves to tea and biscuits when he gets to the kitchen.

'All right there, lads?' he says, by way of a greeting. 'That was dramatic.'

'We came to check you over, see if anyone else needs to go to the mainland.'

Fraser thinks of Rachel's bruised hip and the graze on her head and thinks she really probably should go to hospital, but the thought of letting her out of his sight now, even for a moment, is something he can't bring himself to contemplate.

'Hi,' Rachel says, coming into the kitchen.

She looks almost normal: big grey jumper, black leggings, thick green socks, red hair hanging in thick, damp ropes. She's still pale. She's very definitely alive.

One of them, Paul, is a paramedic in his day job and takes Rachel to one side to check her for concussion and various other things.

'How's the casualty?' Fraser asks the other one. 'I've not had time to radio the coastguard just yet.'

'She's okay, surprisingly enough.'

'What the hell was she doing out there in this weather?'

'Sailing round the coast single-handed.'

'Ah – not any more, she's not. Did you see the boat?'

'Aye, it's pretty much gone. She had a lucky escape, right enough.'

'She did.'

Rachel comes back with Paul. 'I'm fine,' she says, as if she's been repeating those two words on a loop for the past hour.

'She's in good shape, considering. And you're trained in first aid?'

'Aye,' Fraser says, in a voice that allows for no argument, 'I am.' It's been some years since he was certified, and it's probably out of date, but he's not going to admit to that. Marion has been pestering him to get it updated and he has been blatantly ignoring her.

'So you know what to look out for, right – drowsiness, disorientation, dizziness ...'

'Aye, I'll keep an eye on her overnight; if she deteriorates in any way I'll radio the coastguard again.'

'I'd still rather take her to the mainland and get her checked out,' Paul says.

'No,' says Rachel. 'Honestly, I'm fine.'

'Well, I can't make you go, I can only advise ...'

'I appreciate the advice,' she says firmly. 'I'm quite happy to take the risk.'

'Apparently you rescued a lone female sailor,' Fraser tells Rachel.

'I *thought* it was a woman! I saw her face, just quickly, as she jumped. How is she?'

'We think she's doing okay,' says Paul. 'We'll hopefully get an update, but we don't always. It's nice to know.'

They all sit around the table drinking tea. The second crewman – Fraser never finds out his name – makes some jokey comment about Fraser's son being traumatised by all the commotion. Neither of them says anything. He has caught Rachel's eye and now he can't look away, his heart thudding all over again.

He nearly lost her. She nearly died. What would he have done?

He thinks of the loch, of the cold, dark water. He hears it calling to him, calling him home, and inside him a voice roars.

No more. No more.

Rachel

At the door the crew pull on their waterproofs again, but it's stopped raining. The wind has dropped considerably. It's getting lighter again now the storm has passed, the black clouds thinning out overhead, the sea no longer churned up with towering waves.

'Looks like you'll get a smoother ride home,' Fraser says, as they head down the hill to the jetty.

'I'll take that,' one of them says, and with a backward wave they're gone.

Rachel is bundled up in several layers, but she's still cold. She wishes she could have had a bath instead of just a shower, a huge deep bath with bubbles and candles, something to chase away the dark thoughts of the freezing water surging over her head, the roar of the waves and the shingle and the crashing against the stones, the salt water in her eyes, stinging her nose, making her choke and gag.

'I won't keep asking,' he says. 'But just once more. Are you okay?'

She stares at him. 'I'm not sure. I think I am.'

'What you did…' he says. 'I've never seen anything so brave in my life.'

It hadn't felt brave, at the time. It had felt like a compulsion, like something she didn't want to do but had to; and then she's reminded of Emily and that other time she made a rash decision and did something brave and selfless and ultimately rather stupid.

The yachtswoman had been rushed away from them so quickly by the paramedics, it was as if she'd never been on the island at all. As if Rachel had rescued a ghost. It would be good to find out how she is, Rachel thinks, but at the same time she almost wants to forget.

'Did you hear me shouting stop?'

They are back in the kitchen. It's the warmest room, next to the range, and Fraser has closed the door to keep the heat from leaching out into the hallway. He gets one of the tubs of leftovers out of the freezer and tips the contents – a solid brick of something vaguely orange in colour – into a pan and leaves it on the top of the stove to defrost. He's going to start feeding her, she thinks, even though the darkness of the storm has disorientated her and it feels like the middle of the night – it's not quite eight – and really she isn't hungry at all.

'You saw what happened,' she says quietly. 'The boat broke up seconds later. If she hadn't jumped then, she'd have been swept off the rocks and we'd have lost her.'

He shakes his head, his back to her. 'Christ,' he says. 'What a day.'

'I'm glad the storm's died down. Do you get storms like that often?'

'Not this time of year. Maybe once or twice. But later in the year, sure. Big storms. Worse than today's.'

'Really?'

'Aye.'

The pan on the stove has begun to sizzle and the warm, spicy scent of what's probably his butternut squash curry reaches Rachel's salt-seared nostrils, and she realises she could probably manage to eat something after all.

'Are we having alcohol with this?' he asks.

'I think if I started I might not be able to stop,' she says.

'Aye, well, drink some water instead,' he says, and fills a pint glass from the filter jug in the fridge, puts it on the table in front of her. 'You're probably dehydrated.'

All that water, she thinks, looking at the condensation forming on the outside of the glass.

She's thinking about last night, and this morning, and Fraser going out on his own and coming back drenched and freezing. All of it has been somewhat overshadowed by this evening's drama. She watches him moving effortlessly about the kitchen, putting on a pan for the rice, muttering something about not having time to make bread.

He's got it all inside, she realises. All that stillness, all of the tension in the way he carries himself. He holds it all in, all the time. It's all very well pressing those buttons, trying to get him to talk, alcohol or no alcohol, waiting for him to be ready – she's got to the point where she really needs to know. Decisions need to be made.

She thinks she has begun to make them.

Fraser

'Will you stay with me tonight?' he asks. 'In my room, or yours, I don't care which.'

He sees her eyes widen. But everything has shifted after today, and he wants to be clear. He wants to be sure about everything.

'You're only saying that because you're making sure I don't have concussion,' she says, smiling.

'That too.'

'Well, okay. And you're like a giant furry hot water bottle, which is a bonus.'

'I've never been described as furry before, but I'll take it as a compliment.'

He sees the smile fade. There's so much going on behind her eyes.

'Are we going to have sex again, or are you literally just going to watch me all night?'

'That's up to you.' He's not going to push her.

'You said all this had to stop,' she says.

'Aye, I did say that.'

'And yet it keeps happening.'

'I know.'

'Why do you think that is?' she asks.

Oh, God, this woman.

'Because I can't help myself,' he says. 'Because I have no strength. Because I'm stupid. Take your pick.'

She shakes her head as if she can't quite believe she's landed herself here with such an idiot.

'You reminded me of him for a minute there,' he says.

'Of who? Lefty?'

'Like a wee drowned rat. All blue-white skin and bruises.'

She's watching him, with a small frown. It's not the most complimentary way to describe the woman of your dreams, is it? he realises, but he ploughs on; he's ruined things anyway.

'That first night he was on the island, we lost him. He got off the boat and when we went looking he'd fucking disappeared. Robert had to get back, so the boat went. And I looked for him, and then just gave up, thought he'd found shelter somewhere. In the bird observatory, maybe. And there was a storm, nearly as bad as this, and the next morning I found him down in the cottages.'

'That was when he did the graffiti?'

'Not then,' he says. 'Or maybe he did, I don't know. I left him there, see. Left him with a blanket and some water and a packet of crisps. I left him there in the storm. I thought he'd die. I wanted him to die, and for it to just happen, so it wouldn't be my fault, except it would have. It was always going to be my fault, because I left him there.'

She's listening.

'I wanted to kill him. But I wasn't brave enough.'

'What happened then?'

'I went down there to see if he was still alive. He was by the loch, freezing, soaked.'

All she says is, 'And you took him in?'

At last he says, 'Aye. Dried him off and gave him toast.'

'And when the boat came back?'

'He hid again. Fuck knows where. Then I just gave up trying to get him to piss off back home.'

'He told me he wanted to stay here to get free from drugs,' Rachel says. 'And I got the impression he was being threatened by people where he used to live. But that was over a year ago. He can't stay here for ever, can he, working for nothing and being shouted at by you every day?'

'He can go whenever he wants. But, if he goes, I don't want him back.'

'Why not?'

'Because I'm not a fucking youth hostel, right? He's got nothing to do wi' me. I want nothing to do wi' him.'

'You're—' She goes to say something and stops, bites her lip.

'I'm what?' He can feel himself getting defensive. There is going to be a price to pay for this, he thinks. She's going to see into him, see all the filth and the shame and the mess of it all.

'I was going to say, you're all he's got.'

He wants to laugh at that, but he can't even manage a sarcastic grunt.

'You've saved his life,' she says. 'In fact, you are his life. No matter how hard you try to push him away.'

'You make him sound like a wee abused dog,' he says.

'Maybe that's pretty much what he is. All he wants is your forgiveness.'

He can smell the curry starting to catch on the bottom of the pan and gets to his feet, grateful for the chance to look away. *All he wants is your forgiveness.* The absolute pain of knowing that, and realising for the first time that he should be the one asking for forgiveness. He's been a complete bastard to Lefty all this time. He's punished him every single day for something that probably wasn't even his fault. What sort of a man does that make him? The sort of man who wouldn't kick a dog, but would shout and swear at a young lad who's probably never been shown a kindness in his life? And she's seen all of that mistreatment.

Whatever comes next is no more than he deserves. He stirs the curry and waits for her judgement.

There's a weird sort of lightness in him, too. He's carried the weight of it for so long, it's like inhaling fresh air for the first time in years. He breathes in deeply, and out again, feeling so light-headed that he has to steady himself against the counter.

There are other things he's missed out, that he'll tell her if she wants to hear them. How eventually he made the study into a room for Lefty so that he could keep him shut away downstairs. How he used to cook him meals, trying to get him at least a little bit healthier, then eventually got sick of being asked for chips and let him make his own food. How all this time on the island Lefty has asked to look after the chickens, has asked for an Xbox, but has never once asked to go home.

'Fraser?'

He brings two plates of curry and rice over to the table, his mind elsewhere.

'Why's he called Lefty? Did you call him that?'

'He's always been Lefty.'

'But he's not left-handed.'

'Aye, I know. It's just a stupid nickname. Jimmy Wright. Lefty. Made it just a tiny bit easier, to not use his real name.'

12

Redemption

Rachel

'You know Lefty has to go. It's the only way things will ever get better for you.'

'How'd you work that out?'

'While he's still here, you can't move on. He's just a constant reminder of what happened.'

'If you say so. I wish I'd just forced him back on that boat when I had the chance. But see, I'm a coward, Rachel. I'm a filthy, stinking, idiotic coward. I'm afraid of what will happen to him if he goes back there. And now there are other things I'm afraid to lose, too, and I've only just realised.'

He's talking about me, she thinks, and then immediately dismisses the thought.

'I'll look after him,' she says.

'What?'

'Lefty. He can come back to Norwich with me.'

'Don't talk daft.'

'Why not? I'm not saying Norwich doesn't have drug problems, but it would be like another fresh start for him. I'll get him access to support, try to help him get a job, a flat.'

She sees his eyes widen. He's not thought about that as an option.

'It's like you've only had one possible course of action in your head, which is Lefty back on drugs. It's like you've not even been able to think that, actually, maybe things might work out.'

'How are they going to work out?'

She's thought of that.

'Well... you could come too.'

Fraser

'I didn't think you'd want to do this,' Fraser says, later.

Rachel is curved against him, and he's pulling her even closer, as much skin to skin as he can manage. She still feels cold, as if some part of her has turned to ice: a snow queen, a northern goddess. 'I didn't either,' she murmurs. 'But I'm cold.'

'I'm a lucky man,' he says.

'You're a brave man.'

'I'm definitely not that.'

In the darkness of his room, she raises herself on to her elbow so she can look at him, her hair falling over her shoulder. He winds a lock of it gently round his finger.

'What you did for Lefty,' she says, 'nobody else would have done that. You got him through withdrawal. You kept him alive. You kept him safe.'

'Didn't have a lot of choice in the matter,' he says.

'You did. And he knows it, too. He knows what you did for him.'

'Rachel, you've seen what he's like. He's fucking terrified of me.'

'I don't think it's quite that bad. If you were actually going to hurt him, you would have done it by now. He knows that. And he's alive, thanks to you.'

'He's stuck himself on this island like a wee limpet thanks to me.'

'I'll talk to him.'

'Rachel?' he says, his hand moving up the skin of her back.

'Yes?' she murmurs, kissing his throat.

He's going to ask her not to go, but even then the words fail him. Instead he turns his head to kiss her, tasting the salt still on her skin, even after the shower, even after brushing her teeth. It's as if she's made of the sea. As if she's part of the island now, baptised and threaded through it.

'There's something else I have to tell you,' she says, when they come up for air. 'I'm going to ask Robert to take me back to the mainland on Friday. It's only a week until Julia gets here, but I can't wait for that.'

'Why not?'

'I'm going to need emergency contraception. I can't exactly ask him to buy it for me from the chemist, can I?'

'What's emergency contraception?' he asks, feeling stupid.

'The morning after pill. You can get it from a chemist.'

'You can?'

'As long as it's within five days.'

'Right.'

His fingers make their way down her spine. Across her hip, fluttering over the bruise there with the gentlest of touches. He feels her shiver, pulls the duvet up around her shoulders. Her hand meets his, pushes it lower, towards her sex.

Three days. He has three more days with her.

Rachel

Something happened to her in the water. Something entirely unexpected.

It wasn't an out-of-body experience, nothing like that, but perhaps equally dramatic. She recognised herself, as if she were watching from the shore; saw her faltering steps towards the stricken yacht, saw the pause, saw that she was thinking about what she was doing, making a rational choice. It wasn't that what she was doing was stupid, foolhardy; it was that something needed to be done, and she was the only person who could do it.

Exactly like the moment when she had said to Lucy, *I'll do it. I'll be your surrogate.*

In the months that followed, she had told herself she'd been stupid, rash, that she'd ruined her life by making that sudden decision; that it was the latest in Rachel's life of fuck-ups. That she would never recover from having to hand Emily over to Lucy and Rob, knowing she would be a part of her child's life but not the centre of it. She couldn't blame Lucy, or Rob, or Emily – there was nobody to blame but herself.

And then the wave had come and hit her, churned her up and thrown her against the rocks as if to say, *Wake up! This is your life, this is what you've made of it!* The sea had rattled her, drenched her and thrown her back to land again, tossing her on to her hands and knees on the shingle.

She had looked up and seen Fraser grabbing the yachts-woman by her lifejacket, hauling her up, throwing his torch on to the grass and then striding back through the surf to get her. And she'd realised that what she'd done had had a purpose. It had saved someone's life, most probably.

And what she had done for Lucy was to create life, to give her the child she wanted so desperately. How could she think of that as a mistake, as anything remotely resembling a fuck-up?

The depression that has been enveloping her, that has clouded her every thought for the past five months, probably more, has gone. Just like that, the black cloud is gone. She has created a life, and she has saved a life – what's the point of being sad? There is the island, freshly washed and scrubbed by the storm, and tomorrow the sun will probably shine, and on the mainland somewhere is Shona Carter, still alive, thanks to her.

And here is Fraser, trapped and alone and sad, so desperately sad, living this half-life, this miserable existence because of decisions he has made, and because of the way he has thought himself into a narrow wedge with no way out, like a bird flying into the Heligoland trap.

He's behind her in bed, his huge arm draped over her waist, his breath soft and even in her ear. She doesn't think he's asleep, but when she speaks it's quietly, just in case.

'I think it'll be all right.'

He breathes in, holds it for a second. His voice is like a rumble in his chest.

'What will be?'

'Everything. Everything will work out.'

His hand moves up to her breast, cupping it, sliding over the place where her heart's beating. She's still alive. He's still alive. Emily is, and the yachtswoman, and Lefty. Five hearts beating, beating, beating.

'I don't want to lose you,' he murmurs.

She thinks about this for a moment, and twists round to face him. His eyes are closed. She moves her hand over his beard, cups his cheek. 'You don't do relationships, Fraser. And I need one. Maybe not now, but eventually. And besides, you'll be fine.'

'But you're leaving,' he says. 'It's not just a trip to the chemist. You're not coming back.'

'It's not just me,' she says. 'I'm hoping Lefty will come too.'

There is a long pause. His eyes are closed, as if he doesn't want her to see.

'He'll go with you,' he says. 'Of course he will.'

'And you'll be fine,' she says.

A moment later, he answers, 'Sure,' and kisses her ear.

Now that she's out of the dark cloud, now that she's been washed clean by the sea, she can see it for what it is: that Fraser's profoundly depressed, just as she has been. If he cared enough about her to want some sort of commitment, then she would find a way to stay somehow, try to help him defeat it.

But, since he doesn't, then she is going to have to leave. At least she can take Lefty with her, away from the island, give Fraser a chance to heal by himself. The rest is really up to him.

Fraser

Later than usual, for he had woken up with Rachel wrapped around him and he couldn't bear to move, Fraser takes Bess out for a walk.

The sky is blue, cloudless, the sun low in the sky but surprisingly warm, burning off the dampness, leaving a low mist rising from the turf. The birds are out in vast numbers, wheeling overhead as if they're inspecting the island and surprised to find it still here. Fraser is pleased to see them, although most of them will have weathered worse storms.

He makes his way to the north coast of the island, going via the ruins rather than taking the path along the clifftop, which is the most direct route to the northern tip.

He is still not sure what happened, but he has a need to return.

The ruins are, of course, as they have always been: odd bits of grey stone, tussocky grass looking bright acid green in the sunshine, heather blooming between the rocks. The altar stone, with the space underneath it where he had sheltered, cradling Bess against him. He goes towards it and looks back. Bess is sitting on the perimeter of the site, between two pieces of rock that were once part of the outer wall, watching him steadily. He whistles for her, but she stays resolutely still. 'Suit yourself,' he says, placing his hand on the lintel stone. It feels warm, damp, grainy with the lichens that cover it.

He feels as if he should offer some sort of thanks. Fraser has never had a faith, and has felt little curiosity, certainly none since Maggie's death. He has come close to losing his life a handful of times. Once, working on a rig, he was nearly struck by some moving machinery that would have taken his head off if he hadn't ducked at the right moment. Since then he has seriously contemplated suicide five times, the most recent being yesterday morning. But now he looks inside himself for that feeling and it's just not there.

He will not think about that again. Whatever happens, he believes that he will not feel that same yearning. He thinks whatever it is, that urge, has gone.

He turns his face to the sun and allows it to warm the skin on his cheeks, his forehead, breathing in the smell of the rain and the grass and the ever-present fishy undertone of guano, the sage, the salty air, the rich, peaty soil. Then he turns away, whistles for Bess. She joins him on the far side of the ruins, having apparently made her own decision never to set paw on the hallowed turf again.

They head north for a further quarter of a mile and eventually the land slopes down to the rocky shoreline.

The small beach is a mess of dead birds, and the carcass of a grey seal, rising and falling as the waves break, making it look as if it might be still alive. But it definitely isn't. He picks up the dead birds and makes a pile on the grass. Some of them are ringed. They will all be counted and logged. There are a whole load of eider ducklings and those alone make him want to weep. The loss of life is not unusual for a storm this size, but that doesn't mean he can't feel it.

He has felt death very close in the last few days. It has spared him, and Rachel, and the yachtswoman. He feels for the birds, the grey seal, the other casualties that will be littering the harbour and probably the many more that will wash up in the next few days; but he is still here, he is still alive. Rachel is still alive.

That makes him feel unbelievably lucky.

Pieces of the yacht are wedged in the rocks, the mast twisted and broken, rising and falling on the high tide like a drifting limb. He had known there would be little chance of salvaging the boat and now he is only concerned about what's on board and what can be retrieved before it becomes a hazard to the wildlife: ropes, rigging, fuel, plastics. Everything else will be washed away the next time there's a storm, the larger pieces of the hull pulled away to join all the other wrecks at the bottom of the sea.

At low tide he will go out there, take Lefty and Rachel if they're willing, form a human chain and carry as much stuff as they can back to shore. There are likely to be personal items on board, too – things Shona Carter would want them to save. If they can.

Lefty and Rachel, he thinks, trying to imagine the pair of them on the mainland together. Trying to imagine Lefty south of the border, finding a job in Norwich of all places. How's he going to get a job, anyway? But he won't want to go. Or maybe he will, and then he'll change his mind and want to come back. Maybe Rachel will come back, too, although unless Julia doesn't turn up there's no way for that to happen.

In a rare moment of clarity, Fraser thinks that Lefty and Rachel are now the closest thing he has to family.

Rachel

Low tide is at two p.m., and Fraser has summoned both of them to the north of the island to help retrieve items from the wreck of the yacht.

Rachel is eager to see what's left of it, but when she gets there she feels nauseous, despite the bright sunshine and the glowing, jewel-like colours of the grass and the flowers and the sky. There is something unbearably sad about the sight of the yacht, broken into pieces and helpless, as if some giant has taken an axe to it, splintered the wood and severed the mast, leaving the carcass for the birds and fish to pick at.

Fraser orders Rachel to stay on dry land, possibly because he can see that she is feeling uncertain, but more likely because he doesn't trust her to keep her balance on the wet rocks. Meanwhile he is the one up to his knees in the surf, passing items to Lefty, who ferries them up the rocks to her. She collects everything and loads it into the trailer; later everything will be driven down to the jetty to go back on the supplies boat for recycling or landfill. It's Rachel's job to spot anything that might have a value – like the radio, clearly waterlogged but potentially salvageable – and keep it to one side.

She watches Fraser cutting away rigging and heaving things free, watches the muscles in his arms and back, and quite suddenly she cannot imagine being away from the island, cannot imagine what it will feel like to not see him every day. It would be the easiest thing in the world right now, to reverse her rational, logical decision; just the thought of it makes her heart leap in her chest.

But even if she could stay here, if it were possible, somehow, if there were no Julia, no Marion, no Lefty, then she would just fall for him even harder than she has already. And he doesn't want that. He's said it, very clearly, and she has to respect that decision, even if it's not what she wants.

More to the point, whatever she feels, it won't change a thing. Julia is coming. She has no job here any more. Yet again her life is lurching in another direction, beyond her control.

Later, waiting in the kitchen while Fraser makes shepherd's pie, she emails Marion to say she's going to be leaving sooner than planned. A second, longer email goes to Julia, apologising that she's not going to be here for the handover after all. It takes her an hour or two to list all the things she thinks Julia might like to know, everything from the passwords for the island's social media to the list of meals she's batch-cooked and stashed in the freezer.

She doesn't mention Lefty. If he comes with her, then Julia might never need to know about him.

Rachel has done her best, she has worked hard, and now it's time to go.

Fraser

Lefty comes to him on the Thursday night, while Rachel is over at the bird observatory doing a final clean.

Fraser has been waiting for this conversation, and dreading it.

'You're going with her, then,' he says to Lefty, pre-empting what he can see in the boy's face.

He can't even reply. Just nods.

'Ach, you'll be okay.'

'You reckon?'

'What are you going to do with yourself?' Fraser is standing at the sink, side by side with Lefty, who begins to spread butter on a slice of bread.

Lefty shrugs. 'Try an' get a job.'

'Maybe something in the outdoors,' Fraser says. 'That would be good for you. Like a park-keeper. If they have that sort of thing these days.'

'Rachel says there are these big houses, you know, like, open to the public – they have volunteers helping in the gardens. Her mum works at one of them; she thinks maybe I could do that. Just to get a bit of work experience, you know.'

'Sounds good.'

There is a pause. Through a mouthful of cheese sandwich, Lefty says, 'Are you angry wi' me?'

Fraser grimaces. 'Why should I be angry?'

'That I'm leaving.'

'It was going to happen sooner or later.'

'Look. I'm gonnae be good. I'm staying out of trouble. And I'm sorry.'

Fraser doesn't hear the last three words; he never has. And the bit before – well, that's up to Lefty, after all. He can't help him when he's away off the island. He's just a big kid; sooner or later bravado or drugs or threats or something will cross his path, and who knows what will happen then?

'Aye, whatever. Get away wi' you, go on.'

Lefty takes the sandwich and hovers in the doorway. 'I'll be leaving the Xbox,' he says.

Fraser roars, 'Too fucking right you will!'

And the door slams.

Fraser has no desire to begin playing on an Xbox, whatever that involves. But perhaps, if it stays here, Lefty might feel able to come back, if he needs to.

Rachel

Rachel hears Fraser coming to bed. She reaches out a hand to illuminate her phone, which is charging on the bedside table – it's nearly one. She thinks maybe he fell asleep downstairs for a while, or else maybe he's deliberately left it late enough that she'll be asleep.

She hasn't slept, too wired to do anything but think over and over again about tomorrow.

His bedroom door is ajar, the light still on. She knocks and pushes the door so she can see him, sitting on the edge of his bed, T-shirt and boxers, head in his hands. He looks up. Pulls the duvet to one side, by way of invitation.

She crawls into the bed next to him, turns on her side to face him. 'I had a reply from Marion,' she says.

'Oh, aye?'

'Did you not get copied in?'

'I haven't looked.'

'She's doing the whole passive-aggressive thing about me leaving early, telling me they're not going to pay me for the week in lieu of notice. But as there are no birders here, she's not going to insist that I stay.'

'Good of her. I reckon she will pay you, that's just one of her threats. If she doesn't, let me know and I'll sort her out.'

There is a little pause.

'Are we going to stay in touch, then?'

He gives her a long look, as if he's giving it careful consideration. 'If you like. I'm not much good at replying to stuff.'

'I can imagine.'

'Don't take it personally.'

'Heaven forbid. Anyway, if you're going to try and sort her out, it might be worth knowing that Marion seems to think you've done something to piss me off.'

'Well, she's more perceptive than I've given her credit for.'

He leans across and turns out the light. She lies still, looking at his profile, the sweeping beam of the light above them creating patterns in the night sky outside the window.

'Will you take care of him?' he asks quietly.

'Of course I will.'

'And yourself?'

He turns to her, stroking a single finger down her cheek. She can't see his face but she can hear his breathing, slow and heavy. She presses a hand to his chest, feels the warmth of it, the muscle, the beating of his heart beneath it. Then she traces her hand down the swell of his belly, over his hip, over his backside, and pulls herself closer to him.

He's not going to say no. It's the last time, after all.

Fraser

Dear God, this woman.

How is he going to survive?

Afterwards he watches her sleep as it begins to get light outside, her hair russet instead of copper in the silvery light, trying to memorise her face. Time is slipping past faster than he can stand.

He wonders if there's anything he can do or say that might stop her from leaving. She can't stay in her job, of course, because of fucking Julia. And who knows what Marion would say about her staying on the island, if he were to ask. But if he

could just speak up, say the right words in the right order –
what if he promised to change, promised to try? Might she say
yes to staying anyway?

But he will not say anything. It's too much of a risk, too
much of a leap. He has nothing to offer her, and he has no right
to even ask.

Rachel

Fraser brings her backpack down to the jetty in the quad. He'll
need it, because Robert is bringing the week's shopping with
him.

Rachel and Lefty are subdued. Lefty has an old sports bag
that Fraser has given him, with all the clothes he has – which
don't amount to much. Rachel has emailed Lucy, and Mel, and
both of them offered to put up Rachel and Lefty for a while;
it's Mel's offer that Rachel has accepted. She has no idea what
she'll do beyond that. Lefty is going to have to sleep on Mel's
sofa. Apparently he's fine with it.

Although he's actually terrified, of course. She can tell by
the way he's staring at the boat as it comes in, and when she
touches his arm it's shaking.

'Hey,' she says. 'It'll be fine.'

Lefty glances round to look at Fraser, who's managing to
outdo himself in terms of strong, silent, quietly livid and really
quite alarming.

Fraser helps Robert tie up the boat and the engine stills.
Their luggage is handed over. There are some provisions, but
only two crates – still some degree of chinking, she notes, so it's
not as though he's decided to give up alcohol now she's leaving.
Not much of a legacy to leave him with, she thinks.

She looks at the crates and suddenly feels a wave of pain.
What the fuck is she doing? Everything she wants now is right
here on the island.

And she is leaving. This is, surely, the ultimate Rachel fuck-up. The worst ever.

Without warning the tears start falling and she can't wipe them away fast enough. Lefty has apparently not noticed, or perhaps he has, for when Robert beckons him to get on board he suddenly starts forward as if he's had an electric shock, stumbling over the gunwale and grasping at Robert's hand.

A look passes between Robert and Fraser, who's standing behind her. Robert has thus far not given Lefty so much as a glance.

'You coming, hen?' Robert calls.

She looks round at Fraser. One last look. Tears pouring.

He takes a step towards her and that's all she needs: she throws herself at him, buries her face in his chest, arms crushing round his waist as best they can. At their feet Bess whines, pushes her nose against Rachel's thigh.

'Come on,' he says, patting her shoulder. 'There's no need for that.'

She pulls herself away and drops to one knee to cuddle Bess. The dog licks her ear, her cheek, enthusiastically, and Rachel buries her face in the black fur.

Right, she thinks. Enough. Definitely enough.

Robert holds out his hand to her, and she takes it. Her foot leaves the concrete of the jetty and lands on the deck.

She is off the island.

She takes a seat at the side of the deck outside, where she can see Fraser as the boat pulls away. He's alone, she thinks. Completely alone, as he hasn't been for over a year. She has a sudden terror that he's going to do something stupid, that he's not going to be able to cope, and she lurches to her feet, hands against the gunwale. But what's she going to do? She can't stay.

He raises a hand to wave, and then, at last, she thinks maybe he will be all right. Because, in all the weeks on the island, all the boats that have come and gone, Fraser has never waved.

Not once.

Part Three

June and July

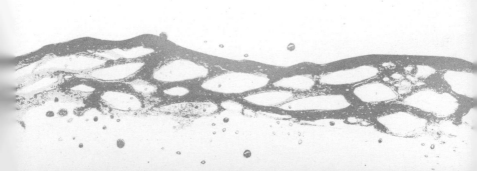

13

And still

Date: Sunday 9 June
From: Julia Jones
To: Rachel Long
Subject: Colander??

Hey Rachel,

How are you doing? How's life back on the mainland?

I'm sad I never got to meet you but you know I'm so grateful to you for doing that long email before you left – I can't tell you how helpful it's been. I can admit this to you (but nobody else) because you'll understand, but there have been a few moments this weekend that I've wondered what the hell I think I'm doing here. I've been on field trips all over the world but this is permanent and I'm in charge and that makes it really different, and pressured. So having your email to refer to has been a real support.

The first lot of birders arrived yesterday and they seem okay but not exactly friendly! They just want to be left to get on with it. I think they think it's really weird that I'm here, cooking for them – yesterday when I came in to do dinner they just stared at me as if they'd forgotten I was catering. Anyway, no complaints so far.

So I wanted to ask if there's a colander – I couldn't see one in the cupboard. Drained the pasta in the little sieve last night and it went everywhere. I asked Fraser but he just shrugged. Does he ever actually talk??

Anyway, if you get a chance to reply that'd be great. I do realise you've got your own life back and I promise I won't be pestering you every five minutes. Actually I can't promise that. Help!

Julia xx

Date: Sunday 9 June
From: Rachel Long
To: Julia Jones
Re: Colander??

Hi, Julia,

Glad you got there okay and that you're settling in. I know it really is a bit full on at first but you'll get used to it. I think the island itself helps. It's a very special place.

Sadly there isn't a colander – it's on a list of things I asked Marion to get including wine glasses and other (matching would be nice) stuff but nothing yet. I just used to use the saucepan lids to drain things.

Don't worry about firing questions at me – any time. It is a bit crazy-hectic here as I'm trying to find somewhere to live and a job etc but I can always do quick replies if you need anything. Although Fraser should be able to help with most things. I know he's a grumpy bugger but honestly he's not too bad when you get to know him.

Good luck with it!

Rachel x

Date: Friday 14 June
From: Rachel Long
To: Julia Jones
Subject: How are things?

Hi, Julia,

Just checking in to see how your first full week went. Did the birders cheer up in the end? Did you find everything you needed? Are you feeling a bit more settled? And how's your mum doing?

I saw you did a blogpost – looks good! I'm sure you'll rake in many more followers than I managed. I loved the pic of the bridled guillemot – I never managed to see one all the time I was there. Fraser kept promising they existed but I honestly was beginning to think he was just winding me up. Has he cheered up a bit?? Hope so.

Let me know if you need anything.

Rachel x

Date: Friday 14 June
From: Julia Jones
To: Rachel Long
Re: How are things?

Hey Rachel,

Thanks for your email, it's great to hear from you – thanks for thinking of me when I know you must be so busy. How're the job search and house-hunting going? The birders were okay in the end – kept to themselves and that was fine. I only went there to do the cooking but it meant I had a whole load of cleaning to do when they left this afternoon as well as all the laundry etc. It's like I have very little to do for most of the week (aside from panicking lol) and then the weekend is manic trying to get everything ready for the next lot.

Sad to say Fraser has not cheered up. He barely says 2–3 words to me a day. When I get back from the bird observatory he's usually in the lounge watching TV or upstairs, I say hello and get a grunt or something. Anyway, doesn't bother me especially but honestly I quite like visiting the birders for a bit more conversation, even if their repertoire is limited!! How on earth did you cope? I've been phoning Mum every evening but it's hard not to sound homesick. Thanks for asking after her. She seems to be having a whale of a time going out with her tennis club mates every day for afternoon teas etc. She had to be really careful about eating and drinking before the transplant, and now she can have everything and she's v excited about that. Can't blame her really.

Thanks again for the email. I do have friends I'm in touch with too, but it's great to have someone who understands just how unique this place is, and what the challenges are. Please do keep in touch.

Love, Julia xx

Date: Friday 14 June
From: Rachel Long
To: Julia Jones
Re: Re: How are things?

Hi, Julia,

No worries – I know it's easy to feel a bit isolated at first, especially if Fraser's not talking! How about over dinner in the evenings? He was never especially chatty when I was there but I think I ended up just kind of forcing him to be sociable ...

House-hunting is going okay, although I've taken the safe option and moved back into Mel's spare room. She is so great. I don't think I ever asked how you know her? She was a real lifesaver when she told me about the interim job, you know. It came at just the right time for me. I needed a few weeks to think about my life and my future, and, although some things are more complicated than they were, you get a real sense of what's important in life when you're on a little rock out there in the middle of the sea. I hope you get that feeling too. No sign of a new job for me yet, but I'm waiting to hear back from a few places.

Take care,

Rachel x

Date: Saturday 15 June
From: Julia Jones
To: Rachel Long
Re: Re: Re: How are things?

Hey Rachel,

Re Fraser – I don't see him over dinner, usually. He's either had it by the time I get back, or he's having something after I go to bed, because I've not seen him eat anything! And I don't know that he's sleeping that well either – sometimes I come down in the mornings and it's obvious he's not been to bed; I think he falls asleep in the living room sometimes. Anyway – quite worried about him, but since he's a bit peculiar anyway I've just been assuming this is normal behaviour for him! I guess it must do things to you, living on the island all on your own. Marion did warn me he's a bit of an odd fish but I wasn't really expecting this. How did you cope??

I was at uni with Mel years ago. We shared a house for a while too so yes, I know she's a brilliant housemate as well as a good friend. We're lucky to have her! And I'm so glad she introduced us. Sounds like it was a serendipitous thing for both of us.

Love,

Julia xx

PS Did you hear about Marion? Craig told me she's been offered another job – apparently she's pissed off about the cottages. Her planning adviser told her not to bother! And the building costs came back three times more than she thought. Apparently she had a stand-up row with them all at the Trustees' meeting, and handed in her notice the next day. Craig seemed quite happy about it!

Date: Saturday 15 June
From: Rachel Long
To: Julia Jones
Re: Re: Re: Re: How are things?

Hiya,

Just a quick one – v weird to hear Fraser's not eating. He's a bit of a foodie. You mean he's not cooking??

Also – good to hear about Marion. Hope she takes that job! She really is v difficult. And Fraser can't stand her!

R x

Date: Saturday 15 June
From: Julia Jones
To: Rachel Long
Re: Re: Re: Re: Re: How are things?

No, we don't have dinner together – most of the time I have beans on toast or I bring back a portion of the dinner I've served to the birders. Like I said, he's usually somewhere else when I get back! Did you used to sit and have dinner with him, then?? Wonder what I've done to upset him!!

J xx

Date: Saturday 15 June
From: Rachel Long
To: Fraser Sutherland
Subject: Hey, how are you?

Hi, Fraser,

Thought I would check in and see how you are? How is Julia settling in? I hope she's doing okay and that you are being super-kind to her. You know it's not easy starting that job – I should know! I hope she's getting on all right and not feeling too homesick.

We are doing okay here. The first few days were really manic. Lefty was in a bit of a state on the journey down, he was all white and shaky, I was worried he was going to do a runner! But when we got to Norwich I think he was just really tired. We were staying at Mel's and we've been spending a lot of time at my parents' house – as you can imagine, that was a bit entertaining. But the weird thing is after a day or so my mum and Lefty kind of bonded – they're thick as thieves now. She has been taking him to Harleton Hall where she works – he's been helping out in the gardens and they're hoping to get him on the official list of volunteers, so he will get some work experience even if he hasn't got an actual job. In any case there's no rush for that as Mum has practically adopted him as her own. In fact she suggested Lefty can have their spare room so that he doesn't have to sleep on Mel's sofa! Anyway he seems okay for now, he's not said anything about you or the island or what happened before, and nobody seems to be asking him probing questions – they're all just cracking on. I'm checking up on him every day. How's Bess doing? I think Lefty really misses her.

No jobs yet but I've signed on with an agency that supplies my sister's accountancy firm – she has put in a good word for me, which helped, I think. Emily is doing well and has grown such a lot. She's like a different baby. Lucy is a bit wired and stressy but that's how she reacts to things. She's going back to work in a few weeks so we are going out for lunch etc while she's still free. She asked me if I wanted to work as their nanny but I said no. Can you even imagine??

Anyway. Write back! How are you doing?

Love,

Rachel x

Date: Monday 17 June
From: Fraser Sutherland
To: Rachel Long
Re: Hey, how are you?

Hi,

Doing fine thanks. Glad L okay. Hope he's behaving.

Julia is doing fine. Doing blogs etc too. Although you should know this since you and her have been emailing.

Good for you for turning the nanny job down. What a fucking cheek.

F

Date: Friday 28 June
From: Julia Jones
To: Rachel Long
Subject: Update

Hey Rachel,

How are you doing? How's the job-hunting?

Had a very busy week with the birders – there were a couple of them who came a few months ago. They were asking after you. A guy called Steve and one called Hugh. I don't think they were impressed with my cooking! They kept raving about a lasagne you made, then I used the recipe in the info sheets that I'm guessing was the one you used, and they were commenting that yours was better!! Couldn't win!!

F has been talking a bit more. I brought back a bit of the lasagne (!!) and went into the living room and asked him if he wanted some, pretended I'd made too much ... so he came and ate with me. Then the next day he made pizza which was really nice. He told me about Lefty – well, told me in a few sentences that he had an assistant here that was a bit unofficial and that he'd gone back with you. You haven't mentioned this so I know it might be a bit awkward if you and Lefty had a thing going on or something, but I wondered if that might explain him being a bit grumpy??

So we have made some sort of progress but, you know, he's still barely speaking and the night after the pizza he went out with Bess and didn't come back until after I'd gone to bed. No idea where he went. Thought it was to the bird obs but they said they hadn't seen him all week, seemed a bit huffy about it.

Otherwise the island is lovely. Did you see my blogs about the terns? Those things are vicious!! The guillemots and razorbill chicks have started to fledge, which is just amazing and terrifying too - the youngsters just launch themselves off the cliff while the adults wait in the sea below and hope they don't hit too many ledges on the way down! The puffins are all hatched now, too - so cute!

Love,

Julia xx

Date: Friday 28 June
From: Rachel Long
To: Julia Jones
Re: Update

Hi, Julia,

That's hilarious about Steve and Hugh - they were my first lot of birders and they were an absolute nightmare. Although the worst one was Eugene - is he there? I can't imagine he'd have anything positive to say about me given he complained to Marion! All because I asked him to leave his boots at the door. I'm sure your lasagne was perfectly delicious - I think they just look for things to complain about.

Good to hear that F is talking (and cooking). Maybe he's just really missing Lefty. (By the way VERY DEFINITELY nothing going on between me and him.) They had a weird sort of dysfunctional relationship. See if you can get him talking some more? I think it will help him. He's a good guy really.

How's your mum getting on now?

Love,

Rachel x

Date: Friday 28 June
From: Julia Jones
To: Rachel Long
Re: Re: Update

Dear Rachel,

Thank you for your lovely email. That is hilarious about Steve and Hugh. There was no Eugene with them but a young guy called Daniel who didn't say much and another guy called Nathan. They were weird!

Hope you don't mind me saying this but I feel like we're kind of friends now, even if we never got to meet ;) but actually I'm pretty sure Fraser isn't missing Lefty. I think he's missing you.

He's not said anything but I'm fairly good at picking up on vibes and every time I mention you (and I talk about you A LOT) he goes all prickly and usually walks off. So it's either that you two hated each other, or the opposite, and from the way you've written about him I'm kind of thinking it's the opposite. Tell me to mind my own business! I'm a bit relieved that I'm not doing anything wrong - I think he's just finding it hard being here without you. And I think me being here is just reminding him that you're not, if that makes sense. After three weeks I'd like to think we'd be friends, but I am very doubtful that's ever going to happen!

So - sorry if this is too personal. Please do let's keep in touch. I'm feeling much better about being here generally but you know it's bloody hard being so far from home.

You're so kind to ask about my mum, too. She got signed off from the hospital with a clean bill of health and she's driving again now. Quite often I phone her in the evenings and she's out somewhere with friends! She was given the name and address of her donor and wrote her a letter to thank her, and has already had a reply. The whole thing makes me so emotional. Altruistic donations are rare - Mum was incredibly lucky to get one. How do you even begin to thank someone for that?

Take care,

Love,

Julia xx

Date: Sunday 30 June
From: Rachel Long
To: Julia Jones
Re: Re: Re: Update

Hi, Julia,

Well, yes, we did have a sort of thing. He's a raging commitment-phobe though, so there was no way it was ever going to mean anything to him. I know you might find this hard to believe but underneath all of that hair and attitude he's really quite a sensitive soul. He doesn't show his feelings easily which I guess is why he's behaving so badly towards you. I'm sorry about that because I'm thinking it's made life so much harder for you on that island than it was for me, and it was hard enough, without having nobody to talk to!! I hope he perks up soon.

I'm glad your mum is doing so well. I can understand how that's a bit of a relief and a bit strange at the same time – but I hope being on the island will help you as it helped me. I was in quite a bad way when I arrived. It's a very special sort of place, the way it carries on regardless, all of this life being created around you, all those different species fitting into their own spaces and doing their own things. You have all the fledgings to look forward to, and the migrations in September and October, and the grey seals breeding – I'll miss all of that.

I'm looking forward to you telling me all about it, to be honest. It's nice hearing about the island even if I'm not on it. And – being honest – about Fraser. I wish he'd cheer up a bit, though.

Love,

Rachel x

Date: Sunday 30 June
From: Rachel Long
To: Fraser Sutherland
Subject: Julia

Hi, Fraser,

Thought I should let you know that I told Julia about us (in very vague terms, don't worry). She thinks you're missing me. I told her that couldn't possibly be the case, since you're so very good at managing your feelings, right? Anyway I don't think you can be, or you'd call me or write to me sometimes. I think you're just being a grumpy bugger, which is a shame because Julia is very sweet and genuine, and is trying really hard and I think you should sort yourself out and be nice to her. Or come and visit me. You know the christening is coming up next month and you promised to come with me, right?

I'm joking. I'm not going to hold you to that.

Lefty is doing well. He's signed up with the gardening crew and he has a name badge – he's very proud of it. My mother is treating him like the son she never had. I told him I was writing to you and he wants to know how the chickens are doing. And I'd like to know how Bess is, and how you are. So – write back?

Love

Rachel x

Date: Saturday 6 July
From: Rachel Long
To: Fraser Sutherland
Subject: Me again

Hey,

You not speaking to me? I've sent you texts as well. I'm sorry if I've said something wrong. Write back?

R x

Date: Sunday 7 July
From: Rachel Long
To: Julia Jones
Subject: Worry

Hi, Julia,

How are you doing? How were the last lot of birders? Hope all's going well.

Not that I want to be making you into a go-between, but is Fraser okay? I've emailed him a couple of times and sent him loads of texts, but he's stopped replying to me. It might be that he wants to break off contact, and I could sort of understand that if he's found things tough, but it would be nice to know one way or the other. It would be really good to speak to him on the phone actually, I've asked him if he could call, but I know there's no point in me phoning him as he never once answered the phone when I was there.

Things are okay here. I've got a temporary job working for an estate agency, which has been brilliant. I love it but it's so exhausting, I'm worn out every night. No idea how I managed walking miles around the island! I'm suddenly really unfit.

Mel has been telling me about your exploits in your uni days. I hope one day we can all get together and have a night out.

Bye for now and take care,

Rachel x

Date: Saturday 13 July
From: Julia Jones
To: Rachel Long
Re: Worry

Hey Rachel,

Have you heard from Fraser? I told him to get in touch with you. He just mumbled something about getting around to it and walked off. I'm afraid we haven't made a whole lot of progress!

The last lot of birders were nice, two really lovely couples called Helen and Karen and Mike and Lindsay. They haven't been before, they were on a birding holiday rather than with one of the orn ithology groups. Fraser was grumbling about them not completing the bird logs properly, since they hadn't done anything like that before, but I managed to persuade him to help them with the count on their second day and after that they did a brilliant job. They logged the first kittiwake fledgling and the first fulmar chick. I think he was expecting them to abandon the bird logs altogether but they were really enthusiastic about it. They were even doing some ringing on their last day. Talk about a working holiday!

Karen is an environmental health officer although she wasn't here to do an inspection (!). Turns out that the person you spoke to at the council – Ellie? – recommended the island to her and she booked it accordingly. Funny where you get the business from, eh? Anyway since you told me all about Ellie in your handover email I thought you'd like to know. (Still haven't had an inspection, and Karen says she doesn't think we've got anything to worry about.)

Congrats on the job!! That sounds great. Bit of a change from cooking suppers and falling down puffin burrows, I bet – no wonder you're tired!!

Love,

Julia xx

Date: Saturday 13 July
From: Rachel Long
To: Julia Jones
Re: Re: Worry

No I haven't heard from Fraser! I don't think he's talking to me. :(

Is he okay though?

Date: Sunday 14 July
From: Julia Jones
To: Rachel Long
Re: Re: Re: Worry

I'd like to be able to say he is okay but actually I'm not sure he is – definitely not sleeping – heard him crashing around in the kitchen at 4 a.m. I spoke to him this morning and he says he's thinking about leaving. Then he went out for the day and I haven't seen him since.

I mean, I don't want to worry you, I'm sure he's fine. I've told him he should call you!

Let me know if you hear from him? I'll keep trying to talk to him my end.

J xx

16 July 11:42

Hi, Fraser. I haven't heard from you :(and I really need to talk to you. Could you phone me pls? Xxxx

16 July 12:50

Hi, Fraser, I left you a really short voicemail, I know you hate answering the phone and honestly I'm not calling to have a go at you. Please call me back. Xxx

16 July 19:25

Okay so I think you're probably having dinner or something. I'm hoping your phone might be out of battery or you've left it somewhere. PLEASE call. Lefty is fine, in case you're worried. I'm going to try again in an hour. Xxx

Date: Wednesday 17 July
From: Rachel Long
To: Julia Jones
Subject: Can I phone?

Dear Julia,

I know this might sound out of the blue but could I have your number? Something's happened and I really need to talk to F. What I'd actually like to do is call you, and for Fraser to be somewhere nearby so you can hand the phone to him - is that possible, do you think? I've put my number below, or let me know yours so I can call?

Thank you!

Love,

Rachel x

Date: Thursday 18 July
From: Julia Jones
To: Rachel Long
Re: Can I phone?

Hey Rachel,

I'm glad the two of you got to have a proper conversation last night
- I hope it helped. We had a chat afterwards and I got the gist of
things. He's very quiet again today but don't worry, I'll talk to him.
I'll call you later with an update, okay?

Take care,

Love,

Julia xx

14

Family

Rachel

'How are you feeling?' Mel asks.

'A bit queasy, since you ask.'

'You look gorgeous, honestly,' Mel says.

Rachel is facing her, wearing a navy cotton dress, strappy sandals. 'I have no clue what people wear to christenings.'

'You should have asked Lucy,' Mel says. 'I'm sure she'd have picked an outfit for you.'

'Fuck that.'

'I'm joking!'

'Just don't. Where's Lefty?'

'Downstairs – he's fine.'

They face each other for a moment. Yes, Rachel thinks, it's fine, even though it isn't really, but she will have to pretend it is.

Lefty has no real desire to go to Emily's christening, and who can blame him? But, since he is now part of the family, his feelings no longer come into it.

Emily is beautiful: so much bigger, smiling and grabbing things and drooling everywhere, sitting up on her own. She looks like Lucy. Rachel had said as much, when Emily had been handed over to her with very little preamble. 'God, Luce, she really looks like you.'

'You think?'

'Absolutely.'

'Well, I guess she's got Ian's colouring – if she'd had red hair she'd look more like you, right?'

'Yeah, thank God she's not a ginger, eh?'

Lucy has lost weight, gained shadows under her eyes, is a wee bit obsessive about things and tense and tired – but then she's just about to go back to work, even if it's just three days a week to start with. Emily is going to go to a nursery, has just had her first taster morning, during the course of which she napped and had a bottle and produced two dirty nappies. Rachel wonders if things would have been easier or harder for Lucy if she hadn't gone to the island at all, and decides that her presence here in those early months would have made everything a million times worse.

Not that everything's been easy for Rachel, either. Far from it. The last week has been particularly challenging.

She has told Mel all about it, of course. Everything. Mel has been party to Julia's emails back and forth, and more recently to the phone calls. Thank heavens for Julia, and for Mel. Between the two of them, Rachel feels an overwhelming sense of love and support, something she badly needs right now.

When she's on her own, of course, it's a different matter. That phone call with Fraser had been difficult, to say the least. Trying to get him to talk. He had said he needed to think. And now she can't get him out of her head – wondering if he's ever going to speak to her again; wondering if he misses her, if he wishes she could have stayed. Some nights it's all she can do to stop herself from going online and booking a train north, but, so far, she has resisted.

Now it's been ten days since that phone conversation. The silence from his end must mean he has thought about it all and made a decision, and that that's it. In which case all she can do is respect his silence, and try her hardest to move on.

From the bottom of the stairs, Lefty shouts up. 'You coming? Taxi's outside. You're gonnae be late.'

Fraser

Fraser is still undecided about the christening. He's thought about it, he knows where it is, but the idea of turning up, confronting Rachel in front of her entire family, is just a bit too much to contemplate.

Instead he's across the road from the church, loitering in an alleyway, uncomfortably dressed in a shirt and tie with a fleece over the top of it so he feels a bit less conspicuous, although it's roasting hot. He has no intention of spying on them, not really, but it has crossed his mind that maybe Rachel won't be there, and then what will he do? Go and look for her? Probably. If he feels brave enough.

His intention, therefore, is to see if she's there – that's first – then see how she looks – if she's well, happy. Whether she's on her own, or if she's got someone with her, because it's been two months since she left and it's entirely possible that she's got herself a boyfriend, despite everything.

The thought of her with someone else makes him feel sick, but there you go. It's his own fucking fault. If she looks happy, he thinks, he will leave her to it. He will turn around and go back up to Scotland.

He watches cars turning into the car park, and then smartly dressed people walking up to the front of the church and going in. Nobody he recognises, until a couple with a pushchair, and he spots Rachel's sister pushing it; he knows her from that photo on Rachel's phone. Lucy. She's lost weight, if that's her.

Then an older couple, the woman wearing a hat, as if it's a wedding – surely that's Rachel's parents? And then a taxi pulls up outside, and Rachel gets out with two other people: a woman and a man. It takes him a good few seconds to recognise Lefty in a suit. In a fucking suit! With a decent haircut, and looking fit and well, if a little shifty. He knows that look. Lefty's nervous, and why wouldn't he be? Fraser doesn't care who the woman is because he's too busy staring at Rachel. Tall, smart, wearing a dress, high heels, her hair up. She looks round for Lefty, says something to him, smiles, then they go inside.

She hasn't seen Fraser, over the other side of the road.

Hasn't even glanced in his direction.

She looks – incredible.

Does she look happy, though? It's only a few seconds. It's impossible to know.

His phone rings, just then. He's still getting used to it actually ringing; it takes him a moment to realise the sound is coming from his pocket.

'Hello?'

'Well?' It's Julia. 'Have you seen her?'

'I have, aye.'

'And? How is she? What did she say?'

'I've not spoken to her.'

'Why not?'

'They've just gone into the church.'

'Get yourself in there! What's the matter with you?'

In the ten days since Julia came into the living room with her mobile phone, handed it to him and walked out again, things have changed. He had always intended to phone Rachel; he just hadn't had the right words. Hadn't trusted himself to be able to speak to her without making everything worse. Had he made it worse? Probably. But, as Julia keeps telling him, he still has the chance to put things right.

Since that evening, Julia has become alarmingly bossy. He wouldn't go so far as to say that this expedition to Norwich – the furthest south he's ever been – was her idea, but she had certainly encouraged him to do it. Maybe he'd needed a bit of a push.

During their phone call, Rachel hadn't mentioned the christening, even though when she was on the island she had invited

403

him – twice – and then mentioned it again in an email. But she'd said that was a joke. She probably doesn't want him here.

'I'm not going in.'

'Just go in, sit at the back. Talk to her afterwards, if you can't bring yourself to do it now. Go on! And ring me later.'

Fraser sighs, tucks the phone in his pocket, and heads across the road.

Rachel

They are in the private function room at the Rising Sun, a gastropub on the river which has a stellar reputation. The lunch they'd served was lavish, and Rachel had mentally tried to calculate the cost of food and wine for the thirty invited guests, but had given up. Lefty, sandwiched between Mum and Rachel's cousin Josh, aged sixteen, has spent most of the afternoon happily leaning over Josh's iPad watching YouTube gaming videos, one earphone each.

Rachel has been talking to her Auntie Jan about the island. Years ago, Jan lived on Fair Isle for a while, and has much to say about seabirds and island life. Rachel is enthusiastically reliving the fresh air and the springy turf and at the same time thinking about Fraser and feeling sad, *again*, when she sees Mel heading towards her from across the room. Mel is striding, fast, eyes on Rachel, who glances across to where Lefty was – to see that he's no longer there.

'You okay?' Rachel asks, as Mel reaches them.

'I'm so sorry,' Mel says to Auntie Jan. 'Can I borrow Rachel for a minute?'

'What is it?' Rachel says, suddenly panicked. 'Where's Lefty?'

'Come, quick.'

Mel takes her arm and they walk fast towards the door, practically running.

'Bloody hell, Melanie, what...?'

And they reach the door of the pub and they are outside in the fresh air, and there is Lefty, hands casually in the pockets of his smart charcoal trousers, bought for him by Rachel's dad, talking to a huge man in the car park.

Fraser.

It's Fraser.

For a moment she has forgotten how to breathe.

'Here she is,' Lefty says, cheerfully. 'What'd I tell you?'

Whatever Lefty had been telling Fraser about her is lost. She is lost. Staring at him, looking so different here, standing on the neat tarmac of the car park instead of on bright green grass, wearing – what is he wearing? A shirt and tie, holding a jacket or something over his arm despite the warm weather; hair cut short, his beard trimmed. And he's staring at her.

'I take it this is Fraser,' Mel says, looking from one of them to the other.

'Yes,' Rachel says, and then collects herself. 'Um, Fraser, this is Mel – Mel, Fraser.'

'Nice to meet you,' Fraser says, holding out his meaty hand.

How is he so calm?

'Hi,' Mel says, shaking it, and adding with a decidedly frosty tone, 'I've heard so much about you.'

Oh, God.

He manages a little smile. 'I expect you have.'

Fraser switches his attention from Mel to Rachel. She sees the flick of his eyes from her face, down the front of her dress, back to her face again. His expression is unreadable. Rachel feels the flush rising from her neck: this is all wrong, she thinks.

Rachel is still staring at him, only half-aware of Mel saying, 'Come on, Lefty, let's go inside.'

Fraser is still here. He's really here.

'You okay?' he asks, eventually.

She nods, and then finally finds her voice. 'What the fuck?'

'Hello yourself,' he says.

'Why didn't you tell me you were coming?'

He shrugs. 'Last-minute decision.'

'Are you coming in?'

He looks behind her into the function room, the crowds of people, the staff clearing away plates.

'Or,' she adds, thinking that for a minute she just wants to have him all to herself until she can work out whether this is really, actually happening, 'maybe we could go in the bar for a drink?'

'Aye,' he says, relieved, 'let's do that.'

They've still got a lot to talk about, she thinks. Best get it over with.

Fraser

He can feel her eyes boring into his back as he stands at the bar. A young barman serves him quickly enough. Mercifully this one doesn't bat an eyelid as he hands over his Scottish twenty-pound note. Everyone else he's paid money to since he came south of the border has stared at the unfamiliar notes and gone to ask a manager.

He takes the drinks back to the table she's chosen in the corner near the window, just about as far from the function room as it's possible to get.

'Here you go,' he says, placing a fizzy water on the table in front of her. He pours the bottle of beer out into the glass he's been given, wondering if he can actually manage to drink it. He feels sick with nerves all of a sudden.

'Thanks,' she says. 'So.'

'So. How have you been?'

'Fine. As I told you on the phone, when we spoke. More to the point, how are you?'

'I'm doing okay. Better.'

He can't keep his eyes off her. He thinks maybe he can see a bump. It might be his imagination, seeing things he wants to see, but, however subtle, he thinks it is definitely, indisputably *there*. And it's his, the baby inside her. It's his. He's been trying to get his head straight about the whole thing, but here it is.

Rachel is pregnant.

'I know I fucked things up,' he says. 'I should have called. Just couldn't think of the right thing to say.'

She sips her drink, her eyes huge. 'It's really very hard to have conversations like that over the phone. Even more so when you have to force someone to talk to you.'

'Yeah. I'm sorry,' he says. 'I thought you might be – you know ... With someone else.'

She stares at him, looks pointedly down at herself. 'Are you kidding me? Of course I'm not with anyone else.'

He still doesn't have the right words. All he can do is look at her.

'I know you're probably pissed off that I had to get Julia involved,' she says.

He shrugs. 'Actually she's got a bit feisty since that phone call. Told me to get my arse down here and tell you what I've been wanting to tell you all this time and haven't.'

'Which is?'

And just at that moment, of course, he hears a strident voice from across the lounge. 'Rachel! There you are! Can you come?'

Fraser turns in his seat. Rachel's sister is heading towards them.

'Perfect timing,' he murmurs.

Rachel takes a deep breath in. 'I'm just—'

'Hello!' Lucy says, brightly, thrusting out her hand. 'I'm Lucy. And you are ...?'

Fraser gets to his feet to shake her hand. Lucy's eyes widen as he towers over her. 'Fraser,' he says.

'Oh,' Lucy says, looking at Rachel and then back to Fraser. 'Oh, I see. Well.'

'Can you just give us a minute?' Rachel asks. 'I'll be there in a sec.'

'Mum was asking...I think they want to go home. Dad wants a photo.'

'Right.'

He looks back at Rachel and sees the eyes wide, the smile huge and bright.

'In that case,' she says, standing, 'we'd better go.' She picks up her drink. Looks back at him. 'You coming?'

'Me?' he says, stupidly.

'Of course you. About time you met my family.'

He watches her as she walks behind Lucy back into the function room. The way her hips move. Those long legs.

And then she looks round, gives him a smile, and he follows.

Rachel

'Mum, this is Fraser.'

Her mother looks appropriately startled, as everyone does when she introduces him. Unsurprising, as he's six foot five and wide as a doorway.

'Oh! Pleased to meet you,' she says, and Fraser tries to shake her hand, but Mum has gone on her tiptoes to try to kiss his cheek, grasping him by both biceps, and Rachel thinks that Fraser's face is really quite hilarious.

She's doing this on purpose, a subtle revenge – forcing him to meet everyone. It's the least he deserves, for turning up unannounced. And for the past ten days, making no further contact with her, after she'd had to tell him about it over the phone.

She had had to explain how she had forgotten all about getting emergency contraception. She had been so busy worrying about Lefty, working out where to live. In the end it was only the fact that she'd thrown up getting off the bus that had made her think about getting a test, and by that point she'd been seven or eight weeks gone. She'd told him all this, trying not to sound apologetic, trying to sound firm, in case he said something she didn't want to hear. Her biggest fear was that he would want her to get a termination – not that she would, but even hearing him suggest it would have just finished her.

Because, actually, she has the strongest feeling that this isn't one of *Rachel's fuck-ups*. This is something far more important. Something precious.

He'd been so quiet, she'd had to say, 'Hello? You still there?'

'Aye, I'm still here.'

'Look, I know this isn't what you want. You don't have to do anything. I'm just telling you because you've got a right to know.'

'That it?'

It wasn't as though he'd been cold. Just – resigned. As if this was another massive thing for him to deal with.

'What do you mean?'

'Do you need anything?'

Overwhelmed with hormones, exhausted and nauseous, that had hit her quite hard. *I need you!* she'd wanted to yell. She hadn't expected him to be overjoyed, exactly. But she had thought that it might mean something.

Deep breath in.

'No. I just wanted to tell you.'

She had heard a heavy sigh from his end of the phone. A long pause. She could picture him in the kitchen, or maybe he was in the living room, feet up. Maybe Julia was still there with him; maybe that was why he was having trouble talking to her. Because this didn't sound like her Fraser. This man was quiet, detached, tired. As though she had just taken away the last bit of life he had left.

'Look, maybe you could call me back? When you've had a chance to think about things?'

'Aye.'

It had hurt. A lot. He hadn't called back later, or the next day, or the next. She'd thought he had gone forever.

And now, here he is, and she's introducing him to her family, and everything is just so... weird.

'... and Dad.'

Fraser gets a brisk handshake and a hard stare. Rachel's father has full knowledge of who Fraser is, and has a damn good idea of what's gone on between him and his daughter, though she hasn't said anything outright, especially not about being pregnant. Her mother also knows who Fraser is, but she's distracted by the christening guests and hasn't quite made the association between Rachel's former job on the island and this huge man who's appeared out of nowhere.

'And this... This is Emily. My niece.'

Rachel borrows Emily from Lucy's mother-in-law, who seems more than happy to reclaim her glass of prosecco from her husband, mutely standing behind her holding their glasses. Emily has been as good as gold today, considering the monstrous christening gown she was forced to wear for the ceremony. She's since been changed into a little pink dress, which is only marginally less awful. The baby regards Fraser with her fist in her mouth, which she then stretches out towards him, leaving a trail of drool.

'She likes you. Want to hold her?'

'I—'

Rachel holds Emily under the armpits and thrusts her in Fraser's direction. He has no choice but to take her, holding her only slightly awkwardly with one hand under her bum. Emily looks up at him, pressing her drooly hand into his pale blue shirt, leaving a nice soggy print.

'Hello,' Fraser says, looking down at her.

The chubby little hand reaches up and grabs at a fistful of beard, and she laughs dirtily, a proper throaty cackle.

'I know, Ems,' Rachel says, 'he's very hairy, isn't he?' She is very close, puts a hand on his shoulder. 'See? Not so bad, is it?'

'I love you,' he says.

'Yes,' Rachel replies. Her heart is pounding. 'Right. Okay, then.'

'Rachel! Come, and bring Emily!'

Rachel stands obligingly for the photos under a string of white fairy-lights twined around a beam, holding Emily, not holding her, then standing with Lucy and Rob and Emily, and then a big whole-family shot that even includes Lefty. She waves to Fraser, trying to get him to come in on the picture, but he stays resolutely still, looking at her with an expression she finds hard to read.

But he said it, and her heart hasn't stopped flying.

Fraser doesn't say things he doesn't mean.

Fraser

An hour later, he's standing in a messy kitchen, with a mug of coffee that is surprisingly not that bad. Rachel has made it, and another one for Mel, who has taken herself off into the lounge. He can hear their hushed conversation through the open door.

'Sure you don't want me to—?'

'No, we'll go upstairs.'

'I can go to Darius's...'

'It's fine.'

Rachel comes back in. Leans back against the kitchen counter.

Now that they're alone, he lets his eyes travel up her body from her bare feet all the way up to her eyes. Feels more unworthy than ever. Wonders what he's doing here.

'So,' she says. 'I love you too. Now we've got that out of the way.'

'Right,' he says, his heart bursting. However blunt the delivery.

'When are you going back to the island?'

'Tomorrow. But I've been thinking I might hand in my notice. Finish at the end of the season.'

'But – why?'

He shrugs.

'You know. Responsibilities. Things I need to do.'

'I can manage just fine, you know. If that's what you're worried about.'

Fraser puts his mug down hard on the draining board, takes a breath, and turns to her. 'Will you just stop?'

'Stop?'

'Stop being so bloody calm about it all! I'm used to you being emotional, right? Not this.'

'Jesus! Sorry that I've got my shit together. And I thought it was me being a constant mess that was hard to deal with.'

He stares at her.

'Fraser, I've had a hard time. When you didn't call me back…I thought you didn't want to know.'

'Aye. And I'm sorry. I'm sorry I made it all worse for you.'

He thinks about how to tell her, how to describe the past couple of months.

'I've been…in a bit of a hole. If I can describe it like that. It's like I've been – stuck.'

She looks at him. 'I know what that feels like,' she says at last.

'I just couldn't get out of it. I thought anything I did would make it worse. I want you to be happy, more than anything, but I didn't see a way I could make you happy. Not the way you deserve.'

'Fraser,' she says, 'the only place I've been really happy my whole life was that island. And that was because you were there.'

She makes a move then – slides one hand around his waist and then the other and he puts his arms around her and holds her tightly, kisses the top of her head.

'I've missed you,' he murmurs.

'My room's a tip,' she says, into his shirt, 'but you'll have to put up with it. Come on.'

He follows her dumbly up the narrow stairs and into her room, which is a mess of unmade bed, scattered clothes, make-up, hairdryer, books – a crazy jumble of colours and fabrics. The room smells of her. It's all he can do not to stand and inhale.

'I don't care where we go,' she says. 'Personally, if I have a choice in the matter, I'd really like to go back to the island, you and me. Lefty will probably want to stay here, with Mum, fuck knows why but they're just best pals now, so we don't need to worry about him. So you don't need to resign. I know you don't really want to, do you? And maybe I can help Julia out next season – I mean, I won't have an official job, and I'm sure you'd need to clear it with head office, but—'

'I don't think Julia's going to stay,' he says.

'Oh,' she says, 'really? Why not?'

'She's seen a job in Orkney. Better lichens. And no bad-tempered nature wardens.'

There is a little pause. 'Maybe I could come back, then,' she says. 'If you want me, that is.'

For the first time he can hear the crack in her voice as the emotion finally gets to her.

'Of course,' he says. 'Of course I want you. That's why I'm here.'

'Because this would be an actual relationship I'm talking about.'

'I know.'

'A permanent one,' she says, her hand over her tummy. 'And there's two of us now. So it's not just me.'

'Absolutely,' he says.

He's thinking of the island, wind-blown, stormy, dark; of Rachel with her hair flying, with a baby, with a toddler, with a child. He thinks of Bess and the loch and the cottages, and the birds soaring overhead, and the light scouring the blackness every night, the whales out there, swimming past in their pods, the grey seals giving birth to their pups on the beach and on the north shore.

He thinks of the yacht breaking up and that moment his soul split in two because he thought she was going to die, and how he knew it then, knew exactly, that he loved her and would absolutely die without her.

And it's taken him all this time to get to the point where he can tell her the truth about how he feels.

'Let's go back,' she says, holding out her hand.

He cups her face in his hands and kisses her, gently at first and then hard and deep, and he thinks, so this is what it feels like. So this is it.

And his heart soars.

Author's Note

The Isle of Must does not exist. Parts of it might bear a passing resemblance to the Isle of May, which does exist, but readers should bear in mind crucial differences and, most importantly, don't try going out to look for it.

Acknowledgements

Thank you to Candida Lacey, publisher, editor and friend, for unfaltering encouragement and inspiration, and for allowing me the creative space in which I can experiment and grow. Very few authors are this fortunate!

Thank you to everyone at Myriad Editions who made this book better: to Linda McQueen for copy-editing, Dawn Sackett for proofreading, and Leah Jacobs-Gordon for the gorgeous cover design. Thank you to my extraordinarily talented friend, Jo Hinton-Malivoire, for her beautiful map at the beginning of this book.

Thank you to my agent, Annette Green, for always being so patient and encouraging, and to Louisa Pritchard for her hard work on rights sales. Thank you to the brilliant sales team at Turnaround for getting my books on to shelves, and thank you to the lovely booksellers and librarians everywhere who do such an amazing job bringing books and readers together.

Special thanks to Joyce (former librarian and bookseller) at the Old Bank Bookshop in Wigtown, who, in response to my vague Twitter request for 'anything on Scottish seabirds', found me a copy of *One Man's Island* by Keith Brockie, which proved fundamental to my research. Thank you, Joyce!

My inspiration for *You, Me & The Sea* came from my obsession with the fanfiction site Archive of Our Own (AO3) and two fics in particular: *Rock Out On The Sea* by Aurora0331 and *Rebound* (part of the *Potential* series) by swimmingfox. My love and best wishes to the SanSan community on AO3 – you are all brilliant and amazing. Thank you.

Inspiration also came from *The Outrun* by Amy Liptrot (and thank you to Abi Hiscock for recommending it), *Swansong* by Kerry Andrew, and the incredible *The Evolution of a Girl* by L.E. Bowman. Thank you to Lauren Bowman for generously allowing me to use a verse from this book as the epigraph. I recommend all three of these books wholeheartedly.

Thank you to David Steel, reserve manager on the Isle of May, for patiently answering my questions about seabirds and island life. He and Bex Outram do fantastic work in taking care of the wildlife and welcoming visitors to the island, as well as keeping up an entertaining and informative blog.

Thank you to Carolyn Cowan, for introducing me to the Isle of May, and to Rosalind Wallace and Janet Emerson for putting us in touch. Janet accompanied me on a memorable research visit to May and I'm very grateful to her for that.

Thank you to Lisa Cutts, Holly Ainley and Nike Lawal, who all allowed me to discuss aspects of the book with them, and thereby helped to resolve crucial issues with the plot. Your encouragement and support has been incredibly valuable to me.

My good friends Samantha Bowles, Moira Tibeau, Linda Weeks, Vicky Allen, Denise West and Lindsay Brown all read various drafts of the story and were instrumental in shaping it thereafter. Linda also kindly loaned me her copy of Munro's *Scottish Lighthouses*, which was most useful. Thank you all for your kindness and your forbearance. I hope you like how it turned out.

Thank you to Donna and Erin Batty for explaining how a quad bike works; to @biggestbossfan (ponyboy) on Twitter for giving me the phrase 'a face that missed a sneeze'; to Susan Nicholson for sharing her experiences working for Nando's (sounds brilliant); to Janice Maciver for last-minute procedural assistance; to my husband David for explaining how lifeboat rescues happen, why modern helicopters don't like hovering, and how marine radios function; and thank you to Erin Kelly, Julia Crouch and Lisa Jewell for their panel event 'And the next twist is…' at Noirwich on 14 September 2019, without which Lefty would never have existed.

Thank you to my dear friend the Rev. Rachael Dines for generously sharing her experiences of altruistic kidney donation. Around a hundred incredible people donate a kidney to a stranger every year, saving lives and dramatically transforming the lives of seriously ill patients and their families. You can find out more about it at GiveAKidney.org. My thanks and best wishes, too, to the members of the Living Donor Facebook group.

Thank you to Natalie Sutherland, brilliant librarian and friend, for both giving me Lefty's name and allowing me to use her own surname for Fraser. Thank you to Ellie Griffiths for allowing me to use her name, and to our lovely mutual friend Karen (EHO extraordinaire) for advice on food safety procedures. Lindsay, Mike, Karen, Helen, Eugene, Susie, Dec, Cristina and Enrique are also all real people, and it's entirely possible that they might enjoy a birding holiday on the Isle of Must, if it existed.

ALSO BY ELIZABETH HAYNES

The Murder of Harriet Monckton
A delicious Victorian crime novel based on a true story that shocked and fascinated the nation.

On 7th November 1843, Harriet Monckton, 23 years old and a woman of respectable parentage and religious habits, is found murdered in the privy behind the chapel she regularly attended in Bromley, Kent. The community is appalled by her death, apparently as a result of swallowing a fatal dose of prussic acid, and even more so when the surgeon reports that Harriet was around six months pregnant.

Drawing on the coroner's reports and witness testimonies, Elizabeth Haynes builds a compelling picture of Harriet's final hours through the eyes of those closest to her and the last people to see her alive. Her fellow teacher and companion, her would-be fiancé, her seducer, her former lover – all are suspects; each has a reason to want her dead.

'This novel will keep you completely hooked and stealing a page at every minute.' – *Hello* magazine

'An expertly crafted slow-burn of a novel, immersing you in the double standards of Victorian Bromley... Perfect sofa fodder for an empty weekend.' – *The Pool*

'What a *tour de force*! I'm blown away. Elizabeth Haynes completely transported me to that time and place. I also found the novel incredibly moving and I'm so glad to know Harriet's story. The novel is an absolute triumph.' – Elly Griffiths

MORE FICTION FROM MYRIAD

A More Perfect Union
by Tammye Huf
Set in 1840s America and based on the true story of the author's great-great-grandparents – Henry, a travelling Irish blacksmith, and Sarah, a plantation slave – this epic tale of a forbidden relationship is a tense, compelling and heartwarming depiction of love and courage, desperation and determination.

Pondweed
by Lisa Blower
A love story in the slow lane about loss and getting lost – two childhood sweethearts take a trip via pints, ponds and pitstops to find their future on a road less travelled from Stoke-on-Trent to Wales. 'Funny, moving, philosophical and wise. Utterly charming and utterly hilarious.' – Emma Jane Unsworth

Noon in Paris, Eight in Chicago
by Douglas Cowie
Chicago, 1947: on a freezing February night, France's feminist icon Simone de Beauvoir calls up radical resident novelist Nelson Algren, asking him to show her around. After a whirlwind tour of dive bars, cabarets and the police lockup, a passion is sparked that will last for the next two decades.

MORE FICTION FROM MYRIAD

Belonging
by Umi Sinha

Lila Langdon is just twelve years old when her mother unveils her father's surprise birthday present – a tragedy that ends her childhood in India and precipitates a new life in Sussex with her great-aunt Wilhelmina. An intense, compelling and finely wrought epic of love, loss and homeland.

Dark Aemilia
by Sally O'Reilly

The orphaned daughter of a Venetian musician, Aemilia Bassano grows up in the court of Elizabeth I, becoming the Queen's favourite for her beauty, sharp mind and quick tongue. But her position is precarious; when she falls in love with court playwright William Shakespeare, her fortunes change irrevocably.

The Longest Fight
by Emily Bullock

Scarred by his childhood and haunted by the tragic fate of his first love, boxing manager Jack Munday is hungry for change. So when hope appears in the form of Frank, a young boxer with a winning prospect, and Georgie, a new girl who can match him step for step, Jack seizes his chance for a better future.

Sign up to our mailing list at
www.myriadeditions.com
Follow us on Facebook, Twitter and Instagram

Elizabeth Haynes is a former police intelligence analyst. Her first novel, *Into the Darkest Corner*, has been published in 37 countries. It was Amazon's Best Book of the Year and a *New York Times* bestseller. She has written a further three psychological thrillers – *Revenge of the Tide*, *Human Remains* and *Never Alone* – two novels in the DCI Louisa Smith series – *Under a Silent Moon* and *Behind Closed Doors* – and a historical thriller, *The Murder of Harriet Monckton*.